THE LAST REFUGE

CRAIG ROBERTSON

SIMON &
SCHUSTER

London · New York · Sydney · Toronto · New Delhi

A CBS COMPANY

First published in Great Britain by Simon & Schuster UK Ltd, 2014
This paperback edition published, 2014
A CBS COMPANY

3 5 7 9 10 8 6 4 2

Simon & Schuster UK Ltd
1st Floor
222 Gray's Inn Road
London WC1X 8HB

www.simonandschuster.co.uk

Simon & Schuster Australia, Sydney
Simon & Schuster India, New Delhi

A CIP catalogue record for this book
is available from the British Library

PB ISBN: 978-1-47112-775-5
EBOOK ISBN: 978-1-47112-776-2

Typeset by M Rules
Printed and bound by CPI Group (UK) Ltd, Croydon CR0 4YY

Praise for *The Last Refuge*

'**Hero**, anti-hero, or **villain**? You'll never be sure until the rain- and tear-soaked conclusion . . .' crimefictionlover.com

'**Craig Robertson** has established himself as one of the most adroit practitioners of the **crime** novel at work today' welovethisbook.com

'I really enjoyed this very unusual and **gripping** book . . . Strongly recommended' eurocrime.co.uk

'Raw brooding **power** runs through the storyline from start to finish . . .' theresbeenamurder.wordpress.com

'Sometimes bleak and desolate, it's an **enthralling** look deep into a man's soul and deep into a **fascinating** place. I highly recommend it' kittlingbooks.com

'A roller coaster ride of **twists** and **turns** that will keep you reading until the bitter end' shotsmag.co.uk

'A carefully-plotted **mystery** . . . You can actually taste the salt-tinged air of these islands' bookbanter.co.uk

During his 20-year career in Glasgow with a Scottish Sunday newspaper, Craig Robertson interviewed three recent Prime Ministers, attended major stories including 9/11, Dunblane, the Omagh bombing and the disappearance of Madeleine McCann. He was pilloried on breakfast television, beat Oprah Winfrey to a major scoop, spent time on Death Row in the USA and dispensed polio drops in the backstreets of India. His debut novel, *Random*, was shortlisted for the CWA New Blood Dagger and was a *Sunday Times* bestseller.

Also by Craig Robertson:

Witness the Dead
Cold Grave
Snapshot
Random

To Alexandra Sokoloff

Nogle stukke med lange spyd,
Og andre med knive skare;
Inver mand gjorde sin dont med fryd,
Slet ingen ænsede fare.

Some were stabbing with long spears,
And others were cutting with knives;
Everyman joyously performed his task,
Nobody noticed danger.

— 'Grindevisen' (Faroese whaling ballad)

Chapter 1

There comes a moment in the wrestle for life when the distinction between opposing sides is blurred to the point of blindness. Did I start this fight or did he? Am I on top or being forced back down? Am I winning or losing? Have I won or already lost? My blood or his blood?

I can see the blood, taste it, smell it. I can feel it lick my skin and hear its rush in my ears. Blood means life but it also means death. My senses are suffocated, drowning in shades of red. All I can do is fight.

Would-be killer and would-be victim, rolling and grappling; life fighting death fighting life.

If he doesn't die, I can't live. If I die, he has won.

The blood's in my nostrils now, not just the scent of it but the liquid reality of it. My bones ache and my lungs burn. Life and living is on the line.

I feel a tiredness that I know I can't afford. He thrashes at me, sending pain surging through my body. It rings in my wrists and my chest, my knees. Then three violent knocks in quick succession against my ankles, an orchestra of pain, all my joints singing from the same hymn sheet.

I'm losing. I'm lost.

My eyes snapped open, seeing the world through a bloodshot veil. They slid closed again, reluctant to see whatever the half-light had to offer. The final, familiar chords of a tune were still playing in the back of my mind, but out of reach.

I moved a hand beneath me, groping blindly for clues. Wet. Smooth, wet and cold. Whatever I was lying on was as hard, as sleek and as unforgiving as marble. It explained the brutal ache in my joints and the throbbing in my back. But they were nothing compared to the pain echoing through my skull.

I tentatively moved one leg then the other, trying to shift from the foetal curl I was locked in, my muscles protesting loudly at the call to action. My right eye edged open again and I saw that it rested half an inch above a pillow of dark grey stone, my cheek flat to its rain-dappled surface.

So cold. At the realization of the raw chill, a shiver squirmed through my body and didn't stop until it rattled my teeth. My bones were as cold as my limbs were stiff. Every little movement was slow and painful. I withdrew back into my curl, huddling against myself, hoping for warmth and salvation. Neither came.

I lay there, cold and disorientated on my unknown bed of stone, drifting back towards sleep. A voice deep inside told me I had to move.

My head was so heavy and the world spun as I lifted it. My brain tumbled inside my skull like a ship cut loose from its moorings in a storm.

I managed to push myself up onto my elbows and looked around, my surroundings a blur. It was almost dark, or at least what passed for dark here. Nearly night or nearly morning? I couldn't be sure. An unnecessary light glowed amber from up above. Shop fronts and vaguely familiar facades slowly came into focus. It was the colours of them that made some sense: red, then mustard yellow; white, then pale blue. I was on Torshavn's western harbour, at Undir Bryggjubakka.

The smells of the sea – salt and seaweed and a faint whiff of oil – came to me on the breeze of that knowledge and I slowly turned to see it lapping blackly behind me, white boats bobbing and oblivious to whatever plight I faced.

I looked below me, a realization slowly dawning. My black stone bed was one of four great slabs on the harbour where the fishing catch was laid out daily. Slate beds for fish and shellfish. Not for drunks.

The canopy above the slab had kept me reasonably dry. Maybe that's why it had seemed like a good idea at the time. I couldn't stay here now, though – too cold, and the fishermen might be due to arrive. I had to move.

I edged forward, inch by aching inch, until my shoes dangled over the side of the slab. I pushed myself to my feet and immediately wished I hadn't, oxygen surging and balance gone. I half-sat, half-fell back onto the stone, my hands reaching up to massage my temples. I pushed again and staggered onto the empty street, veering left, more because of a homing instinct rather than any real sense of direction or purpose. I walked, head low, arms out, weaving my way up Torsgøta, turning my head away from the disapproving glower of the cathedral high to my right, and climbed towards the hills.

The wind had picked up from nowhere and was taunting my ears, whistling cold round them, but helping to keep me on the right side of sleep. The pavements were black wet beneath my feet, the road even steeper than normal, and it made for hard work. I took a stumbling turn left and just minutes later another freezing gust came at me off the sea, making me shiver and forcing me to abandon the use of my hands as balancing aids, driving them into my jacket pockets in search of warmth.

'Shit!'

A sharp pain flashed through my right hand and I tore both of them back out of the pockets as if I'd been electrocuted. Underneath the streetlight, I could see that my right palm was stung with blood.

Cautiously, I reached back into the pocket and emerged with a short, stubby knife. Even in my muddle-headed state, I knew what it was, this wooden-handled dagger with its thick blade. Every adult male on the islands had one. It was a *grindaknivur*. A knife for cutting whale meat at the dinner table.

Except this one had been used for something else. Its blade was coated with blood. Blood that was too dry to have come from the cut to my hand.

I patted myself randomly: hands, arms, head, stomach. I pulled up my shirt, examined the visible flesh. There was no blood and no cut other than the one I'd just made. The blood on the blade wasn't mine.

I stared at the knife, wishing it away. Wishing I could remember where it had come from. What it had been used for.

The street, Dalavegur, seemed more exposed than it had moments before. Standing there with a bloodied knife in my hands, I could only wonder how many curtains were twitching at the sound of footsteps in the middle of the night.

I slipped the *grindaknivur* back in my jacket pocket, turned up my collar, bowed my head and walked on, hoping I was no more than a ghost, unheard and unseen.

The little knife weighed a tonne, though, dragging my pocket down with doubt. Hard as I tried, I could remember almost nothing. Drinks in the Cafe Natur. Then waking up on the fish slab in the rain. Little but blackness in between.

She'd been there, I remembered that much. Laughter. Drinks. Maybe an argument. Then nothingness.

Across the intersection and up a narrow path, the houses were further apart now, the lush green of the hills carved into generous sections by the coloured timber frames of traditional homes. The wind hurled itself at my unsteady figure, spinning me and forcing me to turn and look at Torshavn laid out below me, its odd shapes pushing through the mist. Roofs of turf and rainbow hues, the cathedral spire and swathes of green. All tumbling down towards the sea. Always to the sea.

I don't know whether I was driven by instinct or guilt but I took a few steps off the path and knelt down, the blood flowing to my heavy head and making me think I might throw up or pass out. I grabbed the sharpest stone I could find and began digging at the earth, howking out dirt until there was a hole big enough to contain the little knife.

I pulled my shirt free of my waistband and used the bottom of it to wipe the handle of the *grindaknivur* before dropping it into the newly dug hole. Earth to earth, ashes to ashes. I kicked the dirt back over the knife, filling the hole and stamping it down. Picking up three similarly sized stones, I used them to both mark and conceal the hole. With a final look around, I pushed on up the path to the shack that passed for my home.

It was three hours later, when I'd somehow managed to rouse myself from my brief second sleep and get myself in to work, that I heard. Everyone was talking about it. No doubt the entire islands were.

The stabbing.

The murder.

Chapter 2

Three months earlier.

I was blown into the Faroe Islands on the June wind. Picked up by a squall that dumped me on the first bit of dry land that held fast between the sea and the sky. Due north of where I started. Both zero and 360 degrees north of the place I'd left behind.

It was 435 miles straight up from Glasgow, 415 west of Norway and 400 south of Iceland. It could have been the definition of the middle of nowhere. It could have been anywhere. Just as long as it wasn't where I'd come from.

Emerging from the front door of the tiny airport, I stood and looked. And saw nothing. It wasn't just that the concrete concourse was enveloped in mist and drizzle, it was that there was virtually nothing to be seen.

There was the bus which would take me an hour or so into Torshavn. That apart, there were just the ghostly outlines of a handful of cars scattered around, and beyond them what might have been the vertical shadows of telegraph poles.

My bags stowed in the belly of the bus, I found myself a seat next to the window, huddling myself against it and staring out into the summer gloom until the bus rumbled into life.

A few of my fellow passengers fell into conversation and, despite myself, I tuned into their chat. Not the words, which were incomprehensible to me, but the sound. The accent sang, like the Gaelic. It was like listening to fishermen from Galway on Ireland's west coast or crofters from Lewis. It had a lilt and a rhythm that smiled through the murky evening.

On the connecting flight from Copenhagen, the second leg of my journey from Glasgow, I'd heard the song loudly and constantly. It had been the last flight of the day and more than a few of my fellow passengers had fortified themselves for the journey by downing plenty of beer or wine. The plane's aisle heaved with so many cheery, ruddy-cheeked Faroese that it looked like we were flying to a farmer's convention. The boozing didn't stop there, either. The cabin crew were worked off their feet trying to satisfy the demand as the free alcohol flowed freely indeed.

Perhaps that explained the apparent sangfroid when the weather came calling. Despite our flimsy piece of flying aluminium being pitched and tossed left, right, up and down as we flew through a storm, the locals didn't bat an eyelid, other than calling for fresh drinks.

I watched the wings of the plane flutter like a girl's eyelashes, at times just yards from lush green mountaintops that emerged suddenly and threateningly from the clouds. As we neared the Faroes and circled them, trying to find a way to land, the rugged crags appeared closer and more often, looming up from the angry sea that was occasionally visible through breaks in the porridge-thick fog.

The skyline changed constantly as we rolled, unnatural angles being created and the sea coming far too close. The wind roared as it buffeted against the side of the plane, slapping it like wet towels against bare legs, and hinting at what it could do if it had a mind to. The good slaps sent it sideways, the bad ones caused it to drop alarmingly, leaving stomachs behind.

Tall, improbably balanced rock stacks reached up to us from below. Islands flashed past. If I'd cared about it, I might have seen my life passing before my eyes.

A middle-aged woman across the aisle feverishly fingered a cross round her neck and mumbled a prayer to her god, tears streaming down her cheeks. She, like me, must have been a visitor. The rest had seen it all before or were viewing it through the bottom of a glass. I watched a man in a business suit turn to his companion and shrug, a grin on his weathered face.

Then it got worse.

We must have caught the edge of the jet stream, because the plane tipped almost on its side and glasses and cups flew through the cabin as we dropped further and faster than before. In the long three seconds of freefall, I found time for three thoughts: one, that maybe there was such a thing as karma and that payback would definitely be a bitch; two, that I wished I'd drunk the last of that whisky before the glass went flying on its own; three, that I was going to die.

There is something comforting in that moment, knowing that the end has come. Particularly when your own survival isn't something that concerns you too much. Three seconds to contemplate mistakes and weigh up regrets. At the end of the day they don't amount to a damn thing.

We hit the bottom of whatever it was we had fallen into and the pilot had the thing going forward again, even if only straight to hell. The woman opposite was in hysterics, but the islanders merely laughed, if they bothered to react at all. Most had skilfully managed to hold onto their glasses of booze and little tin soldiers of reinforcements. A man in a grey suit, his tie at a crooked angle, signalled to a strapped-in stewardess that he'd like a refill of his vodka. She said no and he shrugged with equal measures of acceptance and disappointment.

I lacked their confidence in it all working out all right, but I cared as little as they seemed to.

Instead, I found myself mulling over the relative benefits of death and beer. It wouldn't be my choice to make, but it passed the time while fate and the wind decided the matter for us. Death or beer? Die on that flight or get to the Faroes where the beer was said to be particularly good. Both had their attractions, although death was a cop-out and I could hardly choose it without taking a plane-load of presumably innocent people with me. I'd never been one for praying, and although this was probably a good time to start, beer struck me as a pretty frivolous cause for divine intervention. But it didn't matter, as I didn't believe. In anything.

Make a choice, I told myself, shades of Irvine Welsh's *Trainspotting* coming back to me. Choose life. Choose beer. Choose death. Choose to close your eyes and let your whole shitty little existence be chewed up by your conscience till you choke on it. Choose.

As it happened, I didn't have to. An excuse for a runway appeared through the soup and, on the third pass, the wind accommodatingly presented us at a suitable angle and the pilot successfully defied improbability and kept us in line with the landing strip.

The ground rushed at us, tyres hit tarmac with a couple of bumps and a banshee screech. A lone voice triumphantly roared '*Foroyar!*' before a smattering of polite applause rippled through the cabin, reminiscent of – yet a world away from – the drunken clapping that accompanies the landing of a Spanish holiday flight out of Glasgow.

They were home and I was here. It was probably a bad time to start wondering why.

The road from Vagar to Torshavn wound its way through green countryside, rain washing down the windows of the bus. Every so often, hamlets of no more than a dozen homes would appear without warning. The square, weather-beaten houses, most made grimy by the elements, all faced the sea. All the better, I supposed, to see the next wave of weather that would come to torment them.

There were no people. Not one single soul on or by the road. I saw sheep, though, plenty of them. I saw seabirds. I saw horses. I even saw the brown flash of a mountain hare scampering across the lower slopes of a grassy hill. I just didn't see any people.

Suddenly, the road dipped and the bus sailed down a steep

incline into the black mouth of a tunnel. I'd read online that some of the archipelago's eighteen islands were connected by undersea channels but it still took me by surprise. In seconds we were under the Atlantic in a passageway carved out of solid rock. It burrowed its way straight and long as far as the eye could see, like travelling through the stomach of a giant serpent. The concept of a tunnel with no light at the end of it was depressingly familiar.

Finally, slowly, we began to rise then turn, until we emerged gasping from the second mouth of the two-headed snake onto another island.

As a feat of engineering it was incredible. I learned later that we were under the sea for almost five kilometres. As a welcome to these islands, it messed with my head. We didn't island hop. We burrowed.

Above ground, the terrain was a moving feast of greens and browns with russet highlights through the gloom. Hillsides studded with grey rock and cut through with lazy streams running from top to bottom. Regularly the misty showers were pierced by the sight of brilliantly white waterfalls tumbling down from the higher mountaintops, seeking a return to the sea. The landscape was a battlefield for opposing forces; earth and water colliding, with casualties of war everywhere you looked. There was barely a piece of hillside that didn't carry the scars where rain and river had left their mark.

We ran parallel to fjords, verdant hills looking back at us menacingly from the other side, dark clouds low above their tops. When the mist cleared, you could see hill behind hill, peak beyond peak, an endless rolling maul of volcanic eruption now covered in green. Wherever the fjords or the sea made natural bays, there were houses dotted by the shore, communities formed out of opportunity.

Against that backdrop, the first hints of a near-urban sprawl came rudely into sight: a garage; a shop; a flurry of direction signs; houses packed together in rows; the floodlights of a football stadium; industrial units; zebra crossings and offices. The bus careered round a ring road, spun off a roundabout and turned left before dropping us onto a concrete canvas upon which was painted the drizzly shadows of a ferry port. *Welcome to Torshavn.*

I stood on the tarmac, two bags at my side, the rain rushing almost horizontally into my face, and shivered slightly in the chill of what was supposed to be a summer's night. My fellow passengers trooped off to waiting cars or taxis and within seconds I was standing alone. I had wanted remote; I had no right to start complaining.

It took less than five minutes to walk into the centre of town and find the Hotel Torshavn, a tall, red building standing at the bottom of a steep hill and just yards from another section of the port. It was to be home until I found somewhere to live.

Inside, I shook the rain from my jacket and dropped my bags by the front desk. The receptionist, a slim young man with dark hair, smiled politely and asked if he could help me. I told him I had a single room booked and he began to thumb through his reservations.

'Your name, please?'

'It's Callum. John Callum.'

'Ah yes, I see it. Are you in Torshavn for holiday or business, Mr Callum?'

'Neither. I'm here to live.'

The desk clerk's head rose from his paperwork and he regarded me oddly. 'Really?'

The room was tiny but functional. A three-quarter bed pushed up against one side yet floundering halfway along it with no headrest or wall behind. The door of the narrow wardrobe banged against the wall-mounted television and everything was in touching distance of everything else. The windows ran the length of the far wall – a somewhat insignificant feat given the size of the room – and murky light poured through them despite it being so late. I closed the blackout curtains, pretending it was night, and poured myself a generous glass of the malt I'd bought on my way through the airport. After a movie on television and several revisits to the bottle of whisky, I found some sleep, my six-foot-two frame cramped into the inadequate space.

I woke what seemed like five minutes later, snapped from sleep by the sound of banging on the wall. Sitting upright, my head whirled, eyes searching as I tried to work out where the hell I was. My mouth seemed sour with the taste of words that had died on my tongue, a sentence suddenly interrupted and forgotten. I was soaked in sweat and disorientated, my breathing heavy and my system in shock. I sat there, recovering and wondering.

My laboured silence was enough for the angry greeting from the neighbouring room to stop. A final single-word complaint was shouted through the wall, an angry foreign-language protest that I guessed wasn't wishing me goodnight and wasn't particularly complimentary. My sleep, and whatever nightmare it had held, were over.

Getting to my feet, I pulled back the curtains and was dismayed to see the day had already begun. It was going to be a long one.

I tumbled into the shower, enduring the jagged needles of hot water, then put on some clothes and left the room. The receptionist looked up, bemused, as I walked through the automatic doors onto the streets of Torshavn.

I walked where the wind took me. Up one deserted street and down another, daylight and drizzle on my shoulder, in search of something but not knowing what. There was an eerie sense of solitude about the place, disturbed by neither cars nor people, that only increased my sense of confusion.

I stopped to look in the window of a shop that sold locally made knitwear and, above a range of chunky-knit sweaters, I saw a large white clock hanging on the wall. It was 2.30 a.m.

My heart sank at the realization that it was still the middle of the night.

At least my legs were strong even if my morale wasn't. I started walking again.

Chapter 3

I walked for days. Not constantly, but it seemed that way. My wanderings were interrupted by stops for food and short nights of occasional sleep, but little else. The local newspapers, *Vikubladid*, *Dimmalaetting* and *Sosialurin*, whose offices were directly opposite my hotel, had some job listings, but these were, not surprisingly, in Faroese. The phone calls I made yielded nothing. So I walked.

I walked until the fresh air blew away every cobweb except the ones hidden deepest. The wind and rain blasted me and cleansed me. I walked and looked. I avoided people where possible.

In my bad mood, Torshavn reminded me of a Scottish east-coast fishing port; somewhere like Anstruther or Pittenweem. On a Tuesday. In the 1980s. When everything's shut and everyone's gone home. Even to someone from Glasgow it was depressingly grey. I walked through a constant, soul-destroying drizzle, the kind that makes you wish it would just rain properly and get it over with. But it just drizzled. World-class drizzling.

I wandered through the oldest part of town, Úti á Reyni, situated on a rocky promontory by the port. Grey fingers of stone pointed out into the North Atlantic and on them sat remarkable little black-tarred doll's houses with white windows and turfed roofs. Some of these homes dated back to the fourteenth century and were still inhabited. The tiny dwellings were crowded in on each other on narrow alleys paved with stepping stones and sprung with grass, the houses so close that your arms could reach from one side to the other. Further down the hill towards the sea, they gave way to former warehouses, painted blood red and perched on the water's edge. This area was called Tinganes and the former warehouses were now government buildings. Some had corrugated green roofs; others the traditional grass crowning that required the handiwork of a brave gardener to maintain. In amongst them, sitting opposite a covered slipway that led directly into the dark Atlantic, a modest building carried a plaque proclaiming it to be the Prime Minister's office.

It didn't take long to memorize the town: the western harbour at the door of my hotel, where the row of painted houses overlooked the marina with its melee of white yachts and fishing boats; past the white-walled cathedral on the hill, master of all it surveyed; on through the alleyways that fringed Tinganes; past the Cafe Natur with its alluring lights and alcohol, up hills, past shops and hotels and waterfalls. I just walked; my collar up and my head down, bothering no one.

Other days, I climbed high into the hills around the town, and finding no discernible place where the clouds stopped or started, got wet just standing still, despite it not seeming to be raining. I hiked across high moorland and came across an unfinished cathedral which, much like these rain-drenched islands, was badly in need of a roof.

My marches across the hills were accompanied only by the cry of kittiwakes or the screech of fulmars. High-pitched squealing versions of Wagner or Sousa, marking time and territory. Nothing else. All thoughts of anything before Torshavn were banished from my mind.

It took nearly two weeks of walking before I let memories sneak past my guard. I was high on the moorland above the Hotel Foroyar when my mind drifted on the breeze, back to a time and place when I had chosen wrong over right and let violence consume me, control me, define me. And as I thought of it, a little bit more of me died inside, just as it did every time the memory came. I closed the window in my head that it had flown in through, and locked it tight.

I think I became conscious of the movement through the air just moments later, and seconds before I heard the loud, aggressive 'tek-tek' croak just inches from my ear. Instinctively, I ducked. Something brushed against my head and wheeled away. Seconds later, I heard another cry behind me and the air fluttered and hummed. I ducked again and stumbled to the grass as a wide shadow hurtled past.

Getting warily to my feet, I saw a pair of large birds circling way above me. One moved to the left and the other the right. As my eyes tried to follow the movement of both, one was suddenly gone and I knew nothing till it swooped, barrelling straight at me. In the few seconds before I ducked again, I saw that the thing had a wingspan of four or five feet and a ferocious stare in its dark eyes. Its massive brown barrel chest, hooked bill and sharp claws backed up its vicious intent. The other bird followed immediately, its talons dropped to make contact with me, its beak screaming. Just in time, I threw an arm up and fended off the attack.

I'd read enough to know these were great skuas; creatures with a nasty reputation as thugs of the air, attacking other birds in mid-flight and robbing them of their catch, even killing them. They were known to attack ewes and lambs and were extremely territorial. One attacked again, reaching the height of its swing-turn and dive-bombing me, claws outstretched. I managed to sidestep it, but its mate was soon in my face, tearing at my protective arm.

They came again. And again. Screeching, clawing, snapping. Doing everything they could to drive me back down the hill.

My dad kept and bred pigeons where we grew up in Whiteinch. He raced them some, but they never flew fast enough or far enough to win much in the way of rosettes or cups. I was allowed to feed them after school and got to know every one of them by their markings and their cry. The one thing you couldn't tell was whether the bird was a cock or a hen. Until they had chicks to look after. When that happened, the hens would try to take the tip of your fingers off or fly at your face. That was when you had to watch out.

I realized the skuas were attacking because they had a nest somewhere on the flat ground where I was walking. They were protecting their own.

These birds had a duty of care; an instinct to guard those in their trust, whatever the cost. No dereliction of duty for them. They would attack and they would defend. They were the ones in the right and I was in the wrong.

I knew how simple it would be to grab one of these birds as they flew at me. Grab it by a wing or a leg until I could get purchase on its neck. It would be easy to keep its beak at bay as I wrapped my fingers round its scrawny throat, feeling feathers between my fingers, knowing that all that lay below them was soft tissue and fragile bones. My hands would be too strong for that slim neck, my fingers all too capable of gripping, twisting and snapping until life was choked out of it.

My violence would be too much for what little the skuas could offer in return. I could wring the neck of one of them and then the other. But the memory of violence and guilt was what stopped me from doing it. There was still a price to be paid for what I'd done back then, and I couldn't bring myself to hurt those birds for simply trying to protect their young.

Instead, I stood, arms spread wide in supplication, and let them come at me.

My eyes darting left and right, I saw brown shadows flash on the edge of my vision. I kept my eyes open as long as I dared, then clamped them shut as the shadows were almost on me.

The first bird was in or near my face and I recoiled as I felt a rush of air, then the bones of its wings and the softness of its feathers on my skin; the scratch of its claws sharp against my cheek. Its aggressive squawk rang from ear to ear and the earthy, honeyed smell of it filled my nostrils.

My instinct was still to duck or fend it off – or more basic, to kill it. I stood still and fought that urge rather than the bird. The skua revelled in the freedom I gave it and thrashed at me. Then suddenly, breath was thrown out of me and my senses somersaulted.

I felt a huge weight crash into the back of my neck and, stunned, I pitched forward and collapsed onto the ground. My eyes, which had been screwed shut, now saw only blackness sprinkled with stars. Vision blurred and head spinning, I managed to clamber awkwardly back onto my knees but was drunk with disorientation. Next to me in the dirt and as dazed as I was, lay the second skua.

The bird had probably expected me to duck when it launched its attack on me and, not being ready for my sacrificial stance, had crashed into me from behind with its full force. Its senses didn't seemed to have survived the collision any better than mine had, and it flapped pathetically as it tried to right itself.

But the sound of thunder was on me again as the bird's mate returned to the fray with a vengeance, plunging down on me, talons and bill scratching, filling the air with as much menace as it could muster.

It pushed itself off me, arcing away and turning for another assault. The injured bird had joined it in the air again and I couldn't distinguish one angry shadow from the other as they raced down upon me like avenging angels. My arms spread wide as they came, awaiting judgement. It came in the form of a beating of reproachful wings and a brutish peck at my cheek that drew blood.

It was enough. I wanted the punishment I was due, but the physical pain of it forced me into a humbled retreat. When the birds attacked again, I finally ducked away and raised my arms as much in surrender as in protection. I turned and headed back down the hill, the skuas screeching high above me, their braying triumphalism a warning to me to return to my own kind. Whoever *they* were.

Chapter 4

I am deep in the dream. I know that I can't be awake, that it can't be real, because Liam Dornan is there. Alive. Yet I have sunk so far into this bottomless nightmare that I can't climb out of it. Aware of its unreality, I have no choice but to let it play out.

Liam is sitting in the middle of the room, his desk surrounded by the rest of the class, all talking. They are all ignoring me as if I'm not there. Perhaps I'm not, not really. Liam is talking louder and more excitedly than any of them. Pointing and shouting, swearing, winding other kids up, embarrassing the weaker ones, showing off in front of the girls.

I don't want them to make all this noise. It will mean trouble and I don't want that. I'm asking them to be quiet but they can't hear a word because I'm not there. I shout. Then louder. They just keep laughing. I can feel the rage, the frustration, building in me. I'm screaming at them now. Stop. We need to get on with our work. Liam Dornan, this is your doing. Stop them. Now. He doesn't. They don't.

I must be there, though, because he is staring back at me, defiantly, mockingly. I can't do anything to him and he knows it. The smirk. The sneer. That insolent grin. He is laughing louder and longer.

I pick up books and throw them. At Liam. At all of them. Every book in the classroom. Every book in the school is suddenly violently launched at them. They are hit by an avalanche of words but still they stand there, laughing and joking, impervious to everything that I throw at them. Especially Liam. He absorbs it, grows stronger on it, feeding on the frustration and knowing it makes him the winner. I tip up desks and overturn chairs. I turn the room upside down and yet when I look back, every kid is back in their own chair, all laughing.

Liam Dornan is at the heart of it, the eye of the vortex. I don't know how he's doing it but he's putting all that furniture, all those desks and chairs, back in place when I'm not looking. I'm getting even angrier, can feel it growing. I know Liam Dornan shouldn't be alive, can't be alive.

I go up to him, march to his desk, unseen by all. Except Liam. He looks at me, then throws his head back and laughs. My ears are pounding with the noise. It's all I can hear, shutting out everything else.

But then I look closer. Liam is bleeding. How could I not have seen it before? There is blood running down his cheek. It's from a knife wound just below his left eye. There's another, on his right side, a slash from ear to lip. Then one running down the right side of his nose, slicing through the top of his lip, blood pouring from it. There are a dozen cuts, two dozen, three. His shirt is drenched in red; sticky and wet and the smell of it overpowers me. Liam doesn't seem to notice though. He just sits there and laughs, giggling uproariously. His face is all red now; every inch, apart from the white of his teeth, soaked in blood.

I stagger back and Liam sniggers, mocking my reaction. I shout but he still can't hear me. I give in and turn my back on him and walk away.

I can still hear him but he isn't laughing now. He's screaming. I look down. There's blood all over my hands.

Chapter 5

There is only so much fresh air any man can take, and eventually, aided and abetted by the rain, it wore me down and forced me to take refuge in Cafe Natur. The warm orange glow behind the bar's dark wooden facade had been calling to me night after night, whispering sirens that I could ignore no longer.

The sirens didn't lie. Inside, Cafe Natur was everything that outside wasn't. The bare wooden floors and panelled walls rang with the understated hum of people in good spirits. Everything inside was stripped back and basic. Despite my reluctance to mix, it felt strangely good to be in a crowd again.

A large old clock with a yellowed face dominated the wall next to the bar. All the walls were lined with black-and-white photographs and paintings of old Torshavn. Fishermen by the port, men in overalls, washerwomen, boats, the British Army parading through town. I recognized the locations, and not much seemed to have changed except the fashions.

Timber supports ran from floor to ceiling in the middle of the room. Given that there was only a handful of trees in the entire Faroe Islands, Cafe Natur was using up more than its fair share of them.

The shelves behind the bar were in contrast to the rest of the pub. Chic purple backlighting with bottles of expensive vodkas, sambucas and other liqueurs. There was a signed Chelsea football in a glass case, sitting next to a bottle of Tullamore Dew.

I counted eleven taps for draught beer and gave a silent prayer of thanks. The brands seemed to be local, from breweries called Foroya Bjor and Okkara, with names like Gull, Black Sheep, Porter, Klassic, Rinkusteinur.

From behind the bar, a young guy with tousled brown hair and a Nirvana T-shirt smiled and asked what I'd like. '*Bjor, takk,*' I answered in my best attempt at Faroese. It was all I knew and, usefully, *takk* could double as both please and thank you. It would get me by for now.

The guy poured a Klassic and in a generous nod towards my attempt at his language asked me if I wanted anything else. Or at least that's what I guessed he'd said. When I floundered, he asked me again in perfect English.

His name was Oli and we shared the first proper conversation that I'd had since I arrived in Torshavn. The interaction began reluctantly on my part, knowing that barmen, like taxi drivers, hairdressers and journalists, were trained in the art of finding out about people while giving away very little of themselves. The inequity of the deal didn't appeal to me.

'So where are you from?'

'Scotland.'

'Yeah. Which part? The Highlands?'

'No. Glasgow.'

'Oh right. Rangers or Celtic?'

I groaned. 'Partick Thistle.'

Oli looked confused. 'Is that a real team? Or is it just something you say when you don't want to say who you really support?'

He was a smart kid. 'Both.'

'Okay ... So how long are you staying in Torshavn?'

This was a question whose answer would only trigger more questions. However, given that I intended to stay in the Faroes, it couldn't be avoided forever. I hedged.

'I'm not sure. I'm planning to stay for a while. Get a job if I can.'

Oli gave me the same look of surprise I'd received from the receptionist on my first night at the hotel. And the same reply: 'Really?'

'Yes. Really.'

'Okay. How are you finding it here?'

'Wet.'

Oli laughed. 'Yeah. It rains three hundred days a year in the Faroes.'

'That all? I thought it would be more.'

'It only feels like more. You have good weather in Scotland? I don't think so.'

I shook my head. 'Not good weather, no. Just less weather.'

He grinned. 'You get used to it pretty quickly. What else are you going to do? We use cars as raincoats and we stay at home if it gets too stormy. It's not a problem. It's natural.'

'I guess. I'm just not at that stage yet.'

Oli turned and greeted another customer, a balding man in his fifties or sixties, with shorn white hair at the sides and a hippy-looking white beard. '*Hey, Tummas. Hvussu gongur?*'

The man nodded and answered softly. '*Gongst væl, Oli. Gongst væl.*'

The barman began pulling a pint of Gull for the new arrival without being asked and took cash from him. Beer wasn't cheap here and neither was anything else.

'So what kind of work do you do?' Oli asked me as he handed change back to the customer.

Good question, I thought. What I did, what I used to do, was something I could never do again, and that hurt.

'Anything I can get.' I told him the truth, if not the whole truth. As the other customer took his first mouthful of beer he hesitated and narrowed his eyes at the sound of my accent. 'I can turn my hand to most things. You know of any work going?'

The barman thought about it for a few moments before shrugging. 'Maybe. There are jobs. If you don't mind working hard.'

'I don't.'

'Okay. I can ask around. You be in here again?'

I took a long sup on the Klassic ale in my glass. It was dark, cold and malty. 'Yeah. I'll be in again.'

My virgin conversation over, I took a seat at a wooden table with my back to the wall, all the better to watch without being watched. I had a thing about having my back covered. Part paranoia, part self-preservation. Wild Bill Hickok always sat with his back to the wall while playing poker, until the day he played in Nuttal & Mann's saloon in Deadwood in the Black Hills of Dakota. Hickok got shot in the back of the head that day, and I was damned sure it wasn't going to happen to me.

To be fair, the customers of Cafe Natur didn't seem likely to pose such a threat.

Three young guys sat at one table, moodily staring into pint glasses and occasionally gesturing at each other in as unthreatening and undemonstrative fashion as you could imagine. At another table, an older group of men chatted away furiously, but still any kind of fight seemed beyond them. Opposite me, three young women were giggling with their heads bent over tall drinks. One of them, a pretty dark-haired girl with an outrageous 1980s quiff under a porkpie hat looked over and caught my eye, measuring me up before turning back to the company of her friends.

The man, Tummas, who had come in just after me, sat on his own on the mezzanine level, surveying the scene below. Or at least, he was surveying me. He was leaning back in his seat, a leather waistcoat over a white T-shirt, with blue jeans and what seemed to be cowboy boots, slugging on his pint and looking down to where I sat. Maybe he'd never heard a Scottish accent before. I turned side-on and let him look at the back of my head.

Even allowing for Tummas's scrutinizing, the bar betrayed a distinct lack of any threat, of any of the latent aggression that I was used to looking out for in pubs in Glasgow. Maybe it's all about what you are accustomed to, knowing how quickly a lively discussion can become a heated argument. Maybe it's all about spending too much time in pubs where it's wise to sit with your back to the wall. This wasn't Deadwood.

I drained my pint of Klassic, replaced it with a Gull and resumed my watching brief from the position of safety. Through the far window, beyond the wooden stairs that climbed to a second floor, I could see the harbour. White boats bobbed and the grass-roofed red buildings of Tinganes winked at me through the smirr. Free from the drizzle and with the warming buzz of the beer inside me, I grudgingly admired the beauty of the scene. Take away the rain, and the wind, and I had to admit the Faroe Islands were beautiful. The beer must have been stronger than I thought.

Suddenly a raised voice from the table opposite interrupted the idyll and made me turn my head. I saw the dark-haired girl with the quiff gesturing extravagantly, her entire body angrily animated. One of her friends, a short girl with long fair hair, sat with her back to me, but I could tell by the way her arms were spread out, palms up, that she was either apologizing or simply failing to understand what she was being berated for.

Whatever it was, the argument had seemingly sprung from nothing. The three of them had been laughing over drinks just seconds before and now were at war. I knew I shouldn't look, but the dark-haired one was oddly hypnotic. Her green eyes were on fire, staring at her friend furiously. As I watched, her hand shot out and she slapped the other girl across the face.

The sound rang around the little pub, the sharp smack of flesh on flesh.

The dark-haired girl who had delivered the slap sat frozen in her chair, the only movement being her mouth falling slowly open, as if she was confused by what she'd done. The third girl covered her own mouth with a hand, her eyes wide.

The three of them sat dazed for a fleeting eternity, until tears began to roll silently down the cheeks of the girl with the quiff. It burst some communal dam and in seconds all three were in tears and hugging each other over the table in either apology, forgiveness or consolation.

After a bit, they must have remembered that they weren't alone, and looked around to see people watching them. It prompted a fit of nervous giggles then the swift finishing of their drinks. They stood and headed sheepishly for the door, all cloaked in their embarrassment, except for the dark-haired girl, who turned and stared defiantly at the other customers before she left. If this was Deadwood after all, then Calamity Jane had a black quiff and a porkpie hat.

I drew breath on their departure and recommenced my people-watching, albeit aware that the most interesting of the Natur's clientele seemed to have gone. The speed with which the girl's mood shifted had fascinated me. She'd flipped a switch from fun to furious, then another from apologetic to defiant, all changing faster than the Torshavn weather.

Sipping slowly on my beer, I watched the world inch by, slower than the drizzle but just as constant. People ghosted past the pub window, unhurried shadows on their way to or from the sea.

The ageing white-bearded rocker Tummas left too, although not before returning his glass to the bar and bending in close conversation with the barman, his head flicking back in my direction. Whatever was said was brief and the man took the front door towards the harbour. However, as soon as he was outside, he paused and turned to look back in at me, his eyes narrowed in concentration. This time his stare immediately bothered me, sending paranoia spiralling through my bones. Maybe this guy wasn't fascinated by my Scottish accent. Maybe he was trying to work out where he knew me from.

He left and I tried my best to settle, convincing myself that I was reading something into nothing. Some old guy was curious about a stranger in town. Nothing unusual about that. It would have been more surprising if he hadn't been.

After a while that could have been a minute or an hour, I became aware of a voice at my shoulder. It slowly dawned on me that my name had been said, and it was only on the third calling that it registered. 'John?'

I looked up and saw a man of about forty examining me from behind a greying beard.

'Oli says you are looking for work.'

He was tall and slim, with bright blue eyes that regarded me inquisitively. The grey at his chin and temples seemed at odds with his face, which was tanned and unlined. He wore jeans and a blue checked shirt under a navy-coloured jumper.

'Um. Yes. I am.'

He nodded, continuing to look me over. 'And you are from Scotland, yes? I knew someone from Scotland, a friend. He was a good man. What can you do?'

'Anything. I'm a hard worker.'

He continued to weigh me up, scepticism staring back at me from behind the beard. 'It is not well paid.'

'That's okay. I need a job.'

'And it is hard. But it is honest work.'

What was that supposed to mean? Why would he feel the need to state that it was honest?

'Honest work is the only kind I want,' I assured him.

'You haven't even asked me what the job is.'

'It doesn't matter. I'll take it.'

Maybe I was being too desperate. I could see him regretting the offer that he hadn't yet made. He scratched idly at the hair on his chin.

'Are you a man of God?'

I'd happily have given whichever response would get me the job, but I had no idea what that was. All that I was sure of, as my head whirled, was that it was the defining question of this interview. I looked at the man and plumped for his being a bible-basher rather than a heathen.

'I am.'

He smiled and nodded slowly.

'Do you know anything about fish farms?'

'No.'

'You can learn. You start tomorrow. Where are you staying?'

'The Hotel Torshavn.'

He pursed his lips disapprovingly. 'It is expensive there. I will pick you up outside the hotel at eight. I am Martin Hojgaard.'

'John Callum.'

He shovelled a large hand towards me and I shook it gratefully. I had a job. And one less reason to leave.

Chapter 6

Hojgaard arrived as promised the next morning. I'd been awake since six, partly because of the infernal light but also due to an overwhelming nervousness at what lay ahead. I hadn't started a new job in eight years, and hadn't been sure that I ever would again.

The rear door of a steel-coloured Citroën C4 opened and I clambered inside. Hojgaard was driving and two other men, both in their early twenties, nodded a greeting at me and Hojgaard made the briefest of introductions. '*Gooan morgun*. This is Samal and Petur.'

'Callum.'

We fell into silence as Martin negotiated the narrow streets and drove past the ferry port to the ring road. The morning was dry and there was even a hint of sun behind the thin layer of cloud. It counted as a heatwave here.

We were heading north, the sea on our right all the way, until we swung west along the shore of a fjord. At its head, we crossed overland, emerging on the other side of a large headway. We climbed further north and finally crossed a 100-metre long bridge. It was my first indication that we were going to one of the other islands. The sign on our emergence told me we were now on Eysturoy.

On we went in silence, until, at the sign for the village of Eidi, we turned north then east along the coast a short way. Hojgaard signalled right and pulled onto a single-track road that dipped down towards the water's edge. Way out in the bay was a series of large circular contraptions that I took to be salmon cages, rising and falling with the surge of the sea. A long, low navy-blue warehouse lay off to our left, a taller white building at its end, and two container bays beyond that. Two boats were moored by the wooden jetty and a couple of large, cylindrical aluminium tanks sat nearby.

'Risin og Kellingin fish farm,' Hojgaard told me. By way of further explanation, he turned to his left and pointed out to sea, where I saw two spectacular rock stacks, both over three hundred feet high, at the foot of a large headland. 'Risin and Kellingin. The giant and the witch. Come.'

He led the way while I looked back over my shoulder at the stacks as I walked. The one furthest from the headland was tall and bulky; it was easy to see the curve of broad arms at its side and the protrusion of a head looking towards its mate. The other was slightly the shorter of the two and triangular in shape, seeming to be standing on two legs. The giant and the witch indeed.

Samal and Petur disappeared to their stations while Hojgaard gave me the guided tour of the factory. The floor of the first room we passed through ran with water as people in blue overalls and white hairnets busied themselves. The chug of conveyor belts cut through the chill of the air, muffled only by the sound of running water, the sharp smell of fresh fish all-pervasive. Gleaming silver-grey sides of salmon shone on steel-grey tables.

'At Risen og Kellingin we have farmers, handlers, packers and shippers,' Martin explained. 'You will do different jobs depending on what is needed. Okay?'

I nodded, my senses overwhelmed by my surroundings.

'You will be in here on the production lines or out there. On the cages. You can swim, right?'

Martin saw the look of wariness that spread across my face and laughed, the first time I'd heard him do so.

'It's okay. We have boats. We don't like losing workers in the cages.'

I allowed a laugh of my own to break out. I realized I had signed up for something I had no knowledge about whatsoever.

'We farm wild Atlantic salmon. We look after the fish. We look after our workers. And we look after the environment. It is important to the owners, the Poulsen family, that all three are cared for. They make sure that our fish are reared and harvested ethically. As a result, the taste is the best. No antibiotics, no stress in the meat. Nothing but premium salmon. We are very proud of our fish.'

We'd moved into another room, where five workers in yellow waterproofs were tending to large white containers of fish as a machine passed above, dropping shavings of ice onto the fish below. Behind them, crate after crate was stacked to the ceiling, each bearing the company symbol of the giant and the witch.

'You will learn how we work and why. The company likes everyone to understand why we do things the way we do. It is all about protecting the quality of the fish and the environment here. We operate what is called the all-in, all-out strategy. The government says each production site is limited to only one generation of fish. When the generation passes though, everything is dismantled, cleaned and then left crop-free for at least two months. It is a very good regulation. The salmon are protected from the spread of disease and the ocean currents clean the site. Come.'

Hojgaard led me into another room by a connecting door. A bank of TV screens was against the wall, operators sitting in front of them. On each screen, I saw shoals of salmon swimming this way and that, their silver flesh sparkling in the murky dark of the Atlantic.

'We watch them twenty-four hours a day,' Martin told me. 'They are important to us and we watch them as if they were our own children. And like children, we feed them when they are hungry. The cameras also show when the fish are rising to the surface and we can activate the feeding pipes in the cage by computers from here. It means we only feed them when they want it and we do not waste food.'

The sight of the salmon fighting against the tidal waters was hypnotic. They muscled their way through it effortlessly, their black-speckled flanks pulsing with the vitality of natural athletes. Hojgaard saw my fascination with them and smiled quietly to himself. I guessed it was a reaction he was used to.

'The cages are thirty metres deep and those furthest from shore are two kilometres out. We want them as close to open water as possible but it would be too risky to put them any further out. You see the cage here?' Hojgaard pointed at a screen showing the surface section of a cage, waves thundering up and over its curved aluminium edges so that it rocked with the movement. A corrugated standing area on its outer edge bucked like a crazed fairground attraction.

'The waves are wild like the salmon. Out there they can be six metres high and we cannot take the risk of the cages breaking free. Okay, come. I will get you clothing. You will start loading and stacking the crates.'

The work was hard and laborious but it felt good to use muscles that I hadn't flexed in a while. A comforting ache soon hummed in my biceps and calves as I strained to find the best technique, matching brain with brawn and enjoying doing so. My fellow workers seemed a friendly enough bunch. They were relaxed and went about their work quietly and seemingly contentedly. Or at least most of them did.

Late that first morning, as I hefted crates that seemed to grow heavier with every one that I stacked, I suddenly felt a rough edge of hard plastic barge into my lower back. I took an involuntary step forward, before turning to see the back of a short, sturdy figure striding away on powerful legs, carrying a loaded crate as if it was made of balsa wood. It wasn't, though – the ache in my back was testament to that.

He didn't pause, and I had to think that he hadn't realized the crate had caught me on the way past. A few minutes later, the same guy was coming back, and I saw that he was as wide as he was tall, a scowl plastered across thickset features. I raised my head in greeting but got only a glare in return, and had to step aside as the now-empty crate was thrust into the space that I'd been occupying.

'Nice to meet you,' I called after him.

He stopped in his tracks and slowly turned round. Dark-eyed and dark-haired, he glowered at me under heavy brows. He spat out a sentence in angry Faroese then stood for a moment, seemingly demanding a response. When one didn't come, since I didn't understand a word he'd said, he sneered and turned away.

I was left bemused. Maybe something had been lost in translation and he had just been welcoming me to the fish farm, albeit in his own gruff manner. I doubted it though.

Samal sidled up to me, a wary look over his shoulder to make sure that the man had gone.

'That is Toki Rønne,' he explained with a shake of his head. 'He does not like anyone. He is always in a bad mood.'

'It's not just me then?'

Samal smiled apologetically. 'Well, no. Not just you. But it is true he has decided he does not like you.'

'Great. Why is that?'

The man's shoulders rose and fell. 'With Toki, who knows? But he has a friend he wants to work here. He has spoken to Harra Hojgaard many times about it. Now you have a job . . .'

Samal's voice trailed away but it left little doubt that he thought Toki blamed me for his friend's lack of employment. I wouldn't have minded so much if Toki didn't give the impression that he could easily pick me up and snap me in two.

For a while, he wore a path across the wet factory floor as his crate-hauling duties took him directly past me each and every time. He was careless, or more likely aggressive, with his load, charging past me without any care.

I said nothing. The last thing I needed was unnecessary confrontation or hassle. Not now. This idiot wasn't going to spoil the good feeling of that first morning. Anything else, I decided, I'd deal with, if and when it happened. As it turned out, he disappeared, either fed up with my refusal to rise to his bait, or simply working elsewhere in the factory. I wasn't disappointed.

At lunchtime, I took advantage of a day without rain and ventured outside to take another look at my new surroundings. It also meant I avoided any inquisitive questioning from my workmates. A low profile seemed like a good idea.

It was a beautiful day. The breeze was light and fresh and there was even something approaching heat emanating from the sun. Kittiwakes flew overhead, their shrill calls the only sound apart from breaking waves and the bleating of a flock of black-and-white sheep as they defied gravity by scampering across an almost vertical hillside. I picked out a grassy spot facing the beguiling basalt stacks of Risen og Kellengin that rose out of the blue swell and sat to eat the sandwiches I'd brought with me – ham, and a cheese that I'd never tasted before – and to enjoy the view.

I was at the end of the world. A piece of it carved from the dramatic collision of nature.

There was the sound of footsteps from my right and I looked up to see Martin Hojgaard approaching, sandwiches of his own in hand.

'I can join you?'

I nodded and waved a hand to the grass beside me. 'Of course.'

Hojgaard took a bite out of a sandwich, his face contorting slightly as he chewed. 'My wife Silja always puts mustard on them. I don't really like mustard, but I love my wife so I don't tell her.'

He nodded in the direction of the stacks. 'They are interesting, huh?'

'Yeah. It's an amazing view.'

Martin nodded. 'It is easy to forget when you work here every day how special it is. The legend is that the giants in Iceland were jealous of the Faroes and wanted the islands for themselves. So they sent down the giant and the witch who were instructed to take them back with them. They reached the mountain and the giant stayed in the sea while the witch was sent to climb the mountain armed with a heavy rope with which she was to tie the islands together so she could put them onto the giant's back and he would carry them home. Tying islands is hard work, though, and they toiled through the night and didn't realize how much time had passed. Of course, even the smallest shaft of sunlight shining on a giant or a witch will turn them to stone. When dawn broke, the sun hit them and they were frozen on the spot. They've stood there ever since, staring across the ocean towards Iceland. Now, geologists say that the witch will fall into the sea in the next few decades, brought down by the winter storms. Maybe it will. Who can say for sure? We *are* talking about a witch, after all.'

'You believe in that?'

Martin didn't look at me, but grinned as he continued to look out to sea. 'Why not? It is a poor country that does not have legends. You have come here to live?'

'Yes.'

'Why?'

'I wanted to get out of the city and make a new start somewhere not so cluttered with cars. Somewhere I could see the sky and breathe fresh air.'

'But you have such places in Scotland, of course. Your Highlands. Islands too. Why not go there?'

Caught out. Nailed in one.

'I wanted to go further. Get away from Scotland completely.'

'Did you need to? Not my business, of course.'

'I . . . I felt as if I needed to.'

'So you came to somewhere that rains even more than Glasgow. Are you crazy?'

'I like rain.'

'That's lucky for you. You're *really* going to like it here. But you need somewhere to stay. You cannot live in the Hotel Torshavn. Not on the money we pay.'

'I'm looking for somewhere.'

'My wife and I have a spare room. We take in paying guests. If you want it. If you don't mind children. We have a daughter too.'

'No, I like children. And yes, that would be great. Thank you.'

'Okay. You have ten more minutes then back to work. You don't want to be turned to stone.'

Now I had a job and a place to stay. My new life was taking shape. All I had to do was find a way to put the old one behind me.

Chapter 7

Hojgaard and I drove mostly in silence up a steep road accompanied by the inexorable drizzle, homes of all shapes, sizes and colours on either side.

I'd walked up Dalavegur before. Its steep incline had tested my calves and its spectacular views had tested my cynicism.

To my left there was a striking timber house, tall with dark, herringbone wooden panelling. To my right, a large handsome home on two levels; the upper in dark wood, the lower resplendent in white; the window frames and roof were in ruby red and there was a huge, well-kept garden out in front. Up the hill was a low, pale-blue wooden house with white window frames and a roof of sun-bleached turf. The residents of Torshavn loved colour.

Perhaps it was the product of living in an environment often dressed in shades of grey that drove them to brighten what they could of their surroundings. The houses came in rainbow hues of cheery pastels and vivid primaries. Walls and roofs, when the latter weren't made of grass, often contrasted but rarely clashed. It reminded me of the houses and restaurants that strung along the harbour-front on Tobermory on the island of Mull. A palette of brilliance that lit up a dreary day and dazzled on a sunny one.

Finally we reached a sturdy, square house built of wooden boards protected by corrugated iron, painted daffodil yellow and topped with a bright red roof. Martin waved a hand in its direction.

'My home.'

A sheepdog bounded across the neat garden to meet us, its black-and-white coat rippling with the wind and the enthusiasm of its greeting. Its mouth hung open and its tail wagged furiously, but it didn't let loose a single bark.

'Hvirla!' Martin crouched and ruffled the dog's mane and rubbed its ears. The beast celebrated by whirling on the spot, nose to tail, in delight. 'In English it means like a cyclone or tornado. It suits him, no?'

The door opened and a woman stepped out, a young girl tucked shyly in at her side, arms around her.

'This is Silja. My wife. And this . . .' he strode towards them and plucked the girl from her mother's waist, '. . . is my *prinsessa*, Rannva.'

The girl giggled as she was swung though the air, her blonde hair flying, pretending to try to escape the kisses that her father aimed to plant on her cheek. She failed, and Martin kissed her noisily.

Silja Hojgaard was an attractive, rather weather-beaten woman in her late thirties or early forties, her straw-blonde haired pulled behind her head into an unruly ponytail. She smiled warmly and nodded. 'Nice to meet you.'

Those turned out to be pretty much the only four words of English she used, apart from *please* and *thank you*, both of which she uttered regularly. Martin later told me that Silja did know more English but lacked the confidence to use it. Rannva was only six and knew no language other than Faroese. She seemed fascinated by and suspicious of my presence in equal measure.

I was shown to a simple room: clean, tidy and all in white but for the dark wooden furniture. From the sole window there was a stunning view back down the hill towards the town centre and the ocean. A cross hung on one wall and a painting of Jesus on another. This was to be my new home and I had the dubious benefit of Christ the redeemer watching over me.

Silja had prepared the table for dinner and Rannva was in the kitchen along with her, occasionally peeping out from behind the door to look at the new guest. Martin sat with me and made small talk about how long he had worked at the fish farm and how he had become foreman. His dedication to his job was total and his eagerness to extol its virtues knew no bounds.

The Hojgaard dining area was bright and cheerful. The windowsill was dotted with indoor plants in colourful pots, the blinds above rolled up as high as possible, to allow the maximum amount of daylight. Three open cupboards hung on the walls, stacked with plates and bowls, jugs and mugs. Lining the table was a vinyl cloth resplendent in swirls and ferns, which would have graced a Scottish kitchen in the 1970s. I didn't dare to ask whether it was meant to be retro.

If truth be told, and regardless of manners, I'd girded my loins in anticipation of my meal; part fearing, part hoping that it would be the traditional Faroese fare that my trawl through the Internet had led me to expect. I knew about *tvost og spik*, whale meat and blubber. I'd read about the Faroese eating puffins. And wind-dried mutton and fish which hangs outside for weeks on end. My stomach and my curiosity were at war over whether any of this was a good thing.

As it turned out, I needn't have worried, as Silja served up a delicious plate of white fish and boiled potatoes. It and the company of the Hojgaards were enjoyable. We chatted, Martin occasionally translating for his wife, until the effects of the meal and the day's work took its toll. I excused myself and made for my room. After pulling the double curtains across as best I could to shut out the never-ending light, I fell into my new bed content, and properly ready for sleep for the first time since I'd arrived in Torshavn.

My eyes broke open and I sat up in bed, drenched in a cold sweat. My breathing was fast, my heart racing. The last thoughts going through my head still lingered, ghostlike. The boy: his screams, his knife wounds, his broken bones. He still stood there on the edge of my nightmare, but was slipping away as consciousness won.

Something moved to my right and my head swung after it, thinking it might somehow be him. Instead, Martin Hojgaard stood by the doorway, staring at me, his mouth open in disbelief. Behind him, I saw Silja retreating, guiding Rannva back to her bedroom with a protecting arm.

Martin said nothing but it was obvious he was angry. I sat still, trying to let my pulse decelerate and regain some control of my breathing. I was aware of sweat slowly trickling down my back.

'What happened to you?' Hojgaard's voice was low and insistent. He closed the door behind him but didn't step any closer. 'What made you like this?'

I still didn't know quite what he was talking about. The rude awakenings and the sweats were something I'd become used to. The nightmares were sometimes remembered, sometimes not, but I suspected they always involved the boy.

I knew I was drowning in guilt, scarred by my memories. But until now I'd been a tree falling in a forest with no one to hear the sounds I made. Now Martin had heard them, his family too. The look on his face told me they did not make for pleasant listening.

Lips pursed and eyes opened wide, I shrugged, trying to convey my confusion. Hojgaard didn't buy it.

'You were screaming. Shouting and screaming. Foul words. Some words I didn't hear before. You were afraid. But you were also saying violent things. What happened?'

I ran a hand through my damp hair. 'I don't know. A nightmare.'

'More than that, I would say. I have never heard anything like it. I thought you were being attacked. Or were attacking someone.'

'Just a nightmare.'

Hojgaard's eyes fixed on me, his jaw now clenched.

'At work, I asked you if you needed to get away from Scotland. I ask you that question again.'

'Martin . . . I . . . I don't know what you heard.'

'Perhaps not. But you know what you were dreaming about.'

'No . . . well, some of it. It was like I . . . was fighting.'

He stared before finally nodding. 'A fight, yes. And more. Some words you shouted a lot. "Kill" was one of them. You shouted "kill" many times. And "murder". Is there someone you want to kill?'

I shook my head vigorously. 'No. Of course not. Martin, I'm sorry. I didn't mean to wake your family.'

'But you did. And you scared them. Rannva is in tears.'

'I am so sorry.'

Hojgaard dropped into a chair by the door, his head falling into his hands. At length, he sat up and looked at me.

'This cannot be. I cannot have this in my home. You must understand, Callum. You frightened my daughter. And my wife too.'

I began to speak but he held up a hand to signal that I should stop and listen.

'You are a troubled man. I can see that. I do not know what your troubles are but I cannot have them here. Rannva doesn't speak English yet. That is a good thing. There were words said that I wouldn't want her to understand. You must go before she learns.'

I could only nod, my head full of more questions than answers.

'You can keep your job,' Hojgaard continued. 'I will not judge you by your dreams. But I will watch you. I will have no trouble at work either. If you bring trouble, you will bring shame on me.'

'I won't be any trouble. I promise.'

'I promise you that too. You must move out tomorrow. We have a place that you can move into. It isn't much, but you can have it for the same rent. It is further up the hill and on its own.' He paused and looked at me, genuine concern in his eyes. 'If you scream there, no one will hear you.'

'What did I shout, Martin? What else?'

Hojgaard shook his head with a firmness of certainty. 'No. I will not repeat them. They are between you and God.'

Chapter 8

The Hojgaard place in the hills turned out to be little more than a shack. It backed into the hillside itself, a jutting piece of overhang forming a natural turfed roof and supported by wooden beams. The black-tarred walls and white windows made a bleak statement against the browns and greens of the hill. An intruder, despite the native crown of grass.

Inside it was basic. Basic as in rudimentary. As in primitive. In Scotland it would have passed for a bothy – a simple shelter, usually in remote areas and usually left unlocked for anyone to use. There was one small room, an ancient cooker in the corner, with a toilet off it and a shower that looked temperamental at best. The bed was bereft of covers and sagged depressingly in the middle. Cobwebs battled for wall space with dust, and the room was stagnant with the odour of dead air.

Martin Hojgaard, decent man that he was, shrugged apologetically as he gave me the grand tour. Silja stayed close to his side, eyeing me warily, the previous night's drama clearly still fresh in her memory.

'Don't worry. It is fine,' I assured her husband. 'I'm grateful.' And I meant it.

Silja said something to him in her lilting Faroese, waving her arm and pointing here and there. Martin nodded and explained. 'Silja will fix it up. When you return from work tonight it will be better.'

I dropped my bags and turned the key in a lock that wouldn't stand up to any determined effort to break it. I shook hands with my hosts then got into the back of Martin's Citroën and we headed for the fish farm.

That evening, the sun having worked its way across the sky, traversing Torshavn's broad panorama, I returned to my new abode. Silja had indeed worked wonders.

The bed still sagged and the shower appeared as temperamental as before, but the shack sparkled. The cobwebs and the dust might never have been there, and in their place were three vases stuffed full of vibrant flowers in pinks and purples, sweet peas from the Hojgaard garden. The bed was dressed in fresh white linen and a small pile of fluffy towels perched neatly upon it. There was even a chocolate placed on the pillow as if this were some five-star hotel. Three paintings now hung on the walls, one of Jesus on the cross, of course, and two scenes of Torshavn. The air was heavy with the fragrance of the flowers and ... something else ... Silja opened the oven door of the newly clean cooker and produced a steaming dish of stew that looked and smelled delicious.

'Silja! Thank you. I don't know what to say.'

The look on my face must have been enough, as Silja beamed happily and nodded, tapping the casserole dish to suggest I eat it while it was hot. She left me to it and I sat on the bed, wondering how it had come to this, me sitting alone in a shack in the hills, miles from home, but thankful for the chance to shut the door on the world and have somewhere to rest my head.

Chapter 9

I am underwater. I'm in deep, my hands carving their way through the dark, letting me twist this way and that, flipping somersaults effortlessly, diving and rising as I please.

I can feel the cool of the water against my face as I push through it. The water is dense and I can feel the weight of it against me. It's pleasurable though. Soothing. Reassuring. I kick and pull with my arms and I surge forward, powering through the water.

There's a shape up ahead. Somehow I know what it is even before I can make it out. I kick again, but no matter how hard I push, I get no nearer. The water's getting darker too. And thicker.

It's Liam Dornan who's swimming ahead of me. I know it's him. That's when I know I must be dreaming. Is he trying to swim away from me? Or is he leading me somewhere?

There are other shapes around. Moving through the water faster than me, faster than Liam. They're dark, darker than the water. But I look again and I'm as dark as they are. I'm cutting through the water easily, eating it up, born to it.

Liam is looking back now, seeing the sharks descend on him. Part of me wants to shout out and warn him. But I can't. Can't shout underwater. Can't open my mouth.

He's panicking, kicking faster and losing oxygen. There's blood trailing from his heels and it's that that's making the water so dark and thick. We're all swimming in it. Me and the other sharks.

Liam is surrounded now. We are encircling him, waiting for the right moment, knowing that he is getting more and more tired, knowing that he is losing energy and blood and any chance of a way out.

I can see the fear in his eyes. We all can. We can smell the fear as well as the blood. It enflames us. We want to kill. Kill. Kill.

One of my shark brothers swoops first, tearing at a leg, shearing flesh. Then another follows, gripping and biting an arm clean off. There's more blood. The sea all red now, rippled with the boy's blood, and yet I can see clearly as we pounce, one after the other and then all at once, ripping him to shreds. Even when he's in pieces, even though he's deep below the sea and swimming in his own blood, even then he manages to scream.

It's the screaming that wakes me up.

The times of sunrise and sunset in Torshavn are little more than a technicality. The tables tell you that in mid June, the sun will set at 11.22 p.m. and rise again at 3.36 a.m. This ignores the fact that it will not be dark in between those times for any more than an hour, and even then it will be a poor excuse for darkness. It also ignores the fact that the sun often appears over a horizon that is obscured by cloud or mist. Or rain. Or all three. Sunrise, sunset, who can tell the difference? The Faroes in summer is the land of eternal sunshine, except the shining part is far from guaranteed. But the light, the light that fights sleep and guards against slumber, it is always there.

I think in those first few weeks in Torshavn I managed maybe a couple of hours sleep a night. My eyes and my mind were forced into stumbling false dawns by the damnable glow that wouldn't go away. Night was no more than a blink of the sun's eye and darkness was found only under the covers or behind eyelids clamped shut. Daylight stretched for days on end and it chewed at me, eating me up. I found myself listless and struggling to concentrate, bingeing on coffee and food, while wearing the telltale signs of puffy eyes and sallow skin.

Consoling locals were quick to point out that the summer doesn't last forever, but for me it was hell while it did. Once June and July slip away, it accelerates downhill towards winter. The day is three hours shorter at the end of August than at its beginning. Like a summer's night, summer itself is a blink that is easy to miss. Gone before you know it.

Yet back then, the interminable dog days of June and early July stretched out beyond my endurance. The window of my new home faced the sea as almost every other did in Torshavn. The sea was east and so was the arrival of the sun, visible or not. It got so that I was awake waiting for it, like the condemned man waiting for the dawn. Yet for me, the dawn itself was the penance, not the executioner's axe or the hangman's noose. Either of those would have been sweet relief.

This day, a day that had barely begun, I watched the first straw of sun edge its way into the left-hand corner of the window frame and I knew I was done for. It was a little after 3.30 in what was laughingly called morning, and nothing approaching darkness had found its way into my room.

The sunbeam inched left to right, taunting as it travelled. Hard as I tried, I couldn't tear my eyes away from it. It was so visibly the source of my torture. The one bloody thing I didn't want to see, and I couldn't stop looking at it. Day after never-ending day of being awake. Tormented just as much by a lack of sleep as what happened when I managed to achieve it.

The truth was I wasn't sure which kept me awake more. The constant light or the prospect of the nightmares that inevitably awaited me. The sun was my rescuer as much as my tormentor.

I kicked the blanket off the bed and dropped my legs over the side, determined not to be a prisoner to daylight. I pulled on shorts, a T-shirt and running shoes and locked the shack behind me. At the front door, the hill spilling forward before me, I was arrested by the sight of the phenomenon that plagued me.

The glowing orb was rising above the peak of the neighbouring island of Nolsoy, its rays tumbling down that island's slopes and turning them into fields of gold. Above, rolling cirrus clouds burned as if fresh from heaven's oven, and the sky was backlit in a blue that went on forever. The sea was a silver swell and Torshavn's rainbow homes reflected the glory from above.

The sunrise was a lover that you couldn't live with and couldn't live without. I turned my back on her and ran into the hills, determined to exhaust myself.

Chapter 10

It was a Tuesday evening and I'd sought out what passed for a sports bar in Torshavn, with the idea of getting out of the rain and watching Wimbledon with a beer or two for company.

I wandered up the steep, narrow incline of Grims Kambansgøta to where The Irish Pub sat. It was effectively two pubs in one: the mock wood panelling, couthy signs and manufactured alcoves of the theme bar upstairs, while downstairs was the Glitnir, a different beast altogether, and my destination of choice.

It did seem an utterly unsuitable place to be watching something as healthy and outdoorsy as tennis. It was dark and gloomy, a claustrophobic underground lair better suited to snooker or ritual torture. The room was lined with television screens including a vast flat-screen that filled the main wall to the left of the bar.

The walls themselves were draped with huge flags in the livery of Manchester United. The bar was clearly a meeting place for Faroese fans of the English football club. The reds and blacks and images of red devils did nothing to undermine the impression of an altar of sacrifice.

However, for all that it was dark and enclosed, the Glitnir was perfect for its real purpose. Not the monotonous rallies of men knocking balls over a net, but drinking. For the patrons, the tennis was a pretext, an excuse given to either their partners or themselves for congregating in the shadows and easing beer down their throats. Not that I was judgemental of any of that, far from it.

It was the barman there who explained the place's name to me. *Glitnir* meant 'splendour' or 'shining' in old Norse. It was the hall of Forseti, the Norse god of law and justice, and the seat of justice among gods and men. It had pillars of gold and was roofed with silver. The modern-day version had pillars of televisions and was roofed by an Irish bar. I applauded the owner's sense of irony.

The patrons sat almost exclusively round the fringes of the room rather than at any of the tables in the centre, a fact I only realized once I'd taken my own place in the middle. The others, my fellow drinkers and tennis fans, had their backs securely to the walls, like one of those centrifugal-force rides that you get at a funfair. No matter how fast the room spun, they'd never fall off into the middle.

They sat in ad hoc groups of two or three, dropping in and out of each other's company with each visit to the bar to replenish their glasses. At some point – beer three, I think it was – I noticed that one pair of eyes in the half-light was concentrating on me rather than a television screen or the bottom of a pint. I ignored it, but when I turned back minutes later, I was still being watched by the same person.

Rather than stare back into the gloom of the far wall, I waited patiently for my stalker to come into the light, as he would surely have to do. Sure enough, I became aware out of the corner of my eye of the man getting up from his seat and venturing across the floor to the bar. He didn't look at me as he passed, but I had every opportunity to see him.

It was the same guy that had taken such an interest in me in the Cafe Natur. The balding man with the white beard. Tummas Barthel. He was wearing the same leather waistcoat, this time over a black T-shirt. I stared at his back, wondering what the hell his problem was.

He turned, pint in hand, and walked back to his seat, this time looking at me openly. I could feel a familiar anger growing in me, uncomfortable at being an exhibit in a zoo, and barely resisted the temptation to stick a leg out and trip him up.

Barthel retreated into the darkness and I fixed my own gaze firmly on the tennis, determined not to give him the satisfaction of seeing me turn to look at him. If anything, it made it worse. The irritation festered, beer going down my neck quicker, my patience shrivelling.

As the evening wore on, the darkness of the room engulfed my mood. I imagined my hands round the man's throat, demanding answers. Demanding that he fuck off.

When he finally lumbered unsteadily from his seat and made not for the bar or the toilet but for the exit door, I made an instant decision to go after him. I sat still for a minute or so then threw the last of my glass down my throat and got up, discovering that my own feet weren't much steadier than Barthel's.

Emerging blinking into the half-light, I looked left and right until I saw Barthel a hundred yards ahead of me, steering a wayward ship. I set off after him like a dog chasing a car, with no particular idea what I would do if the pursuit was successful. I gained on him along Sigmundargøta, not wanting to alert him to my presence.

The darkness of Glitnir was still in me, an indignant rage boiling over, urging me to ask him what his problem was. Every step closer multiplied my need to know why he looked at me the way he did. I knew full well that I probably wouldn't like the answer, but I still needed to hear it.

I was close enough now to smell the beer on his breath, but he seemed no wiser to my being there. I knew what I was going to do now: the only question was how much I was going to regret it. Up ahead was a corner drowning in shadow and solitude. It seemed the perfect place.

Barthel was much drunker than I was, weaving one way then the other. That was why I saw it before he did. It was why I moved quickly, as quickly as I could, throwing myself at him with every effort I could muster.

The sounds and the movement all rolled into one, tumbling over each other in a blur. I was going through the air, lights blinding me from inches away, the violent shriek of a car's brakes, air choking out of Barthel as I crashed into his midriff, pulling him with me. We crashed onto the ground together, dust coming up and concrete bruising bones. The car was still coming to a raucous halt as we tumbled, two as one, to the safety of the other side of the narrow road.

Barthel was groaning and clearly in shock, but he had landed like a baby, relaxed enough not to suffer any harm. He rolled and sat upright, looking around bewildered.

The car's driver, a bulky dark-haired man with bushy eyebrows, jumped out, red-faced and panicking. When he saw Barthel sitting unscathed at the side of the road, he breathed a huge sigh of relief, but quickly let loose a furious string of Faroese that didn't sound remotely complimentary. There was a lot of pointing, mainly at the older man, but also a couple of gesticulations in my direction.

Barthel reacted with upstretched palms and then with his hands clamped firmly over his ears, shutting out the admonition. He was still in denial of the man's fury when the driver gave up with a final bellow, slamming the car door behind him and driving off with a crunch of gears and complaining tyres.

As the car spun into the distance, Barthel and I were left in the surreal vacuum of a Torshavn night. No daylight, no dark, no sound. We might as well have been sitting by the edge of a road on the moon.

All I could hear was my own breath coming fast and the probably imagined sound of my heart beating faster than necessary. He sat strangely ashen-faced, yet with the ruddy cheeks of a man who'd been drinking all night. Somewhere overhead I heard wings beat and looked up to see the white shadows of a pair of birds slipping across the skyline.

'Are you okay?'

Barthel looked up, seemingly as surprised by my question as he was at my being there. He focused long enough to ascertain who I was and what I meant and at last gave me a lazy nod of agreement. 'I am okay. I am. I'm just groovy.'

I pushed myself up and walked over to him, stretching out an arm and offering it as a help to get him back on his feet. He waved it away airily and instead placed his hands on the ground and tried to lever himself up off the road. After a brief effort, he collapsed back onto his haunches and admitted defeat with a deflated flutter of his lips.

When my hand reached out to him a second time, Barthel grasped it and I hauled him upright. 'Are you okay?' I asked a second time.

'Groovy, man. Just groovy.'

'What did the guy in the car say to you?'

Barthel stared back at me, clearly making an effort at concentration, and I was reminded of the first night I saw him in the Natur and the look he gave me as he left the bar. I got the feeling he was looking at me from behind his eyes, trying to overcome first impressions. Then he answered:

'I know who you are.'

My heart missed a beat. Until that moment, I hadn't realized it was anatomically possible. But I felt it then.

I tried for deflection. 'That's what the guy told you? That he knew who you were?'

Barthel laughed. It was dry and throaty and came from deep inside him. A laugh borne from cigarettes and booze and having seen it all before.

'No. He told me that I was a fucking idiot and I was lucky he hadn't killed me. He said he would have gone to jail and I would have gone to hell. He was half right, I think. And he told me that I would have been dead for sure if it wasn't for you. He said you saved my life.'

I said nothing, as I'd already known all of that. It was what I was less sure of that bothered me. And I both wanted and dreaded to hear it from him.

Barthel straightened up as if ready to make an official pronouncement and extended his arm towards me. I stretched out my own hand and he took it and shook it forcefully.

'Thank you. Thank you for saving my life.'

'You're welcome. Will you be okay getting yourself home from here?'

He smiled and tapped a finger at his forehead. 'I will.'

'Okay then.'

The man turned away, wheeling on unsteady legs and walking a couple of paces before stopping in his tracks. He turned painfully and faced me.

'Oh and Mr Callum . . .'

I breathed deep. 'Yes?'

'*I know who you are.*'

Chapter 11

'Whisky?'

His near-death experience seemed to have sobered Barthel up and he was intent, clearly, on changing the situation. The bottle of Johnnie Walker Blue he was brandishing was 80-proof of that.

We were in the main room of his house, a red-walled building topped with a green roof just off Skiparagøta. The apartment was a shrine to a lost world of rock. Framed concert and festival posters were dotted across the walls: The Who at K. B. Hallen, Copenhagen, in 1972; the Rolling Stones in Cologne in 1973; the Stones again in the Olympiahalle, Munich, in 1976; Radiohead at Glastonbury, 1997; Nirvana in New York City, 1993. A large white bookcase stood against the far wall, but it didn't hold a single book; instead album covers were placed on it, looking out like favourite paintings: Lynyrd Skynyrd, Pearl Jam, Jimi Hendrix, Bad Company, Red Hot Chili Peppers.

Books were piled on the floor to make room for the album display. Biographies, roadies' tales, photographic memoirs, chart listings. Anything and everything the rock junkie might need for his fix. A computer sat in one corner with more books piled beside it. In pride of place on a pristine white table sat a small but powerful looking CD player, which on closer inspection turned out to be a Krell Cipher and probably cost as much as the house.

'Just a small one,' I told him, having little doubt that what Barthel regarded as a standard whisky measure would fill the glass.

'Water?' The question was loaded with judgement and it was obvious which answer he would approve of.

'No, thanks.'

'Good. Water is for fishing and bathing. You know what W. C. Fields said about it, right?'

I nodded. 'Don't drink the stuff, fish fuck in it.'

Barthel laughed as if he'd never heard the line before. 'That's it. That's it. Fish fuck in it. When people ask me what I take in whisky, I say "more whisky". The more the merrier, right?'

I wasn't entirely sure that was going to be true, given the amount he'd poured into the glass. The liquid gold winked at me through the crystal, promising good times and a price to be paid.

'Did you go to all those gigs?' I nodded towards the posters.

'Sure. And others. Cost me a fortune, but it's my thing. Are you into music?'

I took the glass of whisky he offered me and chinked it against his own glass. 'Yeah. But not as much as you, I'd say.'

Barthel shrugged and moved the glass to his mouth, before hesitating when almost there. 'A toast. To lives lost and lives saved.'

All I could do was stare back at him before filling the silence and my mouth with Johnnie Walker. I let it swirl round, bathing my tongue and tonsils in escape. Only once I'd swallowed it did I raise my glass in silent agreement to the toast.

'So, do you go to the G! Festival at Gøta?' I asked.

He knew I was changing the subject but he let it go. 'Of course. I've been every year since it started in 2003. From Bomfunk MCs to Karin Park. Seen them all. I've been all over the world but it's probably my favourite festival.'

'So where else have you been?'

'I lived in New York for a few years so I had plenty of choice. And I lived in London for a bit too. So Wembley, the O_2, Hammersmith Palais. But also Berlin, Rome, Los Angeles. All over.'

'And you played?'

He narrowed his eyes then shrugged modestly. 'Yeah. Not at Wembley, though. The Half Moon in Putney was as big as it got for me in London. Great venue. U2 played their first sell-out gig there. I was a drummer. Played with a few bands.'

'Must have been a great life.'

Barthel laughed, a sound like gravel being churned. 'It had its moments. It wasn't throwing televisions out of hotel windows or trashing rooms, none of that. But we did lots of things we shouldn't have and we had some fun.'

'So how come you came back here to be a fisherman?' I'd learned a little about Barthel from Oli the barman, keen to know something about the man who seemed so interested in me.

His laugh dried up and he looked for an answer in the bottom of his whisky glass, scooping up a mouthful of its contents. 'My father got sick. He couldn't work the boat and I had to come home to help out. He made me promise I would stay and keep the family business going. Then he died on me.'

A bigger gulp of Johnnie Walker washed down the one before. 'I don't break my promises.'

He picked up the bottle and splashed whisky first into my glass and then his. There was something reassuring about the sound, something infinitely preferable to the words whose place it filled. We both sipped in silence.

'Why were you following me home?' Barthel asked at last, reluctantly voicing the question that must have been trying to break free from the moment he saw me by the roadside.

'Why were you staring at me in the Glitnir? And in the Cafe Natur before that?'

Barthel nodded and drank some more. 'Fair enough. I think we both asked questions we know the answer to.'

'It's why I followed you out of the bar. To ask you that question. I'll admit I was annoyed at you. I was angry. But I decided I had to know. Even if I didn't want to hear it.'

He scratched at his cheek contemplatively, looking at the floor then back up at me. 'Like I said, I know who you are. And what you did. Or what they said you did.'

A sinking feeling enveloped me. Just words, just confirmation of the expected, but depressingly sickening. I had fled to the middle of nowhere, but my past had come with me.

Barthel must have read my mind. 'It's a long way from Scotland, I know. But the world is a much smaller place these days. I like to keep in touch with as much of it as possible. I guess I'm not like most people here. I moved away, didn't think I'd ever come back. So I need to travel still, even if it's only in my head.'

He walked over to the corner of the room and tapped the computer monitor. 'This is all that keeps me sane. Or reasonably sane. This and music and good whisky. I am probably the only person in the Faroes who keeps up with the Scotland page on the BBC news website.

'Why Scotland?'

'I lived in Edinburgh for two months once. It was full of English people.'

'And you must have a good memory for faces.'

He shrugged. 'I guess I must have. Although it took me a while to put it together. With your name and all . . .'

I tried to fight the resentment I could feel running through me. Anger at being recognized. Uncovered. He was the only man in the islands who knew me. Who knew who I had been.

Gulping at whisky, I urged myself to calm down. I wasn't that person any more, wouldn't be him again. I needed to say something, offer some kind of reply that didn't beg more questions. Or worse, more answers.

'I came here for a fresh start. A quiet life. I move crates of fish and watch salmon swim.'

He nodded. 'Most people look at a cage of salmon and see thousands of them swimming there. They think they all look the same and certainly couldn't pick one out from the shoal. They can't see that they have different spots and individual ways.'

'It would probably need someone who knew the fish to point it out to the others.'

He held my gaze long enough that I knew he'd made a decision. 'If they can't see it then it's not my place to inform them.'

Barthel raised his glass to me again. 'Here's to lives saved.'

Chapter 12

It was a few weeks before I felt the need to seek the haven of Cafe Natur again. I'd settled into a restless routine of minimal sleep then long days at Risen og Kellengin; stacking, cleaning, filleting, rinsing, icing, lifting, shifting. I'd even spent uncomfortable hours out on the skirts of the salmon cages, rising and falling with the irresistible swell, and hanging on for dear life when the waves threw themselves at me, seemingly determined to finish me off.

I lived with the fact that Tummas knew about my past, relaxing a little more with each day that passed without the sanctity of my secret being breached. It wasn't mentioned the couple of times I saw him on the streets of Torshavn, polite nods being exchanged instead.

In the warehouse, I largely kept to my own company, for fear of too many questions. The one other worker who I could not seem to avoid was my nemesis, the squat and ever-glaring lump of bad temper that was Toki. We seemed to get paired together regularly and never once did he speak to me in English. I'd learned from the others that he knew the language well enough, but he never deigned to use any of it on me. When he spoke at all it was in guttural stabs of Faroese followed by expletives of disgust at my ignorance for not understanding. In my mind, there was a fish hook with

Toki's name on it, with its point and barb driven through his lip and the scruffy moustache that adorned it. In reality I ignored him and didn't rise to his taunts.

I knew that the lack of sleep was affecting me. I was grouchy, lethargic and lacking in energy. The black circles under my eyes were as much testament to my sleeplessness as the strange, displaced feeling that was becoming familiar to me. The only answer that I was sure I could rely on, other than awaiting the arrival of autumn, was alcohol. I could drink myself into either sleep or oblivion. I wasn't too fussed which.

The walk down the hill towards town took me about fifteen minutes, time enough to practise my few newly acquired words of Faroese in my head. Time enough to consider the pros and cons of continuing to keep myself separate from the community. Time enough to gather a thirst.

Oli, the barman from my previous visit, was not on duty, but a girl in her early twenties expertly poured me a pint of Gull and equally knowledgably realized that I hadn't come for a conversation. I poured myself into the same seat I had taken up before, the wall protecting my back from sharpshooters and well-wishers alike.

It was just after nine and the place was busy for a school night. Groups of friends made the pub ring with chatter and laughter, beer flowed freely and the rain washed the windows to make everyone all the more glad that they were inside.

I'd bought a Lee Child thriller from the English section of the bookshop in the SMS shopping centre, just ten minutes' walk away, and was working my way through it. Reading a book wasn't the way I'd have spent time in a pub back home, but then I was a long way from there. I read and I refilled my glass. Twice.

Then, from the corner of my consciousness, I heard the chair opposite me scrape back on the floor. I looked up to see a pretty face smiling back at me under a quiff of dark hair and a hat. It was the girl who had slapped her friend.

She let loose a string of melodic Faroese that inevitably meant absolutely nothing to me. Neither *beer, please* nor *thank you* seemed to be among the words. If it was one of the handful of phrases I'd learned at the fish farm then the speed of delivery floored me.

When she saw the look of confusion on my face, she slipped effortlessly into English.

'Hi. If you're on your own do you want to come and sit with me and my friends?'

I glanced over and saw a table of two other girls, one of them the short girl that had been on the receiving end of the smack, and two guys. All of them were, like her, in their mid to late twenties. On the table in front of them was a tall Perspex funnel containing beer, which descended into a copper bottom with a tap, something like a samovar.

Company wasn't what I'd come looking for, and although there was certainly something beguiling about the girl, I knew it wasn't a good idea.

A line came back to me from *The Great Gatsby*, read in a secondary-school classroom, about how bad drivers are only dangerous when two of them meet. The last thing I needed was a head-on collision.

I shook my head at her. 'No. *Takk*. I'm happy just sitting on my own.'

The girl's nose wrinkled in confusion and her mouth twisted to one side as she weighed up whether to leave it at that. Decision seemingly made, she broke into a coy smile that nearly destroyed my defences.

'Oh come on. It will be fun. Even if you don't like me, my friends are nice people.'

'It's not that I don't like you . . .'

The smile widened and my defences creaked further. I had to be cruel to be kind.

'No. I'd rather sit alone.'

Her green eyes flamed and her mouth tightened until the enticing smile disappeared and was zipped away. The shrug of her shoulders was like twin stiletto blades being flourished in warning. 'Fine. Your loss.'

The chair was pushed back and she spun on her heels, retreating to her friends but leaving a simmering trail of rejection behind her. I couldn't help but notice the skinny jeans that clung to slim legs and showed off a fine rear. I cursed myself silently, but knew it had been the right thing. Even if she wasn't really that bad a driver, I was bad enough for both of us.

She returned nearly an hour later.

I looked across the room to see her sitting with her elbow on the table, chin on her hand, looking at me through narrowed eyes. She pushed the porkpie hat back on her head a little, then siphoned off a pint of beer from the Perspex-and-copper contraption and got to her feet. Weaving her way through two other tables, she reached mine, turning the chair opposite round so that it faced her and straddling it in interrogation mode. She leaned her head across the table till it was near mine.

'So. I'm Karis.'

'Hi.'

She waited in vain for me to offer my name, and when it didn't come she just shrugged casually, the knife sheathed but ready for use.

'Do you not like people, or is it just me that you are rude to?'

Her tone was playful but with an edge to it, like a cat flicking a mouse around and not yet resorting to using its claws.

'I'm sorry. I didn't mean to be rude. I just felt like being alone.'

She tilted her head to one side, making a show of studying me. 'I do not understand that. You are a good-looking guy. So why are you on your own?'

'Because I'm not with anyone.'

'Funny guy, too. So where are you from? Are you English?'

Inside I groaned, as much at the continued conversation as the nationality muddle. 'No. I'm Scottish.'

A strange look crossed her face, something mischievous, and she ducked her head under the table, looking mock perplexed when she re-emerged. 'But if you are Scottish, where is your kilt?'

This girl was going to prove difficult to shake off.

'It's in the dry cleaners. I got it covered in haggis blood during the last hunt.'

'That is disgusting. Scotland must be full of strange people.'

'I can't argue with that.'

Karis was wearing a sleeveless red tartan shirt open over a black rock-music T-shirt. The black porkpie hat sat back on the lustrous dark hair, the extravagant quiff protruding in front of it. Her face was very pretty but almost boyish; gamine, like a young, dark-haired Twiggy. Like a Faroese Audrey Hepburn.

Her look was topped off by a purple scarf coiled high round her neck, and purple fingernails. A tattoo, something Chinese by the look of it, peeked out beneath the capped sleeves of her T-shirt. Boyish or not, welcome company or otherwise, she was beautiful. That wasn't what interested me, though; something else about her intrigued me, and I knew I'd been dragged into this conversation whether I liked it or not.

'So what do you do?' I tried to sound interested enough to be polite, but not so interested that she'd tell me her life story or ask me mine.

'Well, I guess I'm an artist.' She said it shyly, almost dismissively. I couldn't help but like her.

'What kind of stuff do you do?'

'Stuff?' she laughed. 'I paint.'

'People or places?'

'Whatever interests me. You interest me. So you have come to Faroe Islands for a holiday?'

I felt like I'd answered this question more than once, and my irritation crept into my voice.

'No. I've come here to live.'

'*Here?* Why?'

I dodged it. 'Why not? Don't you like your own country?'

She blew out a sharp breath coated in anger.

'Yes, I love it. And I hate it. It's why I came back here to paint.'

'Back?'

'From Denmark. I studied in Copenhagen. Most young people who go to Denmark get their eyes opened and don't come back. Maybe I shouldn't have but . . .'

'But . . .'

'But it's where I'm from. It's in my blood. I want to . . .' She paused. 'Promise me you will not laugh.'

'I promise.'

'Okay. I want to change things. Through my art. Crazy, huh? You think I'm crazy.'

Maybe I did a little. 'No. Of course not.'

'Ha. You do! And that's okay. I don't mind being a little crazy. It's good for the soul. Especially if you paint. Maybe I should paint you.'

That wasn't a good idea at all. 'But I'm not from the Faroes.'

'True. But you interest me. You didn't tell me why you came here.'

I forced a smile. 'But if I tell you then I might not be interesting any more. I'm going to get another drink. Do you want one?'

Karis looked down at her glass and shrugged. 'Why not? No more beer, though. Vodka and Coke, please, Mr Scotsman. What's your name?'

It couldn't be avoided any longer. 'It's John Callum. Just "Callum" would do.'

'Okay, John. Put some ice in it, will you?'

So we talked. We talked about her art and her time spent in Copenhagen. About her schooling in Torshavn. About how she felt women were given a raw deal on the islands and that this was the reason why so many left and didn't return. And about how the Church had so much control over what was said and done and how she hated that, saying it wasn't the way the world should be.

A lot was said and I was impressed by my ability to make so little of it about me.

There was some game being played whose rules I didn't entirely understand. Cat-and-mouse courtship? Maybe, but I was sure enough of my own intention to steer a solo course, and I wasn't really sure that she was trying to win me over. Despite myself, I was enjoying her company. That was the easy bit. She was passionate when she spoke and I could see the same fire in her eyes that had flamed when she'd had the argument with her friend. It coursed through her when she talked about Torshavn and the islands, and it was almost mesmerizing to watch.

'It *is* the most beautiful place on the planet.' The broad smile with which she delivered the statement was utterly convincing. She meant it. 'And we have to maintain that beauty as we drive the islands into the future. That is our duty, as much as it is our duty to make this place somewhere for all the people of the Faroes to live. Especially the young. Especially women. We must harness everything that we have here and make this somewhere the rest of the world is jealous of.'

'And you think that can be done?'

'What? Of course it can. We have every natural asset that we need. Wind, wave, water. We have a youthful populace that we can convince to return with the promise of change. We can be at the forefront of renewable energies and wireless technologies. We maybe have oil out there, too, to fund it. We can be whatever we want to be.'

'Then you choose carefully. Remember, with great power comes great responsibility.'

'Don't make fun of me. Are you making fun of me?'

'Sorry. I think it's great that you . . .'

As I spoke, I became vaguely aware of the door opening and the chill of the night sneaking in. But it was only when I saw Karis's eyes open wide and stare in that direction that I became fully conscious of someone else having entered the bar.

I was still talking, but followed her gaze and saw a tall, broad-shouldered man at the door, a blue woollen hat pulled over his dark hair. He must have been about thirty, good-looking in a rough-hewn kind of way. His dark eyes were on Karis, his face expressionless.

She wasn't hearing a word I was saying, and there was a worry in her eyes that I hadn't expected. The wild, free spirit that I had been chatting to hadn't suggested a tendency towards anxiety.

'You okay?' I had to repeat myself.

She turned back towards me, as if remembering that I was there. Her hesitancy gave the lie to her sudden smile. 'Yeah. I'm fine.'

'Your boyfriend?' I asked.

Her green eyes were at once hot and cold. 'I don't have a boyfriend.' Her tone could have frozen the ocean. 'If I had a boyfriend I wouldn't be sitting here talking to you. I'm not like that. Anyway, I should get back to my friends. I only came back so that I could say no to you rather than you say it to me. Goodbye.'

Karis pushed her glass away from her, stood up and turned away. She brushed past the big guy without looking at him and sat back down at her own table, her back to me as well as the newcomer.

Any doubts on my part that it was he who had spooked her were dispelled when I watched him stare at her as she went by, then turn his head towards me. If looks could kill, I'd have been pushing up daisies on the turf roof of one of the local houses.

Chapter 13

Karis and her friends left just half an hour later, the beer samovar drained of its last golden drop. As they passed by, I heard one of them mention Sirkús, the funky Seventies bar upstairs on a corner of the western port, across the road from the Hotel Torshavn. Part of me wanted to follow them there. Follow her. But it made no sense to do so.

I also felt like I was trapped by the hulking, glowering presence of the guy who had scared Karis off. He stood leaning against one of the vertical support beams, beer in hand, daring me to match his stare. If I left it would be as if he had scared me off, too, and I wouldn't give him that. The only options were to challenge him or to ignore him, but I was angry at being forced into either.

Another man came into the bar and sidled up next to him. A slightly shorter, slightly slimmer version. The same dark hair and eyes. The same sculptured jaw. A brother maybe. Whatever the bigger guy had said, little brother turned and sneered at me. Then a glare of intent. Going out on the street after the girl seemed like a doubly bad idea. I didn't want to be in the dark winding alleys of Tinganes with these two.

Fight or flight. An old dilemma.

My mind was just about made up when a third figure wheeled

unexpectedly into view. A slender, blond-haired man in jeans and a white cotton shirt with a broad grin on his tanned face cut across the other two men and sat himself down next to me. This was becoming a familiar occurrence.

He put a hand across my shoulder in greeting, as if we were long-lost friends, and pressed down harder when I tried to shrug it off. He moved round to sit opposite me, smiling widely, and leaned in close.

'Hey. You're the Scotsman, right? I'm here to save your ass.'

'What? And how did you . . .'

'It does not matter.' The accent was French. 'What matters is that you do not get your ass kicked by that Neanderthal and his brother. You do not want that, do you?'

I glanced over at the pair who were watching me and my would-be saviour. They were whispering conspiratorially and nodding in my direction.

'You know them?'

'The one who scared off the beautiful Karis Lisberg, his name is Aron Dam. He's a hothead. The other one is his brother, Nils. They are trouble. You do not want to know them, believe me.'

'They seem to want to know me, though.'

He laughed. 'Sure looks that way. My name is Serge Gotteri. I am your new friend.'

Gotteri offered his hand and I warily reached out to shake it. He laughed again.

'There are very few foreign nationals in Torshavn,' he told me. 'We should stick together. Let me buy you a beer. And I will have a word with the damn Dams.'

'Look, I can sort this myself. You don't have to . . .'

Gotteri grinned and looked at me, surprised. 'You think you could take them? Both of them?'

I didn't need this.

'I don't want to fight them.'

Gotteri gave a Gallic shrug. 'A wise decision. I will speak to them.'

'No. Wait . . .'

He was gone, suddenly standing beside the two men, their heads deep in conversation. There was some glancing over and some shaking of heads. I got a final glare from the taller brother, Aron Dam, then both men downed what was left of their pints and pushed their way through the door and onto the street.

Gotteri stood there, his arms wide, as if to say, 'See. I told you.' He smiled again and turned to the bar. A couple of minutes later he was back with two beers.

'So what did you tell them?' I had to ask.

'You don't want to know.'

'Yes I do.'

'I told them that you were gay.'

'You did what?'

'It's okay, you don't have to thank me. Now tell me, why have you come to live in this godforsaken place? This is even colder and wetter than Scotland.'

'Why did you tell them I'm gay?'

'To save you from a beating, I told you. *Are* you gay? I think not, I saw you looking at Karis. Never mind, why are you here?'

'Are all Frenchmen as crazy as you?'

'Yes. I think so. They are not all as handsome as me, though. You must be a little crazy, too. At least I came here to work. I know you only found a job when you got here. You have no excuse.'

Gotteri's accent was as thick as a pall of Gauloise and as smooth as Camus Cognac. His constant smile was as beguiling as a kitten and equally irritating.

'What do you do?' I asked with a deep internal sigh, wondering why I was even in a conversation with this guy.

'I am a photographer for *National Geographic*. I have been stuck here for five months already and it seems like five years. I can't wait to get back to New York. No wonder I'm crazy. If you aren't completely insane by five months then I will be surprised. This place does it to you. Are you sleeping at nights?'

An answer began to form on my lips but my hesitation proved fatal to my intent to give a false answer.

'No, I didn't think so. Drives you fucking crazy, huh? The only thing worse than winter here is the summer. If you can tell the difference. It is beautiful, though. No man can deny that. My camera loves it. And the people, they are pretty cool. Well,' he nodded his head in the direction of the door through which the Dam brothers had departed, 'most of them.'

'So you're on assignment here?'

'Yeah. Photographing birds. Hey, it's a job, right? Talking of birds ... what happened to your face? Looks like claw marks.'

My hand went instinctively to my cheek, feeling the scars where the skuas had attacked. 'I disturbed a nesting pair in the hills. My own fault.'

Gotteri looked at me inquisitively. 'Seems you are not very good at defending yourself.'

I took a deep gulp of my beer and shrugged. 'I wasn't paying enough attention.'

'Hm. You need to be more careful. So you go into the hills. You have a car here?'

'No. I just walk.'

'Ha. That is no good. The hills round Torshavn are all very well but there is much more to be seen. Let me take you. Show you around the islands. And,' he pointed at my face, 'I'll make sure the little birdies don't hurt you.'

I laughed despite myself. Maybe I did need someone on my side.

'Okay. Why not?'

Gotteri's smile broadened even further. '*Bon!* We will go tomorrow. It is Saturday, you will not be working, right? Right. I will pick you up at eight. I am going to the Ambadalur valley on the northern tip of Eysturoy to begin with. You will like it. And it is the Faroes, so dress for all four seasons. Just in case.'

I glanced at my watch. 'Okay. There's time for another beer. But ... maybe you could tell me something. It's um ...'

Serge laughed. 'It's about Karis, right? Ha. I'm right. She is quite some girl. Very sexy, no? But she is something of a strange one. I don't know what it is. You like her? Of course you do.'

Was it that obvious? The change of mood and the vanishing act just added to her appeal. I liked her.

'I guess so.' I told Gotteri. 'Do you know if she is seeing someone?'

He grinned. 'So what if she is? I don't know, but she was seeing someone. Aron Dam. God knows what she saw in him.'

'Really? She told me that he was not her boyfriend.'

Gotteri shrugged. 'They fell out, I think. No matter. He is bad, that one.'

'Tell me about him.'

'He is a fisherman, like most people on these islands. His brother used to be, too, but now he works for the oil company that is drilling offshore. Most Faroese people are very friendly, you will know this already. They are quiet, they are not ruled by their emotions, and they make an effort to get on with each other. The Dams are different. Aron and Nils are always angry, it seems. The catch is bad, the weather is against them, the government is doing nothing for them. Always someone else's fault and always they are angry about it. I think all the bad temper in the islands was given to just two people. Anyway, you were going to buy beer, no?'

I bought beer. We drank it then stumbled out into the pale night with loud promises to meet on the quayside near Cafe Natur at eight. Serge wandered his way and I mine up the hill past the Hotel Hafnia and onwards to what passed for home.

Twice I thought I caught sight of someone standing watching me in the shadows of the hotel, but I couldn't be sure if there was anyone there or if it was simply the alcohol or my paranoia. Both times I stood and looked at the shadows, which never moved. If someone was following me then they did so only when my back was turned.

Chapter 14

The new day dawned surprisingly sunny and unsurprisingly early. I fought it, and lost, before finally catching some sleep just in time to be woken by my alarm. A cold shower shook off the last vestiges of my broken slumber before I walked into town to meet Gotteri.

The Frenchman arrived on time, infuriatingly upbeat in the driver's seat of a black four-wheel drive Skoda Yeti. He chatted incessantly, pointing out this and that, giving his opinion on all things Faroese and beyond, his hands waving manically in a manner that made me fear for our safety.

We headed north, across the bridge to Eysturoy, past Eidi and the fish farm, east to the picturesque village of Gjógv, and from there we dumped the car and hiked west again to the Ambadalur valley. It took us three hours in sight of the two highest mountains that the Faroes have to offer, Slættaratindur and Gráfelli. Oystercatchers, snipes and curlews flew above and below as we climbed, unaware of or indifferent to our presence. There were great skuas, too, and my eyes followed them warily in case word had been sent from their cousins in Torshavn.

Finally, the rise disappeared into thin air and we stood on the edge of oblivion, the ocean suddenly stretching away before us framed by a wispy blue. Gotteri had obviously been here before, as he knew exactly what lay over the lip of the hill.

'This is why we are here.'

In front of us as we peeped over the rise of the cliff was a huge sea stack, an astonishingly tall, rounded thumb of black basalt that rose majestically, if improbably, from the ocean. It was thick at the base where it emerged from the swell, then narrowed as it grew, a striking sheer mass of greys and greens almost as high as the cliff top itself.

'That is known as Búgvin,' Gotteri explained. 'It is 188 metres high, the highest stack in the Faroes, and it is at war with the sea. Every day the ocean comes and hurls itself at that rock. Every day for a million years. All the stack can do is stand there and take it. Waves six, maybe eight metres high – in a storm maybe twenty – crashing against it, the full force of nature unleashed. Over and over again. You could stand on this spot for twenty years and swear that the rock was winning, because it would seem that the sea is unable to land a telling blow. But if you could stand here for a thousand years then you'd see that the ocean will win. Grain by grain, it will wash Búgvin away like a sugar cube dissolving in coffee. And the ocean has boundless patience.'

It struck me that I had a lot in common with that rock. Life hammering at you day after day, chipping away at your resistance and wearing you down bit by bit. Sometimes it was easy to wonder how many more hits you could stand.

We walked further along the cliff path until the giant sea stack was immediately in front of and below us, a sea monster rising from the swell. The stack was home to thousands of nesting seabirds: fulmars, guillemots and puffins. Wherever there was a ledge or a nook or a cranny, however precarious, a bird made its home and reared its young.

Gotteri and I sat in silence, a light breeze and a warming sun making the day almost perfect as we watched the waves attempt their daily destruction of the stack. It was a long war but the battles were mesmerizing. In time, Serge took his camera and stalked the periphery of the bluff, shooting the nesting seabirds with deadly accuracy. One by one, they fell prey to his camera.

Then, out of nowhere, the mist rolled in – but only below our feet. It rose from the ocean and snaked up the sides of Búgvin, encircling it. In just a few minutes, the sea was gone and we were staring into a crater of candyfloss, only the top five metres or so of the *stakkur* protruding through the lather. On the cliff top and all around us, the sun shone from a clear blue sky. Below, a cauldron of cloud brewed up *double, double, toil and trouble* for the unwary and the foolish. At once both enchanted and enchanting. Haunted and haunting.

'*National Geographic* have done a feature on the Faroes before,' Serge told me, as we sat and watched the mist at work, his camera rendered redundant by the impenetrable haze. He reached into the pocket of his jacket and produced folded sheets of paper. 'I have a photocopy. I like to refer to it and use it as a sort of template. So I can compare then to now. A guy called Leo Hansen wrote it in 1930. He was here for over a year, poor guy.'

Gotteri held it up and I could just about make out the heading, but he read it for me anyway. 'It is entitled "Viking Life in the Storm-Cursed Faroes". So true, huh? Listen to this. "Basalt cliffs rise majestically on all the islands. Some tower nearly two thousand feet above the restless sea, and against these black barriers the Atlantic sends her mighty waves, to break with explosive force and burst into probably the most remarkable clouds of spray and surf to be found in all the world."'

Serge grinned broadly and flourished the photocopies at the stack below us, its top peeping out above the cloud. 'If Hansen sat here with us today, he would see the same that we see, the same that he saw then. Nothing has changed except that there is some less of Búgvin than there was. You see? It is nature. It always wins. We are insignificant against it.'

A change came over Gotteri's voice, a bitterness that twisted the seemingly permanent smile. 'We are supposed to be custodians of this world, but we do not do a good job of that. If there were a God he would sack us. This ... this is what he gave us to look after. Out here on the edge of the world, it survives as it is meant to do. Only at war with itself, without the interference of man, and therefore it inches to its destruction rather than racing there, as it does in cities polluted by fast-food joints, choked with landfill sites and drowning in their own aspiration. We do not deserve what we have been given.'

The volume had risen with every word of Gotteri's bluster, until he was almost shouting. However, as soon as he reached the end, it subsided like tidal surge falling back into the sea, and the smile spread across his face again.

'I get angry sometimes, my friend. Forgive me. I am French. It is my nature to love beauty and hate anything that might change that. Come on. I have more work to do. We are going to Gásadalur. One of the most beautiful waterfalls you will ever see. And a view across to Mykenes. Come.'

We were halfway back down the hill towards the car, black clouds gathering over our heads, when a raucous sound burst from the inside of Gotteri's jacket, a mobile phone ringtone that I'd never heard before. Serge had taken a few calls in the time we'd been on the road, but this one was entirely different. It screeched and screamed its urgency. He scrambled inside his pocket, the desperate claws of his fingers matching the phone's demand to be heard immediately.

'Yeah?' Gotteri's voice was hopeful, almost pleading.

I could hear the distant chatter of the voice on the other end, an excited and extended relaying of information. I watched Gotteri's eyes widen as he took it all in.

'Okay. Okay. Thank you. I am on my way.'

The call was ended and the phone stuffed back into his jacket pocket. Gotteri broke into a run.

'Serge, what's up?'

'There's a *grind* happening. Just run.'

The word meant nothing to me. 'A what? What's a *grind*?'

'A *grindadráp*,' he shouted impatiently. 'A whale hunt. There's one happening at Hvalvik. We need to hurry!'

Gotteri threw the Skoda into gear and screeched onto the road, leaving Gjógv behind in a pall of dust kicked up from the road.

'The *grindadráp* has been taking place on the Faroes for hundreds of years,' he explained, without taking his eyes off the road. I noticed his hands gripping the steering wheel fiercely. 'They consider it an important part of their culture and history.'

Gotteri drove as fast as the road allowed, cutting corners and overtaking where he could, taking chances, pushing the black Yeti to its limit.

'When pilot whales are spotted off the coast, the word goes out to boat owners and they put to sea. They get their crafts behind the whales and slowly drive them towards shore in one of the authorized villages. It is only allowed in places where the whales can be driven ashore so that they can be killed from the land.'

'What? They beach them?'

Gotteri laughed but there was no pleasure in it. 'Of course. They slaughter them. Wade into the water and cut them open in the shallows.'

'An entire school of whales?'

'Yes. The lead boats throw stones attached to lines. Anything not on the ocean side of the rope will be killed.'

'Who does the killing?'

A car in front was slower than Gotteri expected and he had to abruptly pull out and accelerate past it. 'The islanders do the killing. All the men of the island are expected to participate. You will see.'

I did not want to see a slaughter. I knew that already. The thought of spilled blood was already creeping over me like a rash, anxiety mounting with every bend in the road.

*

Rain was coming down hard now, lashing the windscreen from leaden skies as we dashed south through Eysturoy before we would head west in search of the bridge taking us over the sea to Streymoy. At last, a sign for Hvalvik reared up in front of us and a pretty village of multi-coloured houses soon followed, tumbling down from the fells towards the fjord. There were cars everywhere: far more than you'd expect in a village of just four hundred people.

We found a tight parking place and Serge was out of the car in seconds, jumping down from the driver's seat and grabbing his photographic gear from the boot before hurrying towards the sea. I followed in his wake, noticing that he didn't even bother to lock the car now that his camera was out of it.

We'd run only a matter of yards when Gotteri came to a halt, standing stock still but for his shoulders slumping in defeat. I caught up with him seconds later and immediately realized what had stopped him in his tracks.

The sight was incredible.

There were pilot whales, dozens upon dozens of them, lined up in neat rows upon the rain-lashed grey concrete of Hvalvik's quayside. Every one of them dead.

The tarmac was streaked with blood as well as rain, muted drags of red where each whale had been moved into its position in the serried ranks of death. We walked closer, silently stalking towards the already stricken prey. The closer we got, the larger the beasts seemed, six or seven metres in length and glistening grey against the tarmac. Each bore a gruesome but mesmerizing slash across its back, towards the head, where their spinal cord had been cut, forcing the flesh apart and almost severing the head from the body.

I couldn't take my eyes off the cuts. They'd left each whale with a deep, gaping wound that resembled a mock smile across its sleek dark-grey back. It made me think of the Joker from *Batman*. The cuts that killed the whales also mocked them.

The sight stirred memories and guilt. My breath hid inside me, not daring to come out until it had to, only emerging in stilted gasps.

I did the calculation, counting the carcasses of the whales in front of my eyes. There were 105 of them. We had missed the hunt and had arrived only in time for the funeral procession.

Gotteri was furious. He muttered bitterly in French, his mouth contorted and eyes ablaze. At last he fixed a lens on his camera and, almost reluctantly, photographed the kill.

I walked in between the corpses, both fascinated and repulsed by what I saw. The cuts to the spine revealed a gory glimpse of the meat and blubber inside. To the other side, the whale's snub nose, dark eyes and mournful mouth. All dressed in mundane grey but for the lighter anchor-shaped patches under the chin and a saddle behind the dorsal fin.

Serge had told me on the drive down that Hvalvik meant 'Whale Bay' in Faroese. There seemed a grotesque irony about that now.

I saw he had begun walking away from the rows of carcasses towards the quayside and then beyond it to where the fells met the sea, the grass and rocks giving way to the shallows of the ocean. I followed, seeing his camera lifted towards his eyes again.

I stood beside him, seeing what he saw. I was equally aghast and enthralled. The sea was red. Dark, blood red.

It pooled out forty or fifty yards towards the horizon, where a small flotilla of boats bobbed peacefully in a semicircle on the water. My stomach turned at the sight of it, unwelcome memories flooding my mind, drowning reason. I was lost, enduring another nightmare, but this time with my eyes wide open. It was as if the islands were taunting me, with sleep and the lack of it, night mirroring day.

Gotteri's camera whirred as he fired off shot after shot, his trigger finger thumping down fiercely.

'Serge,' I said at his shoulder. 'Are you so angry because this happened, or because you missed it?'

The camera fired off more shots before Gotteri let his arms drop to his side and he whirled to glare at me.

'Just get back in the fucking car. We're leaving.'

Chapter 15

After the long day spent outdoors and the exhaustion of Gotteri's company on the silent drive home, I should have been ready only for food and bed, but I felt the need for something more. I needed to wash the taste of the whale hunt from my mouth and my mind.

It was doubtful that there was enough alcohol in town to wipe away the sights from the quayside, which continued to bother me long after my eyes were closed. Memories, new and old, swirled together, disturbing me. As if my own guilt wasn't enough, there was some shame at just being part of the human race, and I felt compelled to drown it in beer.

The Cafe Natur was busy inside, a young, happy crowd, oblivious to my sensitivities. No one batted an eyelid at my entrance and that suited me just fine. I nodded at a draught tap of Klassic, not having the energy for words, and looked around.

At a table near the window was Karis. She looked up and held my gaze for a brief moment, her face expressionless, before turning back to her friends and ignoring me.

Fine. I didn't need any hassle about her boyfriend who wasn't her boyfriend, or whatever all that nonsense had been about. There was something about her, no doubt about that, an intriguing mix of dark and light. Whether it was worth the aggravation was something else.

I downed a greedy mouthful of beer and let my eyes slide shut for the length of a heavy sigh. Long enough, it turned out, to see ranks of dead whales carved with bloody smiles.

Minutes turned into a half-hour or more as I worked my way down one pint and most of another, my nerves settling like the head on a beer. The bar hummed around me and I allowed myself to feel safe in the company of strangers, people who either didn't know who I was or didn't care.

Then the door opened behind me and I knew the newcomers for who they were immediately. Even the laughter that burst into the pub with them came with accents. Mostly from north-eastern Scotland, Aberdeen and beyond, but there were a couple of Glasgow voices too. Glottal stops. Fucking this and fucking that. In seconds, I was back in Whiteinch and the hairs on the back of my neck were standing on end.

I turned, as casually as I could, and saw six of them coming through the door. Loud and lairy, obviously full of drink but looking for more. Ruddy-cheeked fishermen, some with hair gelled as if for a Saturday night on the pull, likely lads here for a good time not a long time. I knew Scots boats headed north towards Icelandic waters, and with growing unease I realized this was a stopping-off point. This wasn't good, not good at all. I felt panic rising inside me.

One of them, a heavy-built and heavily bearded guy in a red jumper, pulled a wad of notes from a pocket and flourished it before the others. He had the kitty, the key to their next round of booze, and so he was their king for now. Orders were made and taken and he swayed towards the bar to fulfil requests.

I turned back round, away from them, staring into my beer and wishing I was anywhere else. Above and in front of me I heard the man ordering up the round. Definitely from somewhere near Aberdeen, his vowels pitching and turning like the North Sea. I could feel his eyes on me and looked up to see him tilting his head to one side in amiable greeting. 'A' right?'

I shrugged as if I didn't understand and went back to my beer. Just before I did so, I saw the fisherman's eyes narrow in a shade of confusion, a man unsure of what he might have seen. Then he too shrugged and turned back to the bar to pick up pints of beer.

This wasn't what I wanted, far from it. I needed out, away from the Scots. These guys always trawled nets behind them and could catch fish even when they didn't know they were looking for it.

Most of them were in a clump near the front door, but a couple had spread out in search of local talent, spreading their charms in a way that only those who have swallowed their self-awareness can.

One of them, a lanky type with close-cropped dark hair, was at the door at the far end of the pub, drooling over a local girl with long blonde hair. She was laughing at or with him – either was enough encouragement for him to continue. The guy had positioned himself as close to her table as he could, but with another table behind, there was no way past without going right through him.

Cafe Natur suddenly seemed smaller than it had ever done before. The walls were closing in on me, noise tumbling over movement, the narrow corridor teeming with threat. I had to get out of there, but the very process of doing that offered me up as someone to be seen. Someone to be recognized. Scots were the last people I wanted to see or be seen by.

The bearded guy in the red jumper was looking at me again, curiosity knotting his eyebrows as some cogent thought struggled to be heard among the swill of booze in his head. He was trying to join some dots in his addled brain and I knew it couldn't be a good thing for me.

I turned away from him to find something interesting behind the bar, making myself count the beer taps and then the bottles on the shelves. If he couldn't see my face then there was much less chance that he'd work out where he might have seen it. And if he couldn't do that, then hopefully he'd just shrug his shoulders and give it up. Pinning my hopes on the logic of a drunk was like hoping for sunshine on a Torshavn weekend.

The biggest thing I had going for me was that he hadn't heard me speak and so had no reason to think I was Scottish. Maybe that was enough to keep him from making the connection. Why would he think he might recognize some Faroese guy sitting in a bar? All I had to do was not talk, and hide my face. Out of the corner of my eye, I could see Karis looking at me oddly. She must have wondered why I was taking so much interest in the fixtures and fittings of the Natur bar. I was staring at them like a drunk in the desert, eyeing up a mirage of booze. Shit, was she going to come over and talk to me? Any other time I might have welcomed it, crazy as she was, but not now. The last thing I needed was her to call me 'Scotsman' or say anything that meant I would have to answer out loud. I focused back fully on the beer taps and threw my last scrap of hope at the wall.

She was to my left, while the Bearded Wonder was behind me. The lanky guy was guarding one door and another four or five were near the other. I was surrounded by threats and my own paranoia. Stick or twist, stay or try to leave?

As I watched, the bearded man's eyebrows rose in surprise and his mouth fell open in a round O of disbelief. His hands gripped the side of his chair and he began to push himself to his feet. I turned to my left and saw Karis staring back at me, clearly aware of the growing panic that must have been stitched across my face. Even if I got up and marched straight past her, the lanky guy was still on duty at the far door, and he was taking up even more room than he had before.

I could feel it building inside. A familiar feeling coloured in reds and blacks, an anger fathered by anxiety. My hands balled into fists and my breathing quickened. I didn't know where it was going, but I knew it was spilling out and I had no control of it. I had to get out of there – it was as if I was claustrophobic, and maybe I was. The walls and the people and the talking and the laughter were like a straightjacket that was winding itself ever tighter round me.

I turned back to the bearded guy, seeing him advance on me through the crowd. He clearly had something he wanted to say, but I knew I didn't want to hear it. I scraped back my own chair and was on my feet instantly, heading straight towards him, head down. When I was a couple of feet away, I looked up and saw that he'd made his mind up about who I was. I knew I had to change that.

I raised my head questioningly, gesticulating as best as I could to demand why the hell he was looking at me.

'*Helvitis spassari!*'

I spat the only Faroese swear words I knew at him as ferociously as my poor Torshavn accent would allow. 'Fucking moron!' The guy wouldn't have understood even if he was sober, and there was no way he'd see past the accent in his condition. Confusion crawled all over his face, but his mouth opened to speak.

I jammed my left foot down violently onto his right, trapping it mid stride, and slammed my shoulder into his bearded chin, feeling a satisfying crunch as my flesh and bone hammered into his face. He recoiled from the impact but could go nowhere as my foot held his tight and he fell straight back until his head rattled off the floor of the Natur. He wasn't out cold but he clearly didn't know if it was Torshavn or Thursday.

It had all happened in the blink of a drunk's eye and I was as sure as I could be that no one had seen me do it. I stood above him, gesturing with my hands as if it was all his fault and I'd no idea what he'd been doing.

'*Spassari!*' I repeated, this time for the benefit of his friends, shaking my head at the idiot on the ground.

'Jesus, Malky. What the hell you up to, big man? Sorry, mate, sorry. He's had a few. No harm done, eh?'

Two of the other fishermen tried to pick Malky up while two others held their hands up, first in apology and then with inebriated offers of handshakes. With my head down looking at Malky,

I accepted their hands and eased past them with a shrug of my shoulders.

One of the Scots opened the door for me and I strode past them onto the street, dragging in lungfuls of air and looking to the sky. I pulled my collar up and started to walk up Áarvegur, without daring to look over my shoulder. The reds and the blacks were slowly slipping from my mind, but my breathing still juddered.

Then to my right, I became aware of a pair of eyes staring at me from the throng inside the bar. Despite myself, I let my head swing round as I walked, and saw her, Karis, standing by the window and studying me carefully. When she had looked at me moments before, she had been curious, maybe confused at the way I was acting. Now, she was interested.

Chapter 16

I woke slowly on Sunday, hung-over and unsettled, finding that I'd slept right through into the afternoon. Not that it was a night of sleep. There were hours spent staring at the ceiling and hours more punctuated by dreams of whales and hunts and sex and blood and Karis. Finally, exhausted by the daylight and dreaming, I fell fast asleep at the time I should have been getting up.

At last awake, I was disorientated at first, unsure whether it was the middle of the night or the middle of the day, and uncertain what was bothering me most about what had happened the night before. I knew I was charged with blood, and couldn't shake off the restlessness that brought.

Pushing myself to my feet, I headed for the shower, eager to feel clean. The plastic handle turned in my hand and a trickle of water began to make its way from the shower head. Then nothing. I reached up and shook the head, forcing a couple of drops to fall. I turned the handle off then on again. Nothing. Bloody thing. Again I turned it off and on, but it wasn't for playing.

My rudimentary plumbing skills only extended to finding the stopcock and making sure it was turned on, and it was. I checked the sink and got no water from the taps. I tried to flush the toilet but it wouldn't.

There was nothing for it but to talk to Hojgaard. Martin would know what to do. Slamming the door closed behind me, I stomped off towards his house, and fifteen minutes later, he was rooting around in the undergrowth near the shack.

'The pipe comes in along here.' He was crouching, feeling with his hands in the grass that covered the narrow ditch. 'Some of it is underground and some is not. It is not the most modern system and sometimes someone will stand on it. It goes all the way along here . . .'

He traced a path in the grass with his hands, moving sideways as they felt where he couldn't see. He stepped a yard to his right away from the shack, then another. Then he moved back on himself, dropping to his hands and knees and pulling the grass back.

I saw the look of confusion spread across Hojgaard's face. His eyebrows furrowed and his mouth tightened. He came up from the ditch holding a lump of rock that was big enough that it took two hands to clasp it. He turned to me, offering it up, as if needing another pair of eyes to see it and make it true.

'The pipe is broken here. With . . . with this.' Martin managed to balance the rock in one hand and thrust the other back down, wiping it across the ground and holding it up again, brown with mud, as if to prove his point.

I stepped over to where he crouched, kneeling down into the ditch with him, seeing the severed pipe as he held the grass at bay. It had been hacked open by the force of the rock, water spilling into the earth.

Martin was shaking his head, his face a study in indignant concentration. He weighed the rock in his hands and mimicked it crashing down onto the pipe.

'What happened here, Martin?'

He frowned, pursing his lips unhappily. 'It is possible that someone stepped onto the rock and forced it onto the pipe. It is possible.'

I nodded. 'And it is possible that they didn't feel the rock breaking the pipe. Or hear it. And it is possible that if they did then they didn't know who to report it to. It's such a big place, after all.'

Hojgaard shrugged. 'We have many tourists in Torshavn. They walk the hills but they do not know where they walk or who lives here.'

'Yeah.' I let the sound of doubt fill my words. 'So many tourists. So many places they could walk.'

Martin stood up, throwing the rock into the grass. 'Come. You can have a shower in our house. I will fix the pipe.'

He turned away, his back denying me further questions, and headed towards the path and down the hill.

He was right, of course. The pipe could have been broken accidentally. But I doubted it.

Chapter 17

The next week proved long and frustrating. Work wasn't enough to occupy either my body or my mind and I was left prowling my cage with excess energy. I constantly replayed my dreams through open eyes. Whales and hunts and sex and blood. It was enough to drive me crazy and I had to fight the temptation to go down into town and act on it.

I managed partly because I couldn't be sure if the Scots fishermen were still in Torshavn but also because I was worried about the nature of my attraction to Karis. Much as I'd tried to kid myself, since seeing her look back at me through the window, I knew we were drawn to each other in a way I could not quite understand. By the following Saturday, I was ready to explode and could resist her no longer.

I hit Cafe Natur just after ten, thinking that would have given time for people to have arrived and the place to heat up. I was wrong. There were only a handful of people inside and Karis wasn't among them. As I fretted over a pint of Rinkusteinur, I filled my time by willing more customers to come through the door, but precious few did. Giving in, I pushed the empty glass back across the bar and nodded a farewell to Oli.

I climbed through the narrow alley of Rektaragøta towards the white cathedral on the hill and the western port beyond it. Crossing the road past the striking statue of Nólsoyar Páll with its massive seabirds flying over the hero's head, I saw the bizarre frontage of Sirkús ahead of me.

The building sat on an oddly angled corner with the entrance at its centre, the walls painted in sand yellow, then aquamarine blue to shoulder height, then sky blue above. Either side of the entrance and at each corner, a tall painted palm tree grew from the yellow 'beach' painted below. Above the entrance hung the bar's name in block yellow capitals outlined in red, each letter traced in white light bulbs. Three young bearded guys stood outside, smoking and joking in the night air.

The place got even more eclectic when you climbed the narrow wooden stairs to the bar on the first floor. The vibe was Seventies blending into Eighties, with a detour via psychedelia. It was dark and moody but with fairy lights draped along the junction of wall and ceiling, hanging just above some remarkable tree-print wallpaper. The perimeter was lined with small, round tables and guarded by a mixed collection of wooden chairs upholstered in everything from zebra print and Mondrian squares to floral abominations straight out of your granny's catalogue. Blondie's 'Heart of Glass' was blasting out from the speakers.

There were eight people sat in three groups, all in their early twenties and clearly nearer the beginning of their night rather than the end. I got an Okkara and took a table on my own, but soon found myself in a conversation with two of the guys nearest to me. The Faroese tendency to chat to strangers still surprised me, although I was reluctantly warming to it. We talked football and rain and Scotland. The temptation was to ask if they knew Karis Lisberg and if they'd seen her that night, but I managed to resist. I had my one drink and left; there was more of Torshavn to search.

She wasn't in either The Irish Pub, nor in its downstairs neighbour Glitnir, where Tummas Barthel had watched me from the darkness. Nor could I find her in Cleopatra or the Manhattan, although neither bar seemed quite her kind of place. With heavy heart and thickening head, I moved on to Bar 11 then Hvonn, each place busier than the one before as the night grew older.

Out on the street again, I walked up Myinugøta with the imposing countenance of the cathedral high on my right. I had performed my loop of the town centre and was faced with the choice of another circuit or going home. Home, I decided. She was not supposed to be found. Not by me, at least.

I heard the arguing from the car on the other side of the road long before I saw who was in it. The voices were raised and the tone combative. I couldn't make out much more than the odd word, but it was enough to pique my interest. That, and the fact that one of the accents was unmistakably familiar.

Drawing level with the car on the other side of the road, I saw Serge Gotteri in the passenger seat and next to him Nils Dam. Both men were gesturing furiously, a swirl of arms amid angry expressions. Dam's finger was jabbing at the Frenchman, accusatory stabs that were parried by Gotteri's dismissive wave. I heard the word 'no' quite often. Definitive, uncompromising nos, followed by more fevered argument.

I fell back into the shadow of a shop front, a reluctant spy, but with a spy's unwillingness to be caught. I wondered if the two men were going to actually fight. I couldn't see Gotteri's eyes but Dam's were bulging and it would have been no surprise if he'd swung a punch or launched into a headbutt.

Gotteri suddenly hammered his hand into the dashboard and the thud easily carried across the street. I heard Nils Dam laugh, a scornful snigger that so enraged the Frenchman that he battered his fist into the moulded plastic a second time.

More heated words were exchanged, the volume increasing. 'You promised me!' Gotteri ranted. 'You said you would do it.'

I didn't catch all of Dam's reply but I made out the end of it: '. . . so you will have to wait.'

Gotteri swore, opened the door and began to scramble out of the car. I took two steps back and retreated into the darkened doorway of the shop behind me. He probably wouldn't have seen me anyway as he slammed the door and stormed down the street towards the harbour. He'd taken no more than a couple of steps when Nils Dam crashed his foot down onto the accelerator, the engine roared and he sped up the hill with a squeal of tyres.

I waited until Gotteri had turned right at the foot of the hill and disappeared out of sight along Torsgøta before I stepped back out onto the street. I had no idea what business my new friend had with Nils Dam but it didn't seem to be going well. My mind drifted back to Gotteri's intervention in the Natur when the brothers seemed intent on starting a fight with me. There had seemed to be no trouble between him and the younger Dam then. I wanted to know what had changed.

Still, the memory of the Cafe Natur and Karis storming out after Aron's arrival reminded me of the purpose of my walk round Torshavn's streets and pubs. My intention to go home was dismissed, and in a triumph of alcohol-fuelled hope over experience, I decided to make for the Natur again. In a few minutes, like a one-legged drunk going round in circles, I was back where I'd started the evening. Except this time, Karis was there.

She and three other girls were at a table just behind the area where the band would be playing. I saw the pork-pie hat before I saw the rest of her. Below it, she was smiling widely at her friends, her eyes alive and shining. I pushed my way to the bar and wondered what the hell I was going to do now.

My dilemma was solved before I got the chance to order. I felt a tap on my shoulder and looked round to see her smiling up at me.

'Hi,' she chirped. 'How are you, Mr Scotsman?'

'I'm good. Um . . . how are you?'

'Still crazy.' She grinned at me beguilingly. 'Listen, I'm sorry about last time. I was a total bitch. It wasn't your fault and I shouldn't have bitten you. Give me another chance? Let me get you a drink.'

'No, I'll get it. What do you want?'

'Vodka would be good. With Coke.'

'Okay.' I nodded. 'I'll bring it over.'

She returned to her friends and I signalled to the barmaid. 'A vodka and Coke, please. Plus just a Coke with ice.' I'd had plenty to drink already and needed to cool it.

I took the drinks over to be met by four expectant faces. Like Karis, the other girls were all young, pretty, arty and effortlessly stylish.

'Girls, this is John. John, this is Marisa, Petra and Elisabet. Come, we're going to sit up the back.'

I waved and shrugged and the girls giggled as Karis led me by the hand to a table next to the window. A voice in my head was telling me that I'd come to the Faroes to get away from people, to be on my own and not get involved. Another voice popped up to tell me that if that were the case, I wouldn't have been trawling Torshavn in the hope of finding her.

'So you've been out tonight before you came in here?' she asked when we'd sat down. I guessed there was something in my eyes or my voice that gave it away.

'Yeah. I was in Sirkús for a bit then the Irish Pub. They were both pretty quiet though.' I thought it better not give her my entire itinerary.

'Of course they were quiet,' she laughed. 'No one goes out that early, not on a Saturday. This is going to be a long night, Scotsman. I hope you're up to it.'

I knew she was teasing, but I hoped the same thing. I'd been up since 6.30 and awake a fair bit of the night before that. Cafe Natur was open till four in the morning at weekends, like the rest of the bars in town. Could I last the pace?

'The band on here tonight are pretty good. You going to stay and hear them? They won't even be setting up till midnight though, and the bar will be jumping till four. Then . . .' she looked at me coyly, '. . . my friends and I will be moving on somewhere else.'

I suddenly felt old, tired and hopeful all in one go.

'How old are you?' I asked, the words out of my mouth before I'd considered them. She sat back and regarded me with what I hoped was mock disapproval.

'Is that not a rude question in Scotland? It is here. I'm twenty-four. What about you?'

'Thirty-three.'

Karis leaned in, her face inches from mine across the table. 'That's *old*.'

'I guess it is.'

She leaned even closer. 'I like older men.'

My lips began to open in reply but Karis moved again and kissed me, full and hard. She lingered, meeting no resistance. Finally she sat back, smiling at her own boldness.

'You taste of beer,' she told me. 'I like the taste of beer on a man. I guess that makes me weird.'

'Good weird, I'd say.'

'I think so.' She laughed and raised her glass to chink it against mine. '*Skál!*'

'*Sláinte!*' I responded.

She raised her eyebrows enquiringly. 'It's Gaelic,' I explained. 'It means "health".'

'Like old Scots?'

'Yes.'

'I like old Scots,' she giggled. 'I want to draw you. Let me get paper.'

In moments she was back, her eyes darting from me to the paper she'd procured from behind the bar, her hand moving quickly, confidently. 'Don't look at it,' she scolded. 'Just look at me.'

'Not a problem. I like looking at you.'

'Smooth talker. So you live in the Faroes now?'

I hesitated. 'Maybe it's still too early to say. But I don't live in Scotland any more.'

She smiled. 'So you're a nowhere man.'

'That sounds about right.'

'I think so. So what did you do in Scotland? What was your job?'

She was studying me intently. She'd see the look in my eyes if I lied. She'd probably already noticed the hesitation.

'I was a schoolteacher. English.'

'Really? Wow. I wouldn't have guessed. Why did you give it up?'

Maybe I should kiss her again. Stop her asking questions. Her hand and eyes continued to work together, drawing me out.

'I think I'd just had enough of it. The budget was always getting cut and we had no money for books or pencils for the kids. We spent half our time photocopying books so they could be shared around. Until we ran out of paper for the photocopier.'

'Don't you miss working with children though?'

I let the question roll around my head before answering.

'I suppose so. They could be annoying though. Anyway, that's all in the past. I've fish to farm now.'

She held my eyes. She knew. She changed the subject.

'Did you have a girlfriend in Scotland. A wife, maybe?'

'No wife. There was a girlfriend but that ended. What about you?'

She didn't look up. 'I told you. I have no boyfriend.' I could hear the dismissive tone. It was all I was getting, for now at least.

'Tell me about your art. Are you famous?'

The smile was modest, disarming. 'A little, I guess. Only in the Faroes. And that doesn't mean much.'

'But you sell elsewhere? Like in other countries?'

'Hm. Yes. I have sold to New York, Los Angeles, London. But the Faroes is where matters to me. Here, what do you think?'

She held the sheet of paper up and I saw myself staring back at me. Broad, assured strokes and a definite style. She was good. Too good, actually. She'd caught a sadness in my eyes that I'd hoped to have disguised better. She made me look handsome but . . . vulnerable. Damaged, perhaps. Dark, definitely.

'I think you're flattering me,' I told her. 'I must look older than that.'

She laughed and teased. 'You do, but I wouldn't get many commissions if I did portraits the way people *actually* looked. I did you a favour.'

'Ha. Want to do me another favour?' Sometimes these words came out before I recognized them.

'Oh yeah? What is that then?' Her eyes danced and dared me. I chickened out.

'Get us another drink.'

She looked disappointed, but only half as much as I was. Still, she bought them and we sat, we drank, we chatted, we flirted and we got up and moved to the music of the band when they came on. Time swirled round us, passing easily, my doubts crumbling with each hour, each drink and each smile from her. It came as a surprise when they announced it was four in the morning and we found ourselves falling into the street.

It comes as something of a shock to the system to leave a bar and find it light outside. If you are Scottish, there is a slap of Calvinist guilt at having imbibed before dark. If you are Faroese and it is summer, then you are used to it.

'It is still early,' Karis instructed me. 'Now we go to Mica. Everyone will. You'll see.'

We wandered haphazardly up Aarvegur past the Hotel Hafnia and the City Hall, buildings blurring by. I knew Mica was on the pedestrianized street of Nils Finsens gøta but even if I hadn't, I would have located it by the chatter before we got there. Karis was right.

Everyone in town under the age of forty must have been milling outside Mica. It was like wandering across a nightclub in the middle of the desert. The only equivalent I could think of in Glasgow were the throngs that congregated at taxi ranks at Central Station or Byres Road when the licensed premises would serve them no more. There was a similar sense of drunken camaraderie, but the underlying threat of getting your head kicked in seemed to be missing.

'We come here to meet, to talk and to eat,' Karis told me, her head resting on my shoulder. 'People will go and get pizzas or French hotdogs and come here to meet friends. And there will be parties. Private parties. Some of them will go on for a very long time. They will be arranged here. You will like it.'

The mass gathering outside Mica wasn't the end of something; it was a beginning. The crowd were open, friendly and extremely chatty. Karis was pulled gently and laughingly from my grasp by two of her friends from the bar, Petra and Elisabet. I wasn't alone for long, though, as first a couple of guys, then some others, made conversation, seemingly knowing who I was.

'Hey, man! Are you with Karis? Cool. She's great, huh?'

'Hey, you're the Scottish guy, right? I went to Edinburgh once, man. *Great* city.'

There was more booze, too, happily shared and lazily drunk. I was in a haze of acceptance and an unfamiliar sense of contentment, albeit it largely borne of alcohol. Between the beer, the vodka and weeks of sleep deprivation, I was feeling no pain and happily let Torshavn spin before me.

Then something jarred. As the square circled us in a mid-night, mid-morning whirl, something put on the brakes.

It was because of the constant movement of people around me that the still figure stood out. He was staring at me. Glaring at me. Someone tugged at my arm and forced me to turn, shaking my hand and talking nonsense in broken English. Someone else wanted to know about football in Glasgow, and by the time I turned back, the still form had moved away. Then I saw him again. A shadow in the half-light, standing motionless and facing directly towards me.

I moved to my right so that I could see better, making use of the almost redundant street lighting. The tall, broad silhouette was Aron Dam, a drink moving to his lips and a stream of smoke escaping from the cigarette held close to his chin.

Karis saw me looking, saw the expression on my face. She followed my gaze and saw her former boyfriend standing there and staring at us. At me.

She excused herself from her friends and hurried over, placing a calming hand on my arm. 'Let me speak to him. Please. Stay here.'

Karis marched across the square until she was in Aron's face. Her slight figure looking diminutive next to his in the pale light of the newly risen sun. Whatever she said, he took a step back and began waving his arms about demonstratively. I felt the urge to go over, but Karis stepped forward again until Dam had nowhere to go, his back against the wall, and I saw a tiny hand come up and jab him in the chest.

He gestured some more in protest, but when she leaned in close and said something that only he could hear, he threw his arms high then turned away, seemingly defeated. Yet again someone else was fighting my battles for me. It couldn't carry on that way.

She walked back, head down, with her hat covering her face. I saw her shoulders drop as she sighed, and knew that the conversation had cost her. Still, when she came up to look at me, she was smiling. It was as much apology as explanation.

'It is over. He knows I am with you now.'

This was news to me. 'You are?'

'Yes. If you want me to be.'

'Yes, I do.'

She smiled. 'Good. Now take me to your place. I don't want to go on to a party. We can have our own.'

It had been a long day but I was happy for it to get longer. She slipped her arms through mine and I felt the heat rise from her body as we kissed.

As we turned away, Karis hugging me close, I looked to the other side of the square and saw Aron Dam staring back, the tip of his cigarette glowing furiously in the shadows.

Chapter 18

We were in Karis's flat and she was curled up with her back to me, her hair inches from my nose, the smell of her making me feel almost drunk. This was our third night together in a row and I was getting used to it, sharing my space and my body heat. More than that, I was getting to like it, and that in itself unsettled me.

It had become obvious to me the previous two nights, both spent in my shack, that I still wouldn't sleep much, but at least now I had something useful to do while awake. In fact, rather than struggle to sleep, I fought to avoid it. I was ever mindful of the potential consequences of slumber, wary of the dreams and the words and the shouts that might betray me in the night.

Instead, I wrapped myself around her, content to look at her while she slept. I watched her breathe: gently in, gently out. She lay so still, her face expressionless, as if she knew she was being watched and didn't want to spoil the illusion for me. She was perhaps even more beautiful asleep than awake, even devoid of the mischievous spark that lit up her eyes.

The chaos of her flat, which doubled as her studio, was all around us. A mess of canvasses and materials strewn seemingly where they fell. Yet I'd watched her step between them effortlessly, picking a path without a sideways glance. Brushing my lips past her ear, I lifted my head so that I could see the half-finished painting that sat on the easel near the window.

The soft light caught half of it, making it appear even more brooding than she'd intended. Half of my face in light, half in darkness. The broad strokes had partly been filled in and colour added to my jaw and cheek, my mouth set fast in defiance. I recognized my hair, dark and unruly in its sweep to the right. Noticeably untouched were my eyes, just blank spaces waiting to be filled.

Her other work was scattered round the room, some finished, some seemingly abandoned halfway through, waiting for inspiration to reappear. There were more canvasses, dark works in variations of oil, acrylics and charcoals. Others seemed to be experiments in mixed media using paint and collage. These depicted raging storms or menacing clouds hanging over various island scenes. I recognized the dramatic sea stack at Drangarnir, with its amazing natural arch in the middle of it; the dumpy Lítla Dímun island with its vertical cliffs; and the ruins of the unfinished Magnus Cathedral at Kirkjubøur. All of them under attack from glowering skies, cowering beneath Nature's rage.

I didn't know much about art. I wasn't even sure that I knew what I liked. But I could see that these were startling works. There was an intensity about them, something driven. This wasn't someone just playing at painting things; her work shouted out that she was compelled to do it. The canvasses were brilliant, and even I could see why she had sold to Los Angeles and London.

They were dark, though; there was no escaping that. Just as there was no getting away from the menace from above depicted in almost every piece. What did they say about her mindset or how she really felt about her country? I decided it was better not to know.

My head sank once more, my lips against her shoulder, and she flickered momentarily before she settled again. I watched some more, wondering how the hell I had got myself into something I'd sworn to avoid, and wondering how the hell I'd done so well as to find myself with her. Tiny little breaths escaped from between her lips, making the slightest whistle, and I was the only person in the world that could hear it.

I could feel the comfort and the calm getting the better of me, and I knew I was swimming into a half-sleep, carried away by the warmth of her skin and the smell of her natural perfume. I wasn't sleeping, though, I was sure I wasn't. Instead it was fitful serenity; a workable compromise, some kind of sleep mode where I could retain some control. That was what I told myself as I drifted deeper.

The next thing I knew I was being nudged out of my non-sleep by her ass grinding against me as she stretched, catlike, her smooth skin working against me, a distinct purr rumbling in her throat. I was suddenly and noticeably awake.

She turned, a huge triumphant smile on her face, and pushed me away from her until I was flat on my back. I was aware of her crawling on all fours towards me from my feet, stalking her prey with confidence. A hand grabbed me, stroked me, owned me. Her face told me what we both knew; she could do what she wanted. And she did.

She sat above me, positioning herself just where she wanted. I ached for her but she remained on her knees, an agonizing inch or two above me. She looked glorious in the half-light, her hair partly over her face, her skin pale in shadow and her figure lean yet curvy. When she'd satisfied herself that I'd suffered enough, she swooped and engulfed me.

She set the pace and the rhythm, I just did my best to keep up. It was a race, but only Karis knew where the winning post was.

The smile on her face told me that she was in charge, she had me. But the truth was that I couldn't care less. If this was subservience, I'd take it. In the end, I wasn't sure if she pushed or dragged me over the finishing line, but we crossed it together.

As she collapsed on top of me and we both drifted off on a sea of satisfaction, I took a brief second to look over her shoulder and see an indefinable light leaking through the window. I couldn't place the time within a few hours either way and it didn't matter. This was sleep I could handle.

We were in Etika, the sushi restaurant opposite the Hotel Hafnia on Áarvegur, Karis with her porkpie hat perched cockily on her head. She looked great, in a skin-tight red T-shirt and black skinny jeans, a long hooded red raincoat hung over the back of the chair setting off the urban Little Red Riding Hood look.

We were sitting on the lowest level of the restaurant, next to the floor-to-ceiling windows that held up Etika's thick turfed roof; she facing down the street and me up. She was picking energetically at a plate of halibut, yet still found time to gesture furiously, and there was no let-up in her arguments.

'People say things have changed, but we women still aren't given the chance to express ourselves or to get the best jobs. We're not given enough respect. My eyes were opened in Copenhagen, like so many others. Once you have seen true equality, you do not settle for less. Other young women stayed away because of it. I came back to fight against it.'

'Look, I understand that—'

'No, you *don't* understand. You don't live here, so you can't. Women have never been given a fair chance in the Faroe Islands. It has been the way of the society. We are forty years behind Denmark. *Forty years*, I'm telling you. Oh, and because we now get to hold positions of State we should be grateful? Ha. Men here think they can do what they want and get away with it.'

'Okay, but . . .'

'But? It is not okay and no "but" can make it right. How dare you try to justify it? What is this "but"?'

She glared furiously at me, her green eyes blazing, as she shovelled a mouthful of raw fish into her mouth and clamped it shut like a vice. I should have known better than to even try, but I'd already dug the hole for myself.

'But things have changed some. You had a female Prime—'

Karis thumped the heel of her hand against her forehead. 'Oh, my God. Oh, my God. I cannot believe that is your argument. We had a female Prime Minister so that makes it all right? That was in 1994. I was five years old. Marita Petersen was a wonderful woman, but she was Prime Minister for one year and since then, no other woman. And where did she go to get educated? Denmark. And where did she begin work as a teacher? Denmark. One female Prime Minister and that makes everything all right? Is that what you are saying?'

I wanted to slump onto the table, head first into my sushi, in submission. 'No. No, I'm not.'

'Good!' The word was spat at me, slapping me across the face. Something lit up inside her when she was as angry as this, or when she enthused about something, or when she passionately wanted something. And usually at least one of those three things was happening. She was so alive, so vibrant, so maddeningly animated.

Another forkful of halibut was washed down with a gulp of beer, and as soon as she'd swallowed it a burst of Faroese followed under her breath. I didn't want to know what it meant.

She gave me a final glare over the rim of the beer bottle and sat back, satisfied that I had been vanquished, and taking my silence, quite accurately, as capitulation. I'd been slain by her wrath and I'd liked it, so much so that I was fighting a smile that threatened to sneak onto my lips. I knew it would be the end of me.

I let the conversation roll into art and out again, to the sushi and the beer, to where we were staying that night. But before I could start my own argument, we both became aware of someone looking at us from outside the restaurant. I turned and saw a man just inches from the window, staring straight at us from the rain-sodden pavement. He was short and gaunt, a ghost with close-cut dark hair flecked with grey, and piercing blue eyes.

As I looked at him, I caught sight of Karis's reflection painted over the man's stare. She was open-mouthed, caught somewhere between surprise and fear, an expression I'd last seen when Aron Dam had made her run out of Cafe Natur that first night.

By the time I turned back to her she had composed herself, her mouth closed and her focus regained.

'Who the hell is he?'

'Just ignore him.' Her attention was back on the food in front of her. 'He will go away.'

'Do you want me to get rid of him?'

'No!' Her reply was unnecessarily over the top, and I shifted in my seat to get a better look at the wraith on the other side of the window. He was on the move, though, striding up the street and, for a few moments, I thought she'd been right to ignore him, that he was just some local weirdo. I thought that right up until he opened the door to the restaurant and walked inside.

Karis hadn't been watching him, but there was no doubt she could tell what had happened by the look on my face. She seemed to shrink in her seat, hiding within the folds of her own clothes. The man was in his mid fifties, well-dressed, and walked with the certainty of the supremely confident or the misguided. Whatever it was he wanted, he had no doubt about it.

I pushed myself out of my chair ready to confront him, but Karis hissed at me frantically. 'Sit down. Oh, my God, sit down. Please.'

Reluctantly, I slid back into my chair just before the man got to our table. His jaw was set firm but his eyes alternated between me and Karis, as if he couldn't make his mind up who to glare at.

He stopped by her chair and looked down at her, while she stared up almost obediently.

'*Hvør er hesin*?' he asked her, his hand waving at me.

'*Dáma, Pápi. Dáma . . .*'

'*Hvør er hesin*?' he repeated, louder this time. I balled my fists and got ready to get up, but was put back in my place by a wordless plea from Karis, who shot a despairing look in my direction.

'*Vinur*,' she told him. '*Bert vinur, Pápi.*'

Her answer wasn't enough to satisfy the man and he let loose a string of angry sentences, albeit in more hushed tones than his opening salvo. He was obviously aware of the other diners. She replied, her voice equally low and insistent.

They batted their argument back and forth. At one point, the man grabbed the red raincoat hanging on the back of her chair, half picking it up, as if to say she should put it on and go with him.

'*Nei, Pápi. Nei. Dáma.*'

Karis continued to talk to him, her voice more relaxed now, soothing and pleading. She was winning. I could hear that in the man's own voice now, a reluctant concession.

Finally he sighed hard, breath and will leaking from him. '*Júst. Júst.*'

He shot out an arm and I flinched, wondering what was happening, but he just ran his hand lightly through her hair. Her own hand came up and caught his, clasping it gently. She released him and the man spun on his heels and trudged back out of the restaurant without a backwards glance.

When he'd left, Karis let her head slump forward into her hands, her face obscured from me, her fingers rubbing at her eyes. Her head moved rhythmically from side to side and I heard what I thought was a single sob escape from her.

She sat back up, eyes red, and took a hefty swig of her beer before attacking her plate with a fork.

'Why is it,' I began hesitantly, 'that men round here are aggressive to me when I'm with you? Is it me?'

Karis gave a small, mirthless laugh. 'No, it's not you. It's me. It's because you are with me. They all love me and so they all hate you.' She laughed again, but shrilly this time.

'That was my father. He wanted to know who you were. He is very … protective.'

'Karis, you're twenty-four. Surely he–'

Her eyes flared hot. 'Don't criticize him. Do not. Don't say he shouldn't protect me.'

'I'm not. I … Look, are you okay?'

She sank slightly in her chair, the fire going out of her again. 'Yes.

Sorry. I'm fine. He is a good man. He just forgets how old I am sometimes. And it's his job.'

'Being a father?'

'No. Well, sort of. His actual job. He is a minister in the church. He is the sainted Esmundur Lisberg. The most Lutheran of the Lutherans. The keeper of all our consciences.'

She suddenly looked a little shamefaced. 'I do not mean it. He is a good man. Since my mother died . . . he has to be everything for me and for his church. Sometimes it is too much for him. He just wants to make sure I am okay. I told him that I am. It is not you, Callum. It is me.'

'So you *really* don't approve of the Church.'

She sighed and rolled her eyes. 'No. Of course I don't. The churches here, they have too much of a say in people's lives. And they are too stuck in their ways. They are good people, but I don't think they have changed their views in a hundred years. Do people listen to the churches in Scotland?'

Too much and not enough, was the answer that sprang to mind. I'd already noticed how busy most of the churches here were on Sundays, the Evangelical Lutherans and the Plymouth Brethren, much busier than they would be in Scotland. There, religious affiliation came too often in the form of supporting football teams rather than any deep-held beliefs.

'Not so much,' I told her. 'Is it wrong that they listen to them here?'

'Yes! They think women should be in the home, tending to children or the kitchen. They say homosexuality is a sin and show no human kindness for the persecuted. And it is because of them that the state doesn't help those that are in need. The church says oh the government shouldn't give money to this or that, even though it is needed. They say God will look after them. Well, I am looking and I can't see God doing such a good job.'

'So why don't people change things?'

She laughed at me. 'Because nearly everyone is a member of one church or another. All life on the islands is ruled by the church and the sea.'

I took a deep draw on my own beer, letting the cool liquid swill around in my mouth, savouring the taste of it.

'Tell me about you and Aron Dam.' It was the first time that I'd let on I knew the name of the thug who had spooked her that first night.

Her lower lip dropped momentarily.

'No.'

I took another mouthful of beer, letting the moment simmer.

'Just "no"? That's it?'

'Yes. Just "no". Please, Callum. It is done. Aron is from my past and I want to keep him there.'

There was more. There was so obviously more, but she didn't want to give it.

'Okay,' I conceded. 'But is he someone that I need to worry about?'

'No. He isn't.'

I wasn't sure which of us was the least convinced by her answer.

Chapter 19

A strange thing had happened to me. I was aware of it even though I couldn't be sure when or how it had taken place. I came to think that I had simply been worn down by these islands, chipped away at by the sea, like the giant basalt stacks.

My initial downbeat impressions of drizzly, uneventful Torshavn had been lost on the wind. I now saw a different town, full of colour, vibrancy and charm. I saw calm, friendly, undemonstrative people who would go out of their way to help you. Not that they would do that or anything else quickly. On the Faroes, they said that people were only ever in a hurry for whaling and that only the church started on time.

I had even grown to love the rain and shrug at the wind, as they did. The weather wasn't a foe, it was a friend, something that you could always rely on; only the form of its appearance was in doubt. If the rain and the mist weren't there then you couldn't truly appreciate the blue of the sky and the views to be seen when the weather cleared.

Gotteri took me to cliff tops, fjords, sea stacks, mountain peaks, uninhabited islands and islands with only one family on them. I saw views that took my breath away and others that reminded me why I ought to be grateful for the chance to breathe.

Martin Hojgaard taught me about the history, culture and traditions of the place. Like most Faroese, he was fiercely patriotic and never tired of telling me about the Faroes' heritage as we drove to and from the fish farm. It was he who told me that the first people to settle on the islands were thought to be monks from Scotland and Ireland back in the sixth century AD. It was two hundred years later before the Vikings arrived: Norsemen not only from Scandinavia but also from their communities on the Irish Sea and the Western Isles of Scotland. I now understand why the accent reminded me of Galway or Lewis.

'But now maybe we could find out for sure,' he was telling me on the drive back to Torshavn. 'Last year they began a programme to DNA-test everyone in the islands, the entire population. It is very controversial, as you would imagine. They are deciphering the complete DNA sequence for every person and they will use the information for medical treatment. They say the data will be held securely and only the individual will know. Of course people do not believe this. What do you think?'

I shrugged. 'It's a bit scary, I guess. Someone else knowing everything about your make-up like that. And people are bound to find out things about themselves that they won't like. Inherited diseases, things like that.'

'Exactly. But we are the first in the world to have it done. An entire population. Incredible. But they have done DNA tests before to find out our ancestry. It was interesting. It told us that the men and the women of the Faroes come from different places and in different ways. The women, 84 per cent of them, had Scottish or Irish blood in them. Like you. But in the men, 60 per cent had Nordic blood. You see what that means?'

'The Vikings went raiding Ireland and Scotland and brought the women here to live?'

Martin allowed himself a wry, almost apologetic smile. 'Yes. It is doubtful that women came willingly. But that was a long time ago. We were two peoples, Celtic and Nordic, and now we are one. But even today, the words we use for domestic animals are derived from

Celtic words, because that was the women's domain. Like *ketta* for cat or *hundur* for dog. But wild animals take their names from Norse words, because man was the hunter. We don't have deer but we still call them *hjørtur* or *rádýr*. Strange, perhaps, but logical too.'

'But you feel completely Faroese?'

Martin shifted in the driver's seat so that he could look at me properly. He seemed perplexed.

'Of course. Of course. That is because we *are* Faroese. How can you even ask such a question? We are not Celtic or Nordic and we are certainly not Danish. Never that. They may have sovereignty over us but we are our own people.'

I'd hit a nerve. It hadn't produced anger but pride. And some astonishment that I could think otherwise. 'Will the islands one day be fully independent?'

He shrugged, his eyes back on the road. 'It is inevitable. One day. But to me it does not matter so much. To me, we are already independent. We are independent in our minds and our hearts, and that is more important than anything else. More so than some treaty or a seat in the United Nations. It is nothing against the Danes, they are fine people. But they are not us and we are not them.'

'And . . .' I hesitated. 'Can you afford it?'

Martin laughed. 'I am a fish farmer not an economist. I leave that to others. Yes, Denmark gives us money. But when you are independent in your mind, do you swap that for being more independent but poorer? Maybe not. But then there is the oil. If the oil is found then we can have it all.'

Oil was the thing. It was to turn the Faroes into the new Kuwait, make everyone on the islands a millionaire. The seas that brought fish and wind and rain were now also thought to bring riches. Major companies were drilling off the coast and it was said to be just a matter of time until they struck black gold. The estimate was of public revenues of half a million US dollars for every person in the Faroes. Yet the grim tone of Martin Hojgaard didn't suggest it was such a good thing.

'You don't sound like you believe that, Martin. You don't want them to find oil?'

His hands came up off the steering wheel briefly. 'I don't know. Maybe there is no oil anyway. No one here is sitting on their behind waiting to find out. But if there is ... once they turn that tap on there will be no way to turn it off. Everything will change. Yes, there will be money. Wealth. But will that be such a good thing? It will bring change that can't be undone.'

I'd heard the argument before in town. Some craved the jobs and riches that oil would bring, others feared it. They were wary of the influx of migrant workers, possibly thousands of them, as well as the possible environmental impact.

'It will change our society,' Hojgaard continued. 'How could it not? Now there is not a world between the richest person and the poorest, but if oil comes that gap will grow. When a whale hunt is successful and we have meat, it is divided equally. Everyone gets their share. With oil? That will not happen. We have the sea, we have lived from it for hundreds of years. Do we really want it to turn black?'

I was still thinking about Hojgaard's independence speech and his wariness, when he dropped me off in town and I went for a coffee at Kaffihúsið. The western port was bathed in warm sunshine and I took a seat outside to enjoy it.

The statistic that I had learned – that it rains in the Faroes for three hundred days a year – had turned out to be less bleak than it sounded. If it rained for one minute on one spot on one island, that was enough to count as a rainy day. Yet, on these islands, it could be blowing a gale on one side of a hill but be statue-still on the other. Turn a corner and you moved from drizzle to brilliant sunshine. On a landscape shaped by time, tide and wind, every corner offered a different perspective.

I was enjoying my current one. The warmth of the sun on my skin was cooled by the hint of a breeze off the sea, while the cries of the seabirds were soothed by the water gently lapping against stone. My eyes closed, letting the sensations wash over me. I might even have drifted off, until I heard the sound of a coffee cup clinking against the table top.

Sitting upright, expecting it to be the waitress, I instead found myself facing Aron Dam across the table. Despite the sun, he still had his trademark blue woollen hat tugged low over his head, hair peeping out from beneath it in stray curls. His dark chunky-knit sweater was smeared in oil and he was unshaven. He wore his usual sullen expression, but it was set off by a self-satisfied sneer that forced one corner of his mouth to rise.

'Why are you still here?' His accent was heavy and his voice gruff. I realized it was the first time I'd heard him speak.

'I haven't finished my coffee.'

'In Torshavn. Why are you still in Torshavn?'

I could feel my pulse quickening. What the fuck did it have to do with him?

'I like it here. And I like the people.'

He didn't like that. Bullseye. I saw his eyes widen and mouth tighten. Didn't like it at all.

'You should leave Karis alone.'

'That is up to Karis, don't you think?'

Dam put his arms further forward on the table and leaned in closer. 'She doesn't know what she wants. Better for you that you stay away. You understand?'

'No, I don't. You tell me. What is it between you two?'

He stared at me. He was much bigger than I was, broader and heavier. His hands were like shovels and I got the distinct feeling that he liked to use them. He didn't scare me, though. I scared me.

'None of your business. I told you, you should leave her alone. So. You say you like living here.'

'Yes.'

'In that shitty little house on the hill?'

My skin itched and the hairs on the back of my neck stood on end.

Aron Dam was smirking – a know-all, pleased-with-himself look that bothered me. The temptation was to wipe it off his face with my fist. I could feel that urge rise in me like water on the boil, and the feeling troubled me. I wouldn't give in to that again. I couldn't.

'Yes. I like that shitty little house. And I'll be staying there.'

He made an ugly grin and spread his arms wide, shrugging his shoulders. 'Okay. Your choice. But you will want to move soon, I think.'

'Why don't you fuck off?'

Dam reached out and tipped my coffee cup over, getting to his feet in the same movement. When I didn't get up to face him, he laughed, turned his back and walked away.

The walk back up the hill took the edge off the rage Dam had made me feel, if not my anger at myself. My only compensation was that I'd be hating myself even more right now if I'd responded as I had wanted to.

I found myself kicking at loose stones like a child, booting them as far from me as I could, and imagining Dam's smirking face on every one. There were clouds gathering, threatening to snuff out the sun along with all the earlier good feeling.

The dark shape about five yards along the path from the shack sneaked its way into my consciousness. I saw it but didn't process it fully until I was closer. There had been a puddle there that had stubbornly refused to disappear, loitering in a dip in the track, and at first I thought that was all I was seeing. Slowly, uncomfortably, it percolated through to my brain that it was something else.

As I got closer, I could smell it too. The familiar scent of death.

The puddle was still full of water but the stagnant pool was now flushed out with the bloated, decaying figure of a dead sheep. In truth, it was barely recognizable as one of the thousands that dotted the hillsides. Its coat was thickly wet, the curls lank and lengthy, like a doll's tresses brushed out by an over-enthusiastic little girl. Its limbs were soft and shapeless, forming a greenish mush where they lolled at the surface.

The poor beast's dark matted chest was half in, half out of the water. Its eyes had been pecked out and the soft bones of what remained of its head lay in a soggy misshapen mess, with no obvious point defining where it ended and the water began.

It was stinking. The afternoon heat had dragged the rancid stench of death from the carcass and left it floating in the air above it.

I didn't know much about anatomy or decay or the rate of decomposition of a Faroese sheep. But I knew I would have noticed this rotting corpse if I'd stepped over it that morning. And I knew enough about death to know that it didn't accelerate at this speed. The sheep hadn't died where it lay; it had been placed there afterwards.

All I could think of was Aron Dam's knowing smirk. The one I should have punched from his face.

Chapter 20

A week passed without any further incidents at the shack. Aron Dam was largely out of sight, if not out of mind. On one seemingly accidental occasion we passed on opposite sides of Tinhusvegur, swapping glares as we did so. I swallowed the temptation to confront him and paid the price of seeing him assume a satisfied sneer.

Karis and I had fallen into an uneasy rollercoaster ride that managed to twist, dip and soar, even without Dam's malice oiling the wheels. Karis managed to do that all by herself. She was gloriously volatile, irresistibly unpredictable. This was particularly true when she was painting, and I told myself it was an artistic-temperament thing, but the truth was it could happen at any time.

I was reading in the small room in her studio, lying on the sofa with its Indian-design throw in sunburst oranges and yellows. Karis was painting next door and I could hear the occasional mutter of discontent amid the faint swish of paint being laid down. For my part, I tried to turn the pages of my book quietly so as not to disturb her concentration. It was an unnecessary courtesy on my part, though, as a brass band could have marched through the room and she wouldn't have noticed. When she was painting, Karis was part of her canvas.

I'd been lying there for four chapters, immersing myself in the thriller's small-town Nebraska, and felt the need to move and get a drink. I knew she had orange juice in the fridge, and pushed myself off the sofa in search of it. Halfway there, I stopped and wondered which she would perceive as the greater fault: disturbing her, or not offering to get her a drink.

I knocked quietly on the doorframe but she didn't respond. As I walked across the bare wooden floor, the canvas slowly appeared over her head, and I caught sight of blue skies painted above what looked like the slate roof of Torshavn Cathedral. The weather and mood seemed much improved from her normal scenes and I had to wonder if there was a storm on its way somewhere out of the frame.

Standing behind her, I reached down and put my hand round her upper arm, squeezing gently. The reaction was instant. Karis inhaled sharply, a choke of breath disappearing inside her as she nearly jumped out of her chair. She jerked her arm out of my grip and whirled in her seat, my vision clouding as the air turned white and something crashed violently into my chest. I took an instinctive step back, realizing I'd been sprayed with paint from her brush and a palette lay at my feet, its contents smeared across my shirt.

Karis had her arm drawn back as if ready to punch me, her mouth fierce but already slumping into confusion as she saw me standing there. She looked at me and seemed surprised at what she'd done. The hesitation only lasted seconds though.

'What . . . what are you doing?' There was a shake in her voice and in her body.

'I only wanted to ask . . .'

'Don't creep up on me. Don't . . . not when I'm working. Get out! Get out of the room.'

'Karis for fu–'

'I said get out!'

I stood my ground for a while, staring back at her and shaking my head. She got out of the chair and thrust her hand flat into my chest, the white paint leaking onto her fingers. She pushed me back until I reversed out of the room, the door slamming shut in my face.

Standing on the other side, freckled in white and drowning in bemusement, I didn't know whether to roar or laugh. I was still contemplating it when the door opened again, just enough for a green eye to peer at me through the gap. She stared then blinked and the door eased open far enough for her head to poke through, looking at me sheepishly.

Her teeth nibbled at her lower lip and her eyes said sorry before her lips mouthed the same word.

'Forgive me?'

'Karis, look at the state of me.'

'Sorry. I got a fright. And you know I don't like being disturbed when I'm painting. Let me make it up to you.'

My disturbing her was a poor explanation for the way she had reacted. But I didn't resist when she slipped through the door and put her arms round me. The paint on my chest imprinted itself on her black T-shirt, just as the flecks on my face found their way onto her cheeks as she kissed me.

'Am I forgiven?'

'Of course you are. Aren't you always?'

She smiled sweetly, drew her index finger through the paint on my shirt and daubed it on the end of my nose.

It wasn't about her looks, pretty as she was. It wasn't about her mouth or her legs or her figure, any more than it was about her quiff or her clothes. It was because of – and in spite of – her volatility and her vitality; it was about her sense of life and the uncontainable wholeness of her. I'd never been one for believing that a person's lifespan could be measured by some spurious crease in their palm, but I was prepared to accept that they could be judged by the amount of life inside them. Karis would have needed an entire zoo to be built to contain the life inside her. She was bursting with it.

She was hot then cold; she was exciting, irritating. She was so passionate about her home and its people, their rights and its wrongs, that it would burst from her in angry rants that mesmerized and amused me in equal measure.

She was as unpredictable as the Faroese weather. You could never be sure what you would get, but you knew there would be lots of it.

Yes, there was sometimes a sense that not all was right, that something in her was misfiring; but there was so much of it. A life so overflowing that some of it could be spilt without loss. Karis had life to spare, even if she didn't always seem to know what to do with it.

It was not about how she looked or how her skin felt when I touched her. It was all about what was inside.

Chapter 21

As soon as I walk out the back door, I recognize the smell. November. The aroma is cold and earthy, smoke drifting on the breeze and leaves starting to rot, damp grass turning evening-crisp. The smell of winter is on the wind, too, the sting riding on autumn's tail.

As I go deeper into the garden I can make out the size and shape of the untidy pyramid that sits where it shouldn't be. It's near the far wall where you can catch the last of the day's sun, where the table and chairs ought to be. But then I remember the smell; recognize the darkness of the hour and the chill in the air. November. The strange intruder is a bonfire.

But I didn't build it. This is my garden. Who built a bonfire here? I look around again and I'm not in my garden at all. It's the park and there are people all around, wrapped up in coats, hats and scarves, gloved hands carrying armfuls of fireworks. Bonfire night. That's why we're all here.

The bonfire is huge, one of the biggest I've ever seen. People are arriving all the time and adding ever more wood to it. Sticks and planks and branches. They're adding whole doors and yards of fencing. The bonfire is growing so that you can barely see the top. I'm adding my own timber to the pyramid: an old dining table that came from my mum and dad's kitchen; picture frames that once held photographs of people I loved; a wardrobe that held every piece of clothing I've ever worn.

You can feel the sense of anticipation in the air. Everyone is desperate to see the first flames steal through the wood, watch it rise stick after branch, listen to it crackle then roar until it bursts into a ball of flame the size of a forest.

There's something missing though. The effigy. You can't have Guy Fawkes Night without a Guy. Penny for the Guy. Penny for the Guy.

There he is. Kids pushing him through the crowds in a wheelbarrow, his arms and legs flopped over the side. The crowd peels back, the space forming a guard of honour for four teenagers, big lads, carrying and guiding the wheelbarrow towards the bonfire.

They get to the foot of the huge pile of wood and begin to haul the Guy out and onto the pyre. He's one of the best effigies I've ever seen. So realistic. Almost human. The four of them have got him out of the barrow now, an arm or leg each. As they lift him, the movement makes his head sit up as if he's alive.

Then his eyes open.

He stares straight at me, pleading for help. I recognize him. It's Liam Dornan. His mouth is open, too, moving slowly. Help me. Help me. *Why can no one else see it? It's not a Guy. It's a boy. It's Liam.*

I'm screaming out to warn them but no one can hear me. No matter that I roar until my lungs are burning fiercer than any bonfire, they can't hear a sound. My head whirls round the crowd and every one of them is laughing.

Petrol is poured. A match is struck. The flames lick at the base of the bonfire, they leap up three feet, six feet, up and up. Liam Dornan is at the top of the pile, his head lolling to one side and his eyes on mine. His mouth is open, screaming. The fire is a beast now, a wild animal with a life of its own, unstoppable.

No one will listen so I rush forward. I've got to get him off there, because no one else can see that it's him. I begin pulling at the wood, my hands glowing and my skin almost translucent, so that you can see the blood flowing hot beneath. I throw back a desk, pull away at burning fencing. Looking up, I see that the flames have reached Liam's legs; his shoes and trousers are on fire. I climb towards him, stepping over blazing chairs, tables, boats and beds, throwing them away as I clamber.

He's screaming now. I can smell his flesh burning. See the clothes dropping from him as they turn to ash. He's naked and on fire, engulfed in flame. I can't get any closer. The wood is a barricade. A gate shut to me. All I can do is grasp the scorching timber bars and shake them helplessly, my own skin burning at the touch.

Liam Dornan is burning at the stake in front of my eyes. I clamp my eyes shut and when I open them again, he is only smoke. Just ashes where once he had been.

When I woke, sitting upright and soaked in sweat, I could still feel the heat of the bonfire on my forehead and my hands were still burning. I could still see a wisp of smoke that used to be the boy, disappearing out of the corner of my eye.

And there sitting up, watching me and listening, was Karis. Her mouth gaped slightly, and I wasn't sure which of us was more scared. I didn't dare ask, in case I found out.

Chapter 22

'Are you sure you are not scared? Not even a little?'

She was teasing me, the laughter in her voice just inches from the surface, and delight in her eyes at the expression I was unable to strip from my face.

'No. Of course not,' I lied.

Karis and I were standing on top of Vestmannabjørgini, the Vestmanna bird cliffs on the west of Streymoy, one of the most spectacular spots in the entire archipelago. We were perched on firm ground, lush, green and undulating below our feet. Only a few steps away, the land disappeared and fell to the sea, down vertical cliffs to the rocks 300 metres below. That was where I was going and that was why I was more than a little scared.

'Good. I am glad you're not scared. Because if you were, you wouldn't have to do it.'

The air around us was thick with sea birds and their cries echoed between my ears. They were taunting me every bit as much as Karis was.

'No, I'll do it. I'll go over the edge.'

It was my first trip outside Torshavn with Karis and she was proving to be a different kind of guide from Gotteri. He had at least stopped shy of risking my life when he showed off the Faroe Islands' beauty.

Karis was here to paint and had dragged me along for company. And, it seemed, for her own amusement. Vestmannabjørgini, spectacularly sheer, faced out into the wild Atlantic and was home to fulmars, kittiwakes, cormorants, and guillemots, many of them perched on ledges hundreds of metres below us. The highest point of the cliff rose some six hundred metres above the sea, but we were positioned just halfway up.

In days past, the young men of the islands would descend on ropes held by their companions, abseiling down the vertical rock face to the ledges where they would collect eggs or capture live birds. Both were vital if a village was to be fed. Most times they would come back with food for the larder; sometimes they didn't come back at all. Falling rocks, frayed ropes, loose footing or panicked birds could all be the cause of a young man's death.

Now, enterprising locals offered headlong trips off the cliff edge in the time-honoured manner. In English it was called rappelling. In Faroese, *síging*. In any language, it seemed crazy.

A trio of curious puffins watched as I was kitted out in safety helmet and harness and secured to a rope. The strange little birds gave me a final mildly interested stare before waddling off like three drunken old men, perhaps unable to face seeing another tourist plunge to his death.

Karis kissed me solemnly on the lips. 'It is tradition that I say goodbye in case I never see you again. But I also wish you good luck.'

'Thanks. This was your idea, remember.'

'I know.' She smiled brightly and retreated to the safety of her easel some distance away, where she could take in the whole scene and sketch it. That was my reason for being there, a stuntman for a painting by Karis Lisberg.

I had come to the edge of the world and now I was going to voluntarily walk off it for this woman.

Standing on the lip of the cliff, I looked down at the vertical drop beneath me, a rock face dotted with undercut rookeries and plunging towards a bed of blackened basalt. Some distance down, the view was lost in mist, becoming an invisible abyss from where bird cries rose like the wailing of lost souls.

Off to my right, maybe some fifty metres away, a huge sea stack rose majestically, teeming with birds such that the entire rock seemed alive. Its top was coated in a sward of green vegetation, its middle ringed with the haunting sea mist.

I turned my back on the sight and faced the four men in whom I was placing my trust and my life. I nodded. They gripped the rope tighter then nodded back at me as one. I swallowed hard and stepped off into oblivion. My feet disappeared and my body quickly followed. In seconds, the cliff top had disappeared and all I could see was the rock face in front of me, heaven above and hell below.

Suspended by a thread, just as my life hung by one, I had ten metres of sheer rock above me and still thirty times as much between me and the sea.

I pushed off, away from the rock wall into mid-air and down, the free swinging exhilaration of it coursing through my veins. Down I dropped, kicked and swung and dropped. I fell into the mist and was wrapped in its coolness, disorientated by the sudden loss of the blue above. I halted just for a moment, taking in the strangeness of my surroundings but aware that if I dwelt on it too much I might be stuck there forever. I planted both feet against the basalt and pushed back.

I dropped another forty metres or so and as suddenly as I'd fallen into the mist, I was out the other side. Looking up, the cliff top was gone, Karis and the men who held me gone with it. Below, still far below, I could see the intricate rock formations that had been carved out by the sea, patchwork steps reminiscent of the Giant's Causeway in Northern Ireland. Waves assaulted them thunderously and the noise rose up to greet me, like hands being clapped in encouragement. Go on, be stupid, be brave, be foolhardy.

I was descending the side of a skyscraper, every apartment inhabited by guillemots dressed in black and white. Pushing away from the bluff with my feet, I swung out and down, acutely aware that I was going where others had died before me. Some of the rock hadn't shifted in hundreds of years, but some kicked loose as my feet caught it and tumbled below. If similar rocks were to come at me from above then I'd know all about it.

My heart raced and adrenalin drenched me. This was idiotic. Exhilarating, breathtaking and so enlivening, yet surely crazy.

As I pushed and swung, the sea grew louder as it crashed against the rock, ready to catch me if I fell. The precipice ducked in abruptly, an under-hang catching me unawares. My feet slid into a ledge where a family of guillemots were basking in the sunlight. They were at least as startled as I was and two of them flew into my face in a panic.

My vision was a blur of white and feathers and my ears rang to their frightened squawks. Their wings beat into my face and my mind was instantly filled with memories of the skuas above Torshavn and the damage they had wrought. I kicked out in a fluster of my own, desperate to push away from the winged threats, propelling myself not just out and down but wildly to the side, as I swung haphazardly left and right.

There were shouts from above, worried yells as the men on the cliff top became aware of the irregular movement on the rope. I was swinging out of control and the line above sweeping across ledges as it pleased. I felt a tug as it caught something way above me, then another and a third. Looking up, I saw three dark objects hurtling towards me, big and heavy. I kicked again away from the cliff face and managed to miss the first of them, but the second caught me a glancing blow on the shoulder, a punch hard enough to cause a screeching pain. The third rock clattered full tilt into my helmet and the world crashed through me.

Somehow I managed not to black out, the helmet doing its job, but my hands were shocked loose of the rope and I dangled groggily, suspended by the harness alone. There were more shouts from above and then from far below, too, a futile attempt at conversation against the backdrop of nature's chorus.

Then I was being lowered, inch by helpless inch, down the rock face, only vaguely aware of sliding past further apartments of amused guillemots, each smiling at my plight. As I got lower on the rock, other birds seemed to glide into view to join in the laughter: cormorants and shags, residents of the cheaper accommodation. Finally, I felt hands grasp me and I was lowered slowly onto the bedrock, where I looked up at three pairs of legs and three worried faces.

'Are you okay?'; 'Your head, is it okay?'

The crew of the boat that was to have taken me on a tour round the bottom of the cliffs were clearly worried. But I was more embarrassed than hurt. I'd had worse on a Saturday night in Glasgow. And my head had felt twice as bad on many a Sunday morning.

'I'm fine. How are the birds?'

Karis was still at her easel when I eventually got back to the top of Vestmannabjørgini via boat, car and hike, all while nursing a throbbing headache. If she was aware of the minor drama then she didn't show it. She was lost in the piece before her, her hands moving quickly and her concentration complete.

I moved round behind her to see the piece and froze as I saw what she'd sketched. Sure enough, there I was, over the edge of the cliff, a cloud of guillemots a few feet above my head. But I wasn't dressed in hiking trousers and fleece as I was now. I wore a woollen hat instead of a helmet and was clad in a rough jacket and trousers that seemed to roll into socks just below my knees, like an old golfer's plus fours. The modern safety harness was just a loop around my waist and I held a long pole in my hand with a net on the end. On the cliff top, four men sat one behind the other as if they were in an invisible rowing boat, bracing themselves against the hill as they held the rope and me beyond it.

'Karis, what the hell . . .'

'You survived, then?' Her eyes never left the canvas.

'Yeah. I did. Why am I dressed like that?'

She didn't answer immediately, her right hand busying in a corner, a detail requiring attention.

'I wanted to paint the past but I can only do it in the present.'

'Okay. I see that man is me, but you could have painted anyone going down there.'

'Yes, but I wanted it to be you.'

'Why?'

Again, she worked on her piece before she replied, refining the figure at the heart of it. When she did speak, it could have been an answer to a different question.

'Do you know that when the young men of the villages went out to the cliffs to get eggs and birds for the winter food supply, they could be away for two weeks? Before they went, they would go to all their friends and family and say goodbye. That is how dangerous it was. From the moment they left, until the moment they came back, their family would be in mourning.

'They would go down to the ledges, held up only by their friends, and when they got to the ledge, they would untie themselves, be on the ledge with nothing to save them. The grass grows on the ledges, as you saw, but it is a fragile thing. The puffins nest in holes in the grass and the hunters must grab them from there. The grass moves and they seize it out of instinct. But sometimes all the grass comes loose and they fall to their death. Or the line disturbs rocks and they are hit by the falling stones. What happened to you, being hit on the head like that? It would have killed you if it had been a hundred years ago.'

'Karis . . .'

'The bird-catchers would collect the puffins or the guillemots and put them in the belt around their waist or drop them down to the boat that waited in the water below. It was so dangerous, but they say an expert hunter would catch a thousand puffins in a day. And being in the boat was dangerous too. Being hit by a falling bird was bad enough, but if a guillemot egg landed point-first from such a great height, it would go straight through the bottom of a rowing boat. So many of the bird-catchers died. And so many more of the birds.'

She was still engrossed in her sketch and hadn't set eyes on me since I returned. I was stunned at suddenly being part of the past.

'Usually, the birds would be caught unawares, thinking themselves safe, so high up a cliff face. Others would fly and maybe attack the men to try to save their eggs and their young. So brave, don't you think? What would you do for someone you love?'

It was the kind of trick question that men hate. The sort with no correct answer, and even if there were one it would have to be delivered without hesitation and in precisely the right tone of voice. I made a feeble but, I hoped, safe attempt at responding.

'Anything.'

Karis didn't take her eyes off the drawing but nodded slowly. 'What wouldn't you do?'

'What?' This was a new twist, and I wasn't prepared.

'What wouldn't you do? Is there a line you wouldn't cross? Those birds would put their lives on the line. They would do anything to save their unborn or their chicks. The bird-catchers were feeding their families and keeping them alive by risking their own lives. What wouldn't you do?'

I felt exposed, as if she'd looked inside me and seen the failings in my past. She couldn't possibly know what I had done. How far I'd gone. How could she?

'You want me to jump off the cliff?' It was flippant. An automatic and easy defence mechanism.

'No.' She turned to look at me. 'Of course I don't. And I asked what you *wouldn't* do. Not what you would.'

'Isn't it the same thing?'

'No. Not at all.'

I was uneasy with the conversation, troubled by the place she entered when she was drawing.

'So tell me then. What is the difference?'

Karis looked me in the eyes, seemingly disappointed. 'John, if there was nothing you wouldn't do, then you would already know. You wouldn't have to ask.'

Chapter 23

The pedestrianized street of Nils Finsens gøta was busy, by Torshavn standards at least, with Saturday lunchtime shoppers. I saw a few people carrying bags emblazoned with the name of Gudrun og Gudrun, the incredibly successful sweater shop that now sold its products all over the world, each for a small fortune. At those prices, the buyers had more wool then sense. All around me, people strolled while others ate or chatted. No one in any hurry to get to where they were going, instead enjoying the sunshine under wispy clouds.

I sensed who the short, dark-haired figure on the other side of the street was before I had the chance to recognize him consciously. He had his back to me and was holding court over two middle-aged couples, all four of them seemingly hanging on his every word.

As I looked closer I could see the dark hair was speckled with grey. He was casually dressed, in a light-brown chunky sweater with dark-brown and white diamonds across it, brown cords and a pair of hiking boots with rather ostentatious buckles. For its casualness, there was a sense of deliberate smartness about his attire. I walked a few yards till I was side-on to him, and saw that it was indeed Karis's father, the minister Esmundur Lisberg.

The people listening to him seemed entranced, nodding at whatever he was saying. His hands were gesticulating, but in small, controlled movements, very Faroese and undemonstrative, occasionally making gestures as if to say 'now do you understand?' He came across as kindly but superior, a man more than happy to dispense wisdom to those in need of it.

He looked up and caught me staring over at him, his eyes widening as he recognized me. Cursing myself, I began to walk on, hoping he might not realize that I had been watching him. But he had.

Moments later, I heard footsteps quickening behind me, coming from the only person in the whole of Torshavn who was in a hurry, and a voice calling out in English.

'You will wait. You will wait, please.'

I swore under my breath, having no appetite for the conversation that was to come, and even less for the one that would surely follow once Karis knew of it. I composed my features and turned to face him.

'Yes?'

'I am Esmundur Lisberg. I believe you know that. You are known to my daughter, Karis Lisberg, are you not?'

'Yes. Yes, I am.'

He nodded curtly. 'I wish to ask you some questions, sir. Will you answer me?'

I tried not to sigh. 'If I can. What is it you want to know?'

He was studying me closely, as if trying to see inside, looking for clues, for truth or lies. For a man of God, he seemed keen to judge me. 'I want to know the nature of your relationship with my daughter.'

I nearly laughed in his face, but knew it wouldn't help the situation. The nature of our relationship? Had this man walked out of a Jane Austen novel or had I walked into one?

'Mr Lisberg, with all respect, that is a very personal question.'

His face flushed slightly with anger. 'Karis is my daughter, sir. So yes, of course it is personal. I have a right to know what is going on. You are a foreigner here and I need to know that she is safe.'

'Safe? Of course she is safe. Mr Lisberg, if you want to know the answer to your question, you should talk to Karis. But then you already did that, didn't you?'

He wasn't used to being answered back, I could see that. His eyes hardened and I saw some of Karis in him.

'Yes, I asked her and she would not tell me. Young people have no respect. I would hope for some respect from you, sir. My duty is to look after my daughter and hers is to show obedience to her father and his wishes. Do you understand?'

'I understand, but–'

'My daughter is young and foolish, sir. She has made mistakes in the past and I will not see those mistakes repeated. You are not from here and you cannot understand our ways. It is better for Karis that in time she finds herself a Faroese man who will look after her. That is better, I think.'

I was getting fed up with people telling me what I should and shouldn't do. Particularly when it came to Karis. 'I think that is up to her. If she wants to be with me then that's how it will be. If you want to discuss this, talk to her.'

'You disrespect me, sir. I ask for your understanding and you give me none. You are bad for my daughter. I will not see her hurt again.'

'She won't be hurt by me. Take care that she isn't hurt by you.'

Lisberg's face reddened furiously. 'Do you attend church, sir?'

'What?'

'Do you attend church? Are you a believer or a heathen?'

'If that's the choice then I guess I'm a heathen. Look, I'm sorry, I don't mean to be disrespectful but–'

'The wages of sin is death, but the free gift of God is eternal life in Christ Jesus our Lord. If you do not believe in the Lord then you deny yourself that gift and face eternity in the lake of fire. Think on that.'

He began to turn away from me. 'Look, Mr Lisberg–'

'Think on that!'

The man strode back down the street, leaving me standing there under the gaze of curious shoppers, all doubtless wondering about the foreigner who had incurred the wrath of the kindly minister. They were not alone if they were wondering about my sins.

I had two hours before I was to meet Karis at her studio. She was working on a new piece and had instructed me to stay away until she was finished for the day. Of course she'd given me a time, but we both knew that 'finished' meant when she was done with it, when the inspiration or the energy ran dry and not before. I'd take the chance on interrupting her, and if that meant upsetting her and having to deal with the consequences then I could live with that.

I'd leave any conversation about her father until later, if I mentioned him at all. She wouldn't want to hear it and I wasn't sure what would be gained from telling her. First I was going to have a shower and get changed.

Shutting the door of the shack, I pulled the curtains over and stripped, dropping my clothes in a heap at my feet. Catching sight of the scar above my hip, I instinctively placed two fingers over it and rubbed the old wound, stirring up memories that I quickly moved to shut out. When Karis had asked about it, I'd dismissed it as an old football injury.

The water was warm rather than hot, but it did its job. I let it run over me, standing there for an age, feeling the force of it against my face. The day and the conversation with the minister were eventually washed away with the water.

Getting out reluctantly, I shook the last of the water off me and reached for a towel. Still naked, I walked over to the other side of the bed to grab some clean clothes.

I stood on it before I saw it. My toes felt the softness of the feathers and the brittle straws of the bones in its wings. The recognition raced up my body to my brain, and my heart nearly stopped as I stepped back in fright.

Lying on the floor in front of me was the body of a huge raven, its jet-black wings spread wide and its dark eyes staring into eternity.

I let go of my breath, panting hard. The raven, bird of mystery and magic, harbinger of death.

Bending down, I couldn't see how it had died. No blood, no broken neck. If it had got stuck in here and panicked it could have had a heart attack quite easily.

But how could it have got in? There was no chimney for it to have flown down or window open for it to have got through. The door was locked and I'd have surely noticed if it had got in as I'd left that morning.

I looked at its black beak and heavy throat. It had to have been brought in and left there. And I knew by whom. My hands instinctively formed into fists and I pounded one into the wall. He had been in my shitty little house. I punched the wall till my fist rang with pain.

Chapter 24

My hands still throbbed with the memory the next day as I travelled into work with Hojgaard, Samal and Petur. I was jagged with anger at the violation of the shack, and with guilt that I'd brought it upon Martin's property.

I didn't mention the dead bird to him, but it was the image of it that led me to talk of the whales at Hvalvik. Flightless birds and fish that couldn't swim. Dead in a cause they'd never understand.

'It's not just that it's our culture,' Hojgaard explained animatedly as he drove. 'It's much more basic. The whale hunt has always been a way to eat. As simple as that. Remember we are island people and a long way from anywhere else. In Scotland you have cows in the field or chickens in the farmyards. We don't. We have fish in the sea, and whales. That is what those who disrupt the hunt seem to forget. We need to eat.'

'Who is disrupting it?'

He shook his head bitterly. 'Sea hippies. They call themselves a wildlife conservation group for the sea. Marine Machine. They come in their boats, break up the hunt, scare the whales off, deprive people of the meat. It used to be very difficult for them to do this, because the hunt can happen in any one of twenty-three coves on the islands. So it is hard for them to know where to go. But these last months, they have been much trouble. Turning up all the time. People are worried.'

'But the killing of the whales . . .' My mind's eye saw slaughtered whales with ravens flying above them signalling death. 'It seems so barbaric.'

Martin shook his head bitterly, his eyes still on the road. 'How do you think the cows die that are in your beefburger? Or the pigs that make your bacon? You think they die in their sleep then the cook comes in and slices them up? You are happy that your food is killed out of sight, in some factory, but it does not make it any different. Unless you are a vegetarian, and I know you are not, then you can say nothing.'

'But . . .' I knew my argument was faltering.

'Those animals are killed quickly. Humanely. The cutting of the spinal cord is the most humane way. The quickest way. You think it is better cows are shot in the head with a bolt? And at least the whales have lived free all their lives, not living in cages like factories keep chickens.'

'Okay, it is your tradition, but it is a strange tradition that slaughters animals.'

He shrugged. 'Tell that to Americans who slaughter forty-five million turkeys every year for their Thanksgiving dinner.'

I slumped back into my seat and said nothing more.

When I stepped out of Hojgaard's car at the entrance to the fish farm, I instinctively turned to my left to look out towards Risen og Kellingin, a daily ritual intended to prevent me from taking my surroundings for granted. The stacks weren't to be seen, having been swallowed up by the mist, but there was still a comfort in knowing they were out there.

Samal and Petur and I entered the changing area and found it busy with men and women ready to start their shifts, most of them already in their coloured waterproofs and coveralls. Something about them bothered me, though; as if they had been waiting for us to arrive.

I ignored it as best I could and made for my locker. Petur was just a few feet away, his storage area adjacent to mine. Even as I took the key from my pocket, I caught the first whiff of it. Petur caught up moments later and his face screwed up in disgust. He opened his locker door and the stench fully hit us; at the same time I picked up on stifled giggles coming from behind, the strange behaviour of our colleagues when we had arrived becoming clear.

The inside of Petur's locker was a foot deep in fish entrails and heads, a disgusting soup of blood and innards that spilled out onto his feet. His waterproofs and overalls, hanging up inside, were all streaked in guts and running red with blood. The stink was overwhelming.

Petur took a step back, as much out of surprise as from the smell, his face reddening in anger and humiliation. The movement caused those standing around us to burst out laughing and that in turn caused my own temper to flare. I whirled round accusingly to face the others; it was clear they'd known what was inside. Some of them had the decency to look embarrassed or to turn away, others couldn't contain their enjoyment. Only one person stared back without laughing; instead he had a smirk plastered all over his face. Toki Rønne.

This bad-tempered bully had been a pain since I'd started working in the factory. He'd thrown his weight about, quite literally, barging past anyone unfortunate enough to be in his way. Always sour-natured and aggressive, he had continued to hold some sort of grudge against me and much of the rest of the workforce, particularly those he thought he could get away with tormenting . Now I saw that I'd let his behaviour pass without reply for too long.

He stood there; thick legs planted wide, his brawny arms crossed in front of him, sneering at Petur, daring me to say something in his defence. I'd had enough. I moved towards Toki, any sense of discretion or appeasement gone. A few of the others saw the look on my face and the room was suddenly emptied of laughter. A couple of them tried to walk across my path to stop me but I brushed them aside. Samal and Petur tried in vain to hold me back.

'Callum, do not do it,' Petur urged, his arms grabbing at mine. 'It is what he is wanting. He is very strong. And bad. Do not do this. Not for me. Please.'

'No way. I've had enough of him.'

I was through them, only Toki in front of me, his arms now by his sides. He was a good few inches shorter than me but probably weighed a couple of stones more. He was squat and muscular like a weightlifter. It wouldn't stop me.

I was only a yard or two from him when he grinned like a wolf and held a massive hand up to stop me and spoke in a low growl.

'Nei. Uttanum!'

He gestured behind himself with a violent jab of his thumb. Outside. It was a familiar invitation to anyone brought up in Glasgow, and probably a challenge universally understood. Toki wasn't stupid enough to fight me on the company's premises, something that would most likely lead to dismissal. Instead he had goaded me into going exactly where he wanted. And into precisely the sort of situation I'd been trying to avoid.

No one messed with Toki, that was the word I'd picked up very soon after starting at the fish farm. He was not only bad-tempered and aggressive, he was violent. Samal had told me how another worker, a quiet man named Atli, had been the relentless victim of Toki's taunting, until he eventually snapped and told him where to go, in no uncertain terms. Toki had said nothing, but a short time later he and Atli had been alone in the freezer and when Atli came out his arm was broken in two places. He insisted to everyone that he had trapped it in the door, and left the factory the next day, never to return. Petur was every bit as quiet and placid as Atli. He wouldn't fight his own battles.

I followed in the thug's footsteps towards the tall warehouse doors that led to the dockside. I knew there would be no one out there at this time of the day. It would be me and him and whatever he could use as a weapon. If he even needed one. Toki passed through the thick white strips of PVC curtain into the open air, with me just a few feet behind.

As soon as I was outside, I took a step nearer Toki, who was still walking with his back to me, and crashed the sole of my foot into his calf with as much force as I could muster. I was playing by the rules I was brought up with. If your opponent is bigger and heavier than you, fight dirty.

Toki fell to the ground with a furious roar, bellowing at me as he spun and lay on his back. He swiped a bearlike arm at my legs but I sidestepped it, moved a couple of feet to my left and booted him in the groin as hard as I could. He screamed in equal quantities of rage and pain.

I stood over him, enjoying the sight of him squealing like a stuck pig.

'I know you can speak English,' I told him. 'Now you have learned some Scottish too. You behave yourself from now on or you'll learn some more. The hard way. Understand?'

I was falling to the ground before I knew it. The pain in my shin only registered after I was tumbling through the air. Toki had lashed out with his foot. It might as well have been a tree trunk. Two huge hands were at my neck, grabbing hold of my collar, pulling me up and then slamming me back down again, my shoulders and neck smacking into the harbour concrete, my head catching a glancing blow. He easily picked me up and threw me down again, knocking the wind out of me, following up with a punch to the stomach for good measure.

I was still dazed when Toki lifted me up, propelling me above his shoulders as if I was a barbell. He strode slowly but purposefully towards the quayside, his thick legs bearing the load. The bastard was going to throw me into the ocean.

I reached down with my right arm, straining every muscle to

claw at his face. Toki felt my hand and increased his pace, determined to ditch me. I found his eyes and dug a finger into each, causing him to scream. He squeezed my neck and leg with the hands that held me but I dug my fingers in deeper. He tried to lift to throw but I pressed harder, clawing towards the back of his eye sockets.

With a defeated roar, his knees bent and he dropped me, letting me crash onto the dock. I was on my feet instantly, despite the pain echoing through my hip where I'd landed. Toki wiped at his eyes and hurled himself at me, half-blinded. I took a step to the side, letting him go by me and stamped down hard, but not too hard, on his fibula as he passed. Any firmer and I would have broken it. His face contorted and I followed up with an elbow to the side of his head that dropped him to his knees, the air going out of him like a deflated balloon.

There were white cartons of waste products on the quayside, the very containers of entrails, fish heads and guts from which Toki had filled Petur's locker. I took a large handful of the stuff, the excess spilling from my grasp. Toki was still on his knees when I grabbed his throat in my left hand, forcing his mouth to open wide in protest. With my right hand, I rammed the mess of bloody heads, guts, coils and intestines down his throat.

Toki's eyes popped, he tried to throw an arm at me but I simply squeezed his throat tighter and packed more of the entrails on top of those already there. How much further would I push it?

'Enough,' roared a voice behind me. 'Stop, Callum.'

I didn't relax my grip but looked over my shoulder to see Martin Hojgaard standing a few yards away, a crowd of workers behind him. Martin had the same look of anger and disbelief on his face that he'd worn on the night I woke his family with my nightmares.

The last of the fish guts dropped from my right hand onto the bloody patch of ground beneath Toki and my left released its grip on his throat. The man slumped forward and he caught himself on his hefty forearms just inches before he clattered onto the concrete.

Toki's relief didn't last long as Hojgaard strode over and thumped him on the back with the palm of his hand, causing him to cough up a heap of entrails. Martin followed it up with an angry stream of Faroese that saw an admonished Toki helped to his feet and led back inside.

'I told him that I hit him because I did not want him to choke,' Hojgaard explained, when only he and I were left standing outside. 'It is only partly true. I also told him that he had been warned many times and that if it happened again he would have to go.'

Hojgaard looked round to make sure no one else was listening.

'If it was anyone else but Toki you would be sacked. Immediately. He had that due to him, I think. The others said what he did to Petur. But this must be a warning to you. You understand?'

I nodded, wiping the slimy remains of fish guts against my jeans.

'Good,' Martin nodded back. 'Are you okay?'

'I'm fine.'

'Not a word of this to Silja. She would not approve. But . . . what you did with the fish waste. Ha . . .' Hojgaard shook his head in incredulity and laughed heartily. 'I would have paid many krónur to have seen that. You could have sold tickets. Where did you learn to fight like that?'

I shrugged. Martin really didn't want to know the answer.

Chapter 25

'The thing about akvavit,' Karis slurred, 'is that . . .' She caught sight of the grin on my face. 'No, listen to me. The thing about akvavit is that we . . . what was I saying?'

We were in Cafe Natur, late Tuesday night, and the band was playing below us. Karis and I were at a table on the mezzanine, another couple sharing the space with us.

'You were telling me about akvavit.' I leaned forward and pressed my lips against hers. She had a new hat on, a leopard-skin bowler that only she could get away with, and the brim bumped against my forehead.

'Yes, that's right. The thing about akvavit . . . is that it is really strong,' she giggled. 'No. No. The thing is that the Faroese turned water into schnapps. You know that akvavit is schnapps, right?'

I sighed theatrically. 'Yes, of course I know.'

'Okay, good. Clever boy. In Faroes we drink more schnapps than anyone else in the whole world. It's a tradition at parties. Schnapps for welcome, schnapps with dinner. Okay? But we didn't make our own schnapps. We weren't allowed, because the bloody government, the . . . nanny state . . . it said we couldn't make alcohol above 5.8 per cent. It's bollocks, right?'

Karis stopped mid rant and took a serious sip of her own

akvavit, a single finger politely wiping away a stray drop from her pink lips.

'So . . .' she smiled sloppily, 'the guy who makes this stuff wanted to have our own Faroese akvavit, so he sent Faroese water to Iceland to have it turned into schnapps. Much better than old Jesus turning water into wine, huh?'

'Okay, but . . .'

'I know,' she slurred again. 'I know what you're going to say. I know. Why is it Faroese if it's made in Iceland, right? It's the water, stupid. It's special. It has basalt in it. And salt because of the sea air. And then in Iceland they put angelica in it, which grows here, and cumin. It's good, huh? This one . . .' She tapped the glass as if we hadn't been drinking it for an hour already. 'This one is Havið and it is 50 per cent proof! It's the strongest schnapps in the world.'

She smiled proudly and kissed the glass before kissing me with a noisy smack. Our heads lolled close together, just nuzzling without saying anything, the world's strongest schnapps doing the talking for us. My head was starting to spin, the room with it, but I didn't care, the past seemed far away.

'I can't drink this stuff all night,' I told her. 'My head can't take it.'

She shoved her head right into mine. 'Are you insulting my schnapps?'

'No. I wouldn't dare.'

'That's right. You wouldn't.' She gave a mock slap to my face but then held her hand there, stroking my skin. 'I like you, Scotsman. Even if you are old and can't keep up with me.'

I groaned and let my head slump forward, knowing she was teasing, and playing up to it. 'It's not because I'm old. It's because I don't get any sleep at night.'

She raised her eyebrows mischievously. 'Are you complaining? Because if you are I can let you have more sleep, if you want.'

For a moment, I was thrown. Struck, as was often the case, with fear as to what she was hearing from me while I slept. But the playfulness in her eyes reassured me she was simply suggesting that more sleep would mean less sex.

'Oh no.' I grinned. 'No, no, no. Sleep is overrated.'

'You bet it is.'

I heard the voice coming from above us. It didn't register at first, but then the tone of it worked its way into my consciousness like a knock on the door in the middle of the night.

'Get up. I said get up.'

Karis and I looked at each other before we lifted our heads. She wore the same wary expression that I had seen in this same bar weeks earlier.

I looked up, knowing I would see Aron Dam standing there. He was right up against our table. Either he was swaying or the room was.

'Get up,' he repeated. Louder this time. Angrier.

'Go away, Aron. Get out of here.' Karis's voice was part-pleading, part-ordering. I held his hard stare and didn't let my eyes leave his. He wanted me to blink and I wouldn't give him the satisfaction.

'No. I am not going,' he thundered. 'I live here. He is going. Get up and get out. I told you to stay away from her. I warned you.'

I'd had enough. I smiled at him and he reached down to grab my arm, but I easily shrugged him off, causing him to take an unsteady step back.

Karis let her voice drop low and hissed at him. 'Stop this, Aron. I told you. I told you what would happen if you kept doing this.'

Dam waved a dismissive arm across himself. 'You talk. I don't listen. I want him to go. And I am going to make him go. He just sits there and you fight for him. He is not a man.'

I saw the flame light in Karis's eyes and she was readying herself to argue with Aron, but she didn't get the chance. I swept out my left leg and whipped Dam's feet away from under him. He crashed to the floor with a thud that made the entire bar turn and look. Karis's mouth fell open and her stare turned on me.

Dam struggled to his feet, helped by one of the other customers, who he pushed away ungratefully. His cheeks burned red and the embarrassment made him even angrier. He took a stumble back then moved hurriedly towards our table again. I slipped from my seat, letting him fall into the vacant space, grabbing his arm and twisting it violently behind his back.

Dam yelped then grunted furiously. I twisted the arm further, increasing the angle and feeling the tendons stretch and the bones protest. I was ready to break it. He tried to push back, using his greater size and weight, but every time he moved I bent the arm more.

'Stop it!' Karis was talking to me rather than to him. 'Stop it!' I didn't.

Her eyes squeezed shut momentarily in anger and frustration then opened again as she put her head down beside his.

'Aron, I told you what I would do. I meant it and I will do it. So help my father's God.'

Dam grimaced and I made him whine a little more. He nodded. Then, as I hadn't stopped, he nodded quicker and harder.

I let him go and he stood up before slumping against the wall, nursing his arm as best he could.

'Go.' It was all she said, and he left, head down, everyone in the pub watching his humiliating departure.

I was back in my chair before the door hit his backside. I lifted the glass of schnapps, closed my eyes and emptied it down my throat, the fire and spices warming me yet somehow cooling my rage.

When I opened my eyes again, I saw Karis was sat as far back in her seat as she could. A single tear was working its way down her cheek. Her hands gripped the table in front of her, her knuckles glowing white. I struggled to read the look on her face, seeing confusion, but even as I watched, it turned to anger.

'I told you. I told you to leave it to me. Why did you do that?'

'I couldn't . . .'

'No. Don't talk. There is nothing you can say ... You think violence is the answer? You are as bad as he is.'

She raised her hand and I saw a flash of glass before the remains of her akvavit splashed into my face, stinging my eyes. By the time I had wiped it away, all I saw was the door slamming closed behind her and her shadow disappearing down the street.

I sat for a while, bemused by what I'd done wrong and by her reaction. I'd fought my own battle. I'd bested the beast. Shit, the schnapps was really working on me. Not enough, though, and I now had a problem that could only be solved with more of it.

I managed to get to the bar and ordered another. A double. The problem with akvavit, I now knew, was that it didn't last very long. As my anger and confusion grew, I worked it back quicker and quicker.

It was all Aron Dam's fault. He'd brought me back to a place I didn't want to be. A place I'd already tried to get away from. Karis hadn't helped either. I did it for her and she'd thrown it back in my face. How could she treat me like him?

I threw the last of the akvavit inside me and wiped my hand across my mouth. Pushing my chair back, I got to my feet and pointed myself in the direction of the exit. Faces whirled around me, all looking at me. I waved an arm, dismissing them, not properly recognizing them. Door. I needed to go out the door.

I fell through it onto the street and suddenly knew where I was going. Knew what I was going to do.

Chapter 26

I can see the blood, taste it, smell it. I can feel it lick my skin and hear its rush in my ears. Blood means life but it also means death. My senses are suffocated, drowning in shades of red. All I can do is fight.

I woke somewhere mid fight. A fight I was losing. Suddenly awake, with no idea where I was or when, eyes snapping open in fright. The covers of the bed I lay in were in disarray and my body a tangled, aching mess of limbs. Hojgaard's shack. That's where I was. Morning. The morning after the night before.

My head throbbed and my throat was sandpaper dry. Massaging my temples, I stumbled out of bed in search of water. There were a few inches in a bottle and I eased that down my neck before refilling it from the tap and falling back onto the bed.

Something else was missing. A scratchy memory tugging at my consciousness. Another awakening that seemed like a bizarre dream. The slate fish slabs on Undir Bryggjubakka.

I sat and held my head, trying to separate dream from alcohol from memory. Leaving the Natur. Falling into the night. Then waking . . . not here. There. I woke there first. Didn't I?

It seemed so ridiculous that I couldn't be sure.

Looking down, I saw the cut on my hand. I stared at it, willing it to explain, desperate to know. An attempt to drown my hangover in the shower didn't work, and growing anxiety dressed me with shaky hands, so that I had to clench them into fists to stop it. I dreaded having to speak, practising a few words aloud and hearing them woolly and slurred.

When Martin's car came into view, I took a deep breath and then expelled it again, hoping to get rid of the fumes that must have been lingering on my tongue. I fell unsteadily and uneasily into the back seat, a silent wave to Samal, Petur and to Hojgaard. I feigned tiredness, although it didn't require much acting, and closed my eyes, my head against the window. Maybe I slept, maybe I didn't, but all the time my brain was thinking, 'I'm drunk. Don't let them see that I'm drunk.'

I opened my eyes on bends and turns, seeing waterfalls cascading down the hills into now-familiar fjords. The morning was misty, the low cloud hanging over the fells like the ghost of the previous day's weather. Sheep looked up lazily at our passing, but some stared right at me, their gimlet eyes warning me off. I fell back into my faux sleep, praying that my act was winning over my audience and that conversation would prove unnecessary.

At last I felt the car come to a stop and woke to feel the side of my head wet with condensation from the window and my forehead damp with sweat. Stepping warily out of the car, I saw the other three were well down the path towards the factory and followed slowly and deliberately in their wake.

My fat head hung low as I walked, and I had to force myself to push it up into something resembling a normal position. Martin was a smart guy and I had to wonder if I had fooled him this far. My fetid breath in the small space of the car. Surely he'd noticed.

Inside the factory there was a wall of chatter that assaulted my ears as soon I entered. An ironic thought of gossiping fishwives came to mind as I saw what seemed to be the entire remaining staff standing around talking in one large group.

Hojgaard spoke up at the sight of them, and although it was in

Faroese, I had no doubt by his tone that he was asking what the hell they were doing standing there rather than getting to work.

Five or six of them seemed to answer at once, pupils eager to impress and please the teacher. I heard the name Torshavn. Other words tumbled over each other. I saw Samal's mouth drop open in disbelief. Petur's did the same but as if in slow motion. Hojgaard's hand came up, demanding attention, and his words that followed were firm, calling for quiet and demanding that one person speak. A fat guy named Gudmar did the talking. I followed none of it – except two words. A name.

Petur turned to me, his face blanched.

'They say there was a killing in Torshavn last night. A murder. It is all over the radio, but we didn't have it turned on. They thought we would know.'

My gullet closed over. My head shrank in on itself. Discharged memories nudged me awake. Words forced themselves through the keyhole that was my throat.

'Who was it? Do they know? Who . . . who was murdered?'

It was Hojgaard who answered, his eyes set hard and fixed on me.

'It was Aron Dam. Someone stabbed him to death.'

Chapter 27

Hojgaard's words pierced my guts. Aron Dam's name made my heart stop and my brain freeze. My mouth hung open and my limbs were locked.

With my head stuttering, wondering, arguing with itself, I fell onto a bench, my back glad to have the wall to hold it up. I reached for my work gear, struggling to put it on but glad to have an excuse for not looking up at the others.

Hojgaard had put everyone to work, breaking up the gossip-mongers as best he could. It wasn't easy: the Faroes weren't a place where things like this happened. Glasgow might have a couple of murders over a quiet weekend. The Faroe Islands had had one in the last twenty-five years. Until now.

He didn't say anything to me but I could feel his eyes on me and sense him putting things together in his head and wondering. Just as I was. I strained to remember what had happened between drinking with Karis and waking up outside. Pieces began to drop into place, blurred fragments of memory. Aron. A fight in Cafe Natur. The awakening on the fish slabs that I was now sure I didn't dream.

I got to my feet and made for my work station, legs carrying me there on autopilot. Remembering. The knife in my pocket. The blood on the blade. Burying it on the hillside. So close to the shack. What the hell had I done?

The police would be tracing Dam's last movements, asking around town and finding out where he'd been. It wouldn't take them long, not in a place the size of Torshavn. He was a regular in the Natur: they'd probably already talked to the staff. The fight was bound to be mentioned. *I* was bound to be mentioned.

My hands trembled as I stood on the production line. Not from the alcohol, as earlier. From fear. Some of it fear about what might happen, but more, much more, about what might already have taken place. Fear of not knowing.

My hands were useless, betraying me. Clumsy, fat-fingered traitors. They let fish slip, they squeezed too hard. And there, on the palm of my right hand was the fresh cut where the *grindaknivur* had pierced it. An atheist's stigmata. A wound that might lead to my own crucifixion.

The morning dragged, minutes seeming like hours, the hands of the clock on the wall held back by my guilt and paranoia. Perhaps everyone wasn't looking at me, perhaps it just felt that way. I remembered Karis being angry at me. In my mind's eye I could see her glaring at me, but I couldn't hear the words.

When lunchtime came, I was glad to get out of the suffocating grip of the factory and burst outside, fetching lungfuls of air. It was drizzly and cold but I didn't care. I made for my favoured spot facing out to the ocean and the sea stacks and sat down on the damp grass, mindless of the moisture soaking into me.

I had no appetite but tore into large bites of the sandwich that Petur had given me, eager to fill the void in my stomach. The bread turned into acid, burning me as it dropped inside me and causing my guts to cramp in protest. I ripped the last sandwich into chunks and hurled them into the air, where they were snapped up by greedy and grateful kittiwakes.

To my left, Risen og Kellingin were continuing their hopeless duel with the ocean, the waves relentlessly working away at the colossal stacks, dissolving the basalt, grain by grain. Maybe they should just give in, I thought. Fall into the sea and at least make one final splash rather than meekly fading away until no one remembers you were even there.

Behind me there was a crunch of tyre on gravel and I spun my neck to see a white Mondeo with a blue light spanning the width of its roof and *Politi* written on the side in block lettering. Seconds later a green Toyota pulled up beside it.

Two men in blue shirts and jackets got out of the marked car, one of them large and bulky, the other shorter and stockier. Another man emerged from the Toyota, his back to me and the collar of his long brown coat already turned to the rain below a crop of blond hair. I watched breathlessly as the uniformed men waited for him and they went together into the factory.

My heart beating faster, I turned back to the ocean to see that Risen og Kellingin were slipping from view, the mist and rain eating them from above just as the waves were from below. I knew they were losing their battle, I just couldn't see it.

It was an ashen-faced Martin Hojgaard who emerged from the factory with the police officers behind him. The fair-haired man in the brown raincoat stayed at the door beside Martin while the two uniformed officers moved towards me along the path. I stood as they approached and they quickened their step, perhaps thinking that I was going to make a run for it. But where could I have gone, even if I'd wanted to?

'John Callum?' the large cop asked, even though he clearly knew who I was.

'Yes.'

'Come with us, please. We are taking you back to Torshavn.'

The shorter cop produced handcuffs but I shook my head at the sight of them. 'You won't need those. I won't be any trouble.'

The officer pushed them towards me anyway and I shrugged, my resistance crumbling. I let them tighten the cuffs round my wrists and heard the click as they locked. The bigger guy took my arm firmly but gently and led me back along the path.

The man in the raincoat wore wire-rimmed glasses that he removed and dabbed at with a handkerchief to fight the drizzle. He pushed them back onto his nose when I was a few feet away and regarded me keenly.

'Mr Callum, I am Inspector Broddi Tunheim of Torshavn Police. Enjoying the view there? The stacks are beautiful, are they not? I don't get up this way often enough. My wife always says I should get out of town more, but I don't really get the chance. Today, I do. Mr Callum, did you kill Aron Dam?'

The sound of his name slapped my face, stunned me. I wanted to tell this man that I didn't know. Tell him that I might have done. Could have done. But that I just didn't know.

'No.'

I was lying. If I knew it, he probably did too.

He just looked at me until the rain misted his glasses and he had to wipe them clean again.

'You didn't? Good. This will be easy then. Come, we are going back into town to talk about it. Watch your head when you get into the police car. I will see you at the station.'

I couldn't help but look back as I was led off, seeing my colleagues engrossed in the drama. Hojgaard seemed unable to decide whether to be angry with me or apologetic. He was a decent man and probably felt both. Samal, Petur and a handful of others that I called friends stood by the entrance and watched open-mouthed as I was put into the police car and driven away.

Chapter 28

'You see the time?' Tunheim pointed at the clock on the wall of the interview room. It was five minutes to two.

'That is your enemy and mine,' he explained with a smile. 'A flight from Copenhagen lands at two o'clock and on it will be two detectives and a forensic examiner from Denmark. It will take them perhaps an hour to get to the station and then the case will be theirs. We have one hour and five minutes, you and me. We should spend it wisely, don't you think?'

Tunheim was in his early fifties, his fair hair cut in an untidy fringe and his face lightly freckled and tanned. His glasses seemed a constant distraction to him, being pushed up or down on his nose, or taken off and wiped with whatever he had to hand. There was an air of affability about him that I didn't quite trust. The man who would be your friend.

The larger of the two cops who'd accompanied him to the fish farm sat next to him, across the table from me. This one looked like he spent more time chasing food than he did criminals, a sizeable paunch being evident when he sat down, his podgy frame sinking into the chair.

Tunheim leaned in and lowered his voice, as if the uniformed cop couldn't hear.

'Between you and me? The Danish guys are officious sons of

bitches. And their forensic guys? They don't miss a thing. If there is so much as a hair or part of a footprint or a fibre of clothing near the murder scene they will find it. Sure as sure. Kind of takes all the fun out of detecting.'

He leaned back in his chair and raised his voice again. 'But they are the experts, you see. I'm just a simple island policeman. I am more used to investigating traffic crimes or maybe some vandalism. But so little of it. Do you know it is stated that the Faroe Islands have the lowest crime rate in the world? It is true. For every 100,000 people in the United States, 760 are in prison. In Faroe Islands? The rate is 15 for every 100,000.

'Scotland is not so different from the Faroes in some ways, Mr Callum. We have long winters, little daylight, we drink too much, we have the Viking blood. And yet you have much crime and we have so little. Here there is nowhere to run or to hide, and everyone knows everyone else, or at least someone who knows them. And we are not so poor; even those of us who do not have much, have the sea. The need to commit crime to survive, or because your neighbours do, is not there.

'Now, this is good if you are a citizen, but not so good if you are a policeman. You know, we have only had one bank robbery ever in the history of the islands? And yet now, today, we have a murder. A terrible thing.'

The word had the effect on me that it was probably intended to have. Murder. It rang in my ears, spread through my body like a virus. A terrible thing. It had filled my head since I heard it said in the fish factory. The murder of Aron Dam. I couldn't think about it without wanting to shake.

The inspector took his glasses off and wiped them with the tail of his shirt. Holding them up to the light, he checked they were to his satisfaction then positioned them carefully on his nose again.

'So,' he began again. 'I am thinking you would be doing both of us a favour if you just told me what happened last night. It would go better for both of us. I would get to solve a terrible crime and you would get the benefit of cooperating with the police and the judiciary. You see?'

I saw. And maybe if I'd known then I would have told him. The problem was that I didn't know anything except the possibility of the worst. All I could be sure of was that I had to keep my doubt inside me.

'Yes. But there is only one problem. I didn't do it.'

'Ah,' Tunheim nodded sagely. 'That is a problem indeed. You know what the Danish police will do, don't you?'

I shrugged noncommittally.

'They will look at you. A foreigner. A newcomer. A man who had a public fight with the deceased just a couple of hours before the murder. They will think you did it. Sure as sure. And maybe you did. But maybe you were provoked, you were angry. It happens. We all get angry, even me. Did you get angry, Mr Callum?'

I didn't know. 'No.'

'Are you certain? You don't sound certain. The people in the bar said you were pretty angry. So, are you certain?'

I didn't know. 'No.'

Tunheim smiled warmly. 'So. We are getting somewhere. An hour is enough time, I think. So maybe you were angry, yes?'

'I was angry earlier, yes.'

'Angry at Aron Dam.'

'Yes.'

'Angry enough to kill him?'

'I didn't kill him.'

'Yes, you said that. Where did you go when you left the Cafe Natur last night, Mr Callum?'

I didn't know. I wished the hell that I did.

'I don't know.'

His eyes widened, his expression full of surprise. He was playing me. I knew he was playing me. I'd faced questioning before. I'd cope. Or at least I thought I would. I'd cope better if I wasn't drowning in uncertainty.

'You don't know? Wow. You really don't know? Oh this is bad, Mr Callum. The Danish police ... you know that they won't even give you time to confess, to make it easy for yourself? They are so good at what they do – especially the forensic man, the CSI guy – that before you know it they will have nailed this case, with all their techniques and scientific knowledge. They won't need your confession. They won't even want it. It could mean years more in prison.'

Tunheim took his glasses off again, reaching for his shirt tail and spending an age polishing them, leaving his last statement hanging in the air. I filled the gap with my own fear.

'Did the officers tell you what happened to Aron Dam?' he asked me. 'How he was killed?'

'No. But the workers at the fish farm say he was stabbed.'

Tunheim tilted his head to one side, considering what I'd said. 'Hm. Stabbed, yes. But that doesn't quite cover it. Maybe I should wait and let the Danes tell you. They'd probably like that. Unless you already know?'

'I don't.'

He laughed. 'I'm sorry. Just a little trick by me. You didn't fall for it. I'm not very good at this. No practice, you see. If you stole a fishing boat or broke someone's window ... I'd be fine. Murder ... it's not my area.'

He sat back in his chair and took his damned glasses off again, spreading his arms wide in defeat.

'I give in, Mr Callum. I really should just leave this to the Danish policemen. They will know what to do with you. But it is a pity. I would have liked to have helped you. To have helped both of us.'

I said nothing.

Tunheim made a play of looking at the clock, watching the minutes tick away.

'We have a saying in the Faroe Islands, Mr Callum. Maybe you have heard it. *Hann fær byr, ið bíðar, og havn, ið rør*. It means, he who waits gets a tailwind, and he who rows, a harbour. You understand?'

'No.'

'Well, in this case, you have a choice. You can wait for the Danes, who will be here very soon. Or you can row now and find your harbour. I am your harbour, Mr Callum. Unburden yourself.'

'I told you. I didn't kill him.'

'No? You wanted to, though, didn't you? Was Aron Dam fucking your girlfriend?'

'What?'

'Karis Lisberg. She is very beautiful. Was Aron fucking her behind your back? Humiliating you?'

The flame lit inside me and I could feel my temper rising.

'Fuck you. No, he wasn't.'

'Are you sure?'

'I'm sure.'

Tunheim pursed his lips, his head bobbing slowly up and down.

'Okay. Okay. I'm sorry, Mr Callum. I was fucking with you. It is called "good cop, bad cop", right? I know that I should just play one of them and Demmus here,' he indicated the fat cop, 'should play the other, but Demmus doesn't like to play. So I am being both. I hope you don't mind.'

'When are the Danish police getting here?'

'Oh. You *do* mind. I see. That is too bad. I don't do murder investigations, I told you that. So I am just learning. Is it annoying you?'

'No.'

'It is. I can see. Do you have a *grindaknivur*, Mr Callum?'

'A what?'

'Oh don't lie, please. I know you are lying. You know what it is. Don't you?'

'Yes.'

'Then why lie? Why think it is something you would have to lie about?'

'I am just nervous. That's all.'

'So you lie when you are nervous. Have you been nervous throughout this interview?'

'Yes.'

'And therefore it has all been a lie?'

'No!' I annoyed myself by letting my voice rise. 'Only that. I do know what a *grindaknivur* is.'

'And you have one?'

'No.'

'You know someone who has one?'

'Every adult male in Torshavn has one. And I know a few of them. So yes.'

'If I search your house, will I find a *grindaknivur*?'

'No.'

'Why not?'

'Because I don't have one. And you won't search my house.'

'Oh? And why is that?'

I turned and looked at the clock. 'Because the Danes will be here soon and I am saying nothing else until they arrive.'

Tunheim burst out laughing and rapped his knuckles on the table in what seemed like appreciation.

'So you think you will do better with the Danes?' He smiled proudly. 'That is good. I am flattered, Mr Callum. Thank you. You have made my day. I must go home and tell my wife. But a word of warning. Remember the forensics guy. The CSI. These people are very good. Amazing.'

I just looked back at him and wondered how right he might be.

'Last chance, Mr Callum. Confess. For both our sakes.'

'I would if I could, Inspector.'

'Ha. Very good. I wish you well. Although not if you killed him. Did you?'

'Goodbye, Inspector.'

He stifled a laugh and reached across to shake my hand. He gripped it and looked me in the eye. 'I shall not be going far, Mr Callum. This is my home.'

Before he released my hand, he took hold of my right wrist with his left hand and turned my hand palm-up.

'A nasty cut you have there, Mr Callum! It looks fresh.'

Chapter 29

After a brief respite in a white-walled cell, I was returned to the interview room where the heavy-set local cop Demmus sat silently on the other side of the table. His name badge read D. Klettskarð. It was the only thing I had to read in the ten minutes that we sat there.

I had time to think, though, straining the muddy waters of my mind through a sieve of sudden, stark reality. But the more I tried to remember, the more uncertain I became. I just didn't know. But I knew I could have done it. History told me that.

Had I killed Aron Dam? The thought terrified me. Not knowing terrified me too.

I wanted to scream. Run if I could. Instead I gripped the edge of my chair and tried to drive my fingers through it. I had to have something to hold onto.

Finally the door opened and two blond-haired men marched through it. They didn't even look at me but nodded towards the uniformed cop who promptly left the room. Both pulled back chairs, depositing folders, a brown envelope and a laptop on the desk before sitting down.

The one who sat opposite me had the air of being in charge. He was tall, a good few inches over six feet, with an athletic build and close-cropped hair. With his black leather suit jacket and black turtleneck jumper, he looked like a poster boy for Danish police recruitment. The other was slightly shorter, his blond locks swept back to shoulder length, but equally lean. He was kitted out in a light-brown suit with a pale-blue shirt and darker blue tie.

They both fussed with their papers and the laptop, making me wait. At last, they were both settled in their seats, but the taller of the two still opened and booted up the laptop as he spoke.

'I am Detective Inspector Silas Nymann and this is Sergeant Kim Kielstrup. We are from the homicide department in Copenhagen. You know why you are being held here?'

It was only after he'd finished the sentence that Nymann looked at me for the first time. His sky-blue eyes stared hard.

'Yes.'

'Okay. Good. For the record, I am interviewing you in connection with the murder of Aron Dam in the early hours of this morning. You have the right to remain silent. Please state your name, your date of birth and your address.'

They were both looking at me now, trying to read me. Their faces were blank. I considered remaining silent but dismissed the idea.

'My name is John Callum. I was born on the 4th of March 1981. My address is the Hojgaard residence near Kongsgil. It does not have a number.'

'You real name and your real address, please, Mr Callum.'

My heart dropped into my stomach, despite my having known it was inevitable.

'That is my real address.'

Nymann's expression darkened and his voice got firmer. 'Your full name and your address in the United Kingdom, please.'

'My full name is Andrew John Callum. As for my address in the UK, I don't live there any more.'

'I am asking you for your previous address. It is in your interest to cooperate.'

'Okay. It was 16 Carmichael Place, Battlefield. In Glasgow, Scotland.'

'Thank you. Mr Callum, if you are arrested, as you are a foreign national you can be held for seventy-two hours before we put you before a judge in a preliminary statutory hearing. If you are presented at such a hearing then the judge may either renew the arrest for a further three periods of seventy-two hours, set you free, or take you into custody for up to four weeks. Do you understand?'

'Have I been arrested?'

'Not yet.'

'Then I can go?'

'If you wish. Do you wish to go or do you wish to help the police?'

'I think you need to arrest me so that this seventy-two-hours period can begin. Or I will leave.'

The two cops looked at each other wearily. There was the merest shrug of the shoulders from one to the other. It was Kielstrup who spoke for the first time.

'Andrew John Callum, I am arresting you in connection with the murder of Aron Dam in the area of Tinganes in Torshavn, Faroe Islands. You have the right to remain silent and you have the right to legal counsel. Do you wish such representation?'

'I do.'

'It will be arranged for you, unless you have a lawyer you wish to call.'

'I don't.'

'It will be arranged for you. You have the right to medical assistance and to a telephone call. We have the right to make that call for you. Do you wish to make a call?'

I hesitated, pondering the offer just long enough to realize that there was probably no one that I could usefully call. I was probably, to all intents and purposes, alone on these islands again.

'No.'

'Are you willing to continue this interview while legal counsel is arranged for you?'

'No.'

Elin Samuelsen was in her early forties with a mop of blonde hair that kissed her shoulders, and a funky pair of round amber spectacles atop her nose. She wore a loose-fitting light-brown jacket over a darker brown top and a full figure. A plain gold pendant hung round her neck. Despite flat shoes, she was a good five foot eight or nine. A handsome woman rather than pretty, earnest and anxious in equal measure.

She shuffled through the papers in front of her, puffing out her cheeks in a manner that didn't exactly fill me with confidence. She went through the few printed sheets she'd been given and stopped to shake her head a few times.

'Okay, Mr Callum.' She looked up at last. 'Is there anything you want to tell me or ask me?'

'Have you ever handled a murder case before?'

She laughed, as much out of surprise, I suspected, as nervousness.

'No. Of course not.'

'But you are a criminal lawyer?'

'Yes. I graduated from the University of Copenhagen in 1998. I have been in practice in Torshavn since 2000. Do you wish to see my diplomas?'

'What kind of cases do you normally handle?'

It was her turn to sigh. 'Drunk drivers. Assaults. Domestic disputes. This isn't Chicago, Mr Callum.'

'You're telling me.' I was tired. Weeks of sleep deprivation leapt upon me mob-handed and I could hardly think straight. My mind was riddled with doubt and I was on the verge of panic. 'You're the best they could offer me?'

I didn't mean it to sound as harsh as it did, but there was no taking it back.

Samuelsen's head lowered slightly and I saw some steel as she looked back at me over the top of her glasses. 'Is it because I am a woman, Mr Callum?'

'No. Not at all. It's because you have no experience of this kind of case.'

She sighed wearily. 'I am the duty solicitor. I *am* the best they could offer you. And they could call in every public defendant in Torshavn and you still wouldn't have one who had experience of a murder trial.'

'I'm sorry. It's just . . .'

'It doesn't matter. I understand. Do you have an alibi for the time Aron Dam was killed?'

'No.'

'I see. Okay, this is not good, but it does not matter. They must prove that you did it. Can they do that?'

I hesitated, not knowing, trying to distinguish between possibility, probability and what I merely wanted the truth to be.

'I hope not.'

The lawyer looked back at me for a while before her eyes closed. 'Okay. I hope not, too.'

'Miss Samuelsen, what are the chances of them charging me with murder?'

'I don't know. I have no idea. It depends what else they have and what they might yet come up with. We have to go see what they have to say. I know their forensic is still at the scene. It may all depend on that.'

'Why are you in the Faroe Islands?' This, a short time later from Inspector Nymann, came loaded with a sneer that sounded as if he was asking himself the same question.

'I came here to live.'

'Why?'

I shrugged. 'I wanted a new start. Somewhere . . . quiet.'

Nymann and Kielstrup exchanged quick glances. It was quiet all right, their looks said, backwater quiet.

'You were a schoolteacher in Scotland.' Nymann was looking at the screen of the laptop in front of him. 'Why did you give that up?'

What else was on that laptop? That is what I was supposed to wonder. And their strategy was working.

'I'd had enough. And I couldn't teach here. I don't speak Faroese.'

'So you choose to work in a *fish farm*?' Nymann's voice dripped with exaggerated disbelief.

'Yes.'

'How strange. And you have met a girl here.' He made a show of looking at what was in front of him. 'A Karis Lisberg. An artist.'

'Yes.'

'She is your girlfriend?'

'I think so, yes. Things might have changed.'

'Why is that?'

'We had an argument. You probably know that.'

'Never mind what I know and what I don't know. Just answer my questions.'

'I don't have to answer your questions. I have the right to silence.'

Elin Samuelsen put her hand on my arm. 'It is in your interest, I think, to cooperate where possible. But, Inspector, my client is correct. His rights include the right to silence.'

Nymann regarded her contemptuously and manufactured a fake smile. 'Of course. Why might things have changed, Mr Callum?'

I sighed, shaking my head slowly. 'As I've just said, we had an argument. You will have to ask her.'

'Oh, we will, Mr Callum. We will. But you tell me, what was the argument about?'

'You know what it was about. I was in Cafe Natur last night with Karis. We drank. A lot. Aron Dam came in. There was a fight and she was angry.'

'And she left? What did you do then?'

If only I knew. If only he knew how hard I had tried to remember. But then, I did remember some of it.

'I drank some more. Then I left the bar too.'

'Where did you go?'

'Home.'

It was a big fat lie to two men trained to spot big fat lies. The Danes just looked at each other, then at me, waiting for it to choke me. Even my own lawyer looked as if she didn't believe it. I didn't know what the police knew and that meant they had every advantage. They even had the advantage, though they were surely unaware of it, that I myself didn't know what I'd done or where I'd been.

'Straight home?' Nymann finally asked, a sneer playing on his lips.

'I think so, yes. I was drunk.' A half-lie this time.

Nymann made a note. 'We shall investigate that. Do you have a history of violence, Mr Callum?'

Here it was. The thing I couldn't run from. But I still had to lie. 'No.'

'Are you sure?' He let his eyes drift to the laptop. Maybe it was just a blank screen and he was pulling my strings.

'Yes. I'm sure.'

'I see.' He made another note then gazed at me again. Inspector Nymann seemed to have taken an interrogation course where they majored in the benefits of the strong and silent stare.

'What time did you leave the bar?'

'I'm not sure.'

'What time did you get home?'

'I don't know.'

'Who did you meet or speak to in between those two times?'

'I don't know.'

Nymann turned to Kielstrup and they both shook their heads as if nothing could be done.

'How well did you know the deceased, Aron Dam?'

'I didn't know him. I had met him a few times. Briefly.'

'Last night when you fought with him?'

'And twice before. We weren't on speaking terms. He was hostile to me.'

'Because of your relationship with Karis Lisberg?'

'I think so, yes.'

'Hm. You have a cut on the palm of your hand, Mr Callum. How did that happen?'

The cut began to sing at the mention of its name, the skin pinching and throbbing. I was wishing I'd closed my hand over.

'I cut it on a knife. At the fish farm.'

'I see. Did you report this? To your supervisor, perhaps?'

'No. I didn't. It was only a small cut.'

'I see. It will be reported now. To our crime-scene investigator. Now . . .' Nymann picked up the brown envelope with something of a flourish, looking inside, even though he clearly knew perfectly well what was in there.

One by one, he took several A4-sized photographs from the envelope and carefully placed each one in front of me in turn: face down, like a magician laying down playing cards. One by one, he turned them over. It was a nasty trick.

Aron Dam was barely recognizable. His face and chest were drenched in blood: a dark, red, sticky mess. You could make out the open mouth that made a silent scream, if only because of the flashes of white teeth that shone through the red. And his eyes. Wide open. Terrified.

There was a gaping hole where his throat should have been. That was where the blood was thickest and darkest. Successive photographs showed his neck in grisly close-up. It had been brutally and carelessly ripped open. This wasn't the clinical work of a surgeon's scalpel; it was the artless savagery of a frenzied attack. Whoever and whatever was responsible had done it again and again.

Other shots showed the entire body and I recognized the location. Tinganes. Opposite the Prime Minister's office. Dam was lying on the slipway that sloped through the dark arch into the ocean. With his head near the doorway and his body in the shadows, blood pooled around him and swam with the seawater that soaked the old paving slabs.

Dam's body looked broken, twisted. His arms were helplessly wide at his side, one leg crookedly under the other. So much blood. More blood circled his head, suggesting his skull might have been cracked on the stone slipway.

If the images were intended to force recognition of the scene onto my face, the ruse failed. The only memory chords the photos struck were buried deep inside me. But if they were intended to produce a reaction then they achieved that. I felt sick.

Nymann continued his assault.

'Why have you been calling yourself John since you arrived in the Faroes?'

'It's my name.'

'It's not really, though, is it? It's your middle name.'

'I prefer it.'

'Really? Has it always been that way?'

I ignored him and he ignored my silence.

'You told me that you had no history of violence, Mr Callum.'

'My client has already answered that question, Inspector,' Samuelsen intervened, but I could hear the wariness in her voice. I answered the question again, for emphasis.

'That's right.'

'Is it, though? I have communications from our colleagues in the United Kingdom. You have no criminal record, Mr Callum.'

'I know.'

'And yet . . .' Nymann paused and held my gaze before placing another A4 sheet on the table between us. His ace card.

'You are linked with an incident. An extremely violent incident. Do you wish to tell me about that?'

'No.'

'You don't? Okay, I shall tell you. Four young men, all under the age of twenty, were brutally attacked. All sustained life-threatening injuries and spent much time in hospital. One is not expected to walk again.

You were the chief suspect for the attack on these young men. You, *Andrew* Callum.'

Suddenly I could hear nothing but the sound of the blood pounding in my ears. I said nothing but could see the lawyer's mouth fall open helplessly.

'The report says the incident had much publicity in Scotland,' Nymann continued. 'Is that why you left your own country to come here? Is that why you began using your middle name?'

'I was investigated and cleared. There was no evidence against me.' The words were sticking to the flypaper of my throat.

'That is not what I asked you.'

'I already told you why I came here. I came here for a fresh start. I wanted to live some–'

'Somewhere quiet. Yes, I remember. It is not so quiet for you now, is it?'

I picked a spot on the far wall between the two detectives, far from the lawyer, and stared at it until my eyes slowly closed. I groped for words that would make sense of what he had in front of him. Words that would explain it all away and make it all better. Words that would convince me as much as them. The words couldn't rise from the pit of my stomach where they lay drowning in acid that made me want to vomit.

Nymann continued. 'This information, it at the very least suggests you are capable of the attack on Aron Dam. Do you agree?'

I did.

'I repeat, I was investigated and cleared. There was no evidence against me.'

'Inspector!' Samuelsen's voice had gone up an octave or two. 'My client has told you twice that he was cleared of these charges. They have no relevance to this case.'

Nymann closed the laptop, the click final and resounding.

'The interview is suspended for today. You will be taken to the Faroe Islands prison and held there while we further our investigation. Do you understand?'

Prison. The word hit me like a hammer, forcing my eyes open. I could manage only one question. A question that I wanted an answer to at least as much as they did.

'Don't you want to ask me if I killed him?'

'No.'

Nymann sounded surprised that I should even ask such a question. 'No, Mr Callum. I don't expect you to tell the truth. We will find that out for ourselves.'

Chapter 30

Elin Samuelsen sat across the interview-room table from me, in the seat previously occupied by Nymann. She scribbled furiously on her papers, pausing occasionally to glance up fretfully at me. It didn't seem to be an encouraging sign.

Eventually, she pushed a hand through her blonde hair, a hand that reached her crown then seemed to get stuck as she froze mid thought. 'You didn't think to tell me about the case in Scotland?'

I looked at her defiantly. She was supposed to be on my side. 'You heard me tell him. I was investigated. Thoroughly. And I was cleared.'

'Yes. I did hear you tell him that. But I didn't hear *you* tell *me* about it. Only now am I reading about it. Mr Callum, I must say, it does not read well for you.'

'If I'd been found guilty of it then I'd agree with you. But I wasn't.'

Samuelsen's head fell into her hands, her hair hiding her face from view but not obscuring the exasperated sigh that escaped. When she looked up again she seemed ready for a fight.

'Mr Callum, I may not be—'

The door pushed open briskly and a figure marched through. A small, slender woman with a mass of curly auburn hair tied behind her head. She was casually dressed in jeans and a T-shirt under a waterproof jacket, with white trainers on her feet. She was carrying a large black, plastic briefcase and a camera was slung over one shoulder. She looked at the lawyer and then at me.

'Mr Callum?' It wasn't really a question. 'I am Nicoline Munk of Copenhagen Police. I am here to examine you. I believe you have a cut to your right hand.'

Elin Samuelsen got to her feet, towering over the newly arrived forensics officer. 'Can I see some identification please, Frøkun Munk?'

'Sure.' The young woman breezily flourished a photographic ID attached to a lanyard round her neck. Samuelsen made a show of studying it intently. 'Okay. Go ahead.'

Munk opened her briefcase and slipped on a pair of latex gloves, then another pair on top of those. 'You will agree to be examined, Mr Callum?'

I nodded.

'Good. That makes it easier. You have showered today?'

'Yes, I have.'

She frowned slightly. 'That is not so good but it is to be expected.' I wasn't sure if her tone implied that I'd showered in order to hide something.

'Your hand first, please, Mr Callum.'

I offered her my right hand, palm up. She came in close and took my hand in hers, her head just coming up to my chin. Something told me she was older than she looked. She could have passed for mid twenties, but that was unlikely given the seriousness of the case; nor did her brisk confidence suggest inexperience. She knew what she was doing – and I couldn't be sure whether that was a good thing or not.

Munk snapped shot after shot of my palm, switching angles and checking the light as she did so. I looked at the cut as the flashgun fired and wondered what it was telling her. The cut was small but highlighted in red, the skin sliced where I'd pulled my hand away.

It was already trying to stitch itself together, but not in time to save it from Munk's lens. She dropped a small right-angled measuring scale onto my hand, next to the cut. I could only guess at what she was going to compare it to.

Seemingly satisfied with her photographic endeavours, she delved into her case again. My finger and palm-prints were taken. My fingernails were scraped. A swab was dabbed into my inner cheek and DNA presumably extracted. She worked her way round me, plucking at my clothes with tweezers, like those birds that pick parasites off the back of hippopotamuses, carefully depositing fibres into a clear plastic bag.

Elin Samuelsen was fussing almost as much, edging round us like a worried mother hen. I could see her anxiety growing – probably in inverse proportion to her faith in my innocence.

'Frøkun Munk, you do know that my client has not been charged with murder. He has only been arrested and held in connection with the incident. And that at his own request.'

Nicoline Munk looked up at her, an amused look on her face.

'Miss Samuelsen, I am about to ask Mr Callum to strip naked so I can examine him fully. Do you wish to remain for that?'

My lawyer reddened slightly and retreated. 'No, I . . . no. That will not be necessary. Although it should be witnessed. I will ask one of the local officers to be in the room.'

Munk shrugged casually. 'As you wish. I'd have stayed if I was you.'

Samuelsen blinked furiously, unsure how to take the remark. I thought she was going to come back with some retort, but she snapped her mouth closed and left the room in search of a policeman. I was sure I saw a hint of a smile on Munk's face as she did so.

A few minutes later, a far from happy cop, the fat Klettskarð, appeared in the interview room. Seeing a man strip didn't appear to be top of the list of things he wanted to be doing. Munk, on the other hand, seemed to be positively enjoying the discomfort she was causing. At one point she whistled a jaunty tune under her breath and smiled ironically at me when I looked at her questioningly. My paranoia extended to thinking that she was deliberately distracting my train of thought, to make it easier to get what she wanted. If only I knew what that might be.

I stood there, naked, vulnerable, not knowing if there was something to be found on my person that would incriminate me, not knowing if I had even done anything criminal in the first place.

'Do you get sent to the Faroes often, Frøkun Munk?' I asked, borrowing the form of address I'd heard Samuelsen use.

She answered without looking up. 'I came once with my parents when I was fourteen. It was rainy and cold and we spent all our time hiding out in cafes or marching over wet hills looking for puffins. I hated every minute of it.'

Half an hour later Klettskarð and the other cop who had escorted me from the fish farm, Olsen, led me out of the interview room in handcuffs. Olsen went in front while Klettskarð took my left arm in his meaty hand. We had only made a few paces along the white-walled corridor when we met two figures coming the other way.

The Danish sergeant, Kielstrup, was followed just a couple of paces behind by Martin Hojgaard. His face fell when he saw me, embarrassment and guilt etched all over it. His mouth jammered half open as if to speak but clamped shut again. Hojgaard was halfway through the door of another room when he stopped.

'I am sorry. I have no choice. I must tell them what I know.'

Inspector Nymann was now standing behind him, but made no attempt to stop Hojgaard from speaking to me. My landlord and boss, decent man that he was, was being used, and I knew that the timing of our meeting was no accident.

'It's okay, Martin. It's not your fault. Tell them everything you need to.'

He smiled, awkward and grateful.

Nymann stepped aside to let Hojgaard through, his eyes on me until the door closed.

Tell them what I know, those were Hojgaard's words. The nightmares, the shouting, the cries of murder, the fight with Toki, the reek of alcohol that I must have worn in the car that morning. None of it would serve me well.

The cops led me out of the station into the yard on Jonas Broncksgøta. The same white Mondeo was parked in the corner where we'd left it earlier, and we headed towards it. Klettskarð opened the rear door and made me duck my head as I got in.

The fat cop then got into the driver's seat, but his partner didn't join him in the front. It was only then that I realized the front passenger seat was already taken. I saw the fair hair and the upturned collar of the raincoat, then caught sight of the horn-rimmed glasses in the rear-view mirror.

Inspector Broddi Tunheim turned in his chair, a welcoming smile on his face.

'We meet again, Mr Callum. I hope our friends from Denmark were kind with you. Now, we are your taxi drivers. The Danes don't know the way, and anyway, they are too busy trying to catch a murderer. It is left to me to fulfil the duty. I could have sent Rógvi along with Demmus, but he has had a long day. And it will give us the chance to catch up again. You don't mind, I hope.'

Klettskarð put the car into gear and we moved off.

'We are going to Mjørkadalur,' Tunheim continued affably. 'You know it?'

I shook my head.

'It is at the top of the mountain Sornfelli. Very beautiful. It used to be the American radar station in the days of the Cold War, when we feared we would be bombed by the Russians. Now we don't fear the bomb and the Americans have gone home. The radar station is now the jail.

'Sornfelli is twelve kilometres from Torshavn . . . how is it you say it . . . *as the crow flies*. However, in Faroe Islands the crow must follow the road and climb the mountain, so it is twenty kilometres away.

That is good. It will give us time to get to know each other. Tell me about Glasgow.'

'What?'

'I have never been. They say it is a wild place. Much drinking and fighting over football. Is that right?'

I wasn't sure I wanted any part in this conversation, and that obviously registered on my face.

'Come, Mr Callum. Tell me. I'm interested.'

I sighed and capitulated.

'Glasgow isn't like that. Yes, people drink and yes, football leads to fights, but there is more to it than that.'

'Tell me. Please.'

'Look, why are we discussing this?'

Tunheim ignored the question. 'I read that the football match, the big Glasgow one, the Celtic and the Rangers, is like no other in the world. Is it?'

'It can get interesting.'

'And you have gangs. They can be very violent, I hear. Especially with knives.'

I stared back at the devious prick before slumping back in my seat and turning to look out of the window. Nothing this guy said could be taken at face value.

The police car wound its way onto the ring road – houses and shops going by in a blur – and in just a few minutes we were high above the town and climbing ever higher into the hills. Tunheim was humming irritatingly, the volume going up and down so the noise couldn't easily be consigned to background static.

After a while he turned to me again, as if seeing me for the first time.

'I have another Faroese saying for you. It is from '*Hávamál*', a poem in the words of Odin. I think you will like it: *Tá ið ølið fer inn, fer vitið út*. It means, when the ale goes in the wit goes out. It's true, no? Alcohol, wow. I like it, but, oh boy, it can make you do crazy things. You agree?'

'I guess so.'

'You know it. Let me try another proverb on you, Mr Callum. You know how important a part the *grindaknivur* plays in our culture. It is the knife to kill the whale and the knife to eat it with. Every adult male in the Faroes has one, yes?'

'Yes.'

'Okay. So the proverb is *Knívleysur maður er lívleysur maður*. It means a man without a knife is a man without a life. You understand? It is how important a *grindaknivur* is to a Faroese man. The Danes, they don't understand this so they don't question it. Me, I know it only too well, so it bothers me. I am a strange one, Mr Callum. When I start wondering about things, I can't stop.'

I stared out of the car window, seeing my own face, drawn and anxious, staring back at me. What would Karis make of that face? I wanted her to touch it, console me, kiss me. Did she even know I'd been arrested? Damn it, every man, woman and child in the Faroes probably knew it.

We hit the base of the mountain and began to wind up, the car taking sharp bends at an uncomfortable speed, the steep drop below us only kept at bay by the occasional low barrier. Tunheim gave an intermittent and unasked-for commentary on our progress.

Sornfelli was eight hundred metres high and the road that we were taking only existed because it once held the radar station. As he had said, Mjørkadalur was now an abandoned relic of the Cold War, a former stepping stone in a ring of early warning radar systems that fringed the Arctic Circle on the lookout for Russian attack. In retaliation, the Russians used to keep a warship offshore with its missiles trained on the Faroes, something that scared the shit out of the locals for forty years.

The higher we wound, the more I understood Tunheim's claim that this was the perfect hiding place for a secret radar station that everyone knew existed. The mountain peak and the valley below were regularly covered in fog. You could be standing on top of the place and still not see it. In the half-light I saw ridge behind ridge, successive shadows fringed with mist and dappled with cloud. We had come to the roof of the world or, so far as I was concerned, to the end of it.

Finally Tunheim said something in Faroese and Klettskarð slowed the car to a halt. It was only when I followed the direction of the inspector's outstretched arm that I saw it, camouflaged against the terrain. Below us, perhaps thirty feet down a slope to a levelled-off area, sat five separate buildings huddled together against the wind. All five were long and low, with turfed roofs, dark timber walls and barely a window to be seen. The four at the front partially obscured the longer one at the back. They were bleak and uninviting, shivering in the mountaintop wind.

Behind and beyond the cluster of anonymous structures, peaks rose and fell, sweeping down in rutted greenery towards the fjord below, both sides of the ravine plunging towards the still, black water. Inches above us, the clouds hung around in gangs and plotted.

In front of me, Tunheim had the window wound down and looked at the buildings for an age, shaking his head slowly. 'This is Mjørkadalur. The jail. It's not much to look at, is it? The view from here is wonderful, but of course you cannot see it from inside. And do you know, if you go up the mountain just a little further, fifty metres or so, to where the radar domes used to be, then, on a clear day, you can see almost all the islands of the Faroes. *You* can't go up, of course. And you will see nothing but four walls.'

He took off his glasses and slowly wiped them clean, letting the sounds of the mountain fill the silence in the car. The wind sang a dirge and some unseen birds croaked their indifference. Other than that, there was only the uneasy sound of freedom.

His spectacles seemingly cleaned to his satisfaction, Tunheim turned in his seat and regarded me mournfully. I wondered if he was going to try to shed a tear.

'Mr Callum, you could spend a very long time in those buildings down there. At the moment there is no other prisoner. There will be only you. Solitary confinement. A few days in there and Torshavn will seem like Las Vegas. Have you ever been to Vegas?'

'Yes. Once. I lost a fortune.'

'You are not a very lucky man, Mr Callum. I suggest you let me try to help you help yourself. Once you are inside that place, I can do no more.'

My gaze flittered between Tunheim and the prison. The devil and the deep blue sea.

'I can't, Inspector. I would if I could, believe me, but I can't. If you want me to confess to killing Aron Dam, I cannot do that. It would be a lie.'

'I see. Then help me and you by giving me something to work with.'

'I thought the Danes were in charge of the case now.'

Tunheim fiddled with his glasses, his head tilted to the side. 'They are. In theory it is a joint operation, a partnership. In practice, of course, they run the show. I want to make the partnership a bit more equal. So what can you tell me?'

I stared between the inspector and the jail, to where the mountain slopes ran to the fjord. Whichever way I looked, there seemed to be no way out.

'Nothing.'

Tunheim looked out of the window and avoided my gaze, shaking his head sadly. 'Drive on, Demmus. Mr Callum's new home awaits him.'

Chapter 31

Four walls. It had never been anything more than a phrase before. Now it was all I had. Four walls. White. Unadorned. No natural light. A single bed bolted to the floor. A table and a chair. A double shelf was fixed to one wall and a sink to another. A toilet sat in a corner.

My company was my own. Me, the walls, the bed and the non-stop workings of my mind.

Tunheim's warning about my being the jail's only resident might have had some foundation to it. That long first night, all I heard was the creaking of floorboards and the whistle of the wind. I sat up on the firm bed, listening to the dirge and wondering if the air was trying to find a way out or in.

At least the wind had a choice.

On the second night, I learned I wasn't alone. I was treated to the tuneless singing of a drunken troubadour, a new arrival who had a distinct advantage on me in being brimful of booze. That definitely seemed the way to make this bearable. His singing didn't appeal to everyone, though, as I heard other shouts echoing from slightly further away, shouts which weren't too appreciative.

'Drunks,' I'd been told the previous morning by Mørkøre, a wiry, smiling character who was one of two guards that I'd seen. Being stuck at the top of Sornfelli couldn't have been much fun for him either, and I got the feeling he was glad to stop and chat, perhaps curious about the foreigner who was no doubt the talk of the islands. 'Drunks. That's what we mostly get in here. Men, always men, who have too much then get into a fight. Or who then get into their cars and drive. We don't like that. They go into the cell to cool off then away to the court.'

'You don't get many murderers then?'

Mørkøre's brows furrowed until he realized that I was probably joking.

'No. We had one once before and it made him a celebrity. You are not so famous yet. Before it used to be drunks and only drunks. Now sometimes we get people in who have taken drugs or even some who have committed violence related to drugs. Still, not so much.'

'How many guests do you have?'

Mørkøre laughed. 'We can accommodate up to fourteen guests. All in single rooms. Bed and breakfast. No smoking allowed. Tonight we have four. Normal is maybe eight. You are the VIP guest.'

'Is that good?' I asked him doubtfully.

'Not for you it isn't. It means you will probably be here much longer than anyone else.'

Mørkøre left me with a sympathetic grin and the four walls swallowed me up again.

She didn't call. She didn't write. I was out of mind and out of sight.

A couple of times I asked Mørkøre about visitors or phone calls but he just shrugged and told me 'maybe tomorrow'. I thought that, too; kept thinking it despite all evidence to the contrary.

*

The sun had already come up twice on an unseen horizon, and set twice somewhere over my shoulder. Its invisible comings and goings had got old pretty quickly. It wasn't made any easier by the knowledge that I might have to get used to it permanently.

The sound of a key turning in the lock roused me from an uneasy sleep and I glanced at my watch to confirm it was seven in the morning. The door pushed back and a now-familiar large, gloomy, dark-haired man stepped inside, a tray in his hands bearing my breakfast. It was Jensen, the second and much less sociable of my two jailers.

He gave me the briefest of nods, grumbled under his breath, and placed the tray on the table, before turning round again and locking the door behind him. It was his way. He would bring my food or peer through the hatch in the door with the minimum of conversation or fuss.

I pulled back the covers and swung my legs over the edge of the bed, sitting there for a few moments and savouring the change of scenery. I had a long day ahead of me and next to nothing to do. I'd already learned not to waste what little activity there was by rushing it.

I caught the air, sniffing it. Strong coffee and spicy sausage. And the disappearing whiff that had been brought in on Jensen's back. Fresh air. I hadn't smelled it for a couple of days but that made it more recognizable rather than less.

Pacing across the cell floor, I washed my hands at the tiny sink, scraped back the chair and took a seat at my breakfast table. I wasn't particularly hungry; in fact I'd had little appetite since I'd arrived, but mealtimes at least broke the monotony of the day and gave it a semblance of order that I could manage my sanity around.

The dried sausage was hotter than the coffee so I lifted the cup to my lips first and let a mouthful of the lukewarm brew swill around until I couldn't take the bitter taste any longer. I opened my throat and let the pungent liquid slide down. Starbucks it wasn't, but at least they couldn't be accused of dodging taxes.

I cut the sausage into small pieces with the intention of making the process last as long as possible. The knife wasn't sharp enough to allow me to do myself any serious damage, even assuming that I was of a mind to try to do so, but it accounted for the sausage and let me slowly spread butter on the Faroese rye bread.

Each forkful filled my mind if not my mouth. I picked apart the flavourings, trying to identify herbs and spices, humming the Simon and Garfunkel tune to myself: Parsley, sage, rosemary and thyme. Trying to think of everything *except* time. Trying not to think. Trying and, inevitably, failing.

Each bite was seasoned with memories and questions, some wanted, some not. Images flashed through my mind like newspaper headlines and I struggled to know whether I had read them or written them. Unreliable memories fogged with booze and fear. I remembered staggering onto the street, my eyes blinded with rage, charging through the alleyways with a purpose. I strained to see street signs in my mind's eye, trying to remember where I had been. And where I hadn't been. The bar and the fish slabs were the only two certainties. In between, I was in trouble.

I knew I'd drive myself crazy by obsessing on it. I had to survive the day and would only make it longer and more difficult by dwelling on things that seemed out of reach. Anyway, some things were better forgotten, I knew that much for sure.

So I ate and deflected, trying to force my mind elsewhere. My defences were always breached though, fresh thoughts of Dam and Karis sneaking in through tiny gaps, then flooding my head. His face and hers. His body, bloodied and broken. Hers naked and warm but somewhere else. I tried to push the tide back, damming the breach with desperate memories. Thoughts of home and the past I had been so keen to flee suddenly seemed preferable to the present.

I thought of my dad and the look on his face when he read the newspapers, seeing my name in headlines. The man who had been so proud when he watched me score my first goal for the school football team, or the quiet satisfaction on his face when he was at my graduation, barely able to look at me. I forced the hurt of that memory on myself, donning a protective suit of armour that had spikes on the inside. I knew I didn't deserve to run away from it unpunished.

I was still wrestling with my thoughts an hour later when the door opened, intruding on my solitude. It was Mørkøre, a friendly smile on his face.

'You have a visitor. If you want one.'

I was on my feet in seconds and had to take a moment before I spoke – I knew the words would stutter out as I tried to control my excitement. I'd been waiting for this since the cops turned up at the fish farm. Aching for it every time the door opened.

'I want one. Who is it?'

Mørkøre shook his head apologetically. 'It's not her. I'm sorry. It's a Frenchman. His name is Gotteri.'

My heart sank but I still nodded, grateful for the visit nonetheless. 'Yes. I'll see him.'

Serge was waiting for me on the other side of a large wooden table, a wary look spreading into a forced smile. Mørkøre stood quietly in the corner, looking away but his ears working overtime.

'How are you, Scotsman?'

I spread my arms in response. I'm in here, you see it all.'

'Is there anything I can bring you? Something to make it easier?'

'Sure. A bottle of whisky and my passport.'

A muffled noise escaped from Mørkøre's throat, as if he had been about to respond to my request but stopped himself.

'I will see what I can do,' Gotteri replied, his eyes searching mine for clues. 'This is bad, my friend. Very bad. You are the talk of the islands.'

'There's a surprise. And does everyone think I'm guilty?'

He hesitated. 'Not everyone, I'm sure. The Danish police have interviewed me as they know I'm your friend. They interviewed Karis too.'

My heart jumped at the mention of her name. 'How is she, Serge? Is she okay?'

Gotteri shrugged. 'I don't know. I have not spoken to her. I tried, but her father, the minister, said she wasn't talking to anyone.'

'You must have some idea.'

Another shrug. 'Her father looked very worried. But she will be fine. It is you that I'm worried about.'

'Don't be. Try and make sure she is okay. Will you do that for me?'

Gotteri regarded me strangely. A man trying to make sense of what he was hearing and seeing. 'I will if I can. So what do you remember about that night? I heard you were pretty drunk.'

Whatever I remembered, I wasn't about to share it with Serge. It was my turn to shrug. 'Not much. What else have you heard?'

'About the fight with Aron. Then the argument you had with Karis. People say you staggered out of the Natur like a man on a mission. An angry man.'

I spun on Gotteri's words like a pig roasting on a spit. More unwelcome blanks filled in my memory.

'You know how small it is here, my friend. A place where every person has eyes that they can borrow. Everyone knows someone who saw you leave the bar. It does not look good for you. Surely you can remember something else about what happened after you were on the street.'

'Like, did I kill Aron Dam?'

He held my stare. 'Well, yes, that. Did you?'

'Thanks for the visit, Serge. I'm going back to my cell now. It's been a long day.'

My second and only visitor was Elin Samuelsen who came later the same day.

'You have a date for court?' Mørkøre asked as he led me along the corridor to meet her.

'Tomorrow morning.'

'Okay. I will talk to you tomorrow night then.'

'Thanks for the vote of confidence.'

Mørkøre was still chuckling to himself as he opened the door to the visitor room. The truth was, I expected him to be right.

Samuelsen was nervously fidgeting in the same seat that had held Gotteri, a sheaf of fluttering papers in her hands. She got to her feet and offered me a soft, moist handshake. The woman's nerves weren't doing mine any good.

'How are you, Mr Callum?'

'As well as can be expected. Everyone has been very fair with me. I hope you've brought me some good news.'

She reddened slightly and looked apologetic. 'No. There is none. I'm sorry. I am here to talk you through what will happen in court tomorrow. What you can expect.'

'Can I expect to walk free?'

'It is possible.'

I nearly laughed at her inability to pour more than the minimum of optimism into her words. Never had 'possible' sounded so unlikely.

Samuelsen talked me through court procedure, who would be there and who wouldn't, what I should do and what I shouldn't. I heard what she said on the edges of my consciousness, each word fading like the one before, like ghosts into the night.

'Have you spoken to Karis?' I interrupted.

The lawyer looked up, clearly surprised. 'Karis Lisberg? Um, yes. Yes, I have.'

Of course Karis Lisberg. Who else?

'How was she? What did she say?'

Samuelsen reached for her notes, more out of instinct or self-preservation than any real need to check, because she stopped halfway and looked back to me.

'She was ... upset. This has obviously been very difficult for her. She cried.'

Her words pierced my resistance, tiny arrows fired straight into my conscience.

'What did she say?'

'That she left the bar because she was angry with you. For what you did to Aron Dam. That she was frightened by how you were violent towards him. She went home and did not know any more until she heard the next morning what had happened.'

I took a deep breath. 'Did you ask her the question?'

Samuelsen hesitated, feigning ignorance for as long as she could.

'Yes. I did. She . . . she said that she didn't know. She didn't want to believe it, but in the bar she had seen an anger in you that she had never seen before. She said yes, maybe you had killed him.'

Sitting on a bed, staring at four white walls, and with plenty of time to do so, is not a healthy thing for a troubled mind. Especially if you're locked up in a foreign country for something that you might or might not have done. I sat and stared, hoping for answers but seeing only questions.

My head hurt with the strain of trying to remember what had happened after I left the Cafe Natur on the night Dam was killed. The difficult part was trying to fight my way through the fog of the akvavit. If that wasn't enough I also had to untangle my twisted memories, separate the real ones from the false, those I actually remembered and those I remembered dreaming.

The memory-gaps from events that had taken place inside the Natur had been filled in by what Tunheim and Nymann had told me, and further fragments by Gotteri. The fight with Dam and the argument with Karis were now in my head. So was the sight of the man's lifeless body lying in that pool of blood. I could see that every time I closed my eyes. His ripped throat. His staring eyes. The image placed there either by the police photographs or by reality.

The rest I couldn't figure out, no matter how much I wanted to. Every scrap of recall had to be tested. Was it real or wishful thinking? Was it real or what I was scared of? And I *was* scared. Scared that I'd done it. That I'd murdered Aron Dam.

I was terrified that history had repeated itself.

Four walls. Four white walls. They screamed out at me like a projector screen. Movies played out on them, projected from either my imagination or my memory. When all you have to do is sit and think then time becomes your enemy just as much as thought.

The one thing in my favour was that if I waited long enough the time came for lights out, and for the first time since I'd arrived on these islands, I was in the comfort of darkness. I wrapped myself in it, wearing the shadows like a favourite coat. At least in the dark, I couldn't see the walls.

There were two problems with the darkness however: first, sleep still wouldn't come. Second, eventually it did.

Chapter 32

It's dark. That's my first clue. The second is that the person I am following through the alleys of the old town is myself. Yet no matter how many times I tell myself that it is a dream, I can't wake up and I can't walk away from whatever is about to happen. And I'm aware that I'm walking in the shadows, keeping away from the streetlight, so that the me I'm following can't see the me that is stalking my every move.

There is no noise whatsoever. Neither set of my footsteps makes a sound. Someone has pressed a mute button and turned the whole play into a silent movie. We turn into a straighter part of the street, my shadow and me, and for the first time I am able to see another figure further ahead. I am following me, following him. The first man is bigger, broader. He's familiar. I can't see him properly in the dark but I know it is Aron Dam.

We are getting closer but not too close yet. We want to be deep in Úti á Reyni before we do it. He knows what he's going to do and I know it too. I'm not him though. I'm me. And so is he. I try to shout out and tell him to walk away before it's too late, before we do something that can't be undone, but no sound comes from my mouth.

Dam walks on until we are on the cobbles and the houses are smaller, closer, tighter, no room for cars or the twenty-first century. Nowhere to run now, just the little black houses and the ocean beyond. Up ahead, I see myself close in on the prey. I quicken my own step too.

Then . . . I don't understand. What is he doing? Aron Dam turns and beckons the first me on, a whirl of his arm urging me closer. I stop and watch myself hurrying towards him. Dam is outside the Prime Minister's office, the red walls glowing in the darkness. He walks to the left, towards the slipway that leads down into the water, down to where it is even darker. He stands in the shadow of the open archway, halfway down the slope, his arms open wide, inviting.

I don't want to watch this but can't tear my eyes away. I watch myself walk towards him, quickly, purposefully. Without breaking stride, the first me draws my arm back and punches towards Aron's throat. He staggers back but still stands there. I watch myself thrust towards his throat again. And again. Then again. He is bleeding like a cartoon character who is shot full of bullets then drinks water and sees it gush through the holes. The blood is pouring from him like from a sieve, leaking from every button, every thread, every fibre.

I watch. Horrified. I'm disgusted at myself. Try to scream and shout stop but can't. I have no sound.

As I stand there, I realise that a grindaknivur *is in my own hand. I've no idea where it came from. But I know what I must do with it. I rush forward, heart pounding, until I am just behind the me that is carving Aron Dam's throat. I draw my arm back and ram the* grindaknivur *as hard as I can into my own back. I am stabbing and stabbing and I feel every thrust. It punctures a lung, pierces my heart and slices away a large part of my soul.*

Job done, I turn away from the sea and the scene and head back towards town. Behind me, both Aron Dam and myself are dead or dying. I'm limping, barely able to breathe or pump blood through my body. I'm dying too.

I walk back through the dark, narrow alleyways of Tinganes, on my own except for the people who line the route. Martin and Silja Hojgaard are there, eyes dark and skin sallow. They are both pointing at me. Karis, too, standing beside her father. Both pointing. Told you so. Tummas Barthel is propped against a wall, swaying and shrugging his shoulder helplessly. Serge Gotteri is there and Oli the barman from Natur. Pointing. Nicoline Munk is there, her long hair tumbling behind her, her eyes like shadows, her finger outstretched accusingly.

Liam Dornan is there too. In his school uniform, laughing silently, his finger pointing straight at my heart. Next to him are my parents, sickly white and eyes blindfolded. Then the four horsemen of my own apocalypse: Chilli Ferguson, Shug Faulds, Tam Taylor and Chick Welsh. They point as one, in orchestrated unison, their eyes unseen but I know they are looking straight at me.

I shuffle lamely past them and try to climb the hill, but every step takes me further down, until I can smell the fires of hell being stoked in readiness for me.

Chapter 33

Elin Samuelsen, my accidental lawyer, sat opposite me in a cell below Torshavn's court, looking as if she'd rather be anywhere else. She'd swapped her light jacket for a sober navy suit and had gained an extra couple of inches in confidence thanks to higher heels.

I too was wearing a jacket, along with a shirt and tie, courtesy of Silja Hojgaard. At least I was fairly sure it was down to her. Mørkøre told me that a woman fitting Silja's description showed up at the jail and left the items for me before hurrying off. Martin Hojgaard was much the same height and build as me and the clothes fitted fine. I was to face the judge looking respectable.

'This is just a hearing,' Samuelsen told me, fussing at her collar with one hand and squeezing a sheaf of papers with the other. 'Just a preliminary statutory hearing. If the judge decides to take you into custody leading to trial then we can appeal. If we don't win the appeal . . . and we probably would not . . . then we will get you a lawyer from Copenhagen experienced in murder trials. I have spoken with my colleagues and this is best. You understand?'

I looked at Samuelsen and would have felt sorry for her if I hadn't had enough to worry about. The woman was no doubt proficient in her own field but in this one she was as far out of her depth as I had been when I stood on the fish cages at Risen og Kellingin and the waves crashed at me, threatening to send me into the drink. Samuelsen would have been more at ease with those waves than with a murder trial. At least I'd been through the experience before.

'I have tried to find out what evidence the police have, but no one is talking. I have friends on the prosecution side and we share things, but not this. We will soon find out though. You will not have to say much, I think. The police, the Danes, they will do most of the talking.'

'Are you okay, Miss Samuelsen?'

She looked annoyed at the question, but also slightly embarrassed. Still, she managed a smile. 'I am well, thank you for asking. But I feel bad. This is supposed to be stressful for you, not for me. Perhaps you were right, you should have had better.'

It struck me that the truth wasn't going to do either of us any good.

'Not at all. We will both be fine. Do you know the judge?'

She laughed nervously. 'Of course I do. This is the Faroes, Mr Callum. We all know each other. The judge is Mr Sandur Hammershaimb. He is fair. It is all we can ask.'

'Okay. Let's hope so.'

Samuelsen pushed her hand back through her hair and blew hard. 'How shall you plead? It need not be just guilty or not guilty. You can plead what you think the outcome of the case should be. For example, you can plead that the case should be dismissed. That is perhaps a risk I would not recommend. We should leave a route out if the judge has doubt.'

'I'm happy with not guilty.'

She looked back at me for a bit, taking in what I said, before nodding. It was hard to escape the thought that my lawyer didn't entirely believe in my innocence.

'Yes. Not guilty is straightforward. And the evidence against you, at least that which we know of, is entirely circumstantial. Unless . . .'

'Unless the CSI has found something?'

Samuelsen looked apologetic. 'Yes.'

'But she can only have found something if I did it.'

An awkward silence fell between us. It was Samuelsen's chance to show belief, but she wasn't for biting, and I wasn't for letting her off. The lull stretched until she finally gave in.

'I am not asking you if you did it, Mr Callum. That is not my job.'

'Fair enough.' It wasn't fair and my tone said so.

We made our way into court, a blue-shirted policeman guiding me. The room was more modern than I expected, with laminated flooring and heavy contemporary wooden desks. The back bench accommodated four dark-cushioned chairs, and in front of it two solid desks faced each other in adversarial fashion, with a single table and chair placed in between, for either witnesses or someone to play referee.

Samuelsen and I took our place on one side of the opposing desks, she immediately shuffling, rearranging and generally clinging to her papers, as if they would protect her. I took a deep breath and pulled my chair in close. *Not guilty.* I practised the words in my head so that they sounded confident. So that I believed them myself. *Not guilty.*

In they trooped; the extras in the play of my life. Inspector Nymann's black leather jacket and jumper had been replaced by a sober navy-blue suit with white shirt and navy tie. I felt like standing up and pointing at him as if he was some kind of fake. The sergeant, Kielstrup, was wearing the same light-brown suit he'd worn before. The pale-blue shirt and darker blue tie also seemed identical to the ones he'd worn when they interviewed me, and I wondered if he'd come to the Faroes without a change of clothes.

Perhaps they were so arrogant they thought they'd wrap the case up in a day.

The Danes were deep in conversation with a chunky mid-forties man with close-cropped steel-coloured hair, confidence, and a very expensive-looking suit. My guess was he was a lawyer who had handled a murder case before.

The press were identifiable by their notebooks, pens and digital recorders. Local rubberneckers, the guillotine squad, were trying but failing to hide their morbid fascination. Martin and Silja Hojgaard were there too. Both looked deeply concerned, although I couldn't be sure if it was for me or for their reputation. Serge Gotteri was there, the smile still fixed in place, and giving a carelessly cheery wave towards me.

Three rows back, slumped almost out of sight, was Inspector Tunheim. When I caught his eye, he gave a polite nod. I responded in kind before scanning the courtroom for a second time, checking that I hadn't made a mistake, looking for the one person who wasn't there. A third time I looked, row after row, but there was still no sign of her.

My questions to Samuelsen about Karis hadn't provided any answers beyond what she and Gotteri had already told me. Karis had been interviewed by the police, she was very upset, her father said she wasn't seeing anyone. Wherever she was, she wasn't here. Maybe that was all I needed to know.

With each visual tour I made of the room, there was one face that I kept coming back to. I had no choice. In front of Tunheim and to his left sat Aron Dam's brother, Nils. His eyes were dark-ringed and his mouth locked shut. He stared hard at me; a wild, bitter stare borne of certainty of my guilt. There didn't seem to be any doubt in his mind who had killed his brother. I looked away, to the Hojgaards or the lawyers, to Gotteri or the cops, but every time I glanced back in his direction, Nils Dam was gazing unblinkingly at me. I had to look elsewhere and shifted in my seat until I faced the front bench, but I could still feel his stare burning into my neck.

The judge, Hammershaimb, arrived once everyone else was in place. He was dark-haired and wiry, looking more like a lightweight boxer than a judge, despite being in his late fifties. He fell neatly into his seat, looking around the court to see what sort of circus he was going to have to be ringmaster of.

Two women and a man, all stern-faced in business suits, had come in with him and took their places at his side. One of the women called out in Faroese and the court fell silent. Game on.

Hammershaimb spoke quietly, the kind of big-stick talking that demanded both respect and that people listen. Samuelsen translated for me. It was legal preamble, laying out the do's and don'ts and making it clear who was in charge.

Out of the corner of my eye I saw Nicoline Munk, the petite forensic investigator, bustle in and take her place between the two Danish cops. She seemed to be the only one not dressed up for the occasion. She still wore her waterproof jacket and trainers, only the T-shirt and jeans had been swapped for other models.

She was also swapping words with Nymann and Kielstrup. The three Danes had heads bowed and were on the verge of being animated. The stocky steel-haired lawyer walked over and stuck his head into the mix as well. At one point Munk sat back and spread her arms wide, before crossing them in front of her. Samuelsen was watching the play, too, and I could see the intensity in her eyes as she tried to learn something from it.

The judge raised his voice just a notch and the court fell under his spell once more. Elin Samuelsen got to her feet and he addressed me through her. Hammershaimb spoke a sentence or two then paused, leaving a gap for the lawyer to translate.

'This is a preliminary hearing to decide whether you will be charged with the murder of Aron Dam in the town of Torshavn . . .

'You will be given the right to state how you plead to this charge . . .

'If you are charged with the offence then you will have the right to appeal . . .'

There was a hint of a tremor in my lawyer's voice as she translated the last and most vital of the statements: 'How do you plead?'

Almost as soon as she said it, Samuelsen held her arm out in front of me, as if barring me from replying. Then she froze. She stood still for long enough that the judge had to repeat the enquiry in Faroese and again call on her to translate it.

'*Frøkun Samuelsen?*'

She nodded, obviously flustered, and held a hand up as if asking for more time, before finally bending down and whispering hoarsely and nervously into my ear.

'I am changing the plea. Trust me.'

My head snapped up at her but she was already facing the judge. What the hell was she playing at? This woman didn't know what she was doing. My mouth had dropped open by the time she answered the judge in Faroese. Whatever she said caused a hubbub to spiral round the court. She let that die down before spelling it out for me in English for everyone else to hear.

'My client asks for the charges to be dismissed on the grounds of a complete lack of evidence.'

I wasn't sure if the court fell into silence or if it was just that I could hear nothing above the sound of my heart thumping into my ribcage. Samuelsen dropped into the seat next to mine and picked up a sheaf of papers, moving two sheets from the top to the bottom for no apparent reason other than to busy her fingers. I could see that they were shaking.

'What are you doing?' I hissed at her through clenched teeth.

She didn't look up but kept staring blindly at the papers in her hands. Above us, the judge was making some pronouncement to the court.

'I think they have nothing.'

'You think? You *think* they have nothing? Are you fucking kidding me?'

A flush was beginning to make its way up Samuelsen's cheeks and my swearing had only increased the effect. Her breathing was fast, too, and she was trying to regulate it with regular little gasps, hidden by a hand placed over her mouth.

She turned her head to mine and whispered again: 'The crime-scene examiner, Munk. She is not happy. The officers are not happy with what she tells them. She is not happy with their reaction. In the interview room, she was … Little Miss Sunshine. Here … not so much. I think she has nothing and they are not happy with that. I think.'

I'd seen the sneer on Inspector Nymann's face when Samuelsen had stated the plea. His lip had curled up at one side in a show of superiority. A display of dismissive disbelief. Now he stared ahead at the judge, still a model of confidence, still holding all the cards.

The smart-suited man for the prosecution made a statement and Nymann left his seat and advanced on the opposition bench, neatly tucking the tail of his suit jacket underneath him as he sat down.

Questions were asked of him by his lawyer and briskly answered with complete assurance. He spoke, naturally enough, in Danish and the prosecutor repeated his words in Faroese, even though everyone in the court seemed to understand him first time round.

There was no time for Samuelsen to translate for me as he spoke, but there was no real need. Whatever Nymann had been asked was simply a vehicle to allow him to lay out the police's case. It boiled down to one simple statement, whatever the language. They believed I had killed Aron Dam.

Samuelsen was finally given space in which to interpret, but the words had already been made clear to me in the expressions of the Hojgaards and the press, the local busybodies and the judge.

When I looked back at Nymann, he was smoothing down his suit, like a cat licking its paws and wiping its fur cleaner than clean. Elin Samuelsen, her navy ensemble somewhat crumpled and bulging unflatteringly around the waist, pushed her chair back and got to her feet. She cleared her throat nervously.

The one sentence she spoke squeaked a little. Then she paused and repeated it in English, either for me or for effect.

'Inspector Nymann, I will ask you one simple question.'

The time taken up by the translation gave Nymann time to wonder, and I saw a trace of doubt pass across his face. Samuelsen paused again, composing herself and making him wait.

'Inspector Nymann, do you have even one single piece of physical evidence connecting Andrew John Callum to the murder of Aron Dam?'

The question came first in either Faroese or Danish – the distinction was beyond me – but she translated it quickly enough that I was able to see the look on Nymann's face for what it was. She did so quickly enough that he was forced to give an immediate answer.

Whatever it was he said, it wasn't acceptable to either Samuelsen or the judge. She pushed him. What she said sounded like a demand for a yes or a no. He floundered on in the same vein, but the judge, Hammershaimb, intervened and, it seemed, ordered him to answer directly. That much was clear from the look of unhappiness on Nymann's face.

He tried though. There was an extended statement, a puffed-up, puffed-out defence of his accusation. When he finished, Elin Samuelsen said nothing. She stood and waited, letting the silence hang there for as long as she dared. With a final stare at Nymann, she turned and spoke to me, but it was clear the reiteration wasn't for my benefit but for the court's.

'Inspector Nymann says that there is strong evidence linking you to the murder of Aron Dam. He says you were witnessed in a fight with the accused on the night of the killing. He says you had motive because of a violent disagreement over Dam's ex-girlfriend, Karis Lisberg. He says you were seen to be extremely drunk and aggressive. He says you cannot account for your movements after leaving the Cafe Natur. He says that attempts to retrieve trace evidence from the murder scene were compromised by the rain.'

She paused and reached down to pick papers up from the desk in front of her. My eyes instinctively followed her hands and saw they were still shaking.

'However . . . the inspector has not answered the key question.'

She launched into Faroese again and then Danish, or it may have been the other way round. Finally, in English.

'Inspector Nymann, I ask you again, do you have a single piece of firm forensic evidence that places Mr Callum at the scene of the crime? Do you have even one piece of DNA or one fingerprint or one fibre of clothing or one footprint or one witness? Anything? Anything at all that actually proves my client had anything to do with this dreadful crime?'

The best that Nymann could offer in response was two words: 'Not yet.'

Samuelsen sat down beside me. I could hear the rapidity of her breathing and I saw her grip the seat below her to steady herself. She'd done well though. We both knew it.

Hammershaimb conferred with his colleagues on the bench, their heads close together, speaking low. When he re-emerged to face the court, it was with the grim expression of a man ready to confer a death sentence. My stomach somersaulted in expectation.

He spoke slowly and deliberately. I heard Samuelsen's name and mine, Nymann's too. Hammershaimb was reiterating the points made by both sides as he summed up. As he continued I tried to get some indication from Samuelsen's face, but she was impassive as she intently followed the judge's summation. It was only as he finished that a noise broke out around us and I caught the hint of a smile on the corner of her lips. My eyes flew to the other side of the room, where Nymann looked furious and Nils Dam was on his feet, pointing furiously and shouting.

Samuelsen turned to me breathlessly. 'You are not being charged with murder. You can walk free. The judge agreed there was insufficient evidence to charge you.'

I blew out hard, a release valve being triggered deep inside me. I'd been relatively calm until then, but I suddenly found a shake in my hands.

'*Kortini* ...' Hammershaimb hadn't finished and my heart stopped again.

This time he looked straight at me and spoke in English.

'There remains reason to question Mr Callum's role in this terrible incident. I am ruling that he must give up his passport, stay on the Faroe Islands and report to the police station in Torshavn every day until this court rules otherwise. The police can continue their investigation into the murder of Aron Dam and they have the right to petition this court again with a charge against Mr Callum or any other person. However, if they appear before me again, I hope to see more from them in the form of evidence.'

I nodded my agreement, even though no one had asked if it was okay by me. I had come to the Faroes to get away from the world and now I couldn't leave even if I wanted to.

The Danes, Nymann and Kielstrup, got to their feet, their dissatisfaction obvious. They both glared at Nicoline Munk as if it was all her fault. The diminutive forensic expert wasn't for taking the fall though, and I could see her arguing forcibly with them.

Nymann took a couple of strides in my direction and gave me a curt nod, his dignity and sense of superiority intact as he sneered down his nose at me. 'You will be hearing from us, Mr Callum. Do not go far.'

Nils Dam was being half-pushed, half-encouraged out of the door by a police officer. Wild-eyed and loud, he wasn't easily persuaded, but the cop kept inching him nearer and nearer to the door until his shouts dimmed and he finally disappeared.

Elin Samuelsen got up and I followed suit. She shook my hand and wished me well.

'I will be in touch, Mr Callum. But for now I am going to meet my husband. I need a drink.'

As I left the courtroom, I watched Munk continue her argument with the two detectives, and allowed myself to consider what I saw as the two possible reasons for the failure of the crime-scene investigator to find evidence of my guilt. Either the wind and rain that had toyed with me since my arrival on these islands had come to my rescue, washing away any physical proof of my having been at the scene. Or else I had never been there at all.

I wished I knew which. But I didn't.

Chapter 34

It was raining a bit as I walked out of the court, a welcoming drizzle that wiped my face clean. The air was fresh and I gulped down a lungful of it, hungry for the taste of it in my mouth.

I looked around me, more in hope than expectation. Maybe, I thought, the news would have reached her and she'd coming running through the rain into my arms like we were in some shitty movie. But all I saw was a handful of people regarding me with curiosity and contempt. It seemed I'd been freed by the court of the land but not the court of public opinion. Hushed conversations, knowing nods and suspicious, even fearful, glances.

'Hey, Scotsman.' The accent was unmistakeably Gotteri's, and as I turned I saw his broad smile and his arms spread wide. For a moment I thought he was going to hug me but the gesture was expressive. I was free and he'd known it would happen all along.

'I am thinking that perhaps you could do with a drink, my friend.' His words made me think of Elin Samuelsen, heading off for a drink with her husband, driven by similar yet different stresses of her own. Gotteri was still talking, always talking.

'But maybe not the Cafe Natur, huh? Come on, let's go to Hvonn. They have good enough beer. And you can tell me all about killing Aron Dam.'

'Very funny.'

'Ah, come on, Callum. A little spell at the top of Sornfelli and you lose your sense of humour? I don't think so. This is a thing to celebrate. I am buying.'

I sighed. 'Yeah, okay. I'm Scottish. I can't pass up an opportunity like that.'

Gotteri laughed and clapped me heartily on the shoulder, guiding me towards the bar in Hotel Torshavn. We hadn't gone two steps when Nils Dam stepped out from a doorway across the street. I expected him to run across the road and attack me but he just stood there and stared, making sure that I'd seen him. It was a threat. Perhaps a promise of sorts. His eyes bulged like a madman's and there was a red tinge of fury about his unshaven face.

'Just walk on,' Gotteri implored me, his arm on the small of my back, propelling me forward. 'And don't look back. He won't do anything. Not here in the street.'

'Shit, is that supposed to reassure me, Serge? He won't do anything *here*? He'll wait until no one else is around and I'm not looking? Is that what you're saying?' Gotteri shrugged. 'I'm not saying that, but maybe. He looks pretty mad. And he thinks you murdered his brother.'

'You know the guy. What is he likely to do? What is he capable of?'

'I don't know him. I've spoken to him once or twice, but apart from his reputation for a temper I don't know much.'

I said nothing but fell into stride with the Frenchman, head down, and marching with him towards a beer. Moments later, his words left lying on the pavement behind us, I looked up and studied Gotteri unseen: the perma-smile still plastered to his face, the blond hair bobbing as he walked. In my mind's eye I could see him sitting in his car with Nils Dam in the passenger seat the night Karis and I had got together. The raised voices, the angry gestures. Not a conversation you would have with someone you'd spoken to just once or twice.

Maybe, after being locked up in a sleepless cell, I was seeing lies where none existed, paranoia overruling common sense. And maybe not. I'd drink his beer but I'd be watching and listening carefully.

There were only a few lunchtime customers in the Hvonn, all of whom looked up when Gotteri and I walked through the door. We breezed past them straight to the bar, where Serge ordered two Klassics, then took seats in a quiet corner away from the other drinkers.

He raised his glass to me before knocking back his first mouthful. '*Santé*! So, how was it in Mjørkadalur? I think that, as prisons go, it is not Devil's Island.'

I gulped at my own beer, the way I'd done with the air when I left the court. 'They were fair. But I'm in no rush to go back.'

'No. I am sure you are not. So what do you think happened to Aron Dam? Or was it you? You know that all of Torshavn, all of the Faroe Islands, thinks it was you.'

'I don't know what happened to him. And as for the people here, I'm sure that they do think that. I've seen the looks I've been getting. They'll keep thinking it till they find out who really did it.'

Gotteri nodded thoughtfully. 'You need to hope that the Danish detectives are looking for someone else as well as you. If they only think it is you then you could be the only person they find guilt for. Hey, I saw the forensic expert in court. Wow. She is hot, no? She can take my fingerprints anytime.'

My mind skipped to standing naked on the cold floor of the police station interview room, Nicoline Munk examining me. I decided to spare Gotteri the image.

'Yeah. But that's not really the issue, is it? I need her to do her job. I need her to find something at the scene of the crime – maybe she already has – and I need to her to match it to someone. Someone that's not me.'

I could hear the stress in my voice and Gotteri couldn't have failed to notice it. There was anger underlining every word. I took a bigger swig at the beer and held it in my mouth for a while before letting it slide down my throat.

'You were pretty drunk that night. Everyone who was in the Natur says so. Where did you go when you left the bar?'

I'd answered this question from Gotteri before, and I could feel the heat rising in me as he pushed me to do so again.

'I went home. And that's where I'm going now if I still have one.' I drained the last of my beer and pushed it back across the table. 'Thanks for the drink.'

'Stay!' Gotteri urged me vehemently. 'Have another. You must need it after being locked up in that place. And I could do with some company that isn't Faroese.'

'No. I'm going.' I got to my feet to prove the point. 'I need to find out if I still have a place to live, and there's more chance of the Hojgaards letting me stay on if I don't turn up drunk.'

'Okay, okay. But I'm going across the Postman's Walk to Gásadalur this afternoon. If you don't want to drink it's the best place for you to be. Come with me. Clear your head. And it might be better to be out of Torshavn. Let things cool down.'

Serge had talked about Gásadalur before, telling me about the trek across the mountains to the tiny village and the spectacular waterfall that plunges off the edge of the cliff into the sea. It seemed that the one person I wanted and needed to see didn't feel the same way, so maybe the next best thing was to get away from it all. On these islands, Gásadalur was about as far away as I could get.

'Yeah, maybe. What time are you leaving?'

He put his glass down. 'Now. I'll drive you as near to that home of yours as I can get by road and you can get changed out of those court clothes. Okay?'

Nothing was okay. Neither inside my head nor out. I chose between the seemingly lesser of evils.

'Okay.'

Chapter 35

I approached the Hojgaards' shack feeling like a thief in the night. The key in my pocket wasn't doing much to ease my muddled conscience, not least because I couldn't be sure it would still fit the lock.

Gotteri sat in his car at the top of the road awaiting my return, having urged me to hurry so we could begin the drive out of town. The Frenchman was obviously anxious to get me away from Torshavn, and there was an edge to his constant questioning that bothered me. Maybe I'd just had all the interrogating I could handle for one day.

There had been no sign of anyone at the Hojgaards' house and I'd breathed a silent, cowardly sigh of relief at the realization. If I had been evicted from my home in the hills, I'd rather find out by the door remaining locked than by Martin or Silja telling me in person. My relief was as much for their sake as for mine, as they didn't deserve to be put through such an awkward encounter.

I was relieved to find that the shack looked reassuringly the same, as if I'd expected it to have been reconstructed in my absence. It felt a lifetime since I'd last walked out its doors, rather than the few days that had actually passed. It remained securely fastened into the hillside, a rock in a storm.

Breathing deep, I thrust my hand into my pocket and turned the key through my fingers, glad of the feel of it. There wasn't much that I was sure of any more, neither my past nor my future; not my relationship with Karis or even my own innocence. If I still had one thing to cling onto, one piece of certainty, then maybe the world would stop whirling round my head. I needed the key to turn in the lock. I needed this 'shitty little house on the hill' – Aron Dam's taunt flashed disturbingly through my head – to be the place I could be safe in.

There was a shake in my hand by the time I got to the end of the path and was confronted by the locked door. I knew I couldn't take much more and had to have something go my way. I wouldn't have blamed the Hojgaards, not for a second, but I was praying they hadn't evicted me in my absence.

Even as I manoeuvred the key into the lock, I considered my options if it didn't turn. Depressingly, my gut instinct was that the best of those options was Mjørkadalur. I realized I'd rather return to the four white walls of the jail than take up residence anywhere else on the islands. Except, of course, with Karis. That, I would have taken in a heartbeat, but it wasn't an alternative that seemed to be on offer.

One more breath. Turn the key to the right. Wait. Hold breath and pray. A click. A click. Breathe.

I stood for a moment, silently thanking the Hojgaards and the few lucky stars that looked down on me. This, at least, was something. I pulled the door back and stepped inside, immediately seeing that my blessings were scarce and easy to count.

The place had been turned over. Clothes were strewn across the bed. Drawers were half open and one sat on the floor. The sheet had been taken from the bed and shoes that had lain underneath the bed were now in the open. Toiletries had been moved around the sink. Everything wore the air of having been turned upside down and dropped back in more or less the same place.

I should have expected it, but had probably been so worried

about whether I'd even get inside that I hadn't considered that the police would inevitably have ransacked the place looking for evidence. Evidence. Was there any? I sank onto the edge of the bed and was suddenly overwhelmed by the fact that I didn't know.

The little house could be crossed from end to end in a couple of strides and yet I didn't know it or myself well enough to say if it held something that could condemn me.

My head was in my hands when I heard the distant beeping of a car horn repeatedly calling for my attention. Gotteri's impatience broke the spell I'd put on myself and I got to my feet and grabbed some of the clothes that had been left on the bed. I quickly stripped out of the borrowed court suit and dressed for an escape to the wilds.

Even the one place I had counted on to be a refuge wasn't safe from the doubts and paranoia that were eating away at my mind from the inside.

Chapter 36

Gásadalur was a village on Vagar, the north-westerly island where the airport was. Gotteri drove as far as Bø, where he parked the car and we stepped out into light rain carried on a sharp easterly wind. I could barely hear him, even though we were just a few feet apart. I wasn't sure that was such a bad thing.

He had battered my ears all the way from Torshavn – about the village, about Karis and Aron Dam, about the Danish cops and the price of beer. Serge liked to talk a whole lot more than I liked to listen.

There was now a road all the way to Gásadalur but that wasn't the way Gotteri wanted to play it. The road was still relatively new and he preferred to reach what he was going to photograph by hiking there the way it had been done for hundreds of years. It was known as the Postman's Walk.

Three times a week, the postman had made the steep two-and-a-half-kilometre walk across the mountains and the moor to deliver mail to the villagers. Then he'd make the walk back again. At least his mailbag ought to have been light, as there were only ten houses in Gásadalur. I guessed there were more back in the day, but Gotteri didn't seem to know.

This lasted until 2006, when the government finished blasting a tunnel through the mountain rock and out the other side. For the first time in its existence, Gásadalur was connected to the rest of the world and not separated by a treacherous ocean and steepling cliffs to one side, and the mountain peaks to the other.

Their isolation was so treasured by the villagers, however, that when the road tunnel was originally opened, it was locked by a gate and only the villagers had a key. They had now, reluctantly it seemed, let outsiders use it too.

The white arch that disappeared into the mountain was a thing of wonder, an unblinking eye set into the island itself and surrounded by hillside, brown earth, greenery and stone. We peeped into its belly and saw the road disappear.

The path was steep and strenuous to begin with, but thankfully it evened out after the first hill. Still, we took a breather at what Gotteri told me was *Líkstein*, the 'corpse stone', so called because people had rested there when carrying a coffin from Gásadalur, which had no churchyard, to the village of Bíggjar.

Further on we passed a spring called *Vívd*, which supposedly produced blessed water and gave eternal youth to whoever drank from it. I wasn't remotely sure that was something I wanted, but still gulped gratefully from its waters. Finally, at the mountain's peak, we looked down at the village way below us, its lush green peppered with houses, the new road bursting out of the hillside towards it.

'This is better, though, is it not?' Gotteri roared at me above the wind. 'The way it was meant to be. Walking. Like the postman!'

The rain had come and gone and threatened to come again during the hour and a half we'd hiked from the car. I'd lost my footing a couple of times and the clouds that were gathering in the distance spun dark grey and rolled in our direction. Ahead of it was a fog that inched nearer and grew thicker with every step we took.

'If God had meant us to walk,' I shouted back at him, 'he wouldn't have given us four-wheel-drives. Did the entire twentieth century pass you by?'

I could see his mouth open in laughter but heard nothing. Then he shouted some more.

'I know you don't mean that, my friend. If you had wanted motorways and cars and the rat race, you would have stayed in Scotland. You didn't. You left so that you could do things like this. And to run away from whatever demon it is that is chasing you.'

I ignored him, looking west to where the fog was rolling in. I couldn't see far.

Undaunted, Gotteri pressed further. 'Scotsman, are you ever going to tell me why you came here? I know you have a past that you wanted to leave behind. Why not tell me what it is?'

I looked blankly over at him and shouted to be heard. 'Forget it, Serge. There's nothing to tell.'

'Come on, man! I am here in the middle of nowhere with someone who might be a murderer. Don't I deserve an answer?'

I pressed on down the steep mountainside ahead of him, forcing Gotteri to quicken his pace to keep up. I didn't know the path but I could follow it. If I left him behind that would be too bad.

We picked our way down, scrambling here and there until we were back on flat land. The wind had dropped now and the fog had closed right on top of us, just sitting there refusing to budge, and I couldn't see any further than a few feet in front of me. Going on was madness, but going back would be just as crazy. We had to get to the village and sit it out till the fog cleared.

Gotteri kept his questioning going from a distance. From what I could hear, he was getting more belligerent, more desperate for an answer with every attempt.

'Where did you go when you left the bar? Why did you leave Scotland and come here? What is your secret? What have you told the police? Did you kill Aaron Dam? Just tell me. Did you kill Aron Dam?'

I pushed on faster to get away from it, sick of the words that came after me.

'Come on. I give you one last chance. Tell me, Callum!'

My stride lengthened, mindless of the rocks or irregularities in the path. I had to get away from Gotteri as much as I had to get out of this fog or to the damned village.

'Stop there, Callum! Do not move. I mean it!'

I took one more step, partly out of sheer momentum, partly because I wasn't going to do what Gotteri told me. Then the tone of his voice filtered through to me. It wasn't threatening. It was warning.

I stopped.

'I mean it,' he repeated through the porridge-thick fog, his voice cold. 'Do not go any further.'

'Gotteri, what the hell is this? Are you—?'

'I'm trying to save your life. Stand still and listen.'

At first I thought he meant listen to him, but when he said nothing more, I tuned in to the wind whispering a dirge through the fog. Beyond that I could hear the cry of a seabird, even though there was no chance of seeing it. What else could I hear?

To my left, maybe ten yards away, was the sound of running water. No, it wasn't running. It was *rushing*. Then further off, somewhere below my feet, I heard it roar again. We were on the edge of the cliff.

'My friend, I estimate you are maybe three or four feet away from walking off the edge of Gásadalur into the ocean. Maybe less. The ocean is two thousand feet below us and so are the rocks. *Now* are you listening?'

Chapter 37

'You've got my attention.'

I turned my head but couldn't see Gotteri through the gloom. Was that him there? A darker shade of grey against the light?

'Do not move. Not even towards my voice. The wind and the fog make it deceiving. You could as easily walk off the cliff.'

I could feel my heart thumping and my mind flashed back to my roped descent down the bird cliffs at Vestmanna. I didn't fancy repeating the exercise without a rope. 'Okay. What do you suggest we do?'

'We sit down and we wait. Unless you want to take the chance of going the wrong way?'

'That's the best you've got? We sit down on the edge of a 2,000-foot-high cliff when the wind is blowing and a storm might be rolling in?'

The ghost of a laugh came at me from the ether. His voice was different; he was not making any attempt to charm. '*We're* not sitting on the edge of a cliff. You are. I'm at least ten feet further away. Your choice.'

Swearing under my breath, I crouched down, slowly dropping until I sat. The ground was rough and damp but it was solid. Cautiously, I reached out one arm then the other, patting the earth as far as I could reach all around me. Comfortingly, I didn't hit fresh air.

I shuffled round inch by inch until I faced where I thought Gotteri was. Engineering the fog that trapped us was beyond the Frenchman's powers, but leading us to this spot didn't seem like an accident. I didn't know what he wanted but I was sure I didn't like the situation.

'You know the weather here better than me, Gotteri. How long until this might clear?'

'Who knows, my friend? It could be five minutes or five years. I'm thinking not too long though. Long enough for us to have a chat.'

A gust of wind hit my back and scared the shit out of me. Instinctively, I grabbed the earth beneath me, clutching at straws of grass.

'Why are you so keen on having this chat, Serge? Why so many questions?'

'It is good for me to know these things. It keeps me safe. I am a man who likes to know what is going on.'

Maybe it was the wind. Maybe it was the fog. But Gotteri wasn't quite where I thought he was. Had he moved or had I faced the wrong way in the first place? His voice came at me cold again through the soup.

'What have you told the police, my friend? They must have asked you many questions about that night. They will not believe simply that you got drunk and went home. Would you believe that? Did you do that?'

Those were two wildly different questions. Would I believe that I'd gone straight home if I were the police? Almost certainly not. But was that what I had done? I was getting closer to an answer with every night that passed. All I had to work out was the difference between imagination and reality.

As I hadn't yet done so, I ignored Gotteri's question. 'I told the police what happened. They checked it out. I've been released. What else can you want to know?'

He laughed. 'Everything. I live here. You know how few foreigners there are. A thing like this happens ... they look at me differently too. They know I am your friend and they think "Hey, maybe he was part of it. Maybe the Frenchman killed Aron as well".'

'And did you?'

It seemed Gotteri didn't like that question so much. The lack of a response encouraged me. 'Did you, Serge? You're full of questions about what I did and didn't do. Where were *you* that night?'

He came back at me in quick, angry French that I couldn't keep up with. I realized they were probably the first words of his own language that I'd heard him speak. I'd hit a nerve that had launched him into a kind of Tourette's. After a brief lull for thought, he tried to change the subject. His voice was different though, lower, colder, harder.

'Tell me about Scotland, Callum.'

What was this?

'It rains a lot. We eat too much junk food and drink too much whisky. *Wha's like us? Damn few and they're aw deid.*'

'Not the tourist stuff. Tell me about the kids who got hurt.'

He might as well have reached through the fog and slapped me across the face. My mouth hung open stupidly as I tried to make sense of what he seemed to know. And how he knew it. My heart and my anger raced each other round my body as I considered the possibility that it might be a good thing if one of us, either me or Gotteri, went off the edge of that cliff. How the hell did he know anything about what had happened?

'No more, Serge. I am not speaking again until I can see your face.'

A bitter laugh. 'You like my face that much?'

'No. I need to be able to see it to punch it.' I meant it too. 'Now shut the fuck up. I'm done here.'

Gotteri inevitably tried a few more times, stabbing at me with questions to which I did not respond, until he finally gave up. Not that he went silent. Instead he sang. Edith Piaf's 'Non, Je ne

Regrette Rien' began straining over the breeze, his surprisingly tuneful but still surreal rendition the only thing to be heard apart from the water.

It took maybe half an hour, time enough for the chorus to be repeated, but finally the fog thinned until I could see him, lying flat on his back a few yards away, continuing to sing. I turned my head, and although the fog had not cleared completely, nearby I could see the land falling away into nothing. As he'd said, the edge was no more than four feet away.

Another ten minutes and the fog was gone completely and still not another word had been shared between us. Gotteri was sullen, as if the fog had been his ally and he missed it already. He got to his feet and moved off, giving a brusque wave of his arm for me to follow him.

We quickly walked around the village, a compact huddle of black-tarred houses and outbuildings standing on muddy paths. The remoteness of the buildings was accentuated by their smallness and the space between each one. The wind whistled round protectively, singing or howling as it turned corners, invading further with every passing minute.

Gotteri and I kept our distance from one another, staying yards apart but taking the same circuitous route round Gásadalur's minuscule metropolis. People here had lived on the edge of civilization and only belatedly had been given a connecting tunnel to the rest of humanity.

Having given me the guided tour, Gotteri walked back sulkily towards the cliff. We walked parallel to its edge, not daring to get remotely close, as the wind was blowing hard and driving devilishly back towards the village. At least this time the sun was shining and there was no doubt where land ended and oblivion began. A sheer drop. One step too far would lead to certain death.

Gotteri walked until we were on the opposite arc of the cliff, facing back towards the waterfall and the village. Not saying a word, he dropped his equipment on the ground and glared at me before taking out his camera and lenses. I took it we had arrived at the point where he was intending to work.

I turned back and saw why we'd stopped where we had. The view was mesmerizing.

The waterfall ran to the edge of the cliff top and plunged two thousand feet into the fierce green of the ocean. It arrowed straight down, a brilliant white rush against the dark grey of the basalt, hurtling through the air until it crashed gratifyingly, wet to wet.

Below, dark caves burrowed into the rock, eerie recesses of gloom behind the curtain of falling water. Above and behind the village, the mountains created an intimidating backdrop of vertical greens and browns. The little black houses seemed insignificant dots dropped onto a landscape alien to them. The land and the sea were bigger and more permanent than anything made of timber and pitch.

I was so lost in the sight that I wasn't aware of Gotteri moving off, camera in hand. He eventually crossed my eyeline and I saw him stalking the cliff edge carefully until he lay down flat on a bare bit of scrub ten feet or so from the drop. His lens pointed towards the cliffs opposite, where hundreds of puffins had made their home on a succession of tiny ledges on the face of the rise. The little birds, their blacks, reds and oranges just visible, were dwarfed by their surroundings, but together they dominated the rock face.

I could feel the wind slapping the back of my neck, forcing me to brace myself against it and take an involuntary step forward then a protective one back. The wind rushed over Gotteri, speeding on beyond his prone body, his blond hair fluttering as it passed.

The wind raced on, faster than ever, towards the waterfall. I consciously moved a step further from the edge, fearful of the gale's force. Gotteri was clinging to the earth, his camera surely shaking in his hands. Then it happened.

The Gásadalur waterfall, a creation of nature, was also at the whim of it. It dashed headlong from the top of the cliff and launched itself down towards the ocean, but failed to get there.

Instead, it lifted out and up in an arc, back on itself. It became a water rise, a celebration of the strength of its creator, a phenomenon that was somehow even more dramatic and spectacular than the waterfall had been when plunging to the sea below.

As I watched, open-mouthed, the wind threw the waterfall back until it crashed way back onto the cliff top, one force of nature being overcome by another and sent back to start again.

Chapter 38

Gotteri and I trekked back over the Postman's Walk at the same time but far from together. We were maybe ten yards apart but it might as well have been miles. He seemed to march with a seething resentment, striding out with his mouth tight and eyes staring fiercely ahead.

My own anger was simmering. The only thing that undercut my umbrage about his questioning was that I wanted the same answers. I walked in internal turmoil, furious at him for not believing me and yet incapable of placing that same faith in myself; incensed at him for asking about 'the kids who got hurt', but just as troubled by how they got hurt in the first place.

We climbed in silence, not a word passing between us until we reached *Líkstein*, the corpse stone, and we both had to stop grudgingly for a rest. Gotteri was side-on to me, so I was able to watch him without him having the same advantage, simply because I had done so first. He knew I was looking though, and it infuriated him further.

Suddenly, he couldn't stand it any longer and snapped his head round, glaring at me. 'You said you would talk to me when the fog cleared. When you could see my face. Well now you can see it. So talk!'

I drew in more lungfuls of breath, making him wait. 'Why are you so desperate to question me, Serge? Why so keen to know where I was, what I remember, what the police know? Why drag me up here, miles from anywhere, in order to do it?'

He bristled. 'Callum, I . . .'

'I don't want to hear it, Serge. *You* tell *me* why the hell you're so interested, or we finish this right here. You keep saying how I'm your friend. Friends don't interrogate each other.'

He took a step towards me, jaw clenched, and I was sure he was going to attack. We stared back at each other, standing on the top of the world, each seemingly ready to throw the other off the edge.

I saw the green sward of Gasadalur, behind and way, way below him, and felt the other me itching to hurl him back down the path. Maybe Gotteri saw that in me too, or maybe he just sized me up and didn't fancy the odds. Either way, he fashioned a snarl to his lips and waved an arm dismissively in my direction, before storming past me down the hill again, back towards Bø, where we'd parked the car.

'Not so keen on answering questions as asking them, are you Serge?' I shouted at his back, taunting him as he walked. 'Fine. Don't say you didn't have your chance. Interview over.'

An arm thrown haughtily, furiously, into the air was the only reply I got. I followed in his wake, forming a wordless procession down the mountainside.

By the time we hit ground level and Gotteri's Skoda was in sight, he was maybe fifty yards in front of me, his speed no doubt fuelled by continued indignation. I saw him pull open the car door, clamber up into the driver's seat and slam the door shut behind him.

I was there in under a minute, inwardly dreading the long drive back that would inevitably be made even longer by the brutal silence that would ensue. Maybe I would broker some kind of peace, maybe I would try to change the subject altogether and force myself to talk about his photography or football or the bloody weather. Maybe.

As my hand reached for the passenger door, I heard a roar of acceleration and a squeal of tires. I was grasping at thin air as the car shot forward and ground its way across the rough terrain and back onto the road. Open-mouthed, I watched it disappear from view in seconds.

A sudden, overwhelming silence enveloped me as I stood alone at the foot of the hill, the last strains of the car's engine just a ghost on the wind. I was surprised enough to laugh out loud. I laughed loud enough and long enough that I had to wonder not just how the hell I was going to get back to Torshavn, but also whether I was losing my mind.

Chapter 39

The driver who stopped to pick me up on the road back into town clearly had no idea who I was. It's doubtful that he'd have stopped for a hitchhiker if he'd known him to be a murder suspect. It was only after a mile or two, when my language and perhaps my accent fully dawned on him, that the penny dropped.

I watched a look of dawning realization pass over the man's face and saw his eyes grow wide as he stared resolutely at the road in front of him. Conversation was at a minimum after that and he dropped me off in Torshavn at the first opportunity, no suggestion at all of driving me up Dalavegur as had previously been mentioned. Instead he pulled up in front of the ferry terminal, applied the handbrake and sat looking nervously ahead until I took the hint, opened the door and got out.

'Thanks.' I barely got the word out before he was moving again, leaving me behind almost as quickly as Gotteri had. I might even have found it funny but for my continuing doubts about the sanity of laughing out loud at the mess I was in.

Instead, I walked. Into town and up. As I climbed the steep incline of Dalavegur, I considered taking the coward's way out again and just going straight back to the shack without having to face the Hojgaards. I could take the fact that my key still worked as a sign of acceptance and hide myself inside. It was tempting but wrong. Although I couldn't be sure what kind of reception I'd get from the Hojgaards, I knew they were good people, decent above all else.

However, they also had to live among their friends, and harbouring someone accused of murder might well be asking too much. I remembered Martin's words. If I caused trouble, he'd said, then I'd bring shame on him. It was the last thing I wanted to do.

I breathed deep and made for the square house with the daffodil-coloured walls. Dark clouds, whisked through with menace, were hovering low over the ridge behind.

Hvirla, the Hojgaards' sheepdog, was standing in the garden as I approached, his nose in the air sensing the change in the weather. When he saw me, he let loose a single bark to alert those inside, then bounded over to me, his tail swishing from side to side. At least someone was happy to see me.

As I ruffled the dog's mane and ears, the way I'd seen Martin do frequently, the door opened behind him. Hvirla was still doing his tornado-spin of happiness when Silja made her way down the couple of steps into the garden. She looked troubled and wary. There was no sign of her husband.

'Hvirla,' she called. '*Koma*.' The dog ducked under my hand and trotted off to sit at her side, its tail still wagging contentedly. Silja's straw-coloured hair was tied back and she wore jeans and a chequered Faroese jumper.

'Martin at fish farm.' She was pushing stray strands of hair out of her eyes as the breeze tossed them about. 'You are okay?'

The question caught me by surprise, even though it shouldn't have done. Silja Hojgaard had much more right to worry about her welfare than mine, but it was in her nature to ask after my well-being. If what I feared most was true, maybe she had reason to fear for her safety. I suddenly saw some of that fear. That was what the wariness was, and I felt ashamed. Worse than that, I wondered if I should be there at all, wondered if I was a danger to this kind woman and her daughter.

'I'm okay. Thank you. Silja, I will go away if you want me to. I understand. Or I can come back when Martin is here.'

She toyed with her hair again before giving up and letting the wind blow it as it pleased. She looked at me as if I was some kind of creature she'd never seen before. Her shoulders lifted almost imperceptibly in either acceptance or resignation.

'No. Is okay. You want stay at other house still? If yes, it okay.'

I shrunk a little, embarrassed by the woman's generosity of spirit. In so many ways it would have been easier if she had told me to get lost. If she'd said they couldn't take the risk or face the embarrassment or even stomach the thought of me living in their property. Instead they shamed me by letting me stay.

'Really? Martin doesn't mind? After everything that has happened?'

She hesitated, words unspoken on her lips but sadness in her eyes. 'You stay if you want. It okay.'

The temptation was to ask what it was she wasn't telling me, but I wasn't sure I wanted to know.

'Silja . . . you don't have to do this. I will understand if you want me to go. I don't want to make things difficult for you. You and Martin have been very good to me, giving me a place to live. I owe you for that.'

The sun sprang from behind the cloud and Silja shielded her eyes with the back of her hand. As she did so, I saw something move out of the corner of my eye, and looked again to see Rannva peeking out from the doorway, her body behind the wooden frame and only half her blonde head visible. I waved and after a few moments' hesitation, an arm appeared and waved back.

Silja saw her too and moved a pace to her right, placing herself between me and her daughter, blocking the view from one to the other. I felt something shrivel inside me. Silja's face fell too, seemingly feeling bad about her instinctive reaction, although not so bad that she moved away.

'John . . . court say you go free. That I trust. Not Torshavn people who speak bad things. Please. Stay.'

I wanted to hug her, or at least shake her hand to say thank you, but feared that any attempt would come across badly. I sensed her unease fighting with her decency, and the latter winning. I didn't want to do anything to alter that result.

'Oh . . . other thing.' Silja looked embarrassed. 'You stay for free now. Not pay. You . . . you have no work now. Martin is sorry but he . . .'

'It's okay. I understand that.'

'Later . . . when is over . . . you have work again.'

I nodded, wondering if it would ever be over, but grateful for this little pot of gold at the end of the rainbow.

We left the house just minutes later, Silja with fresh sheets and towels in her arms, politely declining my offer to carry them. Rannva and Hvirla wandered together in our wake, one chattering and the other nuzzling at her hands.

Torshavn fell away beneath us and the clouds edged closer, still holding onto the rain and the threat of unleashing it. Nothing was said between us and any noise was left to Rannva's self-contained conversation, the occasional yap from the dog and the whisper of the wind. Silja was more comfortable in the silence than I was, the stammer of another stilted apology never far from my lips.

The shack soon winked at us from the natural camouflage of the hillside, the sun glinting from the windows the only real clue that the structure was anything other than a natural phenomenon. My uneasy home.

There was something else though. Something that hadn't been there earlier that day. Something that jarred.

I saw it first, courtesy of better eyesight or keener interest than Silja. Even then, though, I didn't see it for what it was. Part of me thought, however illogically, that the Hojgaards had had the door painted for my return. Common sense would have told me that wasn't the way the prodigal son was treated.

As we got closer, I realized the truth and then Silja saw it too, a gasp escaping from her throat and a hand raised to her mouth. She stopped in her tracks, but I walked quicker.

The door to the shack was red. Dripping red. The wood was soaked in it but it had clearly not been done by a brush. And it clearly wasn't paint.

A pool of blood swam stickily on the dirt at the door's foot, soaking into the earth. It stank. Sickly sweet with a tang of rusty nails or old coins. There was a richness about it that turned my mind and my stomach in equal measure, stirring both memories and my guts. Breath caught in my throat and I had to turn away to inhale.

I saw Silja standing there open-mouthed, eyes wide. She had pulled Rannva towards her, her lamb's face buried in the fibres of Silja's jumper. Beside them, Hvirla spun nervously, living up to her name, in a whirl of confusion.

Silja bent down and whispered into Rannva's ear. The little girl took off without a backward look, calling on the dog as she scampered past him and the pair dashed onto the hillside, rolling together blithely in the grass.

The blood had been thrown over the door by the bucketful. It had landed artlessly, drenching the wood and splashing all around. I could only imagine it being hurled angrily. I could feel a similar fury building up inside me.

'Silja . . . I am so sorry. I–'

'No!' She interrupted me forcefully even though her voice was shaking. 'No. This not your do. Is wrong. Is bad. You stay our house this night. Tomorrow we fix. This very bad.'

The woman had an ability to make me feel worse by trying to make me feel better. Every kind act killed off a bit of my soul. I couldn't let her slay the little that was left.

'No. I'll stay here.'

'But . . . you cannot. The blood . . .'

'Silja, you and Martin have done enough. I won't make things worse for you. And I'm not letting whoever did this drive me out. I'm staying here. As long as that's okay with you.'

She looked doubtful, struggling to take her eyes off the blood-soaked door. 'Okay. But I clean this. I go home and get what I need.'

'No. I will do it. It's my responsibility.'

Silja thought for a bit then shook her head grimly. 'We both do. Make work quick.'

Neither Silja's scrubbing brush nor mine made easy inroads into the tacky red mess that had worked its way into the timber. The top coat came away without too much problem, leaving a rusty pool on the earth below, but the rest needed to be attacked vigorously again and again. She worked away at the lower part of the door and me at the top. My hands moved faster, more furiously than hers. Driven by rising anger, I tried to scrub the wood away. She glanced up a couple of times, obviously aware of my fevered exertions, but quickly averting her eyes.

'It sheep blood.' She sounded weary and resentful. 'A terrible thing. In Foroyar, we . . . respect sheep. It feed us and keep us warm with wool. We look after sheep. Sheep look after us. It not right it be killed for . . . for this.'

The mention of the word killed fell into the space between us. Silja had never asked me if I'd murdered Aron Dam. She'd made it clear that I would be judged by her god and no one else. It seemed that hadn't changed. If she was interested in my guilt or innocence, she didn't show it.

We worked in silence for a while until a question that I'd been holding back finally forced its way into the open.

'Silja, when I was away, did I . . . have any visitors?'

She paused and looked at me, hooking up an elbow so that she could push hair away from her face without using her blood-streaked hands.

'Not the one I think you mean.'

'Karis Lisberg.'

She shook her head. 'No. Sorry.'

Ranva and Hvirla continued to play on the hillside, keeping their distance from the blood, the door and me. If Silja wanted to keep the little girl away then it made perfect sense as far as I was concerned.

There was a quiet determination about Silja, a stoicism that was hard to miss. If Jesus himself had been nailed to that door than I suspected she would have been shocked for all of two minutes before setting about washing him down and cleaning up the mess. I envied her calm tolerance and wished I could find some of my own rather than the contrasting emotion that was growing inside me.

Eventually we realized that the door would get no cleaner. It would never pass for white without a new coat of paint; its pink-streaked veneer stood testament to blood being thicker than water.

Both Silja and I were left with raw red hands. I looked at mine and couldn't help but see them painted in guilt or at least the appearance of it. Silja caught me staring at them.

'Hot water inside for you wash. I made hot if they let you free. I go now. Martin, he home soon.'

Silja, her daughter and their dog made their way back down the hill, Rannva running in front of her mother this time, stopping every so often to let her catch up and to sneak curious glances back at the man with blood on his hands.

I went inside the shack, feeling better about being in the cramped, under-equipped confines of the tiny house than I had earlier that day. It wasn't prison. My jail was still the eighteen islands of the Faroes that I couldn't leave, but this part of it at least felt like home. I stretched out on the familiar sagging bed and studied the ceiling.

I wanted sleep, needed it, but dreaded it. Since Dam's death, the nights had got shorter and the nightmares deeper. The sweats and the shakes seemingly knew no end and it was draining me. It was hard to tell how much sleep I'd actually got since my arrest. When I wasn't dreaming about Aron or Liam Dornan or the others, I was dreaming about not being able to sleep. Or at least I thought that's what I'd been dreaming about. It all rolled into one, just like the clouded sun and the backlit darkness that defied you to pinpoint where one ended and the other began.

I fell back and closed my eyes. I might not have been able to distinguish lack of sleep from nightmares but I was ready to face both down.

Chapter 40

I'm sitting. Swaying back and forward but going nowhere. My eyes are shut, my legs crossed beneath me, yoga-style. I look down and see I'm stripped to the waist. I might even be floating a foot or two above the ground. I can't tell.

It's a dream or else things have changed. Rules of science may have evolved. I test them. Yes. Yes! I can float, rise up as I please. I look around and see no one else hovering. No one but me. I can fly if I want to, I know that. No one else can. Maybe I'm God. Or some kind of god. It feels great.

All I know is that it is a good thing. On the edge of my understanding is the belief that I must use this power for something. My arm has a life of its own. It waves loosely, arrogantly, through the air. Bring on the bands. Bring on the clowns. Entertain me.

They appear. As if by magic. Four man-boys. Early twenties going on gnarled forties. They are sullen, resentful. Like beaten tigers, claws shorn yet still fully armed with teeth. They stand in a row, heads bowed, but with a capacity about them. A readiness to turn, spring, attack. They remain dangerous.

I clap my hands and they all look up. There's a slither of sweat trickling its way slowly down my back, crawling over vertebrae one by one, leaving a taint of guilt with every millimetre.

My hands clap again even though I'm barely aware I've done it, and the first man-boy screams as his arm breaks. The noise is quite incredible, a frozen branch snapping halfway up a snow-covered mountain. A bullet fired into a vacuum. An avalanche flows. Space set free.

I like the power.

A leg breaks on the next boy. Then a hip. A thigh. The ankle bone's connected to the knee bone. Crack. Crack. Crack. It's the look on their faces. All four shocked, surprised, outraged. They break, one by one, by one, by one.

There's a thing I remember. Something buried way down deep. The guys who make sound effects for movies. Foley artists. That's it, foley artists. They use peanuts or monkey nuts to replicate the sound. They take either end in their fingers, hold them up close to a microphone . . . and tear. Is that what I'm really hearing? The ripping open of peanuts or the clean – and yet not so clean – breaking of bones?

There's my answer. A femur, the largest bone in the human body, rudely split in half in front of my eyes. A wrench. A pistol crack. The tear of gristle. The rip of tendons. The snap of muscle.

Above all, it's the bones. The broken bones. There's something about the finality of it. Break. Gone. Finished. Snap. Crackle. Pop.

I sit and watch. Impassive. I couldn't care less. In fact . . . truth is . . . I like it. There's something satisfying about the sound.

When I look to my right, I see the broken bones have been arranged in piles. Neat stacks of skinless alabaster. No bone connected to any other bone. Just lying cosily next to its other half. I find myself nodding appreciatively, liking the order of things. No mess. No problem.

But the pile of bones gets higher. It multiplies every time I look at it. I'm wondering why I ever thought this was a good thing. The pit of my stomach is full with it, but the pile continues to mount. Bone upon bone. There is a grating sound as one rubs against another then is sheared from it with a gut-twisting jerk.

The heads, what about the heads? They are lying there. Shorn from the bodies they once clung to. Inexpressive. Poker-faced. I know they're sorry though. They must be. I can smell it.

But I am too. I did it. I clapped my hands and the bones shattered. I did that.

I clap them again. The little toe breaks on my right foot. Then my foot bone. Then my ankle bone. Then my leg bone. I shake dem skeleton bones. One by one I fall to pieces, until all that is left is my brain swilling in gristle and guilt. Dem bones are gonna walk around. They gonna walk around.

Chapter 41

The knock at the door snapped me out of it. Open-mouthed and breathing hard, I threw my legs over the side of the bed and steadied myself for a moment before pushing myself onto my feet. I tried to quell the hope that it was Karis, and it turned out I was right to do so.

Martin Hojgaard looked weary and troubled, doubtless not only due to a long, hard day at the fish farm. He held a plastic container in one hand.

He tapped it gently on the top. 'Fish and potatoes. Mine waits for me. I will not stay.'

Something in his voice bothered me. It was as polite as ever, but curt, verging on irritated.

'Thank Silja for me. She is very kind. You both are for letting me stay.'

Martin's mouth tightened, a purse snapping shut, and he shook his head in quick, sharp movements from side to side.

'No. it is Silja who is kind. Too kind. It is only her that you must thank for being allowed to stay.'

'Not you?'

I struggled to read his face. Sadness certainly. Guilt, too, perhaps. And anger.

'No, not me. I didn't want you to stay. I still don't. I am sorry but I cannot change how I feel. I told you before about bringing shame on me and my family. You have done that. You were charged with murder. *Murder.*'

'The court has let me go, Martin. There was no evidence to charge me.'

His face darkened. 'Not *enough* evidence. That they cannot prove it does not mean it is not so. You have to remain here while they continue their investigation. Do you know how this makes me look in the eyes of the church? Do you?'

'Martin . . .'

'Romans. Chapter thirteen, verse one. "Let every person be subject to the governing authorities. For there is no authority except from God, and those that exist have been instituted by God." You will be not be judged by me or the court.'

'It sounds like I've already been judged. What does the church say, Martin? What does the forgiving voice of God say?'

He scowled at me, obviously irked by my tone. 'The church is here to look after the people of these islands. They have done so for centuries and will continue to do so long after you have gone. Do not mock them, please.'

'But they say that I am guilty. In the eyes of the Lord?'

'No one is saying that.'

'No one? Are you sure?'

Hojgaard flushed with embarrassment. 'Some maybe. But the church does not. "You shall not go around as a slanderer among your people, and you shall not stand up against the life of your neighbour." Leviticus. I shall listen to the word of the Lord.'

'You are very fond of quoting scripture today, Martin.'

He hesitated. 'I reach to the Bible in times of trouble. These are very troubled times.'

'And the church doesn't look kindly on you letting me stay here. That will be making even more trouble for you. I'm sorry. I don't want to bring that.'

Martin sighed heavily. 'You can stay. I am not happy about it but you can. Silja . . . she wants it. I am doing this for her.'

His eyes narrowed. 'Do not give me reason to regret this. And do not give Silja reason to think herself wrong.'

'Is that a threat, Martin?'

He laughed bitterly. 'A threat? Not from me. I told you, you will be judged by a higher power. I quoted Romans to you before. There is another verse in the same Chapter that you would do well to remember.'

'What's that?'

'"For he is God's servant for your good. But if you do wrong, be afraid, for he does not bear the sword in vain. For he is the servant of God, an avenger who carries out God's wrath on the wrongdoer."'

Anger flared in me. I didn't appreciate being terrorized with the wrath of God. I also got the feeling that the quotes were fresh in Martin's memory.

'Is that how it is? Your church knows better than the court? The church has decided I am guilty and you have been sent here to deliver the message from the pulpit?'

'No, I . . . I will not discuss what the church says. Not with you. But no one sent me here. How dare you accuse me?'

'Because that's the way it sounds. I'm sorry, Martin. But if you think I am a murderer, if you really think that, aren't you afraid to be here?'

He stared back at me. 'No. I am not afraid. Are you afraid of what you have done?'

His words slapped me and I had to stop myself from replying 'maybe'. My knees nearly gave way, my head falling into my hands before I realized how guilty it looked and raised it again.

I looked up at him again, my eyes pleading. 'It doesn't matter to me what the church thinks, Martin. It *does* matter to me what you and Silja think. You have been good to me and I respect you. All I am asking is that *you* don't judge me until you know the truth. Can you do that?'

I saw a little bit of the anger leak from him, even as his own conscience fought with his church's. He rubbed at his eyes, his thick fingers working their way from corner to corner.

'John, you remember that I heard your nightmare. The things you said. The words you used.'

A cold fear sneaked up my back. 'Yes.'

'I cannot forget those words. I told them to the police. I had to.'

'And my fight with Toki. And how drunk I must have seemed when you picked me up the morning the police came.'

'Yes. That too. I had no choice. It is the law and . . .'

'The right thing to do. I know. I understand. You had to do it and I don't hold it against you at all. You need to look after yourself first. It is okay.'

He nodded gratefully and the simple act of it filled me with fresh guilt.

'But it is what you said that night that I can never forget. And the way you shouted. Screamed.'

The cold fear was freezing now, snaking its way round my back and weaving inside, wrapping itself around every rib.

'What did I say, Martin?'

He breathed deep, tilted his head to the side as he shook it ruefully.

'No. I don't think–'

'Please. I need to know.'

Martin couldn't hold my gaze and looked away as he spoke.

'You shouted about how there were four boys. How you wanted to hurt them.'

He faltered.

'Kill them. You said that you wanted to kill all of them. Your voice was so angry. So full of hate. You said you were going to break them. You broke their bones. You said you broke all their bones. You were screaming that.'

I was no longer angry at him for judging me. I looked up at him, his face lined with pity as much as with scorn, and had no words to offer in my own defence. He took that as the admission of guilt that it was, and soberly nodded his head.

'You can stay here for now. Until the police have completed their investigation. Stay away from my family. And do not shame me further. You understand?'

I could only let my head bob in submission.

Martin opened the door to leave, but turned before he closed it behind him.

'May God go with you. And have mercy on your soul.'

Chapter 42

The fish and potatoes tasted good despite my mood. After the bland meals of the jail, they tasted of sea and salt and fresh air and freedom. Despite Martin's visit, the mix was heady enough to clear away a little of the fear and depression that had been eating at me.

When the door was knocked again, my breath caught and I wondered which of them it would be, Martin or Silja. It turned out to be neither of them.

Inspector Broddi Tunheim stood a polite couple of paces from the threshold, wearing his familiar brown raincoat and a pleasant smile.

'It is further to walk up here than I thought,' he puffed. 'But my wife is always telling me to take more exercise, so she will be happy. I will go home and tell her that I walked all the way up Dalavegur to speak to the Scotsman. She will be pleased. May I come in?'

By way of answer I stepped outside and closed the door behind me.

'We can speak out here, Inspector. You have been inside already. You know there's not much to see.'

Tunheim grinned. 'Ah, that was not me, Mr Callum. That was the Danes. Very inquisitive people, the Danes. Very efficient. They never give up when they think they have the scent of something. And they are smelling you.'

I didn't offer a reply, but then Tunheim didn't need one. He carried on regardless.

'The inspector, Nymann, and his sergeant ... Wow. They are sure it was you that killed Aron Dam. Sure as sure. They are working the forensic so hard. She is going back over everything. Every inch. At Tinganes. On the way from Natur. In here, of course. Everywhere.'

I looked over Tunheim's shoulder and saw Torshavn laid out below me, its myriad colours and shapes glinting in the newly arrived sunshine. The reds and yellows and greens leapt up, demanding attention, declaring their importance.

'I want the forensic to search, Inspector. I want her to find whatever there might be.'

Tunheim followed my gaze and moved to stand shoulder to shoulder with me, surveying Torshavn as if he'd never seen it before.

'It is beautiful, no? I went to New York once, Mr Callum, and I went to the top of the Empire State Building. An amazing view. All those buildings under your feet. All so close together. And the people like ants and the cars like quicker ants. But you know ... I think this view ... this is as good as New York. Smaller, of course. Sure as sure. But maybe better. And the best thing? That you can find everything. You miss nothing.'

'Inspector? You think the Danish forensic is as good as they say she is?'

Tunheim looked at me as if I'd questioned the Earth's roundness.

'Yes! Oh yes. They are all very good. Like a genius. The things they can do? Incredible.'

'So if there is evidence of who killed Dam then she will find it.'

He smiled broadly. 'Oh yes. Let us hope so. That would be good for everyone, don't you think?'

'I hope so.'

Tunheim laughed, his eyes never leaving the town below.

'Mr Callum, when we were in the car at the top of Sornfelli, I asked you to let me help you. You said no. Are you ready to let me help you now?'

There was something infuriatingly likeable about him. I knew he was trying to trap me at every turn, knew he was playing me and probably putting on some kind of act to put me off guard. But he wasn't Nymann. He wasn't Danish. Somehow I'd become Faroese enough that that tilted the balance.

'Yes.'

Tunheim didn't look at me but he smiled quietly.

'Good. That is very good. Tell me, Mr Callum, the night that Aron Dam was killed – you told the Danes that you went straight home after leaving the Cafe Natur. Is that true?'

I breathed in deep and exhaled hard. Now or never.

'No.'

He smiled again. 'So where did you go?'

'I don't know. All I know is I woke on the fish slabs at Undir Bryggjubakka. I don't remember getting there. Then I went home. That's all I know.'

Tunheim's smile slowly broadened until it filled his face, but there was no glee in it, just satisfaction.

'Good, good. Now we are together in this, Mr Callum. Now I know I can help you.'

There was something else, something behind the words.

'What do you mean, Inspector? What aren't you telling me?'

Annoyingly, he laughed again.

'You know, I'm not investigating this case. Not properly. I think maybe you can call me Broddi, if you want.'

I didn't.

'I'd rather you just told me, Inspector.'

Tunheim held his arms wide, his face looking hurt.

'Okay. We can be together in this now, Mr Callum, because I know you are telling me the truth. Or some truth. You see, I was playing a game again. I am sorry. I already knew you were sleeping on the fish slabs. I learned that today.'

He turned to see my reaction and grinned at the surprise that I must have betrayed.

'The Danes are from Denmark, you see, Mr Callum. I am from Torshavn. When you are from Torshavn, you know who to talk to. And the people of Torshavn, they also know who to talk to.'

'Someone saw me sleeping on the fish slabs?'

'But of course.'

'And do they know when I got there?' My heart skipped faster.

Tunheim's expression answered the question before his words did. 'No. Sadly, no. You could have been there five minutes or five hours. You could have gone there after killing Aron Dam. It does not free you. But … you have been honest. This is good. You will let me help you.'

Maybe I would let him help me, but I had already decided to help myself. I knew what I would do, but first there was something else I had to ask him.

'Inspector … Broddi … have you told the Danish detectives of this?'

Tunheim frowned as if the weight of the world was on his shoulders.

'Ah, no. Not yet. The Danes are a very busy people. So efficient. And so many people to talk to. I am thinking I will not bother them with it. Not yet.'

Chapter 43

The next morning, as I stood on the doorstep waiting for my knock to be answered, I felt I could hear curtains twitch and neighbours whispering to each other. It's him. The Scotsman. The murderer. It seemed the good folk of Torshavn had withdrawn the warmth of their welcome.

The door opened and Tummas Barthel stood there, seemingly unsurprised at my unannounced arrival at his home. Dressed in a classic black Rolling Stones tongue T-shirt and faded denims, he briefly looked over my head before beckoning me inside.

I closed the door behind me and stepped into the Room of Rock, with its posters, album covers and top-of-the-range CD player. A faint air of booze floated warmly, although it wasn't yet noon, and I reminded myself that Barthel had already done a full day's work on the ocean. His sun was well over the yardarm.

I fell into an armchair as directed by my as-yet-silent host. 'I wasn't sure you'd want to speak to me. Not given what they say I've done.'

Barthel grunted a gravelly laugh. 'I spoke to you before, remember. And I knew what they'd said about you then. Whisky?'

'Thanks. You still got any of that Johnnie Walker Blue?'

'Long gone. I have a good bottle of Ardbeg though. Had it flown in. You'll like it.'

He fetched the bottle from the other room, topping up a glass next to the computer, even though it already held an inch of golden dreams, before filling a glass for me. He carried them in one hand, a finger in each and let me take mine from him.

'You'll not only be liking this,' he sipped at his whisky as he sat in the chair opposite, 'you'll be needing it too, I think.'

'I can't argue with that.'

'Did you kill him?'

'What do you think?'

'I think I don't know. I'm thinking only two or three people know the truth. Aron Dam, you and the person who did it. Either two or three.'

'I can't argue with your maths, either.'

We sat in silence for a bit, contemplating the whisky and the world, words an unnecessary distraction. I could hear the wind picking up outside, wind chimes singing nearby and foliage being blown repeatedly against a window, like nature knocking to be allowed inside.

'I hear you're not allowed to leave,' Barthel said at last. 'Like me. Staying here whether you like it or not. My promise to my father, and yours to the judge.' He raised his glass towards me. 'Stone walls do not a prison make, nor iron bars a cage.'

'I hoped you might help me, Tummas.'

'With what?'

'Information.'

Barthel stroked absently at his white beard. 'Why me?'

'Not many people in Torshavn seem to want to talk to me any more. They've judged me guilty. I hoped you'd be different.'

He took another mouthful of the Ardbeg. 'Oh, I'm different all right. What is it you want to know?'

I almost laughed. That was the difficult part, knowing what it was that I wanted. The truth, the whole truth and nothing but the truth? That was a dangerous luxury. A convenient truth? Maybe. I wanted answers that led to a truth I could live with.

'I want to know about Aron Dam. And his brother. And about the Frenchman, Serge Gotteri.'

Barthel nodded slowly. 'Separately or together?'

'Both.'

He paused, sipping at the malt.

'I know some things for sure. Other things I have heard but could not testify to their certainty.'

'Okay.'

'Aron and Nils are not very popular. Never have been. This is a strange business we are in, where men work independently yet we all rely on the same thing, and on each other. We are all, as you would say, in the same boat. Not the Dams. They've never given a fuck about anyone other than themselves. Always angry, always looking for a fight about this or that. They were always a pain in the ass.'

'Plenty of enemies then?'

Barthel regarded me coolly, as if weighing up my meaning.

'Yes. They made more enemies than friends, I would say. Aron obviously made one very serious enemy for himself.'

Perhaps it wasn't meant as an accusation, but my paranoia and my guilt ensured that I took it as one. I'd have been better placed to respond if I could have been sure what I had done. Instead I swallowed down whisky, not enjoying its assault on my throat as it headed straight to my gut.

'What about Gotteri?'

'He is your friend, is he not? Surely you will know more about him than I do.'

'Maybe. I want to know about his involvement with the Dams.'

'Are you sure there is any involvement?'

'Yes.'

'Okay. I can ask around.'

'I'd be grateful. But no one can know . . .'

The laugh gurgled in him, the whisky coughing in disbelief. 'That I'm asking for you? My God, of course not. Anyway, that would hardly help get me your information, would it?'

'Thanks, Tummas.'

'More whisky?'

I looked at the time on the display of Barthel's CD player.

'No. I can't. I need to go to the police station and I have to make a call in town first.'

Chapter 44

I dialled and waited, the delay seeming to last for an eternity, time enough for me to realize I should have thought through what I was going to say.

The unfamiliar ring tone sounded distant, an echo of what it should be. I put it down to the 3,000-plus miles between Torshavn and Washington DC. It rang on frustratingly and I urged someone to answer. At last they did. A woman's voice, pleasant and efficient but showing the wear of having repeated the same phrase a million times.

'*National Geographic*. How may I help you?'

'I'd like to speak to someone in, um, Features, please.'

There was the faintest sigh. 'Of course, sir. Could you be more specific? Which area of publication would your query be addressed to?'

I had no idea and scrambled for an answer. 'Overseas assignments. Birds.'

The sigh was more evident this time, barely restrained. 'Are you an existing correspondent, sir?' The tone of voice made it clear she knew that I wasn't. 'Or do you wish to offer something for publication?'

'Um, well, to offer something. Yes. I'd like to speak to someone about the possibility of an overseas assignment. A features editor.'

'Thank you, sir, but we accept such submissions by mail or email. If you would like to send–'

I cut across her. 'I'd like to speak to someone today, please. It's a matter of urgency. There isn't time for any correspondence.'

'Really?' I had to admire the restrained way she conveyed her doubt, nothing more than a nuance of insult.

'Yes, really.' I was firm and she knew I wasn't going anywhere in a hurry.

The sigh was almost inaudible. 'Okay, sir. If you could hold the line, please, I will try to find someone available to speak to you.'

Silence and she was gone, the line humming with static. I imagined the conversation that I was shut off from. A grouchy editor, or more likely an assistant, complaining that they were the one being dumped on by the switchboard operator. Wondering why she hadn't told the nutcase on the line that he had to write in. She indignantly replying that of course she had. More bitching, then finally, I hoped, a reluctant acceptance. The line clicked again.

'Hello. Bob Dokoris.'

The man's voice was suitably terse, making it clear that he was really far too busy and important to be taking calls like this and it had better be good.

'Hi Bob, thanks for taking my call. My name is James Johnstone and I'm calling from Glasgow in Scotland.'

The silence didn't sound as if it was overly impressed by any of that. 'What can I help you with, Mr Johnstone?'

'I understand that you deal with overseas assignments. I wanted to run a couple of things by you, if that's okay.'

'I'm pretty busy, Mr Johnstone. It would be easier if you could email us with–'

'Yes, I understand that. I'm sorry to interrupt, but I'm up against a deadline of my own. I have a story here that I'm certain you would want to see, but there are other publications showing interest.'

'Okay . . .'

'But my first choice would be *National Geographic*. It's a photo-led article and I don't think anyone else can do it justice the way you could. It also needs a global audience.'

There was interest now, albeit still wary. 'Could you tell me what your article is about, Mr Johnstone? Clearly I can't get into a discussion with you on this until I know the subject matter. And what's your background? Are you a journalist in Scotland?'

'In Scotland, but in London, too, and spells in Johannesburg and Madrid. I can provide you with references from various editors. *The Times*, the *Mail & Guardian* in Jo'burg, *El Pais*, *Le Monde*.'

He was softening, I could hear it in his voice. I'd been scaled up from nutcase to timewaster to possible useful contact. Bob Dokoris was interested.

'Okay, I'm listening. What's the story?'

I paused, as much for effect as to gather my thoughts. I had to get this right.

'I can't tell you the whole thing right now, Bob. It's still pretty sensitive and you'll appreciate that I need to protect some information until we conclude a deal. Like location. I'd need to keep that secret for now, or people will be all over this. But the basics are that I have proof, photographic proof, that a once-native species has been reintroduced to Scotland by an extremely wealthy foreign landowner. A species that will be hugely controversial once this is made public.'

The pause on Dokoris's end of the line was different from the earlier one. This one was his brain working overtime.

'You'll need to give me more than that, James. What species? And why would it be controversial?'

'Well, let's just say that this species is quietly going about the business of killing other native species. Ones that are proving a nuisance on the landowner's many acres, but which he is not allowed to cull. Are you interested?'

More silence. More thinking. 'James ... are we talking about wolves here? Killing deer?'

My turn to let the question hang in the air.

'As I said, I can't tell you the whole thing right now, but let's say that's a very well-informed guess.'

'Wow. And you have photographs?'

'I do.'

'Good quality?'

'Top quality.'

'Okay, James. Let's say I'm interested. But you will also realize I'm not going to talk money until I hear and see a lot more.'

'I appreciate that. I haven't dealt with *National Geographic* before, but a friend of mine tells me that you are very professional to deal with and always fair when it comes to payment. It was him that recommended I take the story to you.'

'Well that's great to hear. We do always try to deal fairly with contributors. Who is your friend?'

'Serge Gotteri. I think he's on assignment for you right now.'

I heard static and Bob's brain whirring. Something had changed in the wind.

'How well do you know Mr Gotteri, James?'

Get this right. Play it carefully.

'Um, not *that* well. I've bumped into him in various places around the world. Shared the odd beer on assignment.'

'Right. So you're not best friends or anything?'

'No. Not at all.'

'Okay. Well I'm kind of glad to hear that. Between us, Gotteri is a bit of a pain in the ass. He's always trying to push articles on green anarchism, real eco-terrorism stuff. You know? It's just not what we're looking for right now. And he's very … insistent. Difficult to deal with, let's say. That's between us, though, you understand?'

'Sure. No problem. Won't say a word. But you are using him. Aren't you?'

'Well, no. That's what I don't understand. Gotteri sure isn't on any assignment from us. We haven't taken anything from him in three years. He knows we don't want his stuff. God knows we've told him often enough.'

Bob Dokoris suddenly seemed a very long way from Torshavn. A long way from Serge Gotteri and his fake job.

'Are you there, James?'

'Yes, I'm here, Bob. I think there's maybe a problem on the line. I'll need to call you back.'

'Okay. Well, do that. I'm interested, and I'm sure we can better the terms of the other publications. Here, take my direct number. James? James?'

Chapter 45

I had to report for my first daily check-in at the police station on Jonas Broncksgøta, the road that ran north from the old fort, Skansin, at the ferry port. It was probably as much a chore for the cops as it was for me, particularly as they knew there was little or no chance of me getting off these islands, short of pinching a rowing boat and taking my chances on the high seas.

Demmus Klettskarð, the heavyweight constable who had picked me up from the fish farm, was on duty and he cheerlessly had me follow the prescribed routine. Procedure, meaningless and torturous as it was, was followed to the letter.

I was signed in and my attendance ticked off like an habitual school truant, albeit one who never ventured further than the back of the school for a smoke. I had bent my knee to their will, and that satisfied them for now. It was all an act of bureaucratic theatre to satisfy their annoyance at my being released by the court.

When the play was done, I half-heartedly asked Klettskarð what his plans were for the rest of the day and, to my satisfaction, got no response. It was a minor victory in a losing war.

I pushed my way through the station door and was hit by a lively breeze that sought to gain entrance. Unlike the wind, I needed to be out. Once I was out in the open I was no less trapped – like a bird with clipped wings – but at least I was able to breathe air that wasn't fogged with the stench of police paperwork.

Like my freedom, my options for the day were limited. I wasn't exactly welcome at some of the places I'd frequented previously. My face wasn't the first one that people wanted to see in the Natur, at Kaffihúsið or on Nils Finsens gøta. I was having to get used to curious stares and suspicious glances, pointing fingers and people crossing the street to avoid me. The irony wasn't lost on me. I had come to the Faroes to get away from people, and now they were getting away from me.

What I wanted to do, of course, was to go to Karis's studio. To bang on her door, demand attention, throw stones at her bedroom window, shout and scream. I wouldn't do that though. Hard as it was, I'd decided she had to come to me. There had been enough opportunities that she hadn't taken. If she thought me guilty then so be it. I could hardly blame her for that, given my own doubts.

As I stood and pondered my next move, male voices came at me from round the corner, getting closer. One loud and angry, the other calmer and more dispassionate. Both were insistent in their own way. They weren't arguing, not quite, but the louder of the two was definitely heated.

Then, amid the tangle of words that I couldn't understand, came one that I knew very well. My own name. Twice I heard 'Callum' rasped out by the louder voice. Then again, this time in the other's clipped accent.

I stepped towards where the voices were coming from, realizing that the pair had stopped walking and were in animated discussion once more. As I turned the corner, I saw them just a few yards away, facing each other, unaware that I was there. One tall, hands on hips, one short and gesticulating furiously.

The tall, athletic type, in the sharpest of sharp steel-grey suits, topped by close-cropped blond hair, was Inspector Nymann. The other was much shorter and wider, thick legs supporting a bulky frame. I could only see him from behind, but his identity dawned on me like a spider crawling over my skin. My abiding memory was of him being picked up from the quay, wiping away the trail of fish guts that I'd stuffed in his mouth.

It was Nymann who noticed me first, seeing me approach over Toki Rønne's head. The shorter man saw the inspector's gaze shift and followed it, turning to look at me over his shoulder. Both watched me approach, the hateful scowl of one counterbalanced by the detached stare of the other.

Toki turned fully in order to face me down, but Nymann stepped forward, his arm held up before him like a traffic cop.

'Do not come any closer, Mr Callum. I would regard it as intimidation of a witness.'

'You're kidding me, right? I get instructed to attend this station and then when I leave you tell me I can't walk down the path to get out?'

Nymann pulled himself up to his full height and offered a well-practised sneer. 'You may walk down the path, of course. But you may not approach this man. Do you understand?'

Toki was clearly enjoying the exchange, his mouth twisting up at the side in some representation of a smile.

'No, I don't understand,' I told Nymann, my patience worn thin. 'Tell me how I can walk that way without approaching him, given that that is where he is standing. And maybe you can tell me what you think he is a witness to.'

The Dane looked as if I'd questioned the likelihood of the sun coming up in the morning. 'He is a witness to your character. And you will walk down that side of the path. We will stand on this side until you have gone by. That is clear.'

I shook my head at Nymann's words and moved infinitesimally to my right, a deference that seemed to satisfy the officer's smug superiority. I walked up to and then by them, at which point Nymann nodded emphatically and turned.

He led the way into the station with a clinical sweep of his arm, striding forward with Toki in his wake. I watched the pair of them going down the path until my former colleague swung on his low axis and turned to face me, walking backwards towards the cop shop.

An evil, crooked grin spread over his face, a light sparking in his dark eyes. Without missing a step, he sucked in the twisted smile and spat heavily onto the ground in my direction. A fat fist came up and a forefinger jabbed menacingly towards me before he turned again, just in time for Nymann to hold the station door open for him.

Chapter 46

For a couple of hours, I sought solace in booze in the Manhattan. It wasn't Torshavn's best bar, but that was why it suited me. It was dark and quiet, with corners to skulk in alone and undisturbed. Their beer was good and their whisky relatively cheap. No one bothered me, other than the odd stare, and I was left to drink and think.

I stopped just short of maudlin drunk and a few glasses shy of recklessly smashed. Just hammered enough to smooth off some of the edges and blunt a handful of memories. It couldn't wipe them out, no amount of booze could do that. Instead, it fuelled the desire to do something about them. I could still smell the blood on my hands from the shack door, and I knew what I wanted to do about it. It was time to get home and get ready.

The steep walk back up Dalavegur did me good, burning off some of the booze and working my body. I kept up a good pace, asking questions of my calves as I marched up the hill. I was getting hotter, breathing more heavily, but liking it. A film of sweat formed on my forehead and I felt as if I was trying to burn everything out of my system: alcohol, guilt, blood, everything. I went faster until the heat came to my knees and Achilles tendons, spreading into my thighs and lungs.

At the top of the hill, the shack in sight through the soft, fading light, I finally relented and eased up. I stood still and panted, eyes closed. When I opened them again, I saw a shadow in the eaves of the shack. Something, no, someone, sitting or kneeling there.

I didn't move. I stood, swallowing my racing breath. I had been seen by whoever it was, no doubt about that. My first thought was of the person who had painted my door in blood, and I instinctively balled my hands into fists.

I began to move quickly again, straight towards the shack and the shadow. I had gone three or four paces when the figure moved, stepping out of the shade to meet me.

Karis! I didn't know whether to go quicker or slow down. As I got nearer I could see tears streaming down her face. She broke into a run and I joined her, taking her in my arms. Her head sunk into my chest and she grabbed me tight. Her head still hadn't come back up when she began tugging at me, steering me inside.

She only let go when she began to pull my clothes off, dragging my shirt over my head and unbuckling my belt, pushing away my feeble attempts at resistance. Not a word had passed between us and I was being pushed back onto the bed naked, Karis standing above me and peeling off her own clothes. Rational thought called to me but I was beyond reach; other faces were banished to locked rooms in my mind. Nicoline Munk, Aron and Nils Dam, Esmundur Lisberg; all shut away where I couldn't see them.

She straddled me, grabbing me with her right hand and guiding me inside her. We were instantly one and yet separate. Karis arched her back and rode me, setting a pace and a rhythm and forcing me to keep up. There was an urgency, a sense of need about her, something extra driving her on. I let her go, rising to meet her and running with her, feeling the need and embracing it.

Her hands were grasping her head through her hair, sometimes shielding her face from me, sometimes facing the ceiling as her back arced away. Other times, I saw her eyes were screwed shut and her face clenched in a grimace. She rose and sank on me, faster and harder. There was no sense of prolonging or indulging in what we were sharing. Instead it was insistent, burning, demanding. She was pushing me beyond control, over an edge of no return. When she saw me arch my back in near defeat, she moved in a blur that carried us both over the brink and into the bottomless chasm beyond.

She fell on top of me, her head on my chest, and I could feel her heart hammering against me. Then little snuffling noises began to escape from her, the sound of sobbing. I tried to lift her head up so I could see her face, but she kept it clamped against my flesh. I got the message and left her to cry softly, not asking why. Instead I just held her, one hand on her head and the other on the small of her back. My skin was damp with her tears.

The light fell further, the sun dipping until only the absence of complete darkness coated the skyline. I reached to the floor where the bedcovers had landed and pulled them over us to keep off the chill. She snuggled closer, silent now but for the occasional sniffle. After a while, I moved to stretch towards the lamp, but her hand came up and caught me. 'No. Leave it. Please.'

So we lay together in the half-light, naked and quiet, until Karis spoke again.

'They say your name is Andrew.'

'It's my full name. I prefer John.' It sounded fake and hollow because it was.

'John, I need . . .'

I'd expected the question, the one I'd waited for since the first moment I set eyes on her that night – but it didn't come.

'No, I . . . never mind.' She sounded tired and frazzled, she sounded small and scared. 'I cannot deal with this. It is too much. I shouldn't be here.'

'I'm glad you are.'

'Because I fucked you?'

She meant it as a joke, but it came across as nervy, almost

hysterical. Having sex with her suddenly seemed completely the wrong thing to have done.

'No, not that at all. Because I haven't seen you since the night it happened. I thought you might have come to the jail, but maybe I'm glad you didn't.'

Her head clamped tighter to my chest.

'I missed you. But I could not come to see you. It has been … difficult. I cannot sleep. I cannot paint. I know that everyone thinks it is my fault. That I am to blame for Aron's death. I know everyone thinks that.'

Again I tried to gently lift her head to see her face, but she refused to budge.

'I have been drinking since …' she was starting to cry again, 'since it happened. No sleep. Thinking about you. And Aron. And me. I am being selfish, but this is a small place. People look at me as if …'

I pulled her closer, tighter. 'It's not your fault.'

The noise she made sounded unconvinced. 'Maybe. Everyone thinks it is. They are all talking about me as if it is. I know it. I know I should say fuck them, but I cannot stand that they think I am to blame for him being dead.'

'Well … maybe some of them do think that. But it isn't true. And what they think of me is worse. They think I killed him.'

I felt her shiver beneath me. The question was unspoken, but I was sure it was going through her head again: *Was it you? Was it you?*

Part of me wanted her to ask so that I could answer, even if all I was going to do was tell her what I thought she wanted to hear. Something that would make her less scared and stop her shaking. Something that would convince her that everything would be all right.

'That night when …' she choked back a sob, '… we were both very drunk. I do not even remember leaving the Natur. Not properly. Do you?'

'Do you remember the fight with Aron? My fight with him, and you being angry at me?'

'Yes.' It sounded resentful. 'I remember that, and I was told about it by others. You should not have done that. It looks bad. Very bad.'

'He was threatening me.' I knew my voice was raised, but I couldn't help it. 'He was trying to warn me to stay away from you and he'd . . . he'd done other things to get at me.'

Karis's head came off my chest for the first time and she looked at me curiously, but she didn't ask. Her eyes were milky red and strained. Her head didn't so much go back onto me as collapse, hitting me with a thud.

'It looks so bad.' Her voice was muffled by my flesh, her lips pressed against my skin. 'What do the police think? I know what happened in court, but what are they saying to you? What do they believe?'

My sigh was deep and marbled with thoughts of Nymann, Keilstrup and Munk, Tunheim and my lawyer Samuelsen, too. A cast of unbelievers.

'They still think I did it. They will keep trying to prove that. I am not allowed to leave the Faroes and must report in to the police station every day. They don't suspect anyone else. Just me.'

Karis pinched me, her nails digging into my skin, as if claiming me. 'Just you? Why do they not think it could be anyone else?'

'The fight, I guess. And I cannot prove where I was when he died. And have no alibi. They don't know of anyone else who had a reason to do it.'

There was a gasp of sorts against my chest, an exhalation of something that I couldn't read. The only thing that I could think of, whatever her actual intent, was that she really wanted to ask the question. *The* question.

'What about evidence? Like from the scene where . . . where it happened? Surely they must have footprints or fingerprints or DNA or something?'

The question troubled me. 'Do you want them to find something like that?'

'No. Well, yes. Of course. To find who did it.' She paused. 'To find that it was not you.'

'Yeah. I'd like that too.'

We fell into a silence that at some point must have become a sleep. I felt her go first. A stillness came over her and I was able to twist my head and see part of the side of her face, beautiful and calm, her lips full and just slightly parted. I stroked her hair and let my own head fall back, until I stared blindly at the ceiling through the gloom. My eyes closed and I drifted.

I am watching myself sleep. Standing over my own curled-up figure, an overgrown foetus, eyes closed and mouth half-open. I can walk all the way round myself and it's fascinating to see me from all angles, see what other people would see.

It's not a pretty sight. Dishevelled and unshaven. Obviously drunk. My long legs coiled under me, my big face bloated with alcohol. Face squashed against the fish slabs, which push it out of shape and make my mouth gape like a trout on a hook. I try to wake myself up by shouting, but either the standing me can't be heard or the sleeping me can't hear.

Everything is in black and white and I wonder if I'm starring in an old movie. My rumpled clothes are in shades of grey and my face is ashen, the pallor of a sixty-a-day smoker. I'd maybe think I was a statue, some grotesque piece of modern art, but for the occasional billowing of my grey cheeks and the faint rise and fall of my chest. I reach down and move my jacket where the movement is coming from and see that not everything is in monotone after all. I can see my heart beating red through my shirt, a glowing fist-sized beast pulsing with life.

Shocked at the sight of it, I stagger back, the jacket falling closed again and the heart disappearing from view. But there's something else. More red. I can see it in the jacket pocket. Crouching down, I can see inside as it opens in front of me. There's a knife, a grindaknivur. *It is in grey like everything else, and the blade and handle are daubed in red. Blood. Bright red blood.*

I can see that the blood is still dripping from the blade. Seeping into my pocket, then my trousers and into my skin. It seeps red then merges into the greyness of everything else and disappears.

As I watch, the sleeping me moves, stretches and wakes, sitting up stupidly and looking around. Gulls and kittiwakes appear and swoop round my head, screeching, wings flapping, trying to peck at my eyes. The me on the slabs is too sleepy to notice, and I have to step in, waving my arms wildly, but one of the gulls still manages a savage nip at the right eye of the other me, scooping out the eyeball and gulping it down in a single bite. A trail of blood leaks from the grey socket and runs red down the leaden cheek, but the dozy, woozy, disorientated me doesn't even notice.

Up. The other me is on his feet and staggering into the street. I run round myself and shoo the other me to the left. My own guardian angel, shouting and screaming to go left, to go home. I stagger left then forward, taking wild lunging strides, one to the right for every two to the left.

On the hill now. I am pushing at myself from behind, palms on the back of the other me and shoving him up the slope. I am heavy and it's a struggle. The hill has never been so steep. Looking around as I push, I see grey heads peeping out at us from doorways and windows, familiar faces that I can't quite recognize. They are all looking at the staggering me. More than that, they are staring at the blood on the knife that can be seen through the transparent grey of the jacket pocket. The blood is running down the leg of the other me now and leaving a spatter behind us as we walk and push and walk up the hill.

When I turn and look back, I see the blood has become a river of red running behind us down the colourless slope, ruby red washing over a hill of slate. So much blood that it cannot all have come from such a little knife. It has come from me. I am not pushing myself any more, I am pushing a corpse. My own.

At the top of the hill, on the path to the shack, I see the spot marked by the triangle of small stones. I let my body drop lifelessly to the ground and take the knife from my pocket. My fingers are long and sharp like talons and I use them to dig a hole big enough to take the knife and hide it away from the world.

But suddenly the little hole is bigger, man-sized, like a tunnel. Or a grave. I drop the knife inside but have to listen for it to hit the bottom. I hear it whistle through the air, becoming quieter and softer, until nothingness, and then finally I hear it hit rocks, miles below.

I look at my corpse and know what I must do. Pulling it by the legs and then the arms, I drag the body across the earth until it is positioned by the edge of the hole. With a swing of my leg, I boot it into the hole and it falls, falls, falls until it crashes onto the bottom of oblivion.

A last look around to make sure that no one is watching, then I jump in feet first, till I am completely inside, swallowed up and on my way down. I pass through the middle of nowhere, hurtling towards the end of somewhere. I know I can hide under here forever, no one will find me, no one will even think of looking for me down here. I fall and fall and there is no end to my falling.

When I woke it was because I had landed, and the shock of it forced my eyes open and my body to sit upright from the waist. I was soaked in a film of sweat, breathing hard, and could still feel the chill on my skin from the fall into and through the earth.

Some realization dawned with the day, and my head snapped to the right. The side of the bed next to me was empty but for a rumpling of the sheets. I looked around but there were no clothes on the floor where they had been dropped in a heap the night before. Karis had gone, left while I slept, and I could only wonder whether she had ever been there in the first place.

Maybe it was for the best. I glanced at my watch and saw that it was nearly time that I should be up anyway. If she had still been there, it would be more difficult for me to get out and do what I had to do.

Chapter 47

One of the few things I knew about my target was where he lived. A red-walled, turfed-roof house just off Hoyviksvegur, no more than a ten-minute walk from the port. Knowing where he lived, I also knew the route he took when he left home in the morning. And I knew when.

Like everything else in the Faroes, his routine was ruled by the sea, by the turning of the moon and the tide. People were slaves to it, just as it was a provider for them – but the sea's demands were greater than those that were made upon it. The sea's very predictability was to be my target's enemy.

I stood in the shadows of a morning gloom, hours stolen back from the waning summer, unseen by the sleeping and the unwary, confident that I wouldn't have long to wait.

The first footstep was enough to alert me and send adrenalin crashing through my body. It was so early that it was unlikely to belong to anyone else.

His footsteps were lazy; unrushed and laboured. He was coming and in no hurry. I held my breath. Last chance to change my mind. I didn't take it.

He passed me, oblivious to my presence, and I let him walk on a full stride so that he wouldn't catch sight of me in the periphery of his vision. I stepped out, quickly and quietly, and brought the wrench down onto his head. The groan that seeped from his mouth as his knees collapsed beneath him was no louder than air escaping from a balloon, but my hand was over his mouth to make sure no one heard. The same hand allowed me to pull him back into the lair of my shadows, while I waited to make sure no one had seen what had happened.

He was limp below me, a crumpled bag of sleeping bones, completely unconscious. I stood, breathing hard now, knowing there was no going back. Satisfied that my attack had gone unnoticed, I pulled my prey down the street and round the corner to where my hired car was parked, and threw him into the boot.

He stirred a couple of times as I tied his hands to the rusting pulley that hung overhead, its rope brown with age. It wasn't enough to wake him, though, and he'd fallen deep again before I placed the balaclava backwards on his head, shutting out the little light that the room offered. He dangled there, his clothing wet and dirty, both from where he'd fallen to the ground when I'd hit him and the dirty floor that I'd hauled him across once I'd got us both inside. Everything was in place, it was time to wake him up.

The water that came from the old tap was as rusty brown as it was freezing cold. I watched it swirl round the cobwebbed bucket and couldn't guess the last time it had been poured. I threw it all over him.

The scream was short-circuited as it caught in his throat. I guessed that the shock of the water had crashed into the pain in his head and the dread created by his blindness. He twisted and turned, seeking light where there was none, not for him.

His feet only barely touched the ground and he was forced to grope towards the greasy floor with his toes to maintain balance. The cry in his own language when it came was an attempt at defiance, a roar of rage but with a foundation of fear.

I walked away as quietly as I could and picked up the second bucket of water that I'd loosed from the tap. He was still shouting as I threw its contents over him, drenching his head and upper body.

This time he screamed fully. A shrill yell that reverberated round the old metal in the room and bounced back upon him. He paused, head cocked, as he tried to decipher the cause of the echo. I had no way of knowing if he'd ever been inside this place but it seemed unlikely. From what I'd learned, it had been abandoned for years.

'Who are you? Tell me.' The shout was much less defiant this time, the bravado all but gone. It was almost pleading. But not quite.

He could hear the water running this time and obviously knew what was coming. He braced himself, his head turned away. The noise that he gave up when the water hit was muffled, his pain swallowed back down, but I could hear him shiver.

If he'd listened carefully enough, he'd have known that I'd refilled both buckets. The scream when the second one hit him suggested he hadn't. Now his teeth chattered and there was the hint of a sob behind the wool of the balaclava.

'Please. Stop.'

I said nothing but retreated to the other side of the room, where there was a heavy metal drum half-full of wood, its base pooleddark with engine oil. I dragged it to within six feet of him and made a point of dropping it heavily to the floor, its clanging echoing round the room.

His head snapped to the side, doubtless wondering what made the noise. And why.

I let him think on it for a bit before I drew the box of matches from my pocket, taking one out and striking it. It sparked and hissed, large in the silence, until it faded to a whimper and died.

'Who are you? Why are you doing this?'

I struck another match and let it drop into the drum. The oil spat immediately and burst into flames that bit into the wood above it. I had made fire.

The contents of the oil drum barked noisily and the smell of burning wood snaked slowly into the fetid air of the room, mixing with the corrosion and grease and decay.

The heat took longer to come, and was nowhere near making its way over to the man, who was squirming and shivering, with his arms still locked above his head. He could hear the fire, though, and couldn't miss it for what it was.

I stood still and silent long enough for him to take it in, and to debate whether fire was a good thing for him or not. He was probably still thinking about it when I kicked him hard in the shin. The yelp was equal measures of surprise, pain and self-pity.

I reached up and pulled the balaclava from his head, feeling him shrink from me, his eyes finally blinking at the available light. Once focused, they opened wide at me. I got the impression that he wasn't entirely surprised at who he saw standing in front of him. It didn't help his fear, though. I was pretty sure it made things worse.

'Why?' It was a whimper in English.

'Come on, Nils. You know why. You must do.'

Aron Dam's brother shook his head fervently. 'No. No, I do not. Let me go. Let me down from here.'

I noticed how pale and raw his hands were now, swollen red above the wrists, but chalk white below, where the blood had drained south. I didn't answer him but picked up one of the old plastic buckets and walked slowly to the rusting tap.

It turned noisily, lack of use cranking up the volume, the screech echoing off the oil cans, wheels, bolts, pipes, buckets, doors and other rusted objects that the place was packed with. I let the water run slower than before, seeing the fear in Nils's eyes as it filled inch by inch.

When the bucket was full, I picked it up and sat it quietly a couple of feet from the metal can and the crackling fire within, before walking back over to Dam. I stood toe to toe with him, my face inches from his.

'You do know why. Don't you?'

He shook his head, less forcefully than before. I laughed in his face.

'Which do you want, Nils? The bucket of water or the bucket of warmth? Tell me what I want to know and I will bring the fire near to you. If you don't . . .'

He screwed his eyes shut, thinking hard and trying not to look at the buckets. When his eyes slowly peeled open again he was defeated.

'The blood on your door. It was me.'

I stared back expressionless. 'Go on.'

'I got sheep blood and threw it over your door.'

'Tell me something I don't know.'

'I did it because you killed my brother.' The words were spat out this time, coated in large dollops of anger and defiance. 'You fucking killed my brother!'

I turned my back on him, not wanting him to see my face screwed up in doubt. Yes, I was more and more sure; probably as sure as I could be. But still . . .

I turned round and faced him again.

'I didn't kill your brother. But you know more about this than you are saying. I know that you know enough to help me prove I didn't kill him. And you will tell me.'

'Fuck you!'

'You know what Aron was doing. The burst water pipe. The dead sheep by my door. The dead raven in my house. And you know why.'

I had to hope he couldn't hear the doubt in my voice. That he couldn't detect the layer of certainty I was trying to coat it with.

He hesitated, words clogging his throat. Now I knew he had what I wanted. I just didn't know if he would give it to me.

'I said *fuck you*. I tell you nothing.'

He meant it. I shrugged at him, as if there was nothing else I could do. Turning away, I picked up the water bucket and slowly advanced on him. As I pulled it back, I paused to give him a final chance. He didn't take it and I launched the cold water over his face and down over his body. He gasped and began shaking, his head slumping on this chest.

'Are you going to tell me?' I grabbed his soaking hair and pulled his head up so he had to face me. Inside, I was begging him to tell me, to stop me from going further.

'No.'

I picked up two blocks of wood, one in each hand, and walked to the oil drum, which was flaming strongly now. Placing a block of wood on each side, I lifted the drum and placed it within a few feet of him.

'There should be enough heat in that to stop you from freezing to death overnight. Probably. I'll find out when I come back tonight. Do you know where you are?'

Dam's eyes narrowed as he looked around him, nervously flitting from sealed rusty drums and tall canisters to ancient spanner boxes and tarnished piping.

'No.'

'You're in the old whaling station at Við Áir near Hvalvik. It's been closed for thirty years, so I'm told. And no one will be anywhere near here all day. Feel free to scream as much as you want.'

'No! You cannot do this.'

'Watch me.'

I turned and walked away, closing the door behind me before hauling three drums in front of it. He did scream, but the wind was already taking it and keeping it for its own.

Chapter 48

I parked the hired Peugeot in town, on a road near the SMS shopping centre, where it wouldn't attract attention. From there I began to walk home.

The early morning start, not to mention what I'd done to Nils Dam, was beginning to tell on me, and the hills seemed steeper than normal. My walking was laboured and my head was heavy.

Just a hundred yards or so from the beginning of Dalevegur, I heard a car behind me and, with a creeping, guilt-borne dread, became aware of it slowing. It edged in front of me and I knew the green Toyota immediately. Inspector Broddi Tunheim.

The driver-side window dropped and he leaned his head forward so he could look straight at me over his spectacles. Surely he hadn't followed me all the way? Could he see the ugly truth written on my face?

'Good day, Mr Callum. You don't seem to be enjoying your walk so much. Get in. I'll give you a drive to the top of the hill.'

I hadn't broken stride. 'No, thanks. It's a fine day and it would be a pity to waste it.'

Tunheim smiled. 'You are learning, Mr Callum. The Faroes are working their own magic on you. But please, get in. I thought we had an understanding now. Sure as sure I did. Anyway, I want to talk to you, Mr Callum. I think it is important that we talk. I have something I want to tell you.'

Maybe it was fear that my guilt would give me away. Maybe I was just worried that Tunheim so often seemed to know more than he let on, and so often asked questions that he already knew the answer to. I sighed and stopped, walking round to duck inside the door that he pushed open for me.

'Did you leave home early today, Mr Callum? I called before but you weren't at home.'

Something heavy dropped in my chest. Tunheim worried me.

'Yes, I just wanted to get out and clear my head. When were you there?'

He looked at me curiously. 'A little time ago. You seem distracted. Is there something I should know?'

A vision of Nils Dam flooded my head as I shook it. It was a snow globe of guilt turned upside down.

'Hm. Okay. Sometimes I think I can tell when a person is bothered by things. Maybe I am wrong. Anyway . . . we are here.'

Tunheim pulled the car to a stop and put on the handbrake. He said nothing for an age, prompting me to do so, despite myself.

'You said there was something you wanted to tell me, Inspector?'

'Ah yes. So there was. Thank you for reminding me.'

Another pause. 'What was it?'

He turned in his seat so that he was looking straight at me.

'I know that you didn't kill Aron Dam.'

Chapter 49

I could barely speak. The huge lump that had suddenly formed in my throat left no room for words.

'Are you okay, Mr Callum? You seem shocked. Should I get you some water, perhaps?'

'What? No, I'm . . . I'm fine. Is that all you have to say?'

Tunheim smiled as he took off his glasses and wiped them clean, prolonging the moment for his own satisfaction.

'No, no. Of course not. As if I would say something like that and keep you waiting to hear the rest of my news.'

Yeah. As if.

'You will remember, of course, Mr Callum, how you told me that you fell asleep on the fish slabs at Undir Bryggjubakka.'

'Of course I do. And I remember how you already knew that.'

Tunheim made a face. 'Ah yes. I apologise. I played a little game. Anyway. You know that the slabs are near the Hotel Torshavn. Of course you do. But do you know that the hotel has a webcam? You know, a fixed camera that people can watch on the Internet.'

'No, I didn't.'

'Not many people do. Unless you live here, of course. Like me. Anyway. The manager of the hotel is a friend of mine, so I went to him and asked to see the webcam footage. And for him to keep the information to himself, as it was very important. You understand?'

'Will you just tell me?'

He smiled. 'Yes, yes. Of course. I went through the film and you were there asleep at the time you told me. Which was very good. You arrived there very drunk. Not coming from Tinganes at all, but from the opposite direction. This made me happy. But I kept watching. It is not moving film, you understand. It takes photographs. Every few seconds. Later, someone else comes. Someone in a long red raincoat, with the hood over their head so their face cannot be seen. This person walks straight to where you are sleeping. And do you know what they do?'

'For Christ's sake . . .'

'They put something in your pocket.'

I had no breath. Tunheim's words punched me hard in the guts.

'Yes. There is no doubt. The person stood over you and put something in the pocket of your coat. Do you know what that thing might be?'

I nodded dumbly and stammered an answer. 'Yes.'

'Then you must tell me, Mr Callum.'

'It was a *grindaknivur*.'

When Tunheim took off his glasses I nearly snatched them from his hands and broke them. He cleaned them slowly and deliberately.

'Tell me about the knife, please.'

I sighed, my stomach knotted with conflicting emotions, my thoughts tumbling over each other.

'It had blood on the blade. Fresh blood.'

Tunheim clapped his hands together happily. 'Now this is good. This is very good, Mr Callum. Ah, but . . .' he manufactured a frown, '. . . I have to wonder why you didn't bring this knife to the police. But no matter, for now. You can tell me that later. For now, you know where this *grindaknivur* is?

I nodded. 'Park where I tell you then follow me.'

I wanted to throw up. I hadn't, *hadn't*, killed Aron Dam. The sleepless nights had provided me with the right answer, in the end. I had been sure, but Tunheim had confirmed it. My stomach burned with acid that threatened to rise up and scald my throat. I hadn't killed Aron Dam. I hadn't killed anyone. Yet.

Nils Dam was tied up, freezing to death in the old whaling station. Fucking Tunheim and his games. Couldn't he have told me this the night before? Couldn't he have let me know before … Christ, I had to get to Nils Dam. What the hell had I done?

Tunheim walked beside me, chattering nonsense about his wife, the Danish cops and the man in the red raincoat with his hood up. All I heard was Nils Dam's name over and over again.

We got onto the path towards my shack – the well-worn, often-trodden track towards what had become my home. The path that Nils Dam had taken to throw blood over my door. Blood.

The three stones lay where I knew they would be, but I still stopped sharply, causing Tunheim to almost bump into me.

'Here? You left the knife here? This was not very wise, Mr Callum. Show me where exactly.'

I pointed dumbly and Tunheim pulled a pair of leather gloves from the pocket of his coat. They weren't exactly the kind of thing that Nicoline Munk would have used, but the inspector seemed happy enough. He crouched down and moved the stones aside before raking at the earth.

After a few moments, he looked up at me questioningly. He rummaged around for a few moments more before standing up, looking far from pleased.

'There is nothing here, Mr Callum. Have you made some kind of mistake?'

Chapter 50

Tunheim and I had walked no more than a few yards towards the shack when we were interrupted. The sound of an approaching car, then a door slamming, made us both turn towards the road. Moments later we saw two heads bob into view. The sight caused both of us to swear under our breath.

Climbing the hill, striding out in unison, were Nymann and Kielstrup. The inspector led the way, his black leather jacket incongruous against nature's greens and browns. The sergeant followed behind, all business-like, giving the impression that he was longing to board the first flight back to civilization.

'Oh fucking wonderful. The cavalry arrives.' Tunheim managed to smile and swear at the same time. He even gave a friendly wave to the approaching Danes.

His seeming affability was not returned. Nymann looked furious. He spoke in English, presumably for my benefit.

'What are you doing here, Tunheim?'

'In Torshavn? My father's fault, Inspector. He was a kindly man and a hard worker, but he lacked any ambition to live anywhere else. I think I caught the disease from him. I was born here and I will die here.'

Nymann leaned forward from the waist, trying to get a closer look at the imbecile in front of him. 'Why are you at this man's home? You are not part of this case and I would take a serious view of anything that interfered with my investigation. I am sure your superiors would too.'

Tunheim's arms spread, the misunderstood man. 'My superiors. There are so many of them, Inspector, that it would take a month to canvass their opinions on such a matter. But let me assure you, the last thing I would want to do is intrude on your case. My God, this is a murder inquiry, after all. I would not even know where to start investigating such a thing. That is why we are all so glad that you and the sergeant are here to take charge.'

I saw the glance that flashed between Nyman and Kielstrup. *They* were Tunheim's superiors. Or so they thought.

'Yes, okay, okay. But why are you here then?'

'A local matter, Inspector. The kind of thing I am more used to dealing with. Mr Callum's property was vandalized.'

'What?'

Tunheim's glasses were in his hand and he was carefully wiping the lenses. 'Yes. Someone threw blood over his door. I am taking it very seriously.'

I didn't let anything show on my face. Least of all my astonishment that Tunheim knew about the incident.

'When did this happen, Mr Callum?' Nymann's gaze switched back and forth between Tunheim and me.

'A couple of days ago. I cleaned it off.'

'This ... this should have been reported. To me.'

Tunheim slipped his spectacles back on his head. 'And it will be, Inspector. As soon as I return to the station. It was most likely someone not happy that Mr Callum had been released from custody. Like yourself, Inspector.'

Nymann's eyes narrowed. 'Are you accusing me of putting blood on that door?'

'Of course, not. What an idea. Someone who, like you, was not happy that Mr Callum was not still locked up. We do not get many murders here. It makes people nervous. Then they can do stupid things.'

Nymann sighed theatrically. 'And that is the only reason you are here, Inspector Tunheim?'

'It is.'

'And you know nothing else?'

'I don't.'

'Then you may as well leave, as I need to interview Mr Callum.'

'Actually, I would like to stay, Inspector. It is unlikely I will ever investigate a murder, but I'd be grateful to learn anything I can from experts like you and the sergeant. It is an opportunity I may not get again.'

Nymann stared at Tunheim for an age before shaking his head and turning his back on him without a word. From across the Dane's shoulder, I caught the hint of a smile on Broddi's face. He and I were now evidently complicit in our lies to the Danes.

'Mr Callum, you will answer questions without your lawyer being present, yes?'

'That depends on the questions. Why don't we see how it goes?'

Nymann didn't like that, but Tunheim did – I could tell by his smirk.

'Okay. I have witnesses saying that you have been violent during your time in the Faroe Islands. Is that correct?'

'You know it is. I had an altercation with Aron Dam in the Cafe Natur the night before he was killed. It was brought up in court.'

'You are correct, of course. And there was at least one other occasion, no?'

I remembered Toki standing outside the police station, his finger jabbing towards me. 'There was a fight in the fish farm where I worked. But you already knew that. Martin Hojgaard told you about it.'

He sneered. 'And he was not the only one. Your victim did so too. And he has told us about other occasions in the workplace where you threatened him or barged into him while he was carrying out his duties. Do you deny this?'

I had known for little more than twenty minutes that I was, beyond doubt, innocent of the murder of Aron Dam. Now I was being neatly fitted up for it. I was far from happy about that, but I was far calmer than I might have been. Toki's claims surely wouldn't stand up in court. The likelihood was that Nymann knew that too. He was here to rattle my cage.

'I do deny it, Inspector. Is there anything else?'

'Yes, Mr Callum, there is. Did you ever publicly threaten to harm Aron Dam?'

What the hell was this?

'No.'

'Are you sure. Think carefully. This might be very important.'

I was thinking carefully. Very.

'I didn't do that, no.'

'It is important because if you had publicly proclaimed your intention to harm, or even kill, Mr Dam . . . well that would be very injurious to your case, don't you think?'

'That is a question I won't answer, Inspector. Not without my lawyer. This interview is over.'

Nymann nodded curtly then smiled. 'As you wish, Mr Callum. We shall arrange for your lawyer to be present. Soon.'

He had rattled my cage. Mission accomplished.

'So, Inspector Tunheim.' He turned to face him. 'I hope you learned something.'

Broddi scratched at his head and then slipped his glasses from his nose. 'Well I think I did, Inspector. I think I did. I will need to sit down and analyse it to make sure. But it was a lesson, for sure. For now I will stay and examine Mr Callum's door.'

Nymann and the silent Kielstrup grinned at each other and turned back down the hill without another word.

'So what *did* you learn, Broddi?' I asked as we watched the Danes depart.

'That although you are a fool, you are perhaps not the biggest fool currently on the Faroes.'

'Is that all?'

'And that we need somewhere quieter for you and I to have a proper talk.'

Chapter 51

'You do understand, Mr Callum, that you are better off talking to me than to the Danes?'

We were in an interview room – actually probably the only room that happened to be available – in the little police station at Miðvágur on Vagar. Tunheim, of course, knew the cop in charge and was related to him in some way that I couldn't follow. Whatever their connection, it guaranteed that no word of our meeting would leak back to Nymann and Kielstrup. That suited both of us – except for one little thing on my part: it took me an hour further away from Nils Dam, an additional sixty minutes during which I could do nothing about whatever state he was in.

'Yes.' The words fell limply from my lips. I sounded defeated for a good reason.

'Good, Mr Callum. Good. We are in some trouble, you and I. It is good that you realize it.'

Tunheim's raincoat hung over the chair behind him, his shirt open at the neck and his tie slung low and to the side. He sat back in his chair and regarded me wearily. He was a laid-back and patient man but I knew I was testing that patience.

'So where is it? Where is the knife?' Tunheim was pulling his right hand distractedly through the stubble on his face, making him look tired and older.

'I don't know. I wish I did.'

Tunheim rubbed at his eyes before getting to his feet and opening a small window located above head-height on the far wall, which admitted the room's only natural light. He stood in front of it for a moment, enjoying the breeze on his face, then went over to where his jacket was slung over the other chair and fished around in the pockets. He emerged with a packet of cigarettes, a lighter and a guilty expression.

'Are you allowed to smoke in here, Broddi?'

He flinched at my use of his first name. Apparently the opportunity for informality had passed with the discovery that the knife wasn't where it should have been. Now it sounded like I was using it to prove I had something on him. Maybe I was.

'No, I'm not allowed to smoke in here, Mr Callum. And neither is anyone else, so don't bother asking for one. You know, I'm not so worried about my friend Berint catching me as I am my wife finding out. She would kill me, and there's been enough of that, do you not think?'

Back by the window, Tunheim's lighter spat once, then again. He drew deep on the cigarette, with the fervour of a man deprived. He filled his lungs then sighed contentedly.

'So who could know where the *grindaknivur* was hidden? I do not think someone found it by accident. I cannot believe in such a coincidence.'

I'd been thinking of little else since we'd discovered its absence. That and Nils Dam were wrestling for space in my head. The man and the knife were rolling around until he inevitably had it inside him and I could see him in front of me, gasping for life, begging for air.

'I don't know. I didn't mention it to anyone. Why would I have done? I thought it might—'

'You thought it might put you in prison?' Tunheim blew smoke in my direction. 'You know that you were interfering with a murder investigation? Now, I'm not a big-city homicide cop, as you know, Mr Callum, but I know enough to know that is very serious. Just trying to hide the knife is enough to put you in prison.'

I nodded slowly. 'Yes. And I'm not a policeman, *Broddi,* but I know that withholding information from the principal investigating officers is pretty serious too.'

Tunheim inhaled some smoke and held it in his mouth, sucking in his cheeks and staring at me. He slipped his glasses off and was wiping at them with his shirt before his mouth opened again and let the last gasps of the smoke slip free.

'I am a simple man, Mr Callum. A small policeman on a small island. I live a quiet life and don't expect much. But I have a guilty secret. I watch lots of American crime programmes on my television. It drives my wife *crazy*. But it is good because I learn things. Like language. Let me try something . . .' He shoved his glasses back on and looked at me. 'Don't fuck with me, Mr Callum. You fuck with me and I will fuck with you.' A long pause and a stare. 'Did I get that right?'

'Close enough.'

'Good. Now, who knows about the knife?'

'I told you, I don't know. I *did not* tell anyone. I couldn't have told anyone, even if I'd wanted to.'

Tunheim dragged a hand through his hair as he took another deep draw on his cigarette. 'Okay, *John*. Why don't you tell me some other stuff then? Why don't you tell me about Liam Dornan?'

My heart sank. This wasn't what I needed. My mind's eye saw Liam sitting next to Nils Dam, both with their heads slumped forward. Both dead. I had to get out of here and back to Torshavn.

'Broddi, I haven't smoked in twenty years. How about we both break the law and you give me one?'

He hesitated. 'Like a last cigarette for the condemned man?'

'Something like that.'

Tunheim threw me the packet and I took one from it. It was clenched between my lips when I joined him at the window. 'Let's see if I remember how to do this.' I dipped my head and he fired his lighter. I inhaled and the smoke hit the back of my throat, causing me to cough ridiculously. It stung but I liked that, deserved it.

I was nodding my head, eyes shut. Memories of nervous smoking behind the school bike-shed, pals on guard-duty to warn of approaching teachers. Teachers. I'd never have thought back then that I'd become one of them. And of course, I never should have.

'Liam Dornan was a pupil in one of my English classes.' I blew out almost as much smoke as I'd exhaled. 'He was the class clown. A really bright kid, that was the annoying thing. He could have been anything he wanted to be, but all he wanted was to show off, act the big man, make everyone else laugh and make me look as bad as possible.'

I took another artless draw on the cigarette.

'I tried with him. I really did. I took him aside and tried to talk to him. Man-to-man kind of stuff. I'd been where he was. Rough area of town. Ran with some bad kids, did some stupid stuff, used my fists rather than my brains. I told him all that and he threw it back in my face. Laughed at me. What did I know? Nothing, as it turned out.

'I just couldn't get through to him. So I tried coming on tough, threatening him with this and that, but I knew I could really do nothing. Even the threats gave him more power. I wanted to knock his head off. I called his parents in but they couldn't care less. Not their problem when he was in school. That's what I was getting paid for.

'And of course the worse he played up and got away with it, the more the other kids thought they could do the same. It's the way of it. So they got louder and more out-of-hand. I came down on as many of them as I could, but it is like putting out forest fires. While you're busy extinguishing one, another's bursting into flames behind your back.'

I sucked on the cigarette, drawing the smoke down my throat and letting it singe my lungs.

'So one night I was walking home. I'd met an old friend and had a couple of pints, not enough to make me drunk. I was cutting through a housing scheme, a bit of a suicidal short cut, but the beers told me it was okay. I heard some kind of scuffle, the kind of thing that makes your blood run cold when it's that time of night and no one else is around. It was the sound of feet, kicking. And a muffled scream. I stood still, listening. Then I heard it again. I knew the sound well enough: someone was getting a doing.

'A bit of me told me it was none of my business. Probably just kids. But I went to look anyway. I got halfway round the side of a building when this guy came out to meet me. They'd obviously heard me coming and he was the advance party, sent to scare me off. I knew him. A big waster known as Chilli Ferguson, who had left school about four or five years before. And he obviously knew me.

'He was all, "Hey, teacher man. Here's a lesson for you. Get to fuck." I didn't. I pushed past him, but a couple of yards later, I saw him. Liam Dornan. Lying on the ground with three guys standing round him. I recognized all three of them, all ex-pupils from the school I taught at. Shug Faulds, Tam Taylor and Chick Welsh. Real bad guys. I saw at least two knives glinting in the moonlight. Welsh was still swinging a boot into Liam's guts.

'Of course, I went to help, but Ferguson was behind me and put a knife to my neck. Just held it there. Faulds and Taylor turned to me as well. Basically they told me it was none of my business. That Liam was getting a kicking because he had it coming, because he was a cheeky wee shite. That if I hung around then I'd get what he was getting and he'd get it worse. They'd stick him. Stab him. And if I went to the cops then they'd make sure Liam died.

'He was looking at me. Pleading with me with his eyes. He tried to beg me, but Welsh just kicked him in the stomach again. I walked away. They were sniggering as I left. When I close my eyes I can still hear the sound of it. Those little bastards laughing at me while Liam squealed.'

I exhaled hard, ridding myself of the breath that was curdled up inside me, and replaced it with a lungful of nicotine. Tunheim watched me calmly, taking it all in.

'I walked away. Maybe a couple of hundred yards. The whole thing eating at me. Hating myself. And then I couldn't take it. Couldn't do it. I knew those guys well enough to know they were bad bastards. Liam was a troublemaker and a pain in the arse, but the others . . . they were serious. I turned and I ran back. There was a plank of wood lying on the ground and I picked it up, ready to use it. But they were gone. All of them. Liam too.

'The next day it was on the news. A boy found dead. Beaten up. Stabbed and tortured. Liam Dornan. I threw up when I heard it.

'When all the details came out, I threw up again. He had fifty-four separate knife wounds on him. They had set fire to his feet. They had pulled out fingernails. They had beat his face so that he only had one eye left. They had broken all of his fingers. One at a time.

'He was a kid. He was one of my kids. They tortured him then they killed him. And I didn't stop them.'

There was a tear trying to leak from my eye but I fought it back. I didn't have the right to cry. This hadn't happened to me: I had no right to feel sorry for myself. Tunheim could see my struggle and in his eyes there was a sympathy that I hated.

He took a final draw on his cigarette, extinguishing the end with his fingers before throwing the stub out of the window.

'A sad story, Mr Callum. Very sad. And I feel your pain. But I need to tell you that I have a friend in the police in Scotland. An inspector like me. He came here two of the times the Scotland football team came to play the Faroe Islands. Your team did not win. I wanted to know more about what happened next in this case. Information I could not find on the Internet or from newspaper reports. So I asked him. He didn't know everything about your case but he knew another officer that did, and I got him to ask for me. Perhaps you will want to remember that before you tell me what happened next.'

If Broddi Tunheim was my only ally, I had no need for enemies. There was a clock on the wall behind his head, and I kept looking at it, making mental calculations about how long Nils had been left on his own, how long it would take me to get back, how quickly I could get out of this room. Tunheim would notice soon enough. He would wonder why I was so anxious.

'What happened next was that I got a phone call. A muffled voice warning me that if I went to the cops then I'd die and so would those around me. I went to the police anyway. Ferguson, Faulds, Taylor and Welsh were arrested and eventually put on trial. My windows were broken, my mother was threatened and my little sister was scared shitless by some thug wearing a hoodie and a scarf over his face. I still testified. But it wasn't enough. They were acquitted on a lack of evidence. After all, even if it had been them that I'd seen with Liam, even if I'd seen anyone at all, I couldn't be sure what happened after I ran away. That was what the defence said. They walked free.'

Tunheim had found another reason to clean his spectacles, breathing on them and wiping them cleaner than clean. 'Mr Callum, that is the information that I got from the Internet. I want to know what happened to the kids that killed Liam.'

'They weren't kids!' I was shouting at him. 'They were grown men. Sure, they were old before their time because of what they did and the environment they were brought up in. Maybe it wasn't their fault that they were like that. But it was their fault what they did to Liam Dornan.'

Tunheim nodded thoughtfully, a hand raised in apology or a request for calm. 'Okay. Okay. So tell me what happened to them.'

'They were set free. They laughed as they walked out of court.'

I heard his tone change. Impatience. Rising anger. 'And *then*?'

I took a last look at the clock over his shoulder. It was six hours since I'd left Nils Dam.

'The four of them were later attacked. Separately. They got off lightly.'

Tunheim sighed. 'One had his knee broken and it was said he would never walk properly again. The second never went to the police or hospital, but was found bound, locked up for hours in darkness. The third went to hospital with internal injuries that left him urinating blood, and also had a broken ankle. He said he fell down some stairs. The fourth was found tied up and gagged on the very spot where you saw Liam Dornan. Local teenagers found him tied up, knew who he was, and beat him.'

'Like I said, they got off lightly.'

'My friend in Scotland, he says that the police there think you did that to those men. In fact, they are sure that you did. Did you?'

I thought of Nils Dam, strung up by his wrists, perhaps freezing to death, maybe dying of thirst.

'No,' I told Tunheim. 'I have no idea who did it.'

Chapter 52

On the drive back into Torshavn after our very unofficial interview in Miðvágur, Tunheim continued to press me for information, albeit in his usual obtuse way. He was clearly worried about the hole he'd dug for himself by keeping things from the Danes. I could have consoled him by letting him know the size of the hole that I myself had dug. A man-sized hole that was getting deeper with every minute I was away from it. But I couldn't say a word.

Now there was no going back, for either of us, and we were in this together whether we liked it or not. Our tacitly understood pact was an uneasy one. Tunheim was stretching his code of ethics to overlook the fact that I had buried the *grindaknivur* and tampered with evidence. I had to accept that he wouldn't tell the Danes about the piece of evidence that would show my innocence.

The inspector and I were up shit creek without a paddle between us.

'Are you in a hurry to get back to town, Mr Callum? A hot date, perhaps?'

I jumped slightly at his words, a twitch that he couldn't have failed to notice. I must have been staring at the clock on the dashboard, watching the digital display race round, and willing the car to keep pace.

'Eh? Yeah. Something like that. A date.'

'With young Karis? A very pretty girl for sure. How does her father feel about it? Esmundur might not be too pleased, I'm thinking.'

'You know her father?'

Tunheim laughed at me. 'This is Torshavn, Mr Callum. Of course I know him. Everyone does. He is a leader in the community and a man of considerable influence. Esmundur Lisberg is a very well-respected man, but he does have . . . what you might call old-fashioned views. An outsider dating his beloved daughter? I am thinking he would not approve – even if that person hadn't been accused of a murder.'

'I'm thinking you're probably right.'

Karis. I didn't know when or if I'd see her again. She was volatile at the best of times, but now . . . She obviously had no idea whether she could trust me or not, and I couldn't entirely blame her. She had been placed at the heart of this whole mess with Aron, and it was the talk of the town. When I'd seen her last it was obvious how on-edge she was. I couldn't know what she would do.

'The Danes will want to speak to you again. Nymann is like a dog digging for a bone. And you are the only bone that he can see. Let me sleep easy tonight, Mr Callum. Tell me that there is nothing else that I need to know. Nothing else that Nymann can find.'

I glanced over at him but his eyes were fixed on the road ahead. He was aware that I'd looked, though; I had no doubt about that.

'There's nothing, Inspector. The sooner that you or Nymann find out who killed Aron Dam the better.'

His response was slow in coming. He raised his eyebrows in slight surprise and pursed his lips.

'Interesting, Mr Callum. But you disappoint me.'

I didn't dare look. Or breathe. Tunheim had an annoying habit of knowing more than he was letting on. I had to keep my voice level. 'Why's that, Inspector?'

Another infuriating pause. 'Because after all we have meant to each other I thought that you would want *me* to find out who murdered Aron Dam. No? Very disappointing.'

We were on the outskirts of Torshavn and all I wanted was to get out of that car. Having Tunheim as my only ally was like sailing the ocean on the back of a shark. I needed to find a way out of this situation that didn't involve being drowned or eaten.

'Could you just drop me off here please, Broddi?'

'Really? I can drive to near your house. It is no problem.'

'No. Thank you. I am going to go for a drink first.'

'Ah. Okay, I understand. And I take no offence at you not inviting me to join you. A police officer is rarely a welcome drinking companion. Particularly if you are on a murder charge.'

'How insightful. Do they teach you that at police school?'

Tunheim smiled. 'Police school? Ah, if only we had the luxury of such things here. Everything I know I learned at my father's knee or by watching the tide. No matter how much the wind blows, Mr Callum, no matter how hard it rains, the tide will go out and it will come back in again. It is all you need to know.'

'You're full of shit, Broddi.'

He popped his glasses back on with a satisfied chuckle to himself. 'Not at all, Mr Callum. Much of it is shit, as you say, but some of it is wisdom. The difficult bit for you is working out which is which.'

'Yeah, I get that. Okay, here is fine.'

Tunheim pulled in at the kerb and turned to look at me. 'Don't go far, Mr Callum. And remember who is on your side.'

I waited until the car had pulled out of sight then changed direction, my stride lengthening, towards the street where I'd parked the rental Peugeot, desperately resisting the urge to break into a run.

The rutted track to the old whaling station was overgrown and bumpy, testing the Peugeot's suspension and my nerves. I could see the three washed-out red buildings growing larger against the background of the rutted hillside across the fjord. Their fading corrugated-iron walls and peeling green roofs were testament to a time lost. Further evidence to its abandonment lay on the approaches: corroded pieces of hulking machinery, cogged wheels and handles rusted fast. Tarnished metal supports lay where they had fallen, propped up by lichen-covered rocks.

Everything reeked of decay, from the obsolete machinery and crumbling, mossy walls to the discarded jawbones of the sea giants whose bodies had been processed here. Oxidized canisters as tall as the roof and a huge orange-coloured boiler as big as a double-decker bus. Massive chain links, great blackened cylindrical tanks and an enormous rusty contraption that I took to be a steam-powered bone saw. Everything was whale-sized.

Hojgaard told me there had been plans to turn the place into a maritime museum but they had been shelved. There had once been over two hundred of these whaling stations around the world, all built to the same Norwegian model. This was the only one left standing in the northern hemisphere.

Inside, I knew there were the blubber tanks, steam engines and the lingering stench of death. And inside the middle building was Nils Dam.

I forced open the heavy iron door as slowly as I could, but it only had to budge an inch before iron echoes rang through the building. It creaked and groaned like a haunted castle, where every ghost was the swimming carcass of a whale. Only the dead wouldn't be able to hear it.

His shadow loomed against a wall, thrown there by the sinking sun. The still figure of a man on the end of his noose, either awaiting or having met his executioner. He hadn't stirred at the raucous opening of the door, nor at the sound of my footsteps across the stone floor. I'd been away too long. I'd left him freezing and without food or water.

His head slumped like a day-old baby. I reached my arm out towards him fearfully and placed a hand flat on his chest. I had to hold it a few moments to be sure it wasn't just my own pulse I was feeling, but then I knew. His heart was beating.

I slapped his face. Not too hard. Cruel to be kind. After a second slap, he stirred, a wet whimpering sounding in his throat.

I'd picked up bottled water on the way over and held it up to his lips. His eyes were still closed but when I gently poured the water into the corner of his mouth, an instinct kicked in and he opened up to receive it, his dry tongue seeking it out. I let him have a mouthful and he choked it down, spluttering into life.

After a minute or two I gave him some more, this lot going down easily and greedily. I felt his wrists and the chill of him crept into me; it was like shaking hands with a corpse. Turning away, I busied myself with the oil drum, placing some more wood inside and preparing to relight it while he slowly regained his senses.

'Fuck you,' he managed hoarsely, the words barely travelling the few yards to where I stood.

I shrugged. 'Up to you. Do you want me to light this for you or not?'

He looked at the drum longingly through heavy-lidded eyes and gave the faintest of nods.

I dropped a match and the wood soon crackled, heat building in the old drum. Picking it up, still cool enough to touch, I placed it near to Dam. He swayed towards it, seeking the warmth and arching out against the pressure of the rope that kept his hands above him.

I'd bought sandwiches along with the water and tore one of them into chunks, offering the bread, ham and cheese up to his mouth. He bit at them, at once resentful and grateful, wolfing down the lot and eyeing up the other sandwich hungrily. I didn't let him have it.

He was alive, and although that answered one question it led to others. What the hell was I going to do with him? How was I going to get out of this mess? I had brought him to this place because I needed information that would prove my innocence;

now I needed information that would allow us both to escape from this situation.

He was staring at the remaining sandwich. 'Give it to me. I am hungry. You cannot starve me.'

'Can't I?'

'Please.'

I placed it in its plastic wrapping on the floor in front of him.

'Nils, you need to tell me what I want to know. You want the sandwich? You want to be warm? You want to ever leave this place alive? Then tell me.'

I saw the look on his face when I mentioned him not getting out alive. It scared him. Almost as much as it scared me. I still had to push it further.

'There are some things I'm sure of and some I'm not. You're going to tell me everything. If you lie, I'll hurt you. Understand?'

He glared at me, sullenly and silently. I got closer and louder, roaring in his face. 'Understand?'

Nils nodded wearily, his eyes sliding over in resignation. It wasn't enough for me though.

'Then say it!'

His eyes flicked open again, his loathing clear. 'I understand.'

'Okay. Good. Let's talk about your brother. About why he took against me the way he did. It wasn't just jealousy about Karis. Aron didn't like me, did he? He didn't like me at all.'

'No. He did not like you.'

'So here's what I'm wondering, Nils. Why? After all, I had barely spoken to him. Yet he set out to get me. And you carried it on. Or were you in on it from the start?'

His eyes closed over and his head moved slowly, wearily, side to side. 'No.'

'Just Aron, then? But you knew about it.'

He nodded reluctantly. It wasn't enough, I needed to hear it. 'You knew what he was doing. Tell me!'

'Yes.'

'You know he vandalised the house that I live in, the one that belongs to the Hojgaard family.'

Nils looked hard at me, making a decision. He made the right one and nodded.

'Okay. So you know that Aron cut my water supply and left the dead sheep and the raven. Right?'

After a faintly defiant pause, he let his head bob in agreement.

'Good. And you know why he did it, don't you?'

He just shook his head dismissively, sneering at me. I took a step towards him, my face fierce. It was enough.

'Okay. Yes. I know,' he said.

'So why?'

'He wanted to scare you away. Make you leave.'

My voice hardened, my frustration obvious. '*Why?*'

He hesitated, the answer stuttering on his tongue, and I had to resist the temptation to grab him by the throat and choke the words out.

'He . . . he think you should not be here. You are an outsider. A foreigner. He hated you.'

'He hated me because I'm an intruder? A foreigner?'

Nils nodded, but I knew he was lying. My foreignness might have been part of it, but it wasn't the whole truth. Something rang false and I knew what it was.

'So what about you, Nils? You feel the same way about outsiders? Hate them? Not trust them?'

He glared at me through his discomfort and fear. 'Yes. Yes I feel same.'

I felt a familiar rush of anger surge through me, a rage borne of frustration and injustice. Stepping forward, I crashed the back of my hand across his face, my knuckles groaning as they caught his cheekbone.

'I told you not to lie to me. Don't do that again.'

Nils yelped in surprise, the pain leaping out of him suddenly and pitifully. I felt a surge of guilt, but swallowed it down quickly like bitter medicine, to get it past my throat before I gagged on it. Before he could recover, I drew my hand back the other way, my open palm slapping hard against his other cheek.

'If you don't like foreigners then why are you so thick with Serge Gotteri? All those secret meetings that you think no one knows about. It's true, isn't it?'

He stared, maybe trying to work out if I was simply guessing. His eyes were narrowed and he chewed at the corner of his lip. If he was trying to decide whether or not I was serious then I could help him with that. I slapped him again, harder this time, catching him just under his left eye.

'Yes!' he yelped before I could repeat the question. 'Okay. Yes. I had meetings with Gotteri.'

Part of me breathed a sigh of relief. Another part wanted to hit him again.

'Now you'll tell me the truth about Aron, too. About why he hated me.' I paused. 'About Karis.'

His eyes widened and I saw fear flash across his face before he could hide it. There was something else, something that was scaring him even more than I was. Resentment rose in my stomach like bile, its bitterness alarming me. I had no choice but to up my threat.

'You will tell me, Nils. The only question is whether you tell me before I hurt you or after. Do you understand?'

'Fuck you.' It was defiant but feeble. I doubted that he'd even managed to convince himself. I willed him to give in and tell me, not to force me to go beyond myself. Out of necessity, I kicked him hard, on the point of his ankle bone.

'*Do you understand?*'

He recoiled at the pain then gave a slight nod, shamefaced and hurt. In turn, I nodded my head more forcibly, displaying satisfaction that we were getting somewhere. I was making a show of being more confident about that than I really was. Inside, I knew it was time to gamble.

'Now tell me, Nils. Tell me what happened between your brother and Karis.'

His eyes slid closed as if he were trying to hide from me. Hide from the question and the answer. I wouldn't, and couldn't, let him. My right leg shot out and booted him in the shin, forcing his eyes wide open. '*Tell me.*'

I couldn't quite read his face. There was fear and loathing of me – that much was obvious. But there was more, much more. Guilt? About what he knew, perhaps – or, I hoped, about what he was going to tell me about his brother. Whenever I mentioned Karis's name, I could see a reaction in him.

He looked at me and I knew he was close to cracking, I could feel it. There was some argument going on in his head, but he was on the verge of spilling his guts. His mouth opened and he hesitated, my heart pausing, but then his trap closed again. He let his head slump onto his chest, swaying side to side as he did so. Hope shrivelled inside me, giving way to anger.

Don't make me do this, Nils. Don't make me. I went up close, close enough that my mouth was just a couple of inches from his ear. Last chance. 'Last chance. Tell me. I know you want to.'

He shook his head, eyes screwed closed, knowing what it would mean. I took a step behind him so that he couldn't see me even if he did open his eyes. My head was in my hands, my fingers pushing through my hair; I was silently screaming, wishing the inevitable away.

Forcing myself to be furious at his stubbornness, I hurried to the other side of the room before I could change my mind. I picked up the items one by one, the metal and the wood scraping across the floor, the noise carrying directly to Nils, as I'd intended. His eyes shot open.

I advanced on him, slower now, giving him time to take it in, to understand the consequences of his silence. When I was in front of him, I held the items up, quite unnecessarily. Then dropped them noisily at his feet, before returning to fetch the next one.

The harpoon. The metal oar. The corroded chain. The rusty knife.

They bounced and rattled and rang when they hit the floor. My face was as impassive as I could manage. I wanted him to read on it whatever he feared most.

Inside me was different. Inside I was churning to the point of vomiting.

This man was standing between me and what I needed to know. He could have given it up so easily and saved us both a lot of pain, but instead he was choosing selfish, pointless resistance. He was making this harder than it needed to be. Harder for me, worse for him. I hated him for it. The son of a bitch was actually going to make me do this.

It was growing inside me. The rage and the readiness to act on it. My mind was becoming black, a darkness closing out the light like a dirty fog snuffing out a church candle. I could feel myself hurtling reluctantly toward a place I'd sworn never to visit again.

When I spoke I barely recognized my own voice, and I didn't like what I heard.

'You can stop me at any time. But only stop me if you really intend to tell me the truth. If you stop me and disappoint me then it will be worse. I told you that you could tell me before or after the pain. Now, it will be after. After how much is up to you.'

I reached down and picked the knife from the floor, its blade having lost the edge that would once have sliced through whale as if through butter. Still, its jagged, tarnished frame would serve my purpose, even if all it did was produce an uglier wound.

Nils began mumbling dissent, incoherent pleas that were wasted on me. I couldn't hear him above the quarrelling voices in my own head. *Do it. Don't. No choice. Don't be that person. Not again. No choice. Don't do this to him or yourself. Hurt him. Slice him.*

Nils had been switching his gaze fearfully between the knife and my eyes, but my face must have changed, betraying my decision. *Hurt him. Slice him.* I knew he'd recognized me for what I was; that he had seen inside me and understood what I was capable of. He was suddenly terrified. Almost as frightened of what I might do as I was.

In a matter of seconds I would be either the person I wanted to be or the one I had tried to run away from. Images tumbled through my head, faces fighting for space in a waking nightmare. *Do it. Don't. There is no other choice. Be better than this. You're better than this. I* am *better than this. But there really isn't any other way. No way out.*

I drew the blade across his throat, its leading edge dull with golden browns, rusty and old and ragged against his skin. Pressing harder, I watched it bite his flesh and saw his eyes widen before my mind closed over, the last remaining light choked out by the darkness inside.

Chapter 53

The beer in the Manhattan was cold, wet and alcoholic. It was all I needed it to be.

I'd only ever been in the place twice before, and on those occasions had found it dark and depressing, but on this night it fitted the bill just fine. My head was racing, my thought-processes out of control, with a dangerous edge that needed to be blunted with booze. Beer would do for starters, then I'd see what whisky or vodka could do to quell the nausea in my stomach. There would be no sleep otherwise, no rest either.

In the blink of an eye, the beer was gone and I needed another. I handed over a ten-krónur note, a slight tremor obvious to me, if not to the barman. Downing a third of the pint before I returned to my corner didn't seem to help. I sat, hands on the table, back against the chair in contemplation. I thought about holes that I'd dug and whether I'd ever learn when to stop digging. I wondered, too, if this current hole was too big to climb out of.

'Do you mind if I join you?'

I looked up and saw Nicoline Munk. The petite forensic examiner was holding a pint of beer in her right hand, a generous mouthful already drunk. Her curly auburn hair was tied loosely behind her and she wore a jumper under her waterproof jacket. She must have seen the doubt on my face in reaction to her question. She wasn't a cop, but she was cop enough to scare me. But maybe a cop was what I really needed.

'It's okay,' she held the beer up in front of her and reading my mind, 'I'm off duty. Can I get you one?'

In my panic, I thought maybe she had followed me from the whaling station; but that made no sense. I'd already be in handcuffs and she'd be extracting DNA not offering beer.

'I'd rather be alone, and anyway I've just got myself a beer.'

Munk looked at my glass and then my face. She must have decided that I looked thirsty. 'I'll get you another one.'

She took off her jacket and dropped it onto the chair opposite and made for the bar before I could say otherwise. She returned quickly, two drinks in hand, and placed them in front of us as she sat down.

She offered her glass in a toast, but I kept mine firmly in front of me.

'I hope you don't mind me joining you.' She was fiddling with her hair. 'No one in town seems very keen to talk to me, because of who I am or what I do. I don't think they dislike Danes, they just don't like Danish police coming in and taking over. I saw you coming in on your own and figured that we are probably two people that no one else wants to drink with, so maybe . . .'

'Are you not in breach of some regulations by talking to me?'

She shrugged. 'Only if we talk about the investigation. And we're not. And anyway, no matter what Inspector Nymann might think, I am very thorough at my job. If you had been at that scene, I would know it.'

'I thought we weren't talking—'

'We're not. We're talking about how thorough I am. It is different.'

'Okay. But just so you know, I wasn't at the scene.' My mind was flashing to Tunheim and the webcam and the *grindaknivur*. Being innocent of the thing everyone thought I had done didn't necessarily make me blameless. Then I thought of Nils Dam. I was far from innocent.

'Like I said,' she was looking at me curiously, 'I know you weren't there. If you had been, I'd have found you.'

All I could think of was the evidence I must have left littered across the whaling station. Footprints. Fibres of clothing. Fingerprints on a rusty knife. Bloodstains.

Sitting next to this woman, I felt exposed. My fingers slowly curled into balled fists so as to hide from her view and my feet tucked behind me.

'How long have you been a CSI?' The words were out of me before I knew it, the kind of banal opening meant for a dull dinner party or an awkward date.

'Seven years. It's the only job I ever wanted to do so I feel lucky.'

'Examining crime scenes and dealing with dead bodies. That's what you always wanted to do?'

She took a sip of beer with a shy grin. 'Yes. Is it strange? I grew up watching *CSI* on television and thought "Wow. That is for me". So I did it. I love my job. How many people can really say that? You work at that fish farm, do you love it?'

This conversation was driving me crazy. Surely she could see I was unravelling as I sat there.

'No. it's just a job. It's not what I do.'

'You were a teacher, right?'

My eyes narrowed and Munk shrugged apologetically. 'I read your files.'

I emptied my glass and slammed it noisily back onto the table. 'Yes, I was a teacher. Another drink?'

It was asked out of nerves, and a courtesy that I couldn't afford, but the offer was out and couldn't be taken back. She nodded so I pushed my chair back, picking up her glass as she drained it, as well as my own. I held them up in front of me so the barman could see, and he began pouring two fresh pints.

What the hell was this all about? I didn't want to talk to this woman, tonight of all nights. I knew I should make an excuse and do my boozing elsewhere or not at all. She wouldn't need a magnifying glass to see my guilt. It was written all over my face. I had to pull myself together. Think. At least if she was here then I'd know she wasn't filling evidence bags at the whaling station and running DNA tests that would lead to me. I recalled advice about keeping your enemies closer.

Seeing a bottle of Lagavulin single malt behind the bar, I pointed at it. 'Two whiskies, *takk*. Large ones.'

There was a look of surprise on Munk's face when I turned up with the whisky as well as the beer, but she shrugged acceptingly. 'Sure, why not? Is it good stuff?'

'The best you will find on the Faroes. *Sláinte!*'

'*Skål*. But that's not saying much, is it? There isn't much of a selection here. It is the middle of nowhere.'

'It's not that bad. You get used to it.'

'I guess you can get used to anything. So did you love being a teacher?'

I sipped at the Lagavulin, savouring its huge tangs of peat and barley, and letting it sting the back of my throat. The hints of seaweed and smoke took me back to a school outing I'd supervised to Islay, where the malt is distilled, sitting round a campfire with singing kids and longing for a quiet dram once they'd all turned in for the night. 'Yes. I loved it. But that's past now.'

'I can hear in your voice that you did.'

Maybe she could hear that, and maybe she was just saying what she thought I wanted to hear. Either way, if she was playing me, I'd play along. For now. A diversion might help keep my mind from festering on things it shouldn't. Either that, or it would make everything worse.

Nicoline took her first sip of the Lagavulin and choked a little. 'Wow. That is so powerful. It tastes very . . . I don't know what it is.'

'It's peat.'

She sipped again but managed not to cough or choke this time. 'I like it. It is very smoky. And it is strong. I can handle it though. Do you miss teaching?'

Her questioning was driving me to distraction, tightening the wires even further. 'Yes. But like I said, it's done now. There's no going back there.'

'Because of what happened to the boy?'

I stopped halfway through a mouthful of beer, placing my glass back on the table. 'You ask a lot of questions.'

She heard the resentment in my voice, she couldn't fail to. 'I'm sorry. But I told you. Off duty. Want me to prove it?' She picked up the Lagavulin and threw it down her throat. She gulped down the last fiery drops and wiped her lips with the back of a finger. 'Do you want another one? Those were doubles, right?'

Maybe this hole was already so deep that I could dig no further. I picked up my whisky glass and nosed it, letting the peat and the sweetness tingle my nostrils. Then I followed her example and downed it.

'Do you know why I don't want to socialize with Nymann and Keilstrup?' She had returned with pints of beer and large whiskies. 'Two reasons. One, all they want to talk about is work and football. The case, the case, the case. And football. Two, they will try to get me into bed. Not together, you understand, but separately. No way. That is *not* going to happen.'

'You could report them. For harassment. Men shouldn't be allowed to get away with that kind of behaviour.'

She snorted in derision. 'No. That's not me. I can handle them. They are just little boys playing at being policemen. If they pushed it too hard I would cut their balls off. I have the equipment in my case.'

'Maybe you would, but it's not like that for other women.' I knew my voice was louder now. 'Maybe they can't fight back so easily.'

She looked at me oddly. 'Okay. That is true. Well, in that case, I'd cut the guy's balls off for them.'

I took a large mouthful of beer to drown my response and wash away a little of my growing rage.

A bell chimed at the front door and we both looked up to see a man blown in on the wind, a familiar, thirsty, unthreatening face that I'd seen propping up the bar in the Natur. Nicoline and I had noticed one another's wariness, the way we had both jumped at the noise, wondering who it was.

For a few moments, we fell into an uncomfortable silence, until she spoke again, words bursting out of her as if they'd been held captive.

'Okay, tell me something. If you want. You and Karis Lisberg. Is that still on?'

The question was so ridiculous in the circumstances that it almost made me laugh. Part of the answer hung in the stale air of the whaling station, a dilemma unresolved. I decided to give her the answer that would work best.

'Yes.'

I could hear my own lack of conviction. A deaf man could have heard it a mile away.

'Okay.' She nodded slightly and sipped long at her whisky. 'Just thought I'd ask. So I know where I stand. Here we are, two foreigners in a strange land. No one else to talk to.'

My paranoia level lifted another notch while my sense of certainty decreased by the same margin. My mind was in a mess and in no fit state to deal with this. I needed yet more deflection.

'Even if we were two strangers alone, should I not be scared that you'd cut my balls off?'

'No. You wouldn't need to worry about that. Trust me.'

Too many thoughts tripping over each other. Holes being dug and no way out. Faces flashing before my eyes, like the dreams I'd been having come to life. She was investigating me. She wasn't Karis. And Karis wasn't all that I thought.

'You live in that odd little house up in the hills, don't you? I am in the Hotel Hafnia. On a different floor from either Nymann or Keilstrup.'

'Nicoline . . .' I realized it was the first time I'd used her name. 'That wouldn't be a good idea.'

'What? Having a drink? Probably not, but it tastes good. And we really don't have anyone else to talk to. Or are you presuming something more?'

This was a game that I might have enjoyed in better circumstances, but right now it made me curl inside. 'No, I'm presuming nothing. Except innocence. That's how it works, right?'

She nodded, lips pursed in thought. 'That's how it's supposed to work, for sure. But my colleagues are presuming your guilt. I have a much more open mind.'

'Nicoline . . .'

She knocked back her glass of whisky. 'All gone. Your round.'

I wanted the booze, I knew that. Needed it. But I feared it too.

'Okay, my round. Last one though, okay?'

'Last one.'

As I stood at the bar waiting for the drinks to be poured, I juggled with wants and needs, responsibilities and guilt. Holes dug deep and tunnels that led out of them. I came to a decision of sorts. This game had to be played my way.

She was closer to me when I sat back down. This time we clinked glasses and she held my gaze.

'I hear you are very good,' I said. 'The local inspector, Tunheim, he says that you are the best.'

A hint of pink blushed on her cheek. 'Does he? I am good. I have been well trained. And I told you, I am very thorough.'

'It can't be easy working here though. With this much rain, crime scenes must be a nightmare.'

She tapped a finger to the side of her nose and slurred her words slightly: 'Only if you don't know what you are doing. A good examiner will always find the evidence, if it is there.'

'And you found some at the scene of Aron Dam's murder?'

It was her turn to be suspicious. She narrowed her eyes and stared accusingly. After a long pause, she looked around, but seeing no one else in the darkness of the Manhattan, apart from a couple of tired-looking older men in the far corner, replied: 'I did. I got some good-quality DNA and all I need is someone to match it with. It is always good to get someone to match with, don't you think?'

'I'm confused though. If you have DNA then what's the problem?'

She slid slightly closer. 'It is not that simple. People have rights. We cannot just DNA test everyone on the islands.'

For the first time in a long time I suddenly felt that something was going my way. I had an answer. Maybe an answer to the whole thing. It was time to play my ace.

'No, I guess you couldn't test everyone. But what if it has already been done?'

Nicoline straightened up and sat back, suddenly a little more sober. 'What? What do you mean?'

'People here have already been DNA tested. They profiled the entire population for a project meant to aid medical research into hereditary illnesses and that sort of thing.'

I could see the wheels going round in Nicoline's head, albeit slowed down by alcohol. 'Okay, yes. I have read about this. There was a paper ... but we couldn't ... the civil-liberties people would go crazy.'

I shrugged. 'I guess. But if the killer was tested then he will be in the national database.'

Nicoline brought her whisky to her mouth, rubbing the edge of the glass against her lips before taking the tiniest of sips. 'You are playing with me here. I shouldn't have told you I lifted DNA from the scene.'

'No. Probably not. But then maybe you were playing with me too.'

She ignored the accusation. 'This database ... I do not know if it is possible. But it is something to think about. In the morning.'

The game had to be ended. 'In the morning sounds perfect. And now I'm going to walk you to your hotel and then go home.'

She gave a theatrical pout then shrugged. 'But of course. What more could a girl want?'

I decided it was best for both of us that I didn't answer.

I walked Nicoline to the front door of the Hafnia, the sound of music and laughter coming up the hill to greet us from the Cafe Natur. She caught me looking towards its wooden shell and held my gaze to let me know that she'd done so. Whatever questions she had were left unasked.

Instead, she moved towards me and made to hug or kiss me. As her head neared mine, I moved it to the side and kissed her softly on the cheek. Nicoline turned and walked away, waving behind her without a backward glance.

I left, shaking my head at the craziness of it all. Even though I seemed to have acquired unlikely allies in Tunheim and now Nicoline, both would disappear like water off a mountaintop if they were to find out about Nils Dam. Worse than that, they would turn on me with the fury of trust betrayed.

I wanted to get back to the shack. I knew I wouldn't sleep, but I was exhausted and needed to lie down and rest my body if not my mind. But before the night turned into another day and another problem, I had one more visit to make.

Chapter 54

I wasn't sure that Barthel had heard me knock at his door above the sound of 'Heart-Shaped Box' booming out of his overpriced CD unit. Nirvana threatened to shake his house more than any Torshavn storm. It left me standing on the doorstep with nothing to do but try to shut out the words of Nils Dam that were torturing me. It was a losing battle.

I knocked again, louder this time, desperate to be inside and get some sanctuary from my own thoughts. Thankfully, this time he heard me. The volume subsided and the door was pulled back, Barthel standing there looking none-too-pleased at being disturbed and less so when he saw it was me. He let loose a sigh and shook his head. 'Come in. And hurry up before any nosey bastards see you.'

Tummas turned back into the house, leaving me to follow. A few strides took him to the CD player and the music was switched off. He dropped into a chair, making his displeasure clear. I wasn't any happier than he was, but could only hope that my shredded nerves didn't show.

Barthel raised the glass that sat beside him and sipped at it before raising it towards me questioningly. It was a temptation I knew I should fight.

'I've had enough for one night, Tummas.'

He shrugged. 'A nightcap for me. The sea will be calling all too soon. What do you want from me?'

'Same as before.'

He scrubbed at his eyes with the heel of his hands and let out a mock yell. 'Jesus, I should have stayed in London. I was never meant to be a fisherman, you know that? I don't even like fish. And I hate the fucking sea. And as for Torshavn . . .'

'What have you found out, Tummas?'

Another sigh. 'I told you before how the Dams made more enemies than friends, right?'

'Yes.'

'Well it seems that included each other.'

The hairs on the back of my neck tingled. 'Tell me. Please.'

He shrugged. 'I hear that they fell out. Aron and Nils. I don't know what the reason was, but they fought. Properly. Punches thrown and both of them hurt.'

My heart was racing. 'When was this?'

Tummas scratched at his head where his hair once was, rubbing his scalp for luck or inspiration or just to help him work out what he should and shouldn't tell me.

'Maybe two weeks before Aron was killed. Another fisherman saw it. He says the Dams didn't know he was there.'

'Would he tell this to the police?'

Barthel's laugh was rough and cheerless. 'No. Of course he wouldn't. No chance.'

'What else did he say?'

'He got the feeling it wasn't a new fight. Not an old one either. A raw wound that reopened. He said Aron was shouting about how he had told Nils what he would do if it didn't stop. The two of them went at it, not caring who got hurt or how much.'

'How bad was it?'

Tummas breathed in deeply. 'How bad? They both said they would kill the other. That bad.'

I let the words sink in, thinking of Nils lying on the floor of the whaling station.

'And no one knows why they fought?'

Barthel spread his arms wide. 'How can I know if no one knows? All I know is *I* don't know.'

'Nothing?'

'Nothing I could say for certain. But maybe, just maybe, it had something to do with your friend Gotteri.'

'Yes?'

'Maybe. It's what I heard.'

'Come on, Tummas. What aren't you telling me?'

Barthel sighed heavily and tapped the glass in front of him. 'That you need to be careful. And that I need another drink.'

He grabbed the bottle of Ardbeg and splashed more into his glass. He didn't seem to take much satisfaction from the mouthful that quickly followed, his lips spreading thin as he swallowed.

'Your friend Gotteri . . . I've heard some things. Not good things. Nothing I can be certain about, but I am asking some more.'

'Are you going to tell me what you know?'

'Yes. Whisky?'

'Tummas . . .'

'I'd take one, if I was you. I think you might need it.'

Chapter 55

A light drizzle fell on Torshavn the next morning as I headed for the hire car, but it wasn't likely to continue for long, judging by the blue sky that extended beyond the low hills of Nolsoy. The clouds overhead were scudding on elsewhere, driven by a westerly wind.

I was reminded of the Faroese proverb that Tunheim had told me: he who waits gets a tailwind, and he who rows, a harbour. I needed a harbour and I was going to row like crazy.

Walking down Torsgøta, my mind full of what lay ahead, I was startled by the blast of a car horn that made everyone within earshot turn and stare. Across the street, the window was sliding down on a black four-wheel-drive Skoda Yeti. I knew the car immediately. It was Gotteri.

He waved maniacally at me, urging me across the street to him. The last time I had seen him, he had sped away in the same car, yet here he was, desperate to speak to me. The words of both the *National Geographic* editor and Tummas Barthel were fresh in my mind.

Even from the opposite pavement, I could see how stressed he looked, worn and anxious. I took a fair amount of pleasure in that, and wanted to know more. I crossed the street to him.

'Hey, my friend, how are you?' He wore his habitual smile, but it didn't sit naturally. 'Where are you off to this morning?'

'Just for a walk. Clear my head.'

I got the feeling that Gotteri was scrutinizing me, trying to read beyond my words. His eyes narrowed, as if he was trying to work something out. 'Yeah? A few drinks last night then? I heard you were in the Manhattan.'

'Yeah. Small place this. Word travels fast.'

He shrugged. 'You know how it is. People talk. So where are you going?'

I matched his shrug. 'Don't know. I'll just see where I end up.'

Gotteri nodded thoughtfully. 'Well just be careful where you walk. Don't go stepping over any cliffs.'

'I'll try not to, thanks.' There was more he wanted to say. I could see it in his face. 'So what's happening, Serge? You look tense.'

The word stung him and the fake smile vanished. 'Me? No, not tense. I do not know why you would say that. I am not tense. I am just . . . looking for someone. Maybe you could help me.'

'Maybe.'

He hesitated, his face darkening. 'It is not important. No, just looking. I wondered if maybe you had seen Nils Dam around.'

I tried not to react to the name. My pulse quickened and I wondered what he knew, what he could know. A creeping sense of dread spilled through me. I did my best to keep my voice level.

'Aron's brother? What is it with you? Do you not think I have been through enough with the Dams? The last time I saw him was after I left court with you. If I had seen him again I would have crossed the road to avoid him.'

He nodded slowly, thoughtfully.

'What do you want with Nils anyway? I thought you didn't know him? That's what you told me.' And it was very different from what I'd heard from Tummas.

'I don't. Not really. But he knows someone I know, and Nils has not been seen for a couple of days. But you have not seen him, no?'

'No.'

'Okay. You be careful.' The window moved up and the car accelerated in one movement, wheels spinning as it sped off up Torsgøta and out of sight.

The rented Peugeot's suspension complained as it bounced along the rutted track to the whaling station at Við Áir. My stomach lurched along with it.

I parked out of sight behind the building on the right, took a bag from the boot and made my way to the middle structure. The heavy door groaned but I made no effort to disguise the sound. I drew as deep a breath as my lungs would allow and went inside.

My eyes quickly adjusted to the gloom and I saw Nils motionless against an old industrial freezer, where I'd left him. Where I'd left him alive.

He'd hurt and he'd bled but he was alive and relatively well. With the knife at his throat, it would have been the easiest and the hardest thing in the world to kill him and yet I didn't do it. Desperate as I was, I'd learned I wasn't the kind of man who could do something like that. It turned out that I *was* better than that, after all.

But I must have been close. Nils had seen the reality of that on my face and had all but shit himself. He'd begun to talk and in seconds I'd wished he hadn't. For a fleeting, maddening second, I wished I'd drawn the blade across his throat instead.

I'd hit him hard before I hurriedly tied both his arms and left him there with the sharp shelving of the freezer digging into his back and guaranteeing that he'd get as little sleep as I would. Then I'd fled.

His head lifted slowly now, scowling at me as I walked across the room, but at the same time it was obvious that he was glad to see I'd returned. Like a whipped dog still pleased to see its master because it meant food. Clearly food with a fist was better than none at all.

I placed the plastic carrier bag a few feet from him and his eyes devoured it, desperate to see what was inside. I was going to make him wait though. Wait, and work for it.

Reaching round behind him, I freed his hands and then the binding round his ankles. Placing an arm under one of his, I hauled him unsteadily to his feet.

'Where are we going?' He sounded scared.

'Nowhere. But you are going to walk or you will seize up completely. And don't try anything stupid or you know what will happen.'

Nils was a little bigger than I was but he was weak, hungry and slow, with rusty limbs and no fuel to fire his belly. He was in no state to flee or fight, but I still had to remind him not to do so for both our sakes.

We did four slow circuits of the room, a marathon for Nils in his debilitated condition, dodging the paraphernalia of the whaling station: cogs, cans, ropes, boxes, tools and pulleys, all set solid with rust and time.

When I returned him to his place on the floor, with his back to the ancient freezer, he collapsed gratefully to the ground and made no fuss as I tied him up again, this time leaving one hand free. Reaching into the bag, I pulled out a bottle of water, seeing his eyes light up. He greedily tipped some of it into his open mouth and I heard the gurgling as it rushed down inside him.

I then produced two ham-and-cheese sandwiches, an apple, a slice of chocolate cake and a bottle of beer. I placed them one by one on the plastic bag, laid out in front of him like a banquet. Nils stared at them ravenously, eyes bulging and mouth open. 'Give me.'

'No.'

His face fell, a child told that there would be no Christmas this year.

'Please.'

'No. Not until you tell me what I want to know. And I mean everything.'

The beaten dog found a little last defiance. 'I tell you. And you did not like.'

I swung the back of my hand at his face and slapped off the smirk that was beginning to appear there, drawing fresh blood from the corner of his mouth. He was right though. The night before he'd begun to tell me what I'd asked of him: he had managed just three words when I could take no more. I'd hit him before he could say anything else.

'I want to hear it. All of it. Not just your edited version of it. Start talking.'

'Food.' He spat the word at me. 'I need or I not strong enough to talk.'

I gave him one of the sandwiches and he wolfed it down, tearing at the bread with his teeth, choking on it. He eyed up the rest but I eased the makeshift tablecloth back, indicating that the remainder was off the menu.

'Now tell me. What happened between your brother and Karis? From the beginning.'

Nils wiped the last of the crumbs from his mouth with his free hand, carefully scooping them into his mouth. 'Aron always liked Karis. He was crazy about her. Never talk about any other girl. Always her. She like him too, I think, but maybe not so much. They went out together here. Like boyfriend and girlfriend. But she always think she too good for him. She and her artist friends and him just a fisherman.

'They both went to university in Denmark, in Copenhagen. She learn art and Aron learn management for to run family business. Aron could have had lots of girls. Any girl. But he like Karis. But Karis she like Copenhagen. She like her new friends and art galleries and museums. And she like the boys who want to go to these. Water, I need more water.'

I gave him the bottle and let him slip some more down his throat but pulled it away just before I judged he would be finished. The glare that I received told me I'd judged right. 'Go on.'

'So Aron would go to her place and ask to see her. He would meet her in bars she like. Sometimes she speak to him and sometimes she too busy with her friends. Like she was embarrass to be seen with him. The daughter of the preacher. The artist. Too proud to be seen with my brother. She *should* have been proud to be with him.

'But she not tell him to go. She still like him. Still want him, Aron say. Just she too proud because he fisherman. They have dinner in restaurant one time and he knows she still feel the same as he. They both drink. Lots. He tell Karis he love her but she laugh and say he not mean it. But he did.

'He walk her home. He tell her again but she say she not love him. Aron he . . . he get angry. He want to show her how angry. And show her how much he love her. Give me food.'

'No.'

'Give me food or I no tell.'

I booted him hard in the stomach and he doubled over, choking out breath. He clutched his free hand to his empty stomach, massaging the pain.

'You will get food once you have told me everything. Now talk. He wanted to show her.'

It took a full minute before Nils could lift his head, hatred all over his face. 'Yes. He show her. He show the bitch how much he want her. You want to hear?'

My stomach knotted worse than his, clenched in anticipation, steeling myself for the words to come.

'He fuck her. Aron fuck her.'

As the anger boiled inside me, I needed to hear the words he'd used the night before. Words that he'd used then as a weapon against me, but now shied away from. I needed to hear them even if I had to say them first.

'He *raped* her.'

'He fuck her.'

'He *raped* her!'

'Yes. He rape her!'

Chapter 56

'He rape her and she liked it.'

I booted him again, my foot slamming into his knee and then his thigh in quick succession, causing him to scream. When his mouth was wide open, I grabbed the apple from the floor and rammed it in as far as it would go, jamming it on his lower teeth, leaving him like a pig set to be roasted.

He screamed again, furiously trying to dislodge the apple, panicking when he couldn't do so, not helped by me pulling his head back by his hair. I let him squeal for a bit, enjoying his discomfort and glad beyond belief not to be hearing him any more. But the absence of words didn't stop them from bouncing around in my head, crashing into my brain. Rape. Karis. Rape.

And the consequences of those words. What they meant and what they might mean. The stomach-churning awfulness of it. But also what it might have left her with. Motive.

Jesus Christ, I couldn't even think it. I had to take it out on Nils.

'Your brother raped Karis. Because she wouldn't have him, he raped her.' I was screaming at him. 'Your brother was a thug. An animal.'

He roared behind the stuck apple, a muffled, incoherent rant, in defence of the indefensible. I put a hand under his chin to support it and battered my fist down onto the top of his head, forcing him to bite clean through the fruit and nearly breaking his jaw in the process.

He choked and sobbed but I couldn't and wouldn't let him rest. I couldn't let myself rest either. Much as I dreaded it, I had to know.

'So what happened next?'

Nils's words came out in a stream of self-pity and resentment. 'He took Karis home. So she was safe. She not tell anyone. Not one person. Aron thank her for not tell. Everything was okay.'

'Okay?' I burst out laughing, incredulous. His head slumped so that his eyes avoided mine. 'Okay? He rapes her and you think it was okay? He thought it was okay? What is wrong with you people?'

'I mean okay because no one know. Aron sorry. Very sorry. But then . . .'

My guts tightened, hearing something in his voice. 'Go on.'

'Then Karis pregnant.'

The words echoed round the room of metal, rattling and clanging, reverberating and ringing off rusted iron and green copper. They rang in my ears and I felt sick.

I myself had no words, and Nils lifted his head to look at me. I dared him to show some satisfaction at my shock: I would rip his head off with my bare hands. Maybe he sensed it, because he just stared at me sullenly.

'What happened?'

'Karis have abortion. She not tell Aron. He very angry. He wanted baby. And he wanted her.'

'What a fucking shame for him.' The words fell from me in a whisper. Since I'd heard about Aron's murder, I'd spent every waking moment, and a few sleeping ones, desperate to find out that I hadn't done it. Now I was wishing that I had.

I kicked Nils on the ankle, a vicious knock that startled him and made sure he got the message. Talk.

'Karis finish her study and come back to Torshavn. Aron too. But not together. They not talk. But still Karis not tell what happen. She not want any person to know. Aron feel bad but he leave her alone. When she meet boys, Aron not like it.'

'And then she met me?'

'Yes. Aron very angry. You not from here and you with Karis. He very unhappy. He say to me that he make you go away.'

I could feel my hands forming fists, knuckles whitening as the skin tightened around them. I watched Nils Dam's teeth as he spoke. I pictured the white of my knuckles on the white of his teeth, smashing through them until they hit the back of his throat.

'Did you help him to try to make me go away?'

Nils looked fearful.

'Tell me.'

'A little. He broke your water pipe. I help him get the sheep to your house. He break in and leave bird inside. He sure you leave.'

'Yeah, well I didn't. Your brother was a bully. A thug. A rapist. You must be very proud.'

'He my brother!' A tear was streaming down his face. 'My brother!'

'I didn't kill your brother. But you know what? Whoever did it deserves a round of applause.'

Nils tried to spit on me but I saw it coming and easily moved my head to the side. 'I didn't kill your brother, Nils. So who did? You?'

His eyes screwed closed and fresh tears formed. 'No! Fuck you!' He shouted and strained against the ties that held him, wriggling like a madman, and I couldn't help but think he was protesting too much. While he was railing against that accusation, I thought it was a good time to try another.

'I know about you and Serge Gotteri. I know all of it.'

His head snapped up, eyes wide and his jaw slack. What I'd said was partly bluff, with little to back it up, but I knew I'd just hit a bullseye.

'I not know what you mean.'

I laughed in his face, making it clear it was the funniest thing I'd ever heard.

'Nils . . .' I laughed again. 'How stupid are you? Do we need to do this every time? Do I need to prove to you that I mean what I say?'

'I . . . no. No. But I cannot speak about . . .'

My head tilted to one side, examining him. 'You remember how I told you that you would tell me what I wanted to know. And that you could tell me before or after the pain? Nothing's changed. The deal is still the same. You will tell me everything. You and Gotteri.'

Chapter 57

When I picked up the rusty knife that I'd previously drawn across his throat, it was hard to miss the look of fearful familiarity that appeared in the man's eyes. Maybe he thought that it would be easy for me to cut out the tongue that had spoken those words about Karis. Slice away the word *rape* as if it had never been spoken.

I'd made the decision that I wasn't the kind of person who would carry out the threat embodied by the rusted blade, but that didn't matter. All that mattered was that Nils still believed that I was.

I knew, too, that it would help if Nils learned that I had knowledge. Knowledge that he couldn't imagine that I'd possess. Thanks to Tummas Barthel, I was armed with just that.

'You will tell me everything about you and Gotteri. And everything about your fight with your brother.'

His mouth dropped, fear temporarily overtaken by surprise. I let the knife turn in my hand, making sure it caught his eye.

'Tell me all of it, Nils. And not a word of a lie. You've no idea what I know and what I don't know. Don't take the gamble of trying to guess. For starters, Gotteri is not here working for *National Geographic*. We both know that. Right?'

He nodded dumbly, confused and uncertain. I could see him

trying to work things out and failing. I let the knife turn in my hand again.

'So why is he here?'

'Gotteri is here for the whale hunt.' Nils let the words slip quietly into the stale air of the station.

Tummas had been right. He said that all he had on Goterri were suspicions and guesses but they'd been accurate.

'Speak up. And tell me everything.'

'He is here for the *grindadráp*. To photograph it. To wreck it. He wants to destroy it all.'

I remembered Gotteri's over-the-top reaction at being late for the whale hunt at Hvalvik, his fury when we arrived only in time to see the bloody carcasses lined up on the quayside.

'Go on. I told you I wanted to hear it *all*.'

'He not work for *National Geographic*. He work for the Marine Machine. The crazy eco people. They send him here to photograph it from inside. So he pretend. He say he here to photograph birds but he a liar.'

Nils paused and nodded at the bottle of water. I grabbed it and tipped some into his mouth so that he could continue.

'He want photograph of the *grind*. To make it look bad. He want to see rules broken. Laws broken. He want it to look . . . brutal and cruel.'

'So you helped him.' I tried to make it sound like a statement rather than a question.

He nodded sullenly. 'I know fishermen and boats, so I know when whales are coming. Before anyone else. So I tell Gotteri.'

'Like when you told him about the hunt at Hvalvik.'

'Yes.'

'And he paid you for that information.'

'Yes.'

'Gotteri didn't just want to photograph the *grind*, though, did he? He wanted to make sure some of the hunts didn't happen. And you helped him with that too.'

Nils grimaced but nodded. 'He told Marine Machine and they got there in time to scare away the whales. Make *grind* not happen.'

I was struggling to focus on what he was saying. As much as I wanted to know about Gotteri and his dirty tricks, I couldn't drag my mind away from what Nils had already told me. Images of Karis were bombarding my head. Karis and Aron. I was drowning in rolling waves of compassion, rage and worry.

I had to force myself to stick with it, concentrate on learning about Gotteri.

'That must have made you popular, Nils. People were very angry at the hunts being disrupted. And you made that happen. You were the traitor.'

He looked away, shame heaped up on top of everything else. When he turned back, I could see that he had made a decision – a decision forged on defiance.

'Not traitor. Not all like that. I tell Gotteri more. Much more.'

I nodded, as if armed with more than I was. 'Go on.'

'From my work. With oil company. I tell him about the report that company do on the whales. Secret report. It made Gotteri very happy. His eyes become like lights when I tell him.'

Nils had the ghost of a grin on his face.

'Company do tests and find whales are full of toxins. If people eat then it poison them. Mercury. More than they think before. And much lead and chromium. Enough to make brain and liver not work. I tell him this and he give me money. Lot of money.'

I kept my face expressionless, forcing him to continue.

'He want copy of report but it not easy to get. So I tell him some information each time and he pay me each time. He kept saying "Whole report. I want the whole report." But you know somehow I just not get the whole report.'

Nils burst out laughing. A manic uncontrolled burst that seemed to cause him pain.

'I not get the report because there was no report. No poison. No lead. No chromium. No brain-failure. Ha. Gotteri, he so excited he not see when he be lied to. *Helvitis spassari!* Fucking moron.'

'You made the whole thing up.'

'Yeah. All of it. I make sure Gotteri pay properly for information I give.'

'Does he know this?'

'No.' Nils laughed again, with as much bitterness and pain as before. 'Aron though, he . . .'

He let his words trail off, catching himself, but too late.

'Aron knew you had lied to Gotteri and made up the fake report. And knew you had told him about the hunt.' I was guessing.

The glare was weak, pitiful really. The truth was too much for him. So too was the sight of the knife that turned slowly in my hand.

'Aron find out about Gotteri. About how I tell him about the *grindadráp*. He angry. Very angry.'

'Of course he was. He was furious at you and at Gotteri for betraying the hunt, betraying the local way of life. That is why you fought. Beat each other up, almost. And you both swore you'd kill the other.'

Nils's eyes widened. Words got stuck in his throat.

'So what did Aron do? About Gotteri.'

'He threatened him.'

'When.'

'A week before he was . . .'

My heart quickened. Possibilities of something better, something less terrible than I'd imagined.

'What kind of threats?'

'He said he would beat up Gotteri. Let everyone on islands know what Gotteri do. Unless he pay him money.'

It was my turn to laugh. 'You Dam boys are two of a kind. Blackmailing bastards. Did Gotteri pay?'

I wanted to hear 'no'. I wanted a reason to feel relief. To be dealing with only one horror rather than the possibility of two.

Nils shrugged. 'I do not know. I really do not know.'

Chapter 58

I didn't know what I was going to say to Karis, but I knew we had to speak. I abandoned the Peugeot at the foot of Landavegur and climbed up the pretty street with its stream and succession of waterfalls. The stream ran alongside, round and even, it seemed, through houses on its way back down to the sea, pausing only briefly to surge over one waterfall then another.

At the top of the hill was the dramatic Vesturkirkjan, the western church, a modernist building that dominated that part of the skyline with its high triangular roof and giant three-sided glass front-piece that soared towards the heavens. In its gardens a stone pillar stood in the middle of the stream as it wound its way downhill, and on top was a statue of Jesus, arms outstretched and head bowed. I stared at him in passing, and thought of a time I might have looked to him for answers. A lot of water had fallen towards the sea since then.

Her studio flat was just another few minutes' walk away, and I braced myself for what was to come. Nils Dam's confession on behalf of his brother had been ugly and shocking, producing an overwhelming anger in me that had no outlet. A villain that I could not reach. A wrong that I could not right.

Still I found myself second-guessing Karis. Did what had

happened to her explain her volatility, her mood swings? Or had they always been there? Was the angry, reactive Karis a product of what Aron Dam had done to her, or was it just a part of her that existed already? She shouldn't have to explain her personality on the basis that that bastard abused her. Every thought made me angrier, and I was trying to get that anger under control before I knocked on her door.

Outside the flat, I stood still and breathed deep. I so wanted to talk to her, but a voice in my head kept telling me to be careful what I wished for. It seemed an age before I got up the courage and discipline to knock.

No response, but I waited, ignoring the cowardly part of me that felt relieved. I knocked again, louder. Still nothing. My hand was lifting to strike the door a third time when it was halted by a voice from behind me.

'Get away from there. Away, I say.'

I spun to see Esmundur Lisberg advancing on me, his face a furious red. He wore a different sweater to the last time I'd seen him, this one dark brown with white snowflakes, but he had on the same brown cords and the same boots with flashy buckles. His everyman preacher's uniform.

This was all I needed.

'What are you doing here? My daughter does not want you here. I do not want you here. Go. Go now. Do not disgrace my daughter.'

'Mr Lisberg–'

'No.' The man was livid. 'I told you before. I asked you to respect me and you did not. You disrespect my wishes and my position. Get away from here. Leave.'

'I am not disrespecting anyone but I need to speak to–'

He cut me off again. Physically, this time, barging right up into my face and getting between me and the door. I wondered whether he was actually going to try to hit me.

'Look, I need to speak to Karis.' I was determined not to back down. 'She's a grown woman. Let her make her own decisions.'

His eyes widened and his face contorted. If we had been in a cartoon then steam would have been coming out of his ears.

'She is not a grown woman. She is my child. You are not a parent, are you? No, so you will not understand. You are accused of murder. I cannot have you near my daughter. Do you understand that?'

I did. Of course, I did. Teaching those kids was the nearest I'd ever been – ever likely to come – to being a parent. I understood the parental responsibility that I myself had failed to show when I'd left Liam Dornan alone with those thugs. This man was protecting his child in a way that I hadn't done. I could hardly blame Lisberg for that, and yet I wasn't ready to walk away.

'I do, but, Mr Lisberg, I am not here to hurt your daughter.'

His face darkened.

'Hurt her? You will answer to me if you do. In Mark 9, verse 42, the Lord says "whoever causes one of these little ones who believe in me to sin, it would be better for him if a great millstone were hung around his neck and he were thrown into the sea." Believe me, I would throw you in the sea.'

I swallowed what I really wanted to say. 'I am here to help Karis, not hurt her.'

He laughed bitterly. 'By shaming her? By making everyone think that man's murder was her fault? If you think that is helping her then you are a crazy man. Karis has not slept since that happened. Leave this place now.'

The man was bristling with a fury that no words of mine were going to soothe. This was achieving nothing.

'I am going, Mr Lisberg. But not because you are angry or because you are ordering me to. I am going simply because Karis is not at home. I will return though. If you see her, you can tell her that from me.'

The man was still blustering and quoting scripture when I turned away. His lecturing voice followed me down the street, but his feet did not; he was satisfied, for now, that I was no longer darkening his daughter's doorstep.

I had met him three times now, and I had yet to see him anything other than angry. For a man of God, he seemed to carry little contentment in his soul. What was it that Karis had said at the Etika restaurant, the time he came inside to confront us? 'The sainted Esmundur Lisberg. The most Lutheran of the Lutherans. The keeper of all our consciences.' The job didn't seem to make him happy.

The Etika. Memories came back to me. Karis and I eating sushi. Her father staring in through the window. Him standing by our table. Karis looking anxious and alarmed. Sitting opposite me with her raincoat hanging over the back of her chair.

The memory nearly made me choke.

Chapter 59

I didn't have room for my daily check-in at the police station. My head was full of so many people, possibilities and problems, it was the last place I wanted to be. I needed to think about Karis, Nils Dam still tied up in the whaling station, Gotteri and Nicoline, not the fat cop Demmus and his paperwork. Yet there was no choice: I had to sign in and go through all the necessary bureaucracy, consigning me to the station for far longer than I wanted.

Demmus was going through his near-silent routine, grunting and checking boxes and identification as if he'd never seen me before. It was a procedure that had got old after day one. It was physical confirmation of my inability to leave these islands, the padlock on a cell with no doors or windows.

As Demmus laboured at the desk behind his counter, I fretted to leave. The voice that dropped into my frustration was instantly familiar. Nervy, out-of-breath tones that signalled pressure, anxiety and a lack of fitness. Elin Samuelsen. My lawyer knew when I was supposed to be at the cop shop, and had met me there a couple of times to keep me up to date with the progress of my case.

'How are you, John? We should talk.'

Alarms bells rang. Surely there wasn't more bad news. There was only so much I could handle.

'What's up?'

'Let's go outside. We can walk and talk.' She rattled off something in Faroese to Demmus and he grunted in reply, presumably meaning I was done and free to go.

We pushed our way out of the front door and headed downhill towards the fort, a watery sun offering us warmth. Samulesen took off her round, amber spectacles, dropping them into the top pocket of her jacket, and replaced them with the sunglasses that had been acting as a hair-band for her blonde mop. She had heels on today and was only an inch or two shorter than I was. She was nervous: there was obviously no correlation between her increased height and confidence. Nicoline, all five-feet-nothing of her, burst with self-assurance, but my lawyer didn't seem to have enough to spread on a slice of bread. Given her daring work in the courtroom, her lack of confidence baffled me.

'So John, is there anything else that you need to tell me?'

I didn't like where this was going. There was so much that I could have told her, but there was no way I was sharing any of it. Yes, she was on my side, but how the hell could I tell her about the knife, and the fact that Tunheim knew about it? Or my chat with Nicoline? And I feared that if I told her about what I'd done to Nils Dam she would have a heart attack on the spot.

'No. Nothing.'

'Are you sure, John? I cannot do my job unless you tell me everything. If the police have surprises for me then I will not be ready for them. I will not know how to fight them.'

I didn't look at her, couldn't. Elin got hot and flustered just being asked her name, but I'd already seen how sharp she was. I had even wondered whether the nervousness was a front to disarm people – judges, lawyers or clients. I looked straight ahead and lied to her.

'Miss Samuelsen, there is nothing else. What has happened?'

She sighed theatrically and raked her hair with her right hand. 'I have heard that the police have a new witness. Someone who is prepared to testify that you spoke of doing harm to Aron Dam.'

I stopped in mid-stride. Nymann's words when he visited the shack came back to me. *Did you ever publicly threaten to harm Aron Dam?* He had been doing more than rattling my cage. He'd been testing the water. I had no choice but to look at her, even though I couldn't control what was on my face. 'What? Who?'

'That is what I want you to tell me. I do not know. All I hear is that they have someone who will go into court and say how you hated Aron Dam and you wanted to hurt him badly.'

'Elin . . . I don't . . . there can't be . . .'

'Are you sure?' The nervousness seemed to have vanished, replaced by accusatory but controlled anger. 'They have a witness. It may be enough for them to go back before Judge Hammershaimb, even without forensic evidence. I have spoken to a colleague in Copenhagen and he says it would go very badly against you.'

'But I didn't . . . I did not kill him.'

'That is not what I'm asking you. Whether you killed him or not does not matter. What matters if someone can say you declared intent. Who could say that?'

I remembered Toki talking to Nymann at the station, but knew I'd never spoken to him about Aron. But then again I had spent plenty of time in plenty of bars. I'd drunk plenty, too.

'I don't know. Honestly.'

Samuelsen frowned intently. 'I have spoken to Inspector Nymann but of course he is saying nothing. But he is so pleased with himself. So smug. So arrogant. I do not like that man.'

She narrowed her eyes at me, the pussycat finding her claws. 'You think, John. And you think well. I do not want that man to laugh at me. Think he knows what I do not. If there is something, you make sure you tell me. Okay?'

'Okay.'

She nodded at me, her eyelashes fluttering furiously. Was she angry at me or at Nymann, or at herself for acting so out of character? 'Okay. Good. Now tell me something else? What is going on with you and Inspector Tunheim?'

Shit. This place was a village. I had to lie again, and she could see it coming.

'Nothing. What do you mean?'

She was marching on again, glaring at me side-on as she walked, puffing with the exertion. 'I have known Broddi Tunheim for a long time. I have been to his house for dinner and he to mine. Many times. But now he cannot look me in the eye and tell me the truth. Like you. So what is going on?'

'He, um . . .' A complete denial was going to get me nowhere. 'He is taking an interest in the case.'

She laughed in my face. 'No shit? There is a murder in Torshavn and Broddi "takes an interest in it"? Ha. You do not know the man. He has probably thought of nothing else since the murder. He is . . . obsessed. He might look like he does not care, but it will make him crazy that the Danes are in charge. John . . . Broddi is my friend and you are my client, but . . . be careful with him. He is very . . . tricky.'

'I've learned that already.'

Elin closed her eyes and shook her head. 'Oh, my God. I do not want to know. I really do not want to know. Okay, I'm going this way. Think on what I said, and stay in touch. My God, why could I not just get a nice traffic case?'

She veered right towards town without another word, just a despairing wave of her arm without turning round. I stood and let her go, floored by the news. A witness. Maybe a liar. *Surely* a liar.

There were people I had to speak to, although I had no idea where any of them were. Still, these islands were just seventy miles by forty-six miles. They couldn't be far.

I found Nicoline in the makeshift incident room outside Tinganes. I wasn't stupid enough to go inside, knowing the implications it would have for her. Instead I stood in a doorway opposite until she came out. The sergeant, Kielstrup, emerged and I had to slide back further into the shadows to avoid being seen by him.

When Nicoline came out of the white Portakabin a minute or

two later, I stepped out into her eyeline and she saw me immediately. Her mouth dropped slightly but she quickly caught herself, looking around to see if anyone else had noticed, before angrily shooing me back into the doorway and signalling that she would be there in one minute.

'What do you want?' she hissed at me when she came over. 'I can't talk to you here.'

'Then meet me somewhere else. The old fort. You know it?'

'Of course I do. I know every inch of this bloody place now. Okay, go. I will be there as soon as I can.'

The fort at Skansin was just a few minutes' walk away on a plateau near the ferry port. Its grass-covered slopes also contained the lighthouse and four old cannons, two of them remnants of a British warship. I went round to the far side of the guardhouse, facing Nolsoy and away from the eyes of the town. I had waited there just five minutes when Nicoline arrived.

Her waterproof jacket was zipped up to the neck to keep out the chill of the rising wind, and her hair, although tied back, rose and fell on the breeze. 'What the hell is it? Are you okay?'

'There is something I need to talk to you about.'

She frowned. 'It had better be important, for you to come to the incident room. Are you crazy?'

'Maybe. But there is something in it for you too.'

She stared hard. 'Okay. I'm listening.'

I took a breath, not sure how this was going to be received. 'I hear that Nymann has a witness who says he is going to testify against me. Saying that I spoke about getting Aron Dam. Hurting him.'

'You are joking me, right? You want me to get involved in that? Come on, Callum. That is asking way too much. Jesus.'

'I need to know.'

'I do not need this aggravation. And I do not know who this witness is. Yes, I know Nymann has someone. He is walking around, what is the expression you use, like a dog with two cocks, so sure of himself. But I do not know who the witness is. And even if I did . . .'

'You *know* I didn't do it. I did not kill Aron Dam. Right? So if Nymann has a witness saying that I threatened to kill him then someone is lying and I could go to jail for a murder I didn't commit. Help me, Nicoline. *Please*.'

She half-turned away, rubbing at her face. 'Jesus. You ask a lot. This is my job we are talking about. The job I love.'

'Well . . . what if I might be able to get you the murder weapon?'

Nicoline's jaw dropped. 'What?'

'I'm not saying I can. Not definitely. But I might be able to. If I can, can I get it to you without anyone having to know where you got it from?'

'Yes. I mean, I think so. You are full of surprises. You think you can get it?'

'You think you can find out who the witness is?'

She held her head in her hands before answering. 'Do you know why I always wanted to be a forensic investigator?'

'Because you watched *CSI* when you were a kid. You told me.'

She shook her head. 'No. That is what got me *interested*. But it is not what made me want to do it. I wanted to be a CSI like them because they got to the *truth*. That is what evidence gives you. The truth. I wanted to be the one who could prove who the guilty person was. And who the innocent one was. I will help you. But if I get into trouble then I will cut your balls off. Understand?'

'Thanks, Nicoline. I appreciate it.'

'Where the hell are you going to get the murder weapon from? You know what . . . I am not sure I want to know.'

'No, you don't. How are you going to get the name of the witness? From Nymann?'

She shook her head, smiling. 'No, that asshole will not tell me. But Kielstrup, he will.'

A gust of wind surged round the point and hurled itself at both of us, making Nicoline stagger to the side.

'Here.' She pulled a card from the rear pocket of her jeans. 'My number. Use that if you need to get in touch with me. I don't want you appearing at the incident room again. It would not be good for either of us.'

I nodded. 'Okay, thanks. I'll let you get back to work. But one last thing. Did you think about the DNA database? How you might use it to find a match for the evidence you got at the murder scene?'

She narrowed her eyes at me. 'Yes, I did. And do not think I don't know that you set that up to plant that whole thing in my head.'

'Well?'

'Well, I have spoken to people to see if it can be done. They are not very happy, but . . . it is possible. We are going to have to go very high up, though, and it may take time. But if we get the go-ahead then, yes, we will find our killer.'

Chapter 60

I had waited outside Karis's flat for two hours, sitting in the Peugeot, before she finally arrived. I gave her fifteen minutes before I went to the door.

She answered my knock almost immediately but her face fell when she saw it was me. Not discontent, more surprise. Something else, too . . . worry. She'd been crying again, that was obvious. With a half-step forward, she recovered, throwing her arms round me and hugging me. 'Come in.'

She led me by the hand up to the studio and we both sank onto the sofa, but she immediately bounced to her feet again. 'Do you want a drink, John? Do I still call you John?'

'No, I'm fine. And yes, call me John.'

She looked disappointed that I had declined her offer. 'I'm having one. Join me?'

'Okay.'

She came back with two full glasses of white wine and a tiny tremor in her hands. This time she eased herself down beside me and took a generous mouthful from her glass. 'Cheers,' she toasted breezily. Too breezily.

I tipped my glass to hers and took a sip at the chilled wine.

'Karis, we need to talk.'

'Do we?' She sounded far from enthusiastic.

'Yes. We have to. I'm in serious trouble and maybe you can help me out of it. I could go to jail for the rest of my life for Aron's murder. You do realize that?'

Another large gulp, this time with her eyes closed. 'Yes.'

'There's the question you didn't ask me. The one you started to ask but didn't finish. You know the question I mean?'

All the sparkle had gone from her. The feistiness and vitality that had once been so irresistible had disappeared. Instead she just nodded dumbly.

'Don't you think you should ask me that question? It would seem the sensible thing to do. After all, you would maybe be in danger if I had done it.'

She tipped her glass back, leaving only an inch or so of wine in it. 'I need a refill.' She began to push herself out of the chair but I caught her wrist. 'No. Stay. You don't need any more.'

Some of the old fire returned to her eyes and she angrily wrenched free of my grasp. 'I don't? You don't tell me when I need a drink or not.'

'Ask me the question.'

'John, I . . .'

'Ask me.'

I could see tears forming in her eyes. Bitter little tears of fear.

'Okay. Did you kill Aron?'

'No. No, I did not.'

She just nodded. No relief, no doubt, no 'thank God', no challenge, no more tears. Just a nod of acceptance.

'I didn't kill him, but I might still go to prison for it. There is a very real chance of that. Is that what you want to happen?'

'Of course not! John, how could you think that? *Reyvarhol! Asshole!* I really do need more wine. Don't try to stop me.'

I didn't. Maybe the wine would work. Loosen her up. The danger was in overdoing it.

She took a long time refilling her glass. I could just see her through the kitchen door, standing still, a hand over her eyes. When she came back they were redder.

'Okay, let's talk,' she sighed. 'I do not want you to go to jail. You must know that.'

'Well, to stop that from happening, I have to find out who *did* kill Aron. And why.'

'What? But that is not your job. That is the job of the police.'

'The police still think it was me. They are still looking for evidence to convict me. They aren't looking for anyone else, Karis. Just me.'

Her eyes closed as she drank, lips clamped tight to the glass.

'If you can tell me anything at all that might help then I need you to do it. Why someone would want Aron killed. Who else might have a motive.'

She looked for answers in the glass, tears running down her face again and sliding into the wine, causing salty little pools to form on the liquid's surface.

'Like who?' The voice was a little girl's, tiny in a big world. Keeping from her that I knew what Aron had done made me feel like a complete bastard. 'Tell me about Aron. Who hated him? Who did he upset? Someone in the fishing industry maybe? Or someone in town? He always seemed so aggressive, to me. Could he have pushed someone too far?'

'I . . . don't know. Maybe, yes. He was always arguing with people. He liked to . . . push people around, I guess. But I don't know . . .'

The wine was going down fast and working faster. There was a definite slur to her words, a catch in her voice. I was going to have to push her further.

'You can't think of anyone?'

'No.'

'No one that he might have hurt?'

A pause. 'No.'

'Okay.' A change of tack. 'You remember the night we were in the Etika and your father came inside?'

A wariness on her face, wondering where this was going. 'Yes . . .'

'Do you remember what you had to eat that night?'

Sheer confusion. 'John? What is this . . .'

'I do. You had sushi. Halibut and cod. And you had prawns. And beer.'

'Okay, but . . .'

'You wore a red T-shirt and black skinny jeans. And your hat, of course. And you had a long hooded red raincoat. I remember thinking that you looked like some rock-chick version of Little Red Riding Hood.'

Her face narrowed in concentration, hanging on every word. But she still looked confused. And lost.

'I know a little of what happened the night Aron was killed,' I said. 'Do you want to hear it?'

She gave just the merest movement of her head up and down, fresh tears forming.

'I didn't go straight home. I was too drunk. I don't know where I did go; wandered round town looking for you, I think. But I know where I ended up. On the fish slabs at the western port.'

She was just looking at me, her mouth wider than her eyes.

'I fell asleep there. Out cold on the slabs. Then in the middle of the night, someone came up to me and slipped something in my pocket. The knife that was used to kill Aron.'

'Oh, my God.'

'And that person was wearing a long red raincoat with a hood.'

The tears were streaming now. I had to push it. Had to.

'Okay, Karis. Let me ask you the question then. Okay?'

'Okay.'

'Did you kill Aron?'

'Yes.'

Chapter 61

You should never ask a question unless you are prepared to hear the answer. I'd got the reply that I'd half-expected, but the world still stopped for a few moments. I had no breath, my heart didn't seem to beat, and Karis didn't move.

There was no noise either. Not a sound inside or out. No howl of wind or passing cars, no voices in the street, not so much as the flap of a butterfly's wing.

Karis finally broke the spell by lifting her head and looking at me for my reaction. I had none.

'Yes,' she repeated, as if I hadn't heard her the first time.

'Why?'

Her mouth opened and closed, groping around for words that wouldn't come. All colour had gone from her and she sat there, bloodless and dazed.

'Why did you kill him, Karis?' I wanted it to come from her. I needed it to be that way. I could hardly tell her how I had learned of her motive.

Her shoulders lifted. Like a child caught stealing biscuits, or a teenager who hasn't done her homework.

'Let's start somewhere else.' I was trying to keep my voice calm, even though my guts were churning and I could feel a rage building inside me. 'How did it happen?'

Her eyes slid shut, trying to remember and trying to forget. I wondered if she was seeing it replayed inside her head.

'I was not thinking properly. I was drunk. So angry at Aron. And at you for fighting with him. I wanted an end to it, so I went looking for him.'

'To kill him?'

'No. Oh, my God, no. I just . . . I do not know. To end it. Once and for all.'

'To end what?'

She stalled, not wanting to give the answer that came first to her lips. 'Just all of it.'

'Karis, that night in the bar. I heard you threaten Aron. You said that you'd told him what you would do. That you meant it and you would do it. What did you mean by that?'

She froze, looking at me with her green eyes moist, pleading for help. I couldn't give her it. I needed her to tell me the truth.

'What had you threatened him with? What did he fear you would do?'

'I can't . . .'

'Karis, come on. I know he was hassling you. And me. But you must have had a good reason to want him dead.'

'He raped me!'

The words finally burst from her in a scream of anger that shamed me for goading her. Words that still managed to shock me as if I'd heard them for the first time. Hearing them from her mouth made it worse. Hearing the pain in her voice.

'Aron raped me.' Quieter now, almost ashamed. 'Okay? He raped me.'

Her hands flew to her face, and she sobbed loudly. I went to her and tried to hold her but she fended me off, her shoulder turning against me, stopping me from comforting her. I couldn't blame her – I'd forced this out of her.

Her hands finally fell away and there was a renewed defiance about her. Eyes red but mouth set firm and angry. She was steeling herself to tell me more.

'Aron was always keen on me, but it was one-sided. He was always too aggressive for my liking. A bully, really. I did date him once, but it was nothing serious, he just wasn't my type. It was a mistake, as he thought it meant we were a couple. Boyfriend and girlfriend. And of course, when it was over, he would become a crazy person whenever I was with anyone else.

'I went to Copenhagen and Aron went too. He basically followed me. I loved university, a new way of life, new friends, new places to go. All the things that Torshavn wasn't. But then Aron started showing up, ruining everything. He would hang out in bars that I went to. Even go to my classes. And at nights he would show up drunk, really drunk. Hassling me and embarrassing me.

'I tried to ignore him but he was everywhere. He kept demanding that I go out with him, give him another chance. He wasn't going to leave me alone until I did. I was sick of it and I made the same mistake again. I told him okay, we would go out for dinner once. If I then said that was it, then it would be over and he would respect that. Of course he said yes.

'Dinner was okay, but Aron was loud and overbearing, trying too hard. I felt uncomfortable and it showed. He was walking me back from the restaurant when he asked when we were going to go out again and I told him we weren't. He got mad but I reminded him about the agreement he'd made. He was shouting. He told me that he loved me. I said I was going home on my own.

'He followed me. Getting angrier and angrier. I told him to leave me alone, but he grabbed me by the arm and pulled me off the street. Down this alley. His eyes were . . . crazy. I tried to shout but he put his hand over my mouth and . . .'

She stopped, trying to compose herself, bracing her hands on her thighs to stop the shaking. It didn't work. She jumped to her feet and made for the kitchen.

'Wine. I need more wine.'

'Karis . . .'

She whirled. 'Do not tell me to be calm or whatever it is you were going to say. I will decide what I do or feel or say. I have kept all this inside me for so long and have only ever managed to tell one other person. This is not easy for me.'

I let breath escape from me when she turned her back, blowing it out in a futile attempt at getting rid of some of the tension that was eating me from within.

When she came back, she sat gripping the wine glass, holding on to it for dear life. When some of it had slipped down her throat and had the desired effect, she continued. 'Aron took me down that alley and he raped me. That was it. He . . . held me and he forced himself on me. It was . . .'

The effort her admission had taken suddenly showed, and her face crumpled, eyes and mouth locked tight, her chest heaving. My movement towards her was repelled by an outstretched arm. The last thing she needed was the unwelcome touch of another man.

When words came they were soaked in tears, choked out one by one. 'It got worse. A few weeks later I discovered I was pregnant. It was . . . terrible. The hardest thing I ever had to do. I could not keep it. Not after . . . So I did it. I had an abortion.'

The word tasted sour in her mouth – I could see it on her face. Just saying it made her burn with guilt and hatred.

'I hate myself. And him. Him most of all. I came back to Torshavn because I wanted to paint here. Get it all out of me. Make this place better, so that it wouldn't produce another Aron. But then I realized it was not Torshavn that made Aron like he was. Aron made Aron like that. And he made me the way I became. After it.'

Her hands were shaking, wine shimmering in the glass.

'But you see I was determined that he would not dictate the rest of my life. I would not be the person he made me. I would become *me* again. Live life on my terms. He would not have the satisfaction of breaking me. I have my friends here. And my painting. And my father. And then you. But when you came, Aron threatened everything again. So the night in the bar, when I was drunk and the two of you fought, and you became as bad as him, I let Aron know I would tell people what he had done. I needed a way to keep him away, to get him to stop.

'But it was only a threat. I would never have done it, because the last thing I wanted was for people to know. When he left, I panicked. I went to my flat, but I could not settle. I knew what he was like and that he would turn the threat round. He would not care if people found out. Under pressure, he would tell people himself, and everyone would know. I was very drunk. I did not think it through. So I went out again. After him.

'I caught up with him in Tinganes, near the Prime Minister's office. I knew he liked to go there at night, hang out at the water's edge. Of course, he thought I was there because I wanted him. I realized it was the first time I had been alone with him since ... since it happened. I tried to talk to him, reason with him. Said it would be better if he left you and me alone and no one knew about Copenhagen. He got mad and said he would tell you how he fucked me. He would tell everyone and see how I liked it then. Then he said that, as everyone would know soon anyway, maybe he should just fuck me again.

'He came at me, tried to grab me. I knew what he meant to do, but I could not let it happen again. I had a knife. A *grindaknivur*. I pulled it out and he just laughed. He lunged at me but I stabbed him. Then again. He fell to the ground and I just kept stabbing him. It was like it was that night in Copenhagen, except I was able to stop him.'

When she stopped talking, there was complete silence again. It crept into the room and fed on the tension, gorging itself on anxiety. I could feel my pulse throb and my heart beat and could hear absolutely nothing.

'Then I got scared. Terrified. I stood up and saw what I had done. It had been like someone else was doing it. I ran. Just had to get away. Then, going home, I saw you. Lying there drunk. And I saw you as part of the problem. I'm sorry. But I was thinking if you had not fought with Aron this wouldn't have happened. I panicked. I needed to get rid of the knife and . . . John, I am sorry. So sorry.'

I reached for the wine glass that I'd placed on the floor. It was my turn to take a hearty gulp. I chewed at the wine, unhappily biting at it and swallowing it down.

'And when I was arrested . . . ?'

There was a long, restless pause. 'I kept telling myself you could not get charged because there would be no evidence. They couldn't prove you killed him, because you didn't. But it was too late.'

'You could have gone to the police. You could have told them it was you.'

She looked away, not willing or able to look me in the eye.

'It was too late and I was frightened. If they had sent you to trial I would have confessed. Believe me, I would never have let you go to jail.'

'Well, I might still be going there. Someone has spoken to the police and said they will testify that I said I would hurt Aron. A court would think it was premeditated.'

Her eyes widened. 'Me? You think that was me? No, John. Please. I swear. I know nothing about that. Nothing. You must believe me.'

'And what else do you know about the knife?'

'What?' I saw the look on her face. Caught.

'You heard me. What else can you tell me about the knife?'

'I took it.' A confession sneaking out between tight lips.

'Go on.'

'When I left you. After I stayed at your place. I went to where you'd buried the knife and took it. Dug it up.'

'How did you know where it was?'

'You were dreaming. Talking about it in your sleep. I could not understand all of it, and some of it scared me, but you said where you buried the *grindaknivur*. The three stones. I knew I had to take it. To . . . protect myself.'

'Really? So where is the knife now?'

Her eyes moved away. Couldn't look at me.

'I threw it in the sea. I had to get rid of it.'

'Where?'

'What?'

'Where did you throw it in the sea?'

'Off the western port. But the swell was high. It could be anywhere.'

'Christ, Karis. What the hell were you thinking?'

She looked shamefaced. Scared. 'I don't know. I just wanted it gone. I know . . . I am sorry.'

When I closed my eyes, I could hear the sound of near-silence in my head. Like television static once a station goes off air. It sounded like loss.

She looked up at me and I could see another thought occurring to her and forcing itself out.

'He said he was going to tell people what he did to me, but that is not why I killed him. It was because of what he did to me. Not because of what he might say. Because he raped me.'

A door closed inside me. Karis and I were finished. Or at least we could never be what I had wanted us to be, I knew that now. What she was, what she'd done. I couldn't be part of any of that. The doubts that had pursued me had been replaced by certainty.

Despite that, though, I knew I'd dragged the information and pain out of her, forced it to the surface and made her confront it. I owed her something for that. I was going to help her, whatever the cost.

'Don't blame yourself. Blame him. He did it, not you. You remember how you used to ask me why I came here? And I never properly answered you?'

She nodded, confused and anxious. 'Yes.'

'I did something I shouldn't have done, and I had to get away from it too. I did something for the wrong reasons and regretted it. You . . . well, if there's ever a right reason to kill someone, then what Aron did to you is one.'

'What . . . what did you do?'

'When I was a teacher, there was a kid in my class who got himself into trouble. I was walking home and saw four other kids, older boys, beating him. They basically scared me off, threatening worse for me and him if I didn't leave. So I walked away. I left him there. Eventually, and too late, I did what I should have done in the first place and went back for him. But they'd killed him. Tortured him and killed him.

'I went to court and testified, but of course that couldn't bring the boy back. And it didn't even put the killers in jail. There wasn't enough evidence and they walked. The boy, Liam, his parents blamed me. Hated me for not protecting their son. And they were right. I hated myself for it.

'So I did something about it. I hunted down the four thugs and hurt them the way they'd hurt Liam. I didn't kill them, couldn't bring myself to go down to their level. But I scared them and hurt them badly. No one could ever prove that I did it. In fact I have never admitted to anyone that I did it. Not until now.'

She was teary. 'So why are you admitting it now?'

'Because I did what I did to those kids for the wrong reason. I told myself it was because they'd killed Liam. Stabbed him. Burned him. That I was doing it because they deserved it. An eye for an eye. But I know that wasn't really true. I was doing it for me. To make up for my guilt. To try and make myself feel better about leaving Liam. I had walked away, and I was massaging my own guilt by hurting the thugs that hurt him.'

'You are too hard on yourself. You did what you thought was right.'

'But it wasn't right.'

Karis flinched.

'What I did was wrong. And the reason I did it was wrong. If you killed Aron because of what he did to you, I can't say that was the wrong reason.'

She collapsed again, crumpling into her seat and dissolving into tears. This time, when I went to comfort her, she let me. Her head fell under my chin and she shook as I hugged her.

'Don't tell anyone. Please.' Her words were spluttered out from beneath me. 'Please, John. I beg you. Don't tell anyone.'

'I won't. I promise you.'

I held her, wrapped her in my arms and in my flawed assurance. Helping Karis by keeping her confession a secret made me a prime candidate for prison. Would that be so bad? If my conviction meant she went free, it wouldn't be the worst thing in the world.

She and I couldn't be together, whatever happened, that much was certain now. But I'd already committed crimes worthy of prison when I'd taken revenge on Liam's killers, and maybe now was the time to pay the price.

Suddenly, something that Tummas Barthel had said came back to me, a whisky toast laden with meaning. *To lives lost and lives saved.*

I had to save one more.

Chapter 62

I'd left Karis an hour earlier, safe in the knowledge that she was in some form of reconstructed stability. The crying had eased, then ended; the shaking had gone, externally at least. She was going to visit her father. That would force her to behave rationally, rather than succumbing to the emotional disintegration that would be so easy within her own four walls.

She would be forced to put on a front of normality that would at least carry her through part of the night, a temporary scaffolding that was better than none at all.

Her visit to her father also presented me with the opportunity I needed. To break into her flat.

When I left her, I drove north to the whaling station to check on Nils Dam and to feed and water him. He was weak and bad-tempered and yet somehow accepting of his situation. He had become conditioned, beaten yet still needy, so that he was easily malleable.

From Við Áir, I drove back into Torshavn, again parking where I could get a good view of Karis's flat without being seen. I was there half an hour before she had said she would be leaving. I needed to make sure she had gone.

I sat, thinking and fretting, the car's clock inching forward. This wasn't something I felt comfortable with, far from it. But I was still going to do it.

Karis emerged from the front door right on cue, looking pensive and tired. She headed off on foot, huddled up against the wind and the world.

I didn't move. Not until the clock crawled on for another five minutes. I couldn't take the risk that she'd have forgotten something or simply change her mind.

I'd never broken into anywhere before. Not even in my rough-and-ready youth, when plenty of the other kids were wide enough to have done their share of thieving. I was stupid enough to be quick with my fists and roam in packs with the other wasters, but I'd never stooped to breaking and entering. That didn't mean I didn't know how to do it.

When the five minutes had passed, I stepped out of the car and quickly across to her door. I had to open it as quickly and unobtrusively as if I had a key. Any neighbours who happened to be watching would probably have seen me come and go often enough not to think anything of it, as long as I wasn't at the door too long. I slipped the thin piece of plastic into the lock, jiggling it into position, desperately trying to get it behind the bolt, as I'd seen others do. It wasn't as easy as it had looked. *Come on.* I was forcing it, panicking over the time it was taking, which inevitably made it take longer. There. Was that it? Shit. Again. The bolt sprung, I turned the handle and was in.

The door closed behind me and I climbed the stairs into the flat itself. I didn't know how many times I'd been in there, but this was different. This was wrong. For the first time, I was aware of the sound of my feet and what I touched. I could hear my own breathing.

I moved between things. I attempted the kind of catlike movements where obstructions are elegantly, effortlessly avoided and glided past untouched – the way I had watched Karis negotiate the room, walking a ninja's path between the canvasses, painting materials and other equipment. In Karis's absence it was a different space. In a sense it was more hers, more intimately and personally her own.

It was trespassing in her studio that was the greatest betrayal of trust. This was her inner sanctum, the place where she bared her soul. Sneaking in there like a thief, like the tearaways in the housing scheme where I grew up – every bit as bad as them and yet worse. I knew she didn't like me inspecting whatever she was currently working on, that she didn't like her work to be viewed until she herself was happy with it.

The easel near the window was covered with a piece of sacking, hiding it from the world, or at least from me. Shamelessly, I lifted the covering and saw my own face looking back at me. The last time I'd caught a glimpse of this painting I'd seen a brooding visage, the features mapped out and partly filled in, with only my eyes waiting to be painted. They'd been done now.

I could see the paint was still wet there. Presumably this was what she had done this afternoon after I'd left. My eyes: the windows to the soul that she hadn't previously been sure enough about to fill in. Now she had finished me, judged me, at last. The eyes that stared back were kind, trustworthy and reliable. In her generosity of spirit – or her gratitude that I wasn't going to tell anyone what she had done – she had lent my eyes a compassion that my current actions were giving the lie to.

I eased the sacking back over the portrait, two protruding pieces of wood keeping it off the still-drying oils, hiding the hypocrisy represented by that face. Better that it was covered and unseen.

On the wall beside it, I found two canvasses that I'd never seen before. Two abstract works that were very different from her usual style. Both were violently scored in reds and blacks, vicious brushstrokes that made me think of war. Or murder. There was a face visible in each one, eyes screaming through the colours, faces either drenched in blood or burning in hell. Both paintings disturbed me immensely.

Karis had an old sideboard against the wall, a faded and battered piece of furniture that was more functional than decorative. I knew its drawers were stuffed with tubes of oil, colour charts, swathes of material and photographs that she'd taken round the islands, as well as old letters and new bills and anything else that had nowhere to go. It was this sideboard that I wanted.

I'd read years before of the theory that when people lie, their eyes move up and to the right. Psychologists say it is a subconscious indication that they are inventing something, attempting a deception, reaching for the part of the brain that facilitates lying. Whether it was true, I had no idea.

But I did know that, earlier, when I'd asked Karis where something was, her eyes shifted. They had moved, if only fleetingly, to the right. I knew she had lied and I had a good idea where the truth lay.

I pulled the drawers out one by one and carefully worked my way through brushes, drawing pads, small tubs of primer, pastel pencils and tubes of oil in every colour under the sun. I pushed aside bundles of charcoal, water-colour blocks, frames and soaps.

I'd promised her that I wouldn't tell anyone that she had killed Aron. I hadn't yet broken that vow, but I had no doubt that I was breaking the spirit of it. The same went for our relationship. Maybe not so much breaking it as taking a wrecking ball to it and smashing it into a million pieces.

There, at the back of one of the drawers, under a piece of linen canvas, sat a plastic sandwich bag, the kind that presses together at the top to seal. Inside was the *grindaknivur*, the little blood-stained knife that she had told me she'd thrown into the sea off the western port while the swell was high. The knife she said could be anywhere.

I held it up in front of the window, the soft light streaming through glass and plastic, making a ruby-red stain shimmer on the blade. Such a small knife. The blood took me back, to bad places and times, to things I should have done and to things I shouldn't. I still wasn't sure which category my next action would fall into.

Chapter 63

When I'd called Nicoline the next morning and said that I wanted to meet, she suggested the dark interior of the Manhattan, the bar that never sleeps.

Our lunchtime rendezvous was still two hours away and so I had time to drive over to the whaling station to check on Nils. I had to finish all of this soon.

As the Peugeot bumped its way along the track, the now-familiar sight of the fading red buildings loomed into view up ahead. I parked out of sight, the building nearest the slipway shielding the car from the road. I stood for a moment, pondering what a sight it must have been to watch the whales be winched up the sloping ramp from the sea. The lingering, stale stench of blubber made it an easy leap for the imagination.

I eased open the heavy old door to the middle building, something comforting, now, about the door's harsh groan, and stepped inside, with water, fruit and sandwiches in hand. The gloom and the rancid smell of old oil greeted me as usual, my feet ringing across the solid floor. But as I took in the room, the pulleys, the drums, the cogs, the oars, the boxes, there was no sign of Nils. The shelves of the old freezer were visible, exposed by his absence. Stupidly, my eyes searched the rest of the room, as if I'd secured him somewhere else by mistake.

The food and water tumbled from my hands, landing on the floor in a clatter. I charged around the room, looking behind every possible hiding place, pulling back cans and ropes, throwing aside old lifebelts. At the freezer, I saw the shackles that had held Nils lying on the ground. I grabbed the door and hauled it open, running blindly outside.

I hadn't been there since the evening before, so he might have twelve hours or more head-start on me. I ran from building to building, the main sheds and the smaller outhouses, down to the shore, across the slipway and beyond. I retraced my steps up the track to the road and across the fields. There was no sign of him.

Then in a panic I thought about the car. The keys were in my pocket, but perhaps he'd managed to circle round behind me and would be able to hotwire it. I ran, breathing hard now, but the Peugeot stood where it had been, and no Nils in sight. I fired the keys and locked it.

This time I stalked round the site more slowly, but the outcome was the same. Nils Dam, however he had done it, had escaped.

If he'd got out the night before then he could have crawled into Hvalvik by now. I couldn't be sure how steady on his legs he would be. I'd supported him during the brief bouts of exercise I'd allowed him, but he could easily have been faking his weakness. And even if he'd only got to the main road he could have thumbed a lift into Torshavn. But if he'd done that, then surely Tunheim or Nymann would have been after me by now.

For all I knew, he had got halfway across one of the surrounding fields – or the fjord – and no further. He could be lying there dead or dying, but there was no way I could comb every inch of it trying to find him. Nor did I have the time. I had to get out of there and back into town.

With a final despairing look around, I unlocked the car again, jumped in and drove off.

*

I decided to make a better job of parking the car this time, secreting it up a side street off Stoffalág. It meant a longer walk back but it was more discreet. I had no idea if the cops would be looking for it, but if they were there was no sense in making it easy for them.

It made the hike over to the Manhattan a nervous one, looking over my shoulder and seeing suspicion in every passing face. If I was going to get picked up for imprisoning Nils then I would be in deep shit, but if the object in my jacket pocket were to be discovered then the depth of the shit would be unfathomable.

Of course, in going to meet Nicoline, I may well have been walking straight into their hands and giving them everything they wanted, but I had to bluff that out and hope for the best. There was no other way.

Climbing the steps to the pub, the black-and-green livery in my face, I took one deep breath and pushed through the doors. Nicoline was where I expected her to be, in the same corner that we had sat in before. She was alone.

There was an orange juice parked in front of her and I pointed at it. 'Do you want another one of those?'

'No. I am good with this. Thanks.'

At the bar, I fretted over the temptation to have beer. Or something stronger. The words orange juice were eventually forced out through gritted teeth.

'You look nervous.' Nicoline was studying me carefully as I slid into the seat opposite her.

'Do I have reason to be?' I knew it sounded defensive and probably paranoid, but I reckoned I had cause.

She leaned forward, chin on her hands, to get a better look at me. 'That depends, I guess. Does being chief suspect in a murder investigation make you nervous?'

'It does today. Don't piss me about, Nicoline. Please. Is there anything else that I should know about?'

Her brows knotted, she was clearly confused, and I allowed

myself to breathe a bit easier. 'Not that I know of. You tell me. Is there anything else *I* need to know?'

I hesitated. I trusted her up to a point, but her job was her job.

'Yes, maybe. But I'm not going to tell you what it is. You might know soon enough, but for now I'm saying nothing. There's no point in trying to change my mind. Anyway, I have something better for you.'

That interested her. I could see her hoping that it would be what she suspected it was. She was on edge, desperate to know if I could deliver on my promise.

'Well? Tell me. For God's sake.'

'We are alone here, right?'

'What? What's wrong with you? Of course we are alone. I am putting myself at risk here, too.'

I looked round, like a drug dealer making a scan of the premises before handing over his gear. My eyes didn't leave hers as I reached into my pocket and produced the object that had been burning a hole there, its plastic bag hot to the touch. I lifted it above the table edge and placed it in front of her.

The blade glinted under the strip lighting and the blood-streak gleamed. Nicoline's eyes lit up, too.

'That's it?' She reached over the table towards the bag, but I placed my hand above it before she could get there. 'Did your parents never teach you it is rude to grab?'

She sat back, a rueful smile playing on her lips.

'I just need to be sure we understand each other,' I said. 'And that we are both giving something here.'

'Okay, tell me.'

'You can't say where you got this from. Say it was left anonymously. Say you found it. Say the tooth fairy left it under your pillow. I don't care. But it wasn't from me. Okay?'

'Okay. But I need to know more about it. For a start, will your prints or DNA be on here?'

'Yes. My prints probably will be.'

'That makes things difficult. For both of us, but especially for you. You do realize that?'

'Of course I do.'

'Okay. So who else's prints will I find on here?'

I shrugged.

'You don't know or you won't tell me?'

'Which would you rather hear? That should be enough for you to work with. And it's all I will give you. But in return, I want the name of Nymann's witness. The person who is going to testify against me.'

'Let me look at it. Oh come on, let me see.'

I took my hand away and Nicoline reached over and picked the bag up, the tips of her fingers gripping its sealed edge. She held it up to the light, turning it this way and that, occasionally frowning, sometimes nodding.

'There are prints, some quite clear. Those on the blood are sharp but . . . well, let's see. It is definitely the murder weapon?'

'I wouldn't want to tell you your job, but you will find that is Aron Dam's blood on there. And, by my own memory of *CSI*, the blade will fit the entry wounds.'

She scowled at me. 'Very funny. But you are right, I will test all that for myself. You sure you won't tell me where you got it?'

'I'm sure.'

'And you won't tell me how I can rule out your fingerprints?'

'No.'

'It is a dangerous game you play.' She paused and sipped her orange juice. 'The national DNA database, the one that you wanted me to tap into?'

'Yes?'

'I think I'm getting the go-ahead. Some people are very unhappy, but that is their problem. I will be allowed to run the DNA I found at the scene against what they stored.'

'So you might not need the knife then?' I began to wonder if taking it, and the inevitable consequences of doing so, had been necessary after all.

'Oh no. Putting someone at the scene is one thing. Putting him on the murder weapon is something else entirely. I need this. And thank you.'

I nodded, still wondering what the hell I had done.

'So ... Nymann's witness ...'

I sat up anxiously. I had a list of names in my head. Would it be the one I expected?

'I spoke to Kielstrup. Men are so easy. Well, most of them. He was not keen to speak, made a big deal out of how Nymann would not be happy. He was overdoing his hand, like a bad poker player, trying to get the most out of a little. Which is always the way I've thought of Kielstrup.'

'Nicoline, are you going to tell me?'

She tilted her head forward in mock admonishment. 'Did no one ever tell you that patience is a virtue? And being so impatient for ... what do you call it ... instant gratification, yes, that's it ... not a good sign at all.'

'For fu–'

'It is Serge Gotteri.'

'What?'

'The Frenchman, Serge Gotteri. He is Nymann's witness against you.'

Chapter 64

I had phoned Gotteri's number three times and got no answer. The fourth time, I got an engaged signal. And the same on the fifth.

Nicoline had left, the prize of the plastic bag and the *grindaknivur* in her possession. I trusted her to keep its provenance a secret. I had more trust in that than in my own ability to act with restraint, having heard what I'd heard.

The Frenchman was a liar. I would drain every drop of truth out of him – I knew there was more to come. The fact that he was in so thick with Nils Dam complicated matters hugely though, particularly as I had no idea where Nils was.

I went to Gotteri's rented home on Hamarsgøta and banged on the door for long enough that a neighbour appeared and asked what the problem was. I told her I was looking for my friend Serge and she informed me that he'd left a couple of hours earlier, but no, she had no idea where he'd gone.

He could be anywhere on the islands, I knew that, and could easily be away all day. Waiting for him to return wasn't an option, though; it would take time that I didn't have.

Hurrying back into town, I decided to check out some of his regular haunts. He wasn't having lunch in the brasserie at Hvonn, or sitting having a coffee in the sun outside Cafe Karlsborg at the port, or gazing out to Nolsoy with his camera round his neck. I charged back up past the cathedral, round the fringe of Tiganes that led to the Natur, to see if he was there.

There were only a handful of people inside, and Gotteri clearly wasn't among them, just a few tourists and couple of girls giggling over coffee. Oli was on duty behind the bar and he seemed as likely to know the Frenchman's whereabouts as anyone. He hadn't noticed me enter the bar and seemed preoccupied with his mobile phone.

'Hey, Oli. *Hvussu gongur*?'

He looked up distractedly. 'Hey. Good, thanks. And you?'

'Yeah, okay. Listen, have you seen Serge Gotteri around?'

Oli shrugged. 'Not today, no. I thought you guys were not talking so much?'

'Where did you hear that?'

He grinned sheepishly. 'It's my job. I hear things.'

'Well, if you hear where he is let me know, okay? It's really important. I need to know where I can find him.'

Oli studied me, seemingly making his mind up about something. His phone beeped again and he dropped his head to read whatever message had arrived. I saw his eyes widen. When he straightened up again he looked round the bar before speaking quietly to me.

'Okay. I might know where he is. Or where he will be going. Him and everyone else.'

'What do you mean?'

Oli raised his phone so that the top of it peeped above the level of the bar. 'I am on Facebook, keeping up with something about to happen. But it is being kept quiet until the last moment. You understand? To keep away the wrong people. But Serge, he will definitely be there, as long as he knows about it.'

'Oli, I have no idea what you are talking about.'

'A *grindadráp*,' he hissed at me. 'There's a *grind* about to take place. They are watching the whales now.'

'Christ. Where?'

'Here. Torshavn. The boats are off the southern tip of Stremoy. They say Skopunarfjordur is heaving with pilot whales. The ocean is alive with them. As many as a thousand, they say.'

'Where will they bring them in?'

'At Sandagerd, of course. They are waiting for the current to change, then they will drive them onto the beach. They won't be able to bring them all in, it just isn't possible. But there will be many, many more than we have seen in a long time.'

'How long? When will they arrive?'

'They are whales not buses. Things can change. But if the current and the whales do as they should, then . . .' He glanced at his phone again. 'Half an hour. Maybe a little longer.'

He leaned forward with a conspiratorial grin. 'Then the killing begins.'

The beach at Sandagerd, just before Argir, was three kilometres away. By the time I got back to the car, I could be halfway there on foot. I would walk. Or run.

Chapter 65

The road to Sandagerd was due south of town, beyond the end of the western port. I strode back over the hill, past the cathedral and the Hotel Torshavn, out past the boats bobbing on my left and the hulking keel of a ship being worked on. I climbed the circular hill past little cottages and neatly tended gardens, across the corner of the road that plunged downhill towards the industrial part of the port and onto the long, straight road out of Torshavn towards Argir.

As I bustled along, I tried phoning Gotteri again but got no answer. I was actually glad. Oli was right, Serge would be there. I remembered his fervour when we were at Búgvin and he got word of the whale hunt at Hvalvik. He had been desperate to get there and was furious at being late. A fury that all made sense now.

There was much more traffic on the road than usual, all seemingly heading in the same direction as me. Looking both back and ahead, I saw men walking in groups of twos and threes, all swarming towards the beach. The further I got along the road, the more I became aware that a small army was on the march. Its uniform was jeans, boots and either thick checked shirts or traditional local sweaters.

Their numbers grew as the word of the hunt spread, increasing with every step, until the road and pavement were thick with people advancing on Sandagerd. I was after Gotteri, but I'd become part of something else: an unwitting recruit in a body of men with fixed stares and set, determined jaws.

After the hospital, the hill tumbled down below us towards the sea. A flank of golden green that fell away quickly, with a long stretch of people already standing by the crescent shore. The tide was bringing white peaks rushing on to the small sandy beach, with the white walls and green roofs of the houses of Argir above them on the opposite shoreline.

As we funnelled down the narrow path towards the beach, a murmur of excitement went through the ranks and we all looked up as one to see a line of dots on the horizon, coming round the bend past Nolsoy. It was the boats.

Somewhere immediately in front of them, as yet unseen among the white horses that danced at the bow of the armada, were the whales. God knew how many of them.

The boats were strung out in an arc, slowly but steadily pushing towards the shore. I remembered that Martin Hojgaard, in his passionate defence of the hunt, had talked of how important it was to drive the whales in at the right speed. If the boats panic the pod, then the whales will turn and get away. If they either drive them for hours or try to get the job done in minutes, the whales will be stressed. This is bad in two ways, Martin told me. First, no one wants unnecessary suffering to the animals. Second, stress damages the meat. He said that when seventeenth-century kings hunted deer with horses and dogs, they would throw the meat to the dogs, as it was not seen as suitable for humans. The purpose of the *grind* was to get meat to feed the family.

As we marched, the boats got nearer. The dots became distinct and soon crafts of different sizes could be identified. In front of them – my heart jumped at the sight – I could see inky black dorsal fins rising and falling with the waves. There were hundreds of them.

The side boats hemmed them in and those behind pushed them on. They would be upon us soon, no place for them to run.

I was on the sand now, standing at the back of the beach alongside other men, some of them looking at me curiously, but most staring straight ahead. I tried to drag my eyes away and search for Gotteri, but was rapt at the sight of the advancing boats and whales and by those I stood guard with.

It was like they were in a trance. They were gaping at their prey, readying themselves for what was ahead. For what they had to do. They were preparing themselves to kill.

Barely a word passed between them. What little I heard them say was to themselves, oaths of intent muttered under their breath, vows to do what their fathers and grandfathers had done. They had walked away from jobs when they got word, left cars or boats, banks, factories and fish farms. Now they stood, grimly waiting, psyching themselves up, as if the execution was to be their own. They were soldiers, ready to go to war.

The rules of the *grind* were simple and ancient. Harpoons were banned, as were spears or guns. It was man against beast, except that man was armed with a hook called a *sóknarongul*, and a knife, the *grindaknivur*. And that the beast, the gleaming black leviathan, was denied the benefit of its natural habitat. These were not whalers in the vein of Ahab and his pursuit of Moby Dick, this was a battle to be fought in the shallow waters of the shoreline.

They were much closer now, the hunters and the hunted. Speedboats and motorized dinghies dodging between sailboats and small yachts. Before them, fins sliced through the water.

The men along the shore held a thick rope that was fed from one man to the next, an umbilical cord that each held for dear life. In the other hand, and attached to the line, each man grasped a heavy iron hook, the *sóknarongul*. It was this hook that would bring each whale to them.

I looked around me, a final desperate attempt to see Gotteri before everyone was swept up in what was to come. There were so many people now; it was hard to pick out faces among the spellbound. They lined the shore and packed the beach. It was hard to see where one group finished and another other began. There were hundreds of people, maybe even a thousand. One for every pilot whale believed to make up the pod.

As I scanned the ranks of grim expressions, I was brought to a crashing halt by one that I recognized. Not Gotteri but Toki Rønne. The short, wide frame of the fish-farm worker was unmistakeable, as was the scowl that scarred his face under heavy, furrowed brows. He stared out to sea with murderous anticipation, and had no eyes for anything or anyone else. I couldn't help but shudder at the relish with which Toki would tackle the task of killing the incoming whales.

There was an intent in him that was different from the other faces lining the beach. Maybe it was just my knowledge of his character, but I could see a want in Toki that was absent from his fellow sand soldiers. They were steeling themselves for what was to come. He hungered for it.

My eyes moved on beyond Toki, seeing most of the adult males of Torshavn standing ready, the blood of their Norse ancestors pulsing through their veins. Instincts, centuries-old and centuries-deep, rising to the surface. I saw Tummas Barthel, a hand rummaging doubtfully through his white beard. Just yards from him was Martin Hojgaard, and further on Oli was there now too, his normally carefree countenance locked firm.

Then I looked back, my attention tugged by something, someone, out of place. A man looking not out to sea but directly at me. Features haggard, drawn and marked by recent battle. A face that made me jump. Nils Dam. He stared at me through the crowd, the hatred in his eyes visible from thirty yards away. His brows low, glowering, as if he was trying to kill me with his glare. Did he get here before me or follow me on the road from town? There were so many people between us that I didn't think I could quickly get to him or he to me. Then the crowd swelled like the ocean and he was swept out of sight.

Everything moved at once. The men beside me began to step forward, a hum of intensity rising among them, earnest and determined. My head whirled back to the boats and saw that the ocean boiled with whales.

The great beasts were thrashing in the shallows, broad flanks of black and flailing fins causing the water to churn into heaving sprays of white. As one, the men were on their way to meet them, striding into the sea until it was quickly to their waists, their generals to the fore, pointing this way and that, both leading and carrying the line.

My eyes cast along the advancing islanders, sensing the awfulness of the collision that was to come. I could feel my own adrenalin pumping, blood surging through me as I felt the most primitive of impulses taking over. *Do it. Join them.* That's when I saw him. Gotteri.

The blond hair above the slender frame was unmistakeable. He was in the middle of the whalers yet not with them. He didn't hold the rope or carry a hook, instead he was armed with something else, which he held close in front of him.

My legs were moving before I realized it. Towards Gotteri. Towards the ocean and the whales. The cold shock of water chilled my legs then my groin and my waist. I was in amongst the swell of sea and man and whales and boats. I was part of it, living it.

The froth of whipped water rose up at me as the whales fought for their lives, soaking me and those around me. Men had crossed between Gotteri and I. Only his head was in view, and then it too was gone amid the tumult. In front of me and to my left, a flinty-eyed whaler with short dark hair was leading with the rope, up to his chest in water and his hook raised at shoulder height.

As I watched, he grimaced, steadied himself, and brought the hook down on the great writhing figure that blackened the water in front of him. The rounded end of the *sóknarongul* struck violently but deftly into the whale's blowhole, where it stuck fast.

The reason for the line fastened to the hook became suddenly apparent. With the gaff lodged in the whale's skull, the men began dragging it to the shore, where its fate would be sealed. I watched open-mouthed as the slick dark shape slid through the foam towards the sand. In seconds, the whale was beached and a knife produced, a glinting reminder of the little *grindaknivur* that had stabbed Aron Dam. It sliced through the air, then through the spinal cord of the beast. Its killer's hand sawed back and forth, blood surging from the whale and coating every finger that held the knife.

The blood poured out. A fountain of red that erupted. A geyser of life gushing out like an uncapped oil well. I could not take my eyes off it, seeing the same almost darkly comic gash carved into its flesh, its blubber and meat exposed. I turned and saw another whale being cut, then another. One by one, they were being hooked and sliced. Knives flashing and blood streaming out. The sea was dark red around me, a blood-red sea thick with bodies, both human and mammal. In seconds, the sea had turned from its dark-blue blackness to a gory soup of fresh blood. When the tide brought waves, their angled flanks resembled a marbled cut of steak.

The sea of blood and the slaughter all around me was making my head spin and taking me back to places I didn't want to be. I saw Liam Dornan's body sliced by the knives of his killers, saw his raw open wounds where they made his blood flow. I could smell it, smell him, smell his death. It surged into my nostrils, filling them, choking them, sickening them. All of my senses were overloaded. The taste of death in my mouth and the sound of it assaulting my ears.

I couldn't move, lost in the mayhem and memories. Maybe that's why I didn't react until it was too late. Perhaps I didn't recognize the hook for what it was until it had rapped my skull violently then wrapped itself round my throat. I was choking and falling into unconsciousness and into the ocean, and yet still I was not aware of what had been done to me.

The last thing I saw before I slipped underwater was the blue of the sky. It spun pale and languid overhead, only a patch of flimsy cloud spoiling the view. I saw that vision for just a second, before my eyes blurred and everything was wet and red.

Chapter 66

There comes a moment in the wrestle for life when the distinction between opposing sides is blurred to the point of blindness. Did I start this fight or did he? Am I on top or being forced back down? Am I winning or losing? Have I won or already lost? My blood or his blood?

I can see the blood, taste it, smell it. I can feel it lick my skin and hear its rush in my ears. Blood means life but it also means death. My senses are suffocated, drowning in shades of red. All I can do is fight.

Would-be killer and would-be victim, rolling and grappling; life fighting death fighting life.

If he doesn't die, I can't live. If I die, he has won.

The blood's in my nostrils now, not just the scent of it but the liquid reality of it. My bones ache and my lungs burn. Life and living is on the line.

I feel a tiredness that I know I can't afford. He thrashes at me, sending pain surging through my body. It rings in my wrists and my chest, my knees. Then three violent knocks in quick succession against my ankles, an orchestra of pain, all my joints singing from the same hymn sheet.

I'm losing. I'm lost.

When consciousness came it was immediate and uncomfortable. I could barely see through the fog of red, and the pain in my head was unbearable. My ears were filled with the surreal echo-chamber sounds of underwater, the booming thrashing of giant bodies and the pitiful wails that they let loose.

There were hands round my neck and holding me under. The world was upside down, and screamed with strange sounds that, though muffled, still managed to be huge and frightening. I kicked and thrashed but I achieved nothing.

My attacker punched me in the neck and the ache of it surged through me, an electric shock or a lightning strike. Not a punch, couldn't have been a punch. My skin stung and my blood pulsed.

Through the blood-red gloom I saw the black shadows of the whales as they fought for their own survival. They twisted and turned and I tried to do the same, spinning my body in a frantic effort to free myself. I threw back my elbows one by one, but the sea cushioned the blow and I was no more than a nuisance to my assailant, barely slowing him down. I tried to scream or shout but all I did was swallow water, sending bubbles of lost oxygen into the sea.

I managed to get an arm behind me. Reaching. Grabbing. There was another punch to my neck and the sea grew thicker with blood around me. I was getting weaker, had to act quickly. My free hand groped feverishly until I found a body part. An ankle. I grasped it, dug in my nails to little effect. Giving it every bit of strength I had left, I wrapped my hand around it and pulled. I felt the foot slide.

The grip on my neck was released and I felt the body behind me move back and away. I was free of the grip that held me, but my respite was short as the foot returned, stamping on me and forcing out air that I couldn't afford to lose. I tried to tumble turn and get my head out of the water, my senses somersaulting with my body. But I saw something glint below and then above me, only just turning my head in time to avoid the knife as it stabbed down on me. I had nowhere to go, desperately trying to see where it was coming from. Then I felt a hand grab my hair, locking my head where my attacker wanted it. Where it could be attacked.

I looked through the veil of whale blood, seeing the sky beyond the surface. The knife was coming down again, plunging at my skull. Then, from the side, something huge and dark closing in fast. It was like a black truck careering off a road and coming straight at me at full speed. I felt its force and went spinning, slipping through the water and into a fresh darkness of my own.

I felt my cheek come to rest on the sand and felt the rough grains scratch my skin. My mind was shutting down, spiralling with me to the bottom of the sea. Blackness enveloping me. Memories gone.

Something squeezed hard round my middle and I spewed water and coughed for air. I was standing. Well, sort of. I was upright. Blurred blue sky above me. An above-water world around me, albeit out of focus.

My head was heavy and I let it slump, staring down at the bloody sea that swam around me. It pitched in red swells, heaving and sinking. I managed to lift my head again and saw that I was being held up by two strangers, one on either side.

The first man wasn't looking at me but at the sight around him. He had a thick head of dark, greying hair and a salt-and-pepper beard. A broad streak of blood clung to his cheek and his mouth hung open in slack-jawed contemplation. The hand that wasn't holding me up was drenched in blood and held a knife; even his gold wedding band was painted in red.

On the other side was a younger man, fair-haired, with rouge-spattered cheeks. He was staring at me incredulously, his mouth opening and closing, but I couldn't take in what he was saying. He tried again, and it trickled through my sodden brain that he was speaking a language I didn't understand.

They continued to hold me, dazed and hurting, keeping me from dropping back into the sea. I knew, now, that that was where I'd been. A whale. A whale had saved me. No doubt more by accident than design, but it had saved my life when it crashed into me and probably my attacker too. I swung my head round the scene but there was nothing alive down there. My saviour was now a carcass, his blood swimming round my waist.

'Mr Callum. Mr Callum.'

My two supporters spun me round to face the voice, and I saw Broddi Tunheim striding through the sea towards me, his face ashen.

'My God, man. I thought you were dead.'

I tried a smile but my head hurt. 'Me too.'

I was sitting on a grassy bank above the beach, my head coming slowly back into focus. Tunheim crouched next to me. His spectacles were bothering him; he fidgeted with them with one hand, as he helped me drink from a bottle of water with the other.

The whales were in my eyeline, row upon row of them turning grey as they dried out, no longer the gleaming black, vital creatures that had surged through the ocean towards death. I let my eye settle on one, imagining it to have been the individual that saved my life. Its head nearly severed, wearing its macabre smile, waiting to be sliced up

At the water's edge, a couple of dozen boats nestled on the blood-red sea, with the same number again moored further out. Below us the beach thronged with people, a sated, patient queue snaking the length of the sand and then back again, every inch of it five or six people wide. There were people as far as I could see, all charged with the euphoric sense of survival that comes from having bested nature.

'They have to queue to get their share of the whale meat,' Tunheim explained, as he eased the water from my lips. 'They all get the same. The officers down there make sure of it.'

At the head of what I saw now were separate queues, men wearing hi-vis jackets were taking down names, clipboards in hand. The town would eat well and long.

'Did you see who did this to you?'

I shook my head and wished I hadn't. A paramedic had treated the wounds to my neck but I'd refused to go to hospital. Seeing how stubborn I was, Tunheim shooed the man away after he'd done his work.

'No. I was attacked from behind me. No one saw it happening?'

'No. Not amongst all that. If he held you underwater and was stabbing at you, everyone would just have assumed he was cutting at a whale. I suspect it all happened fast. No one saw. Those in the water only have eyes for the kill. Those on the land only have eyes for the killers.'

'Yeah, well there was one killer extra.'

Tunheim nodded gravely. 'And that is one too many. So tell me, did you see anyone on the beach before the *grind* began? Anyone who might have had a reason to do this to you?'

I hesitated, seeing again the faces on the sand. Nils. Gotteri. Toki. I shrugged.

'Most of the men of Torshavn were there. There were lots of them I knew.'

'That is not what I asked you. Did you see anyone who might have wanted to kill you? You must tell me.'

My definition of 'must' didn't match Tunheim's.

'There was a guy that I worked beside at the fish farm at Eiði. Toki Rønne. We've had a couple of run-ins. I guess he'd have reason to hurt me.'

'Okay. I know of him and yes, he is a violent man.' Tunheim held my gaze. 'Anyone else?'

I shrugged again. 'There were so many people. I can't be sure.'

The inspector shook his head in obvious disappointment, and when he took off his spectacles again and began to wipe them clean I had a sense of foreboding.

'Oh dear. I am worried about you Mr Callum.'

'Why's that?'

'I think the attack on you must have affected your memory. It is the only thing that can explain why you don't remember seeing Serge Gotteri on the beach. I would have thought he was the one person you would have been sure to have seen.'

'I . . . Yes, maybe. I must have forgotten. All the excitement of nearly being murdered.'

'Yes. That would do it, I'm sure. But in any case, Gotteri was not the one who tried to kill you. Just the opposite.'

Not for the first time, Tunheim seemed to know more than I did. My confusion caused the words to stumble out of me.

'What? What do you mean, Broddi?'

Tunheim spread his arms wide. 'He saved your life. It was him that pulled you out of the sea.'

My head spun anew, this time at the news. 'Are you sure? Maybe he just made it look like that after trying to drown me and stab me. If he thought he was going to get caught?'

'Not according to the men who were holding you up. They told me Gotteri was in the sea, shouting. He hauled you out of the water and then the others came to help him. They say Gotteri saved your life.

'Where is he now?'

'No one knows. He has left. He did not want to hang around, it seems. So, tell me, Mr Callum. If not him, who do you think tried to kill you? And was it the same person who killed Aron Dam?'

My head came up and I returned his gaze, but I said nothing.

'Come on. I know you know much more than you are telling me. But this has gone too far and it must stop now. It must be over. Help me make it over.'

I sighed. 'I don't know who it was.'

'No. That is correct. You had your back to the person. But you have a very good idea who is responsible for all that has happened. And so do I. If we have the same person in mind then I think it is time to visit them, don't you?'

I closed my eyes and wished my life away. I remembered being at the bottom of the ocean, twisting and turning for my life, seeing the glint of metal above and below, and the knife coming flashing towards me.

'Yes. Yes, Broddi. I do. Come on. I take it you know the way.'

Chapter 67

'So how did you know, Broddi?'

Tunheim was at the wheel of his green Toyota, driving us back into Torshavn. He shrugged wearily. 'I live here, Mr Callum. It is my job to know the people. I might not know modern detective techniques or psychological profiling or whatever it is that the Danes are taught. But I know people. *My* people.'

I nodded. 'And the Danes, Nymann and Kielstrup, they will be okay with you knowing things and not telling them?'

Tunheim grinned blackly. 'No, of course not. And that makes it better. I am just a man who investigates traffic crimes and a little vandalism. I know nothing about murder or murderers, I only know about people. But anyway, you talk of knowing things and not telling those who should know. There is much you have not told me, no? Now would be a good time.'

'Maybe. Let's just get there. And anyway, you first. Telling me you *know people* isn't enough. I want an explanation. How did you know?'

'Okay. When you could not produce the knife that killed Aron Dam, that was a big problem. For me, for you, for the investigation. It put me in trouble for not informing the Danes. You . . . it made you the main suspect again. But it also made me think. You are not stupid, you knew how important the knife was. And when it was not where you left it ... you were honestly surprised. I could see that.'

He paused and slowed at a pedestrian crossing, giving a wave to an older woman making her way across the road.

'So I had to wonder who might have taken it. I am sure you must have done the same. It is not the kind of thing you could tell people. That you had the murder weapon and you buried it. You would only tell someone very, very close to you. Or maybe you had not meant to tell them. And that would probably mean that person was even closer. The only person I knew of who could match that description was Karis Lisberg.'

I knew a lot about guilt. It had brought me to Torshavn and it had almost brought me to my knees. My body and soul were scarred with it. Now there was more of it flowing poisonously through my veins.

'With her name in my head, other things fell into place,' Tunheim continued. 'Her relationship with Aron. The time they were both at university in Copenhagen. I asked around town, people I knew I could talk to and trust to be quiet. And, of course, I knew what to ask about. The red-hooded raincoat. Ah yes, people told me. Yes, that's right they said, a red raincoat. It did not make me happy to learn it. You must know that. And now, what you have told me ... my God. It is a bad affair. So sad.'

Sad. Yes, it was definitely that. So much hurt already and so much more to come.

'It must not be easy for you, *Andrew*. I understand that. Knowing such a thing about someone you care for. It is not easy to be the cause of pain to a loved one. I do understand why you tried to keep that secret. But it cannot be allowed to stay that way.'

I knew he was right. We were on our way and there could be no turning back.

'Do what you can though, Broddi. Please? After what Aron did to Karis ...'

He exhaled hard. 'I will try. I will. It was a terrible thing. I do not know how much my voice will be listened to though. Our Inspector Nymann . . . we need to make sure he is not a problem. What you told me about Gotteri, that will help. Nymann's star witness is not to be believed.'

He was right. Gotteri's word wouldn't carry any weight now, not with everything that about to be known. I knew the man had contrived to frame me, in order to avenge the killing of Aron Dam at the urging of his brother, and to prolong their own murky dealings. Neither he nor the Danish inspector had anything they could use.

Instead it was down to Tunheim and me to put an end to it. If this was a *grindadráp*, the boats would have already driven the prey into the shallows and we, the hunters, would be standing there with our hooks ready to deliver the fatal blow.

I'd told him what I shouldn't have told him. Something I had no right to share. I'd told him about the rape, about Karis. About what she'd admitted.

My thoughts gave way to a quiet dread as I realized the car was slowing to a halt and Tunheim had put on the handbrake. We were in the shallow waters and nearing the end of our hunt.

Chapter 68

Tunheim led the way, moving quicker than I'd ever seen him move before, betraying some nerves perhaps. He was at the door in a matter of strides, with me just a couple of paces behind.

He rapped on the door with his knuckles, two quick knocks, followed seconds later by two more. When there wasn't an immediate response, he turned his fist side-on and battered harder.

He grimaced and I knew he was contemplating putting his shoulder to the door or kicking it open. He battered again, louder still. The voice came from behind us, panic-stricken.

'What are you doing? What are you doing here?'

Karis.

We both spun and saw her rooted to the spot, eyes wide and on the verge of tears. She stared at me accusingly. 'You! I trusted you. I begged you not to tell anyone. You promised.'

'Karis, I'm sorry.' I meant it. 'But there's no choice. This is the only way.'

'No!' she screamed it, her eyes locked on Tunheim. 'No. Inspector, I need to talk to you. Need to tell you what I've done.'

'Karis, don't . . .'

She moved across the street, talking as she went, not caring who heard. 'Inspector, I killed Aron Dam. I stabbed him. I did it. It was me.'

She was almost hysterical, sobbing the words out. 'Come away from here. Take me to the station. I need to make a full statement. A confession.'

Tunheim spoke calmly, his voice sympathetic and soothing. 'Frøkun Lisberg, please. We know. *I* know. Everything.'

Her face crumpled, all hope gone. Stuttering, she tried to salvage the situation. 'Yes, you know I killed Aron. Me. I killed him.'

Tunheim slowly shook his head. 'No. We know that it was your father.'

Her mouth dropped and tears formed. She blinked furiously.

'No. You are wrong. Wrong. I did it. It was because he raped me. Inspector, you do not realize. Aron Dam raped me. In Copenhagen. He would have done it again, so I killed him. For what he did.'

I couldn't take any more. 'Karis, stop. You can't protect him. I know you lied to me when you admitted it. I knew at the time. It made no sense for you to plant the knife on me then to take it away again by digging it up. And I knew you'd never have hidden it on me in the first place.'

She snarled, baring her teeth at me. 'You! You took it. You took it from my flat. You bastard!'

She flew at me, fists flailing at my chest. I let her hit me, but Tunheim stepped between us, wrapping his arms round her. I turned away, my hands over my face and rubbing at my eyes. This was even worse than I'd imagined.

'Where is your father, Frøkun Lisberg?' Tunheim tried to wrestle her into calm. 'We need to speak to him.'

'I don't know. He is not here. He has gone away.'

'Frøkun Lisberg, his car is parked right there.'

As I backed away from them, unable to bear seeing her like this, I turned and faced Edmundur Lisberg's house. I had to stop and look again. Then I knew.

'Inspector, keep hold of her, away from the house.'

'What? Why?'

'Just do it.'

I took a couple of paces back from the front door then kicked it above the lock.

'John!' She was screaming. 'What are you doing? No!'

I crashed my foot into the door again and then a third time before it groaned. I lashed at it once more and the wood splintered and the lock gave away. Without stopping to look back I pushed my way inside and through to the room I'd seen through the window.

As the door flew back, I could see him properly for the first time. Esmundur Lisberg. Hanging from a timber beam with a rope around his neck.

Chapter 69

I ran across the room, heart thumping and mind racing, trying desperately to remember anything I'd read about what the hell you were supposed to do in such a situation. I grabbed his legs, finding his trousers and boots soaking wet. Drenched like mine, from where they'd been underwater at Sandagerd beach.

I tried to lift him, to create slack in the rope, but I wouldn't be able to hold him for long. I needed to cut him down. A knife. Needed a knife.

Then the scream behind me. Footsteps running behind it.

'Christ, Broddi. Get her out of here.'

Her head was in her hands and she shrieked like the wind, staring horrified at her father.

'I couldn't hold her.' He grabbed her again, keeping her from moving forward, but unable to drag her away.

I grabbed an armchair and hauled it across the floor until it was underneath Lisberg, propping his feet on it so that at least some of the weight was transferred.

'A knife, Karis,' I yelled. 'Where does he keep a knife?'

'The drawer,' she pointed. 'That drawer.'

I grabbed the wooden handle on the dresser drawer and dragged it so fiercely that it came right out, objects clattering to the floor.

Among them was a large-bladed knife with a serrated edge. Picking it up, I jumped on the armchair, Esmundur's wet body sticking to mine, and sawed at the rope, Karis screaming behind me to hurry.

The fibres gave way and he dropped, my left arm catching him before he hit the floor, and easing him down towards the chair. Karis burst free of Tunheim's grip and was at her father's side, her hand stroking his face. Mine went to his wrist in search of a pulse.

'*Pápi!Pápi!*' Tears were streaming down her face. '*Pápi, góði. Góði.*'

'Karis, he's gone.'

'*Nei! Nei! Pápi, góði!*'

'Karis. He has no pulse. It's too late. He is dead.'

A neighbour, a kindly older woman and a friend of the minister, came into the house and looked after Karis while we were waiting for police officers and an ambulance to arrive. The neighbour sat with her arms around her, the sound of uncontrollable sobbing muffled by the woman's clothing.

Tunheim and I stood near the window, both drained by what had happened, both fearful of what might come next.

Suddenly, unexpectedly, Karis pushed herself away from the older woman and thrust her head up, mouth open in shock.

'It is my fault. All my fault.'

'No, Karis. We know it was your father.' I strived to take any anger out of my voice. 'The forensics will prove it. And you know it. You cannot take the blame.'

'It *was* my fault.' She was confused and in shock, struggling to come to terms with it. Her father lying on the floor, his face and upper body covered by a blanket. 'I told him about what Aron did. If I had not done that . . .'

'On the night of Dam's murder? You told him then?' Tunheim had moved nearer to her.

'No. Yes, then, too, but no, I meant I told him right after it happened.' Her voice fell away, warily looking at the neighbour, but the woman didn't seem to speak English. 'The rape. I told him a few months after the rape. He knew there was something wrong with me. I never wanted to go out. Always crying. In the end I told him. Everything. The rape. The abortion. He … he was so angry. I had never seen him like that. He wanted me to go to the police, have Aron put in jail. But I couldn't. I didn't want anyone else to know.'

'What did your father do, Frøkun Lisberg?'

'Nothing. Not then. I made him do nothing and he agreed. He was not happy, but he wanted to make me better. And in time I was. I became me again. He was so protective after that. Suspicious of men who wanted to date me or be with me. I was, too, but not so much as him. Then Aron … he just would not leave me alone. And *you* …'

She spat the word out and it hurt.

'*You* came and Aron got worse. Everything was going to come out. I tried to threaten Aron but he must have known I would not tell. But *he* would. If he couldn't have me then he would tell everyone what he did. He didn't care. That night … when he died … I went home and told my father. Said that I was scared what Aron was going to do. My father went out after him.'

'And he killed him.'

She heard the judgemental tone in my voice and her head snapped up venomously.

'At least my father did that for me! No one else would!'

I was aware of Tunheim's gaze switching furiously between Karis and me. All she and I could do was stare at each other. Her words were out and couldn't be taken back; but neither I nor Tunheim, it seemed, was brave enough to ask the questions those words demanded.

Memories drifted back to me though. Standing on the cliff top at Vestmanna, as she finished the sketch of the brave and reckless young birdcatchers of the past. She asked me if there was anything I wouldn't do for the person I loved. Her father had proved there was no limit to his love.

Tunheim broke the spell. 'Did you know your father murdered Aron Dam, Frøkun Lisberg?'

She let her head slump again, staring despairingly at the floor. 'I . . . I . . . No. Not at first. I thought maybe . . .' She looked up at me. 'I thought that you had done it. Like everyone thought. I came to see you to find out. Because I was frightened. Frightened my father had done it. For me.'

'None of this is your fault, Karis.'

She nodded her head furiously. 'Oh yes. Yes, it is. All of it. You remember when you told me how you hurt those four boys who had killed your pupil?'

I saw Tunheim's head move in recognition of what she'd said, but he said nothing.

'Yes.'

'You told me . . .' she wiped the back of her hand across her face, 'you told me that you did it for the wrong reasons. For yourself. Not for the pupil. Well, Aron wasn't killed because he was going to tell. Even though he was. It was because of what he did to me. Because he raped me. In the end, it was because of that. I told my father because of that. And he killed Aron because of that.'

A silence fell for a while. A horrible, fetid stillness that magnified everything that was in the room. I broke it in the end.

'Why did your father try to frame me? What did I do, or what did you say, to make that happen?'

She looked shamefaced, some of her anger at me having seeped away. 'It wasn't you. Not really. You were a man, so he did not trust you. And you were a stranger, a foreigner. And he thought you did not respect him when he asked you to leave me. But even then I think it was an accident.'

'An accident? Come on . . .'

'You were there when he walked through town after . . . after what he did. He did not plan it. Not any of it, but seeing you there . . . It was a chance. To get rid of the knife and to . . .'

'And to get rid of me?'

'Yes.'

'And today? At the whale hunt?'

Karis shook her head, but Tunheim spoke up for her.

'I think I can answer that. Harra Lisberg knew you were getting close to the truth. Far too close. He had to protect his daughter and his reputation and his church. He was a desperate man. He saw his chance to put an end to things. Do not think too badly of him, Frøkun. I am a father and if someone had done that to my daughter . . . well, I would seek the strength to deal with it.'

She looked up. 'My father had the strength of his god.'

'Frøkun, sometimes that is just not enough.'

Chapter 70

The road out of Torshavn to the airport at Vagar seemed much shorter than it had when I first arrived. The days were shorter, too, little blips of blue amidst a long stretch of darkness. This part of the world was turning upside down and the undying light of summer was inevitably being replaced by the strong grip of a long winter.

As we drove, I imagined the people of my dark summer lining the route and waving me a thankful goodbye. Martin Hojgaard, full of remorse at his lack of faith in me but equally devastated by his misplaced faith in Esmundur Lisberg. Tummas Barthel, gratefully holding the case of Ardbeg that I'd had delivered for him, the least I could do for the information he'd given me about Serge Gotteri. Broddi Tunheim, the good inspector who had smoothed out many wrinkles and made certain that Aron's rape of Karis did not become public knowledge.

Some of them had left before me. Gotteri, the liar, the fraud. The man who'd saved my life by pulling me unconscious from the seabed. He'd flown back to France, no doubt planning to fight the good fight somewhere new, but not before he and Nils Dam had fought in the middle of town. They had knocked lumps out of each other, both driven by the fury of shame, wanting to hurt and be hurt. Nils never told anyone about his incarceration in the whaling station. He couldn't. He had too many things he didn't want anyone in Torshavn to know about, and his guilt ensured his silence.

The Danish cops had flown home too – Inspector Nymann having the decency to offer me a handshake, which I accepted. Nicoline Munk left me her card, with a handwritten invitation on the back to visit Copenhagen sometime.

The rain hit while I was on the bus, winding my way past now-familiar hills and fjords – soaking the greens and the browns and topping up the waterfalls that cascaded down from the peaks. The driver couldn't have been able to see much more than twenty yards in front of him as the weather closed in, but he knew the road well enough to have driven it blindfold. The rain washed us all, cleansing past sins and leaving the land fresh to start again.

Karis hadn't been to see me and I couldn't entirely blame her for that. As she saw it, if it hadn't been for me then her father would still be alive. And she was right.

But I knew that I'd done the only thing I could. If I'd accepted her confession, knowing it to be a lie, I'd never have been able to live with myself. No one has the right to take another person's life, but Karis had more right than anyone to take Aron's. If I'd thought she had actually killed him then I would have kept her secret happily.

When I'd told her about the person in the red raincoat placing the knife on me, I had seen the look on her face and recognized it for what it was. Genuine shock. Her father's red coat, the one she'd often borrowed. That might have been the moment she knew for sure that her father had murdered Aron. And it was the moment that I knew that she hadn't.

I'd had to save Karis by proving her father to be the killer. A life saved for a life lost. Of course, it also meant a love lost – but it was a love that was beyond saving.

It was almost a happy coincidence that I'd saved myself too. I had stared into Nils Dam's eyes with a knife in my hand when I most needed the truth, and I came up with the right answer. I wasn't the person I'd feared I was. Nils lived, and because of that, I did too.

As the bus pulled into the tiny airport car park in the wilds of Vagar, the rain hammered down, making passengers scurry across the tarmac to the terminal. I walked, letting the rain lash my face and enjoying the feel of it on my skin.

I was almost inside when I heard a car speed into the car park. Turning, I saw it was a familiar green Toyota – Tunheim's. The passenger door opened and a figure stepped out into the rain. Even with her back to me, I saw the dark hair and the quiff and knew Karis immediately.

She ran across the tarmac, puddles splashing at her feet. I dropped my case and she ran until she stood just a few feet away, coming to a sudden, seemingly reluctant halt. She looked so small standing there, the rain soaking her hair and streaming down her cheeks. She made a step as if to come to me but instead stepped back, further from my reach, or me from hers. She stood there, dripping, eyes reddening.

'I can't stay, Karis.'

'I know, John. And I don't want you to. I want to say sorry.'

'Call me Andrew. Sorry for what?'

Her mouth flopped open and it clearly pained her to even think the words she wanted to say. 'Everything.'

'For using me?'

'No, I . . . Yes. Yes.'

'Was that all it was?'

'No! No, I swear. But now I think I know, deep down . . .'

She looked distraught but I wasn't going to spare her this pain. We both needed to hear it. My mind flashed back again to the conversation on the bird cliffs of Vestmanna, when she had demanded a test of honour from me, wanting to know what I would and wouldn't do in the name of love.

'You said to me that at least your father did that for you – killed Aron. Was that what I should have done for the person I loved?'

Karis began to speak, but confusion caught her tongue. Then a sudden realization tied a knot in it.

'It's true, Karis. Isn't it? You wanted me to murder Aron for you.'

Tears streamed down her face and she seemed traumatized.

'Not … not consciously. Oh, my God. I … I have had time to think. Lots of it. And I think I wanted someone to love me enough to take that pain away. To revenge me. To …'

'Kill him. And you thought I was capable of that?'

She shrugged helplessly. 'There was something about you. Something troubled, and I wondered why you had come here. What you had run from. I was drawn to it.'

I felt sick.

'It wasn't exactly a great foundation, was it? Being attracted by each other's demons.'

Her mouth opened and closed, saying nothing, saying everything.

'I did love you, Karis.'

'I am so sorry.'

'Don't be. It's okay. I didn't think I would ever love anyone again, because I had hated myself. You solved both of those things.'

'Can you forgive me?'

'It's his fault, not yours. But I knew we were done the moment you told me you had killed him. Even though I knew you were lying, I also knew you'd been prepared to risk me going to prison for it.'

'I had to protect my father!'

'Of course you did. Because you loved him more than you could have loved me. Because he did the thing for you that you wanted most.'

She stared at the floor and nodded.

'Just go home, Karis. And forgive yourself. Aron did all this, not you.'

Tunheim was walking slowly toward us through the rain, but still a respectful distance away. 'Look after her, Broddi. I need you to do that.'

'I will . . . Andrew. And I need you to look after yourself.'

Karis half stumbled forward and drew her hand softly down the side of my cheek. She smiled and in her eyes I saw something of the wild, mercurial girl I'd fallen for. She blinked and it was gone as she turned away, walking through the rain to the car, Tunheim at her side.

I was still standing, nearly wet through, when the car turned and drove away, Tunheim offering me a wave and a smile from the driver's seat. The car park was empty and there was nothing to be seen but the ghostly outlines of telegraph poles. I remembered the same scene when I'd first arrived, thinking that I'd come to nothing in nowhere.

I'd been wrong. It was somewhere. And I'd found enough of myself that I could go home with a lighter load. I would face whatever people thought, because I'd realized the true source of my fear. It wasn't about what they thought of me. It was about what I knew about myself. Now, I could live with it.

Acknowledgements

This ship sailed under two outstanding editors, Maxine Hitchcock and Emma Lowth, and I owe them greatly. I wish them calm waters and a following wind in their future voyages. I miss them both.

My gratitude to everyone at Simon & Schuster for being so good at what they do; to my agent Mark Stanton for understanding and supporting this book from the start; to the wondrous Alexandra Sokoloff for expert help and for explaining Karis Lisberg to me; and to my family and friends for being who they are.

I want to thank all the people of the Faroe Islands but in particular Jan Egil Kristiansen, Eyvind Akraberg Hansen, Randi Samsonsen and Bob Walker, plus Regin W. Dalsgaard the photographer whose work features in the book *2 Minutes*.

Craig Robertson

WITNESS THE DEAD

Red Silk is back . . .

Scotland 1972. Glasgow is haunted by a murderer nicknamed Red Silk – a feared serial killer who selects his victims in the city's nightclubs. The case remains unsolved but Archibald Atto, later imprisoned for other murders, is thought to be Red Silk.

In modern-day Glasgow, DS Rachel Narey is called to a gruesome crime scene at the city's Necropolis. The body of a young woman lies stretched out over a tomb. Her body bears a three-letter message from her killer.

Now retired, former detective Danny Neilson spots a link between the new murder and those he investigated in 1972 – details that no copycat killer could have known about. But Atto is still behind bars. Must Danny face up to his fears that they never caught their man? Determined finally to crack the case, Danny, along with his nephew, police photographer Tony Winter, pays Atto a visit. But they soon discover that they are going to need the combined efforts of police forces past and present to bring a twisted killer to justice.

Move over MacBride! *Witness the Dead* is the compelling new thriller from Scotland's hottest new talent.

Paperback ISBN 978-0-85720-420-2
Ebook ISBN 978-0-85720-421-9

Craig Robertson

COLD GRAVE

A murder investigation frozen in time is beginning to melt.

November 1993. Scotland is in the grip of an ice-cold winter and the Lake of Menteith is frozen over. A young man and woman walk across the ice to the historic island of Inchmahome which lies in the middle of the lake. Only the man returns.

In the spring, as staff prepare the abbey ruins for summer visitors, they discover the body of a girl, her skull violently crushed.

Present day. Retired detective Alan Narey is still haunted by the unsolved crime. Desperate to relieve her ailing father's conscience, DS Rachel Narey risks her job and reputation by returning to the Lake of Menteith and unofficially reopening the cold case.

With the help of police photographer Tony Winter, Rachel prepares a dangerous gambit to uncover the killer's identity – little knowing who that truly is. Despite the freezing temperatures the ice cold case begins to thaw, and with it a tide of secrets long frozen in time are suddenly and shockingly unleashed.

Paperback ISBN 978-0-85720-417-2
Ebook ISBN 978-0-85720-418-9

Craig Robertson

RANDOM

Glasgow is being terrorised by a serial killer the media have nicknamed The Cutter. The murders have left the police baffled. There seems to be neither rhyme nor reason behind the killings; no kind of pattern or motive; an entirely different method of murder each time, and nothing that connects the victims except for the fact that the little fingers of their right hands have been severed.

If DS Rachel Narey could only work out the key to the seemingly random murders, how and why the killer selects his victims, she would be well on her way to catching him. But as the police, the press and a threatening figure from Glasgow's underworld begin to close in on The Cutter, his carefully-laid plans threaten to unravel – with horrifying consequences.

'If you like Tarantino-esque tales of gangland killings, violent hardnuts and lives spiralling out of control, you'll enjoy reading this' *Madhouse Family Reviews*

Paperback ISBN 978-1-84739-881-9
Ebook ISBN 978-1-84737-987-0